P9-CBJ-697

EVERY VARIABLE ✳ OF US

LINDENHURST MEMORIAL LIBRARY
One Lee Avenue
Lindenhurst, New York 11757

CHARLES A. BUSH

flux
®
Mendota Heights, Minnesota

Every Variable of Us © 2022 by Charles A. Bush. All rights reserved.
No part of this book may be used or reproduced in any manner
whatsoever, including internet usage, without written permission from
Flux, except in the case of brief quotations embodied in critical articles
and reviews.

First Edition
First Printing, 2022

Book design by Sarah Taplin
Cover and jacket design by Sarah Taplin
Cover jacket and title illustration by Kah Yangni

Flux, an imprint of North Star Editions, Inc.

This is a work of fiction. Names, characters, places, and incidents are
either the product of the author's imagination or are used fictitiously,
and any resemblance to actual persons living or dead, business
establishments, events, or locales is entirely coincidental. Cover
models used for illustrative purposes only and may not endorse or
represent the book's subject.

Library of Congress Cataloging-in-Publication Data (pending)
978-1-63583-074-3

Flux
North Star Editions, Inc.
2297 Waters Drive
Mendota Heights, MN 55120
www.fluxnow.com

Printed in Canada

For all the queer Black kids scared of not being accepted:
you belong, and you have it in you to be and do anything.

And . . .

For my mother, who sacrificed everything
to give us a better life.

AUTHOR'S NOTE
WITH CONTENT AND TRIGGER WARNINGS

Like all art, *Every Variable of Us* is unique, and its themes can be at times misconstrued. So I thought I'd add a little note to set the record straight from the jump.

I grew up in Philadelphia, living in neighborhoods from West Philly to Mount Airy. I love everything about Philly (well, not so much driving on 76, but no one's perfect): from its rich history, to world-renowned food (you want a goated cheesesteak? Hit up Jim's or Dalessandro's!), to all the amazing Black people and businesses it has produced (Questlove and Uncle Bobbie's, I'm looking at y'all), to the stunning murals that adorn the sides of abandoned houses, reminding us how beautiful and talented we are as Black people. But much like every major city, there are many neighborhoods and blocks that got the short end of the stick when it comes to the distribution of wealth that has for too long plagued Black neighborhoods across America. The seeds of systemic racism have been planted in the soil of these blocks. In Hargrove, I do my best to depict such a neighborhood. Hargrove is a fictional neighborhood in West Philadelphia. It's a sometimes-exaggerated amalgamation of the neighborhoods that my friends and I grew up on. I bring this to your attention, dear reader, because not every block in the hood is filled with violence and drugs. In fact, many are filled with love and Black beauty. I wrote this book based on my experiences as a young Black, queer kid raised by a single mom, who on some nights would have to apologize to three starving children because she couldn't afford to put food in our bellies. Many Black kids in these neighborhoods will relate all too well to this feeling. And it pains my heart that they do. All my life, I was told I had to be one thing to get a taste of that wealth—an athlete. And more so, I was told I couldn't be queer to get it. My hope is that this book will show that Black kids in any neighborhood, of any sexuality and gender, have the aptitude to be and do anything!

While it does not have a major presence in the book, I also do my best to champion the autistic community. Unlike the Black community, which I am part of, I do not belong to the autistic community, nor do I claim to be an expert on the subject. The autism spectrum is *not* linear. Every autistic person has their own space on the autism spectrum. If you are part of this community, you may or may not see parts of your space represented in Matthew. Being that this is not Matthew's story, I do not go into much detail on how it feels to have to navigate the world in someone like Matthew's shoes. And for this, I apologize, because you are beautiful and every facet of your story deserves to be told. But it is not my place to tell such a story. For more information on autism, and books that deal specifically with an autistic protagonist, please visit www.autism-society.org.

Now, without further ado, I present to you my heart and soul— *Every Variable of Us.*

CHAPTER 1

I've never been one for all the girly shit. You know, lip gloss, extensions, jeans so tight they make your ass look like Nicki Minaj's. I put my hair in a ponytail, throw on some sweats, lace up my ball sneaks, and I'm good to go. Not to mention, all that primping just to impress the guys— nah, I'm good.

So why did I even agree to hit up the corner store with Britt today, knowing damn well she's a klepto with the fashion sense of a broke Kardashian? Because I'm an idiot and really wanted a Kit Kat to eat after our first game. Processed sugar is the perfect postgame snack—win or lose. Also Britt fed me some bullshit line about wanting to meet the new owners. But what she really meant was: "New ownership! Ooh, I know, let's rob the place!"

Britt nudges me with her pointy-ass elbows and looks over her shoulder to make sure no one's watching. Two Black girls in a corner store, one of them wearing a hoodie—oh, they're watching.

"Here, slip this in your hoodie," she whispers.

Told ya. She's about that klepto life.

I look around the store. The aisles are empty, other than a Muslim girl—this isn't racist because (A) she's dressed in traditional Muslim garb under her blue Super Mart apron, and (B) I'm pretty sure she's the owner's daughter, who I'm certain is Muslim because everyone on the block was talking about the Muslim family that bought the Super Mart. People don't buy businesses in the hood, especially in Hargrove Projects, and go unnoticed. The girl's restocking the milk, while the guy behind the register (probably her father) is breaking his neck to keep an eye on us. In his defense, we do look suspicious as fuck. There has to be a joke in there: *Two Black girls walk into a corner store . . .*

Anyway, I used to think stealing things we can't afford was cool (yes, Kit Kats are on that list). We were Robin Hoods balancing the injustice of poverty-stricken households everywhere. Now we're more like shitty martyrs, just playing into the stereotype that every Black kid in the hood is constantly banging Kendrick Lamar and on the prowl to jack someone's shit.

"Fuck you. You steal it," I whisper back. "I'm not trying to get kicked off the team because you need a new weave to impress Jordan. He's corny, anyways. And his jump shot's all kinds of broke. Dude's got no range."

"I can't," she retorts, moving in closer to hide from Muslim Girl, who's moved on to stocking ramen. "I already got three tubes of lip gloss, a bag of Hot Cheetos, and a frozen pizza under here."

Ah, a frozen pizza. I was wondering how her stomach suddenly became so flat. Britt's never done a sit-up in her life. Shit, she spends every gym class eye-banging the boys.

"Now do you want to eat tonight or not?"

I shrug. "I mean, yeah."

"A'ight then. So stop bitching and take it."

She tries to shove it up my hoodie.

"Chill," I say, swatting the weave away like I'm Joel Embiid. We start slap fighting in the aisle because, you know, that's not making things worse. I do want to eat, though. Especially since Mom doesn't actually buy food with our food stamps.

The bell above the entrance chimes, and in walks a fat-ass white cop, who makes his way to—and I'm not making this up—the donuts and coffee.

Well, now we're officially fucked.

Muslim Girl (I really have to come up with a better and more woke name for her) looks up, daring us to try something with the cop here. She clearly doesn't know who she's grilling. Cops don't scare us.

Officer Tubs—as he henceforth shall be named—starts chatting up the owner while running a train on a bear claw.

"Okay, damn. Just chill before you get us caught," I say out of the side of my mouth. "Ol' girl over there keeps grilling us."

"If you had any sense you'd jack one for yourself. Because your hair stay nappy."

I suck my teeth. "Whatever," I dismiss. "I know you're not talking; hair looking like The Weeknd. Just give me the damn thing."

I stuff the weave under my hoodie. (Yes, I realize how ridiculous that sounds.)

We nonchalantly stroll to the front of the store as though we're unimpressed by the selection and are looking to take our business elsewhere. As we pass the Muslim girl, she looks up at me with these big, soft brown, judgmental eyes, a sneer of disapproval etched on her face. Her skin's a half shade darker than mine and she has wavy black hair that runs past her shoulders. The chill from the open freezer sweeps out as she restocks the Hot Pockets. I can tell she knows. So I mean-mug her hard, imploring her to mind her own damn business.

We're almost home free. No going hungry tonight with nappy heads. But then the girl grows a pair and says something in Arabic—or what I assume to be Arabic (clearly I have no clue what Muslims speak)—to her dad.

"Hey, you!" the man reprimands. He points at Britt as if picking her out of a lineup. "What do you have under your shirt?"

Britt cups her hand to her ear. "Huh?" she patronizes, trying to buy us some time. "Speak English. You're in America now."

I have no excuse for Britt. That was mad racist.

Officer Tubs puts down his second bear claw. "Lift up your shirt. And do it slowly. Keep your hands where I can see 'em."

Britt's head snaps back in resentment. "Why, because I'm Black? I ain't lifting up shit."

No, I think. Because we're thieves, that's why.

Tubs grips the handle of his sidearm. "Just do it and shut up."

Britt gives me a cool smirk.

I dread what's coming next. It involves being a cliché, and it's the reason our friend Nassir got shot last year.

Why did I come here with her? No Kit Kat is worth this.

Britt's not as fast as me and needs to lose some of the added weight, so she opens the bottom of her shirt and lets everything except the pizza fall out. As the last piece of contraband hits the floor, Britt and I book it through the front door. The bell jingles and slams against the door behind us.

Tubs pulls out his gun, but fumbles it to the floor, giving us an even larger head start. Thank baby Jesus he was going ham on that bear claw.

And can I just point some messed-up shit out? Two high school girls stealing a frozen pizza and hair extensions, and this guy feels it's necessary to draw his weapon. And they wonder why there's a new hashtag against the police every week.

By the time Tubs retrieves his gun from the floor, I'm well in front. I actually turn and start running backward just to mock him. I know, how mature of me, right? Then again, I am in the midst of stealing horse hair, so I don't think anyone was thinking of using the word "mature" to describe us.

What Tubs doesn't realize is I can do this all day. I've been running my whole life, whether it's from the opposing team's point guard or one of the many gunshots that go off on my block every hour like church bells. No matter what—I run. And I'm hella fast. If you don't believe me, Google me—Alexis Duncan, senior, All-State point guard three years running.

I whip around in one smooth motion and start running forward again. Now's not the time to fuck around. And if he does decide to pop off, I'll be well out of range.

I glance back to assess the situation. I see Britt, who's keeping pace, and the blurred mirage that is Tubs way off in the distance. Damn, he's slow as fuck. You'd think they'd require some level of fitness to become a cop. I guess the only requirement is hating Black people.

"Plan D!" I shout back to Britt, using the commanding voice I call out plays with.

Two things you should know: (1) D stands for Devon's apartment building, and (2) we've had to ditch the cops so many times that we have devised a playbook for each scenario. That's not a brag. It's the sad truth. Coach always says, "Preparation is the first step to success."

I hang a left at the corner and duck down the alley behind the Chinese restaurant, only a block away from Devon's. I almost bust my ass tripping over Moe—one of the local homeless guys who makes his home in the alley—but my reflexes are Black Panther fast and I dodge him.

"My bad, Moe!" I shout back to him. "Cop's on my ass!"

He looks up from his crusty sleeping bag and shakes his head in disapproval.

I shrug like, *What do you want from me? A girl's gotta eat.*

And even if I did bust my ass it wouldn't matter, because I'm basically lapping Tubs at this point.

Once I'm back on the street I weave around some people on the sidewalk and then Rock in *Fast and Furious* slide over the hood of a parked Mazda.

You'd think with such a lead I'd dip into a McDonald's bathroom or something and hide out until the danger passes. But that would be the smart and not fun thing to do. Plus, I want Tubs to suffer for pulling out his gun on us. It'll serve him right if he catches a heart attack chasing us.

I see Devon's drug-infested building.

A horn rings out. My life/basketball career flashes before my eyes as a Jeep nearly clips me. I take a second to thank Jesus, and then I'm back to running.

I'm nearly across the street when *pop! pop!* echoes through the air. Two gunshots. I don't flinch. But then I remember Britt's slow ass and turn mid-stride to make sure it wasn't Tubs firing at her. Next thing I know, a guy the size of Shaq on a bicycle smacks into me. I hit the pavement. Or rather the pavement Ali uppercuts me, because the back of my head slams against the gravel. Seconds later, I'm laid out like Sonny Liston.

And can I just say: What grown-ass man rides a bike?!

Then it all goes black.

I think I only blacked out for a few minutes, because when I come to, Officer Tubs still hasn't caught up. Maybe he had that heart attack a few blocks back. Or maybe that shot was for Britt. God, I hope she's okay. Thinking about Britt being turned into a hashtag has me starting to panic, so I get up off the pavement and haul ass to Devon's.

When I get there, I learn that Britt never showed. I shoot her a text:

> Me: Where u at?

Britt: Went to school instead

(Words I never thought I'd see by her name.)

So not only did she leave me to get booked, but now I'm mad late to school.

Just another morning in West Philly.

I get to school just before Mr. Jones's English class, where I'm currently getting a sweet C-. Just the way I like it; enough to remain eligible.

Since it's already second period I don't have to walk through the metal detectors. James, the head security guard, tells me to move my ass and get to class.

Britt and Krystal-with-a-K are sitting in the back and start cackling like super villains when they see me walk in. Yeah, it's freakin' hilarious that I could've became some woman named Big Brenda's prison bitch. Laugh it up.

I can't even with them right now.

I walk to my seat next to them and don't say shit.

Britt flips her fake-ass hair and leans forward. "They give you time off for good behavior?"

Oh, they got jokes.

Krystal chimes in with, "You see my cousin Shauna in there? She still owes me a dub."

"See, y'all look stupid because I didn't even get booked," I dismiss, keeping my attention on the whiteboard.

Mr. Jones writes some grammar, vocab, synonyms—I don't know, some English shit—on the board. (This frustration brought to you by English and my sweet C-.) As long as I understand seventy percent of it, I'll be all right. Not that anyone cares. Another perk of being on your own is no one gives a shit what you do with your life.

The bell rings.

Britt sucks her teeth. Yeah, like I'm the one who decided to rob a convenience store, then leave my friend to take the rap. "If you weren't being a little bitch and took the weave in the first place, we'd have been out before that ISIS chick could snitch."

"Wow. I don't know what's worse. You being mad racist, or you missing the whole point that I didn't want to jack that nasty-ass weave in the first place. You almost got us shot. And for what, a frozen pizza?"

Britt laughs it off. "Girl, ain't no one getting shot. And you don't have to eat the pizza. I'm tryin' to help you out. Go hungry tonight. See if I give a fuck."

She's not about to play me like I'm stupid. "I heard the shots."

"That was some BM, Crew beef. I wish a bitch-ass cop would shoot at me. I'd shove that donut right up his ass."

I nearly shake my head off my body in frustration. "If you weren't getting shot at, then why the hell did you leave me there and not meet up at Devon's?"

"You were out cold. There wasn't shit I could do. And I wasn't about to get booked because your dumb ass can't watch where you're going. Your mama never taught you to look both ways before crossing the street?"

This is the shit I have to deal with.

I shake my head and go back to trying to decipher Mr. Jones's whiteboard. He might as well be writing in hieroglyphics.

"Aw," Britt says, extra patronizing. "You mad." She pats the top of my head like I'm a dog. I hate when she does that. Just because she's nineteen (she was held back twice, one shy of a hat trick), is taller than me, and was the first kid Marcus fostered, she thinks she can treat me like a bitch.

I knock her hand away. "For real. Cool it with that shit." As an afterthought I add, "And I'm done stealing. I'm trying to get this scholarship. I can't afford to get booked. If I have to go hungry, then I'll go hungry. Won't be the first time."

She grips my arm. (I'd like to take this time to point out that Mr. Jones is still writing nonsense on the board. Like, a little help here, playa.) Because I'm light skin, people think I'm soft. And that's one thing you can't be in our hood. It's not my fault my skin's more Beyoncé and less Kerry Washington. "You don't have an option. Next time I tell you to put something under your shirt, I mean that shit."

She releases my hand and it falls back to my side, limp.

Krystal, with her hoop earrings and gaudy name necklace, gives a definitive "Mhm." She lives on the block, but not in the foster home. She likes to act tough, but her parents don't play that. Her pop is a minister and her mom is a nurse. When she's not around Britt, her attitude changes real quick.

Mr. Jones turns and finally begins class. I never thought I'd be so happy to continue my academic quest to do just enough to get by.

The board looks like a crossword puzzle with all of the English terms.

"All right," says Mr. Jones, taking a seat so we can see the whiteboard. "Take out your copy of *To Kill a Mockingbird* and pass up your assignments. I expect some well-written insights on the final chapters."

Shit! I totally spaced on the assignment. That's what homeroom is for, which I wasn't in today thanks to another Britt kleptomaniac special. Homework is the backbone to my glorious C average. If I don't hold a C average, then I can't play ball, and if I can't play ball I can't get an athletic scholarship and get the hell out of this town.

I approach Mr. Jones's desk, putting on my best starving-African-child face. "Uh, Mr. Jones." He looks up from his lesson plan. Mr. Jones can't be any older than mid-thirties. He still has all his hair and his waves. Unlike Mr. Fletcher, whose hairline is worse than LeBron's and his face looks like a pug with all them wrinkles. "I don't know if you're aware, but Coach Stevens has been kicking our asses all week at practice to get us ready for our first game tonight. So I've been getting home super late and didn't have a chance to do the paper. It's number one on my list of things to do, though. No lie."

He raises his eyebrow and lets out a heavy sigh.

"Alexis, this is that lazy behavior I'm talking about. You're not applying yourself. Colleges don't just look at what you do on the court. They look at your grades. God forbid something ever happens to you and you can't play anymore. What will you do then, huh? You'll be just like every other girl out here on these streets." He studies my face, waiting for his words to sink in. He's wasting his breath. Coach told me Coach Staley from South Carolina is coming tonight. My future's all but set. "And I gave you the assignment *last Tuesday*."

I nod, like, *Yeah, I know. I was there.*

"Well, it's two weeks later . . ." I continue looking confused, waiting for him to get to the point. "You don't think that was enough time to get it done?"

Uh, obviously not.

"I'll tell you what." He smirks. "If you can summarize the final chapter in one sentence, I'll give you an extension."

"For real?!" I say, a little too excited.

"For real."

Damn. Now I really wish I'd read the final chapters, or better yet, any chapter.

Let's see, *To Kill a Mockingbird . . . To Kill a Mockingbird.* I know Michael Clarke Duncan's in the film version. Or is that *The Green Mile*? Shit.

"I got you, Mr. Jones. It's about a little, country-ass white girl and a Michael Clarke Duncan–looking ol' head trying to kill a mockingbird that threatens to infect the town with a disease." Then to really show I know my shit, I add, "It's like *The Walking Dead*, but for old white people."

That was some baller summarization.

He looks at me deadpanned.

"Sooo . . . extension?"

"That'll be a hard no. Now back to your seat."

All right. Damn. He didn't have to be such a dick about it.

I mope back to my seat. I'm actually going to have to put forth some effort to keep my C now. WTF! This day just keeps getting worse. At this point, I won't be surprised if I miss every shot tonight.

Britt and Krystal die laughing. Sometimes I wonder why I'm

even friends with them. But then I remember Britt's practically my sister. When I was about four my mom went off on one of her more serious benders and child services scooped my ass up quick. When my mom gets high, it's never the dope Snoop Dogg high, but the fucked up *Requiem for a Dream* high. And considering no one knows where my dad's been for the past seventeen years, he wasn't an option. There's this middle-aged, Wesley Snipes–looking guy on our block, Marcus Franklin, who runs a foster home. He collects foster kids like Pokémon. I've lived there off and on over the years, but Britt's been there since she was five. We still have dinner pretty much every night together, because both of our parental guardians are terrible at providing anything but ass whippings for when we fuck up or just because they feel like getting some exercise.

Britt's also been there for the major milestones in my life. She was there in first grade when the shelter gave me my first basketball (we stole a nicer one shortly thereafter); when I got my first period in the middle of a game and she threatened to whoop anyone's ass that would dare make fun of me (we stole tampons shortly thereafter); and she had my back last year when these Jersey City bitches tried to jump me after I dropped forty on them (I'm not sure what we stole shortly thereafter, but I'm sure it was something).

"Yo, look who it is," Britt says, tapping me on the shoulder.

I look up to see Muslim Girl from the corner store standing next to Mr. Jones. She's ditched her blue apron for this extra, teal kaleidoscope-pattern Muslim dress that runs down to her beat-up Chucks. The thing has a fucking sash around the shoulders.

"This bitch goes to our school now?" Britt continues, an evil grin curling at the corners of her mouth. "Ay, Krystal, that's the snitch from this morning."

"Oh, for real? The one dressed like she's going to Muslim

prom?" Krystal inquires with a nefarious grin of her own. The back corner is now Grin City.

Mr. Jones takes the girl's slip. She nervously grabs her backpack straps and stares at the tops of her shoes. "Class," Mr. Jones begins, staring at our section to lose the grins and STFU, "we have a new student. This is Aamani Chakrabarti. She's a foreign exchange student." The new girl says something just above a nervous whisper.

Britt and Krystal cackle. They can smell blood.

Mr. Jones leans in. "I'm sorry, Aamani, I didn't get that."

She speaks up. "I said I'm from Jersey."

Mr. Jones nearly swallows his tongue. "Oh my God, my apologies, Aamani. I just assumed . . . that was poor judgment on my part. Aamani here is from Jersey. Let's make her feel welcomed. You can have a seat at one of the open chairs in the back."

Aamani takes the seat in front of Britt. I wince as she sits down. Bad move, girl. She unzips her bag and reaches for her notebook. Britt flinches and nearly jumps out of her chair. The legs of her chair scratch the linoleum and the whole class whips their heads to the back of the room.

"My bad," Britt scoffs. "I thought you had a bomb in there. Had to bust out the survival moves." Random chuckles sweep through the room. "And why are you dressed like you're about to go to Taliban prom?"

Lame. Like, at least come up with your own diss.

"Brittney!" Mr. Jones scolds in his I'm-the-teacher-hear-me-roar voice. "Please disrespect Aamani or any student one more time so I can toss your ass in detention for the rest of the year." He looks gravely at Britt. "Try me."

Britt smacks her teeth and rolls her eyes to the ceiling.

As soon as Mr. Jones turns his back, Britt leans in to me and

Krystal, our faces huddled. She whispers, "After school this bitch is getting stomped."

"Bet," Krystal confirms, immediately. Sometimes I believe she's a minion Britt created in a lab.

I look over at Aamani, who appears to be unfazed by Britt's blatant racism. She's staring ahead, ready to learn. Nerd. But besides being a nerd, she's done nothing wrong. It wasn't her fault Tubs pulled his gun on us. Shooting Black folks is what they do. If anyone deserves to be stomped, it's him. I mean, all Aamani did was protect her family business. We'd have done the same. Well, we wouldn't have snitched, especially to the cops (because seriously, and I can't stress this enough, but in the words of the great American poet Tupac: Fuck the police!), but we would've definitely given her a beatdown for trying to jack our shit. So I guess we too deserve an ass whooping in all of this.

"Nah, it's cool," I say, trying to convince them. "Like, we were actually stealing. We brought this on ourselves."

"The fuck are you talking about?" Britt's whispers grow louder and she scrunches her face. "She's catching this ass whooping. Snitches get stitches."

Damn.

She has a point. Rule number one on the block: Snitches do indeed get stitches.

I have three more classes with Aamani. Essentially it's just three more hours for my guilt to build. The girl's, like, the LeBron James of schoolwork. In math, she enthusiastically raises her hand and answers every question right. I mean, the girl's only been here for a few hours and she's already smarter than Lindsay Ross, the smart-ass white girl who thinks she's the shit because she has the highest GPA in the school, which isn't saying much because the second highest is, like, 3.2. Aamani was the same levels of hype for Mrs. Hall's science class, where she was kind enough to let the rest of the class answer a few questions (and by "rest of the class" I mean everyone not named Alexis Duncan). Mrs. Hall even asked her to stay after class. Probably to thank her for actually giving a shit about science. Aamani also had gym with me. Her math and science skills may be on point, but her ball game is all kinds of trash. She played one pickup game, got clowned after she shot an air ball, and wasn't picked for a team for the rest of the period.

We finally make it to lunch.

But, before I hit up the caf, I beg Janitor Mike to let me use the auxiliary gym. In the end, after a significant amount of groveling, we broker a deal. I get to use the gym for twenty minutes, and in return I have to come to school early tomorrow to sweep both gyms. I waste no time. I set up three cones just outside the three point line, then I weave between them, cutting in and out, alternating my dribbling pattern—under the legs, behind the back, then under the legs. When I get to the final cone, I combine the moves. I explode left, going under my leg, take two additional dribbles to escape my imaginary defender, then quickly maneuver the ball behind my back and cut the other way. I stop on a dime and shoot a pull-up jump shot.

Swish. Nothing but net.

I sprint and retrieve the ball, and do fifteen more sets.

The gym doors swing open as I set up cones for the next drill. I turn and see Malcolm Bridges, the starting small forward on the boys' team. He's six-foot-three, but when they announce him in the starting lineup before games the PA claims he's six-foot-five because of his big afro. He's got about eight inches and a hundred pounds of muscle on me.

"Tryin' to run a quick game?" he asks, all too sure of himself.

I look at him, grinning ear to ear, sweat dripping down my face. I wipe it off with my sleeve. "You sure you want this smoke?"

He cracks a grin of his own and tosses his backpack to the patch of hardwood in front of the bleachers.

"Just check rock, yo."

He steps to me at the top of the key. I toss him the ball and he tosses it back, signifying we're checked and ready to play. "I got the gym for ten more minutes. Game to five. All ones."

"Bet," he says, sitting down in a defensive stance. He majestically opens his six-foot wingspan like a hawk gliding above its prey.

I square him up. I give him a little jab with my right pivot foot to see if he reacts. He doesn't. But he's forcing me left, so I can exploit that. I jab with my right foot again. This time when he doesn't react, I attack his left leg that's ushering me left and blow past him for an uncontested layup.

"One, nothing," I say, catching the ball out the net.

He does this frustrated brow-knitting thing. "Good move. But you ain't gettin' another bucket."

The corners of my mouth tug upward.

We check rock again.

I jab hard to the right. This time he opens his hips out of respect for my speed, so I go left. He's able to recover with his long wingspan, so I hit him with an Elena Delle Donne–esque step-back and nail a jumper right in his face.

"Two, nothing," I update him.

"I know the score. Just check ball," he mutters in frustration.

What he doesn't know is he made a huge mistake giving me

the ball first. I know I can't guard him in the post. He's too big. But he can't guard me on the perimeter. So what he's starting to realize is I'm not going to give him a chance to play offense. Because I'm not going to miss.

The next two possessions, he sags way off because he's petrified of my speed. I easily drain two jumpers. The second one hits the back of the rim and rattles in. I was kind of pissed about that. Should've been all net.

He's fuming now. I can practically see the steam coming off that afro, which he desperately needs to pick, by the way. Hair just nappy. Looks like a bunch of spiders having a meeting up there.

"Game point," I remind him with a devilish smirk.

He doesn't say anything. I go to check ball. He puts his hand out rejecting the gesture. "Just fucking play."

"I'll tell you what. I'll let you choose how you take this L. You want a step-back in your face or a layup?" Again, no answer. He just grunts. I see he has a massive vocabulary. Mr. Jones must love him. "I'll take that as you want a layup, quick and easy. I got you."

I put the ball on the floor and throw it between my legs two times in quick succession. I watch his eyes follow the ball (wrong move, bruh), then I give him a little hesitation dribble with my left hand. When he doesn't bite, I shift my body like I'm going left and crossover to my right hand. His first step is to my left. I zoom by him for a layup, but he recovers quickly and is right on my ass. I see him in my peripheral vision, biting his lip in determination of blocking my shot. I soar through the air gracefully for a right-handed layup. As he leaves his feet to block it, I allow my momentum to carry me to the other side of the basket, where I finish with a left-handed reverse layup.

"Fuck!" he yells as the ball bounces off the backboard and through the net.

"Nice move, youngin," says Janitor Mike, who has appeared mystically in the doorway. "You going places."

"You better get your boy," I say to Janitor Mike, pointing at Malcolm. "I tried to tell him he don't want that smoke. Don't he know I'm about to get an offer to South Carolina? Coach Staley's coming to the game tonight."

"Yeah, I don't know nothin' about no Coach Staley. But I know LeBron Stank over here needs to take his butt to class, and you need to come see where I keep the brooms for tomorrow."

I suck my teeth. "A'ight, ol' head." I go and grab my backpack and sling it around my shoulder, cradling my basketball under my right arm. My most prized possession.

"A-yo?" Malcolm calls from the court, still picking up the pieces of his pride. "Good shit."

"You too," I reply. "Little tip for the game tonight—don't watch the ball. Watch the offensive player's waist."

"Good lookin' out."

I'm eating the strawberry Pop-Tart I grabbed this morning on my way out of the house (Pop-Tarts are the only food my mom keeps in the house; drug addicts love them some Pop-Tarts, I guess) and a bag of Hot Cheetos I stole off some freshman when he wasn't looking. I can't eat that nasty-ass free lunch. I mean, it's "free" for a reason. Britt, Krystal, and Mikayla are playing Fuck, Marry, Kill. I have more important things on my mind, like impressing Coach Staley at the game tonight. I couldn't care less that Jordan's fade makes him look like Michael B. Jordan, which earns him the unanimous status of "fuck" every time they play this stupid game.

Right on cue, Jordan and Trey Davis roll up to our table like we should bow in their presence.

"What up, B?" Jordan says to Britt with what I'm sure he thinks is a smooth I-got-game voice. It's not. Britt nearly melts, though. Sure, he's already committed to Villanova next year—lucky!—but beyond that, the fade, fresh Js, and solo dimple that makes every girl want to bang him don't do anything for me. "Y'all hittin' up Kyle's party after the game tonight, right?"

Britt smirks as though imagining him naked. "Who's all going?"

"I'll be there," Trey adds for incentive.

Mikayla snorts, Britt rolls her eyes then goes back to eye-fucking Jordan, and Krystal perks up in excitement (Trey's always her choice of "marry"). I don't have a problem with Trey. He plays backup shooting guard on the boys' team. The only thing is he looks like what would happen if a piece of coal fucked Lance Stephenson.

Jordan puts their minds at ease with a flash of his dimple. "The whole team will be there. Kyle said some people from Kensington might show up too. Shit's gonna be flames."

Britt fronts like she had no intentions on actually going. "A'ight, I gueeess I'll make an appearance."

"What about you, Lex?"

I look up mid-chew.

"Me?" A piece of Cheeto flees my mouth.

"You're the only Lex here," Jordan teases.

"Maybe. Depends on how the game goes."

If I play bad, I don't want to be around people. And if we lose, I definitely don't want to be around people.

"She'll be there," Britt answers for me.

I give her a stank-eye of my own.

"Say less," Jordan says. "I'll holla at y'all tonight then. Good luck tonight, Lex."

"Thanks, you too."

He laughs like he doesn't need it. "Thanks."

"Peace out, ladies!" Trey says, chucking up the deuce as they go spread the house party news.

We return to our regularly scheduled programs. They talk about boys while I eat the lunch of champions and start getting pumped for my game. Everything is going fine until Aamani walks in. She sits at an empty table by the double doors, pulls out our science textbook that's the size of three Bibles and a four-tier tower of some metal contraption, and proceeds to mind her own business. She opens the metal casing, folding the long stainless-steel brackets to the side, and then she begins deconstructing the tiers, each one breaking off to make a tiny steel bowl of food.

Somehow all of this pisses Britt off more, like, *How dare she read a textbook and eat lunch?*

Britt balls her fists and stands. "Fuck this. I'm not waiting until after school."

I'm not sure when Britt turned into a super villain. Probably around the twelfth time Marcus knocked her ass out. I guess she has to put that aggression somewhere.

I drop my Pop-Tart, which I was really enjoying, and grab her arm. "What are you doing?" She gives me the stank-eye, as in if I don't let her go, she's going to go Floyd Mayweather on my ass. I let go and retreat into my seat. I'm all for doing the right thing, but

I'm not about to get my ass beat for it. I don't even know this girl. "You know you can't do anything with all these teachers around."

"Chill. Lex is right," Mikayla seconds. Thank Jesus someone's got my back. "I'm not tryin' to go back to detention." Mikayla's already had eighteen detentions and it's only November. Two more and it's an automatic expulsion.

I look at Aamani again, reading her textbook like a straight-up nerd. She's a helpless lamb for slaughter. Then I look at my girls and see how bad they want to stomp her. It's all starting to feel kind of hate crime-y.

I panic. "I got an idea."

I do not have an idea.

They look at me in anticipation.

Shit. Think of something before they murder this girl *Hunger Games*-style.

"Well, what is it?" Britt asks.

Think. Think.

"Um . . ." I search the caf for help and see Jordan using his dimple to spread the gospel of Kyle's party. "Let's invite her to the party."

Britt furrows her brow and plays around with the idea for a few seconds. She nods. "Bitch, I knew you was smart. Ain't no teachers gonna be able to save her there."

Not exactly what I was getting at, but it'll do for now.

"You're inviting her, though," she adds. "Because if I go over there, I'm dropping her ass."

I make the long trek across the caf. A couple people say what's up and wish me luck for tonight. I don't know what to say to this girl.

Why did I agree to this again?

I take a seat across from her. She doesn't move. Her head's

buried in the textbook and her right hand occasionally reaches for some bread that she uses to pick up the most disgusting-looking food ever.

I clear my throat and she lowers the textbook.

"Hey, I'm Lex," I say, scrunching my face as she slurps up a brown, barf-esque substance from one of her steel containers. I offer my hand like we're about to do a business deal. "I'm sorry, but what is that and why does your lunch box look like a Transformer?"

Aamani searches for hidden cameras.

"Are you talking to me?"

"Yeah," I say, curling my nose at the food.

"It's chapati with eggplant curry. Would you like some?"

"Nah, I'm good. But why do you have, like, seventy compartments for your food?"

"It's a tiffin. It keeps my lunch warm."

"Well, good luck not throwing any of that up."

She frowns. "Can I help you with something? Why are you here?"

"I just wanted to introduce—"

"I know who you are. You and your friend over there robbed my dad's store today."

I retract my handshake. "Yeah, my bad about that. If it makes you feel any better, I got run over by a bike because of it."

"It doesn't."

Man, tough crowd.

"Look, I won't tell my dad or the cops that you two go to school with me, if that's what you're worried about. Honestly, I feel sad for you that you feel it necessary to treat a felony like sport."

Okay, I kinda want to whoop her ass right now. Where does she get off saying some shit like that?

I bite my bottom lip and take a deep breath like I'm shooting a free throw.

"I know we shouldn't have tried to jack your shit. My girl gets a little overzealous when she sees frozen pizza."

"Frozen pizza?"

"It's a long story. What I'm getting at is I want to make things right and invite you to a party tonight."

"Oh, uh, thanks," she stammers. "This isn't some sort of *Carrie* thing, is it? Sorry, but I don't really trust the person who robbed me less than seven hours ago. Like, this isn't *BVS*. We're not going to all of the sudden become friends after we've spent the entire movie hating each other. And I highly doubt our moms have the same name."

"Okay, first off, I have no idea what you're talking about. And what's a *Carrie*?"

Her light-brown eyes expand. It's the most emotion she's shown since she's been here. "You've never seen *Carrie*? Not even the terrible remake with Hit-Girl?"

For some reason I get defensive. "Have you ever seen *Friday*, *Next Friday*, or *Friday After Next*?"

"No."

"A'ight then." I proclaim myself the winner of this . . . what, movie debate?

"*Carrie*'s a horror movie based off a Stephen King novel."

"Sounds corny. But whatever. It's nothing like that. It's just a regular party."

"I don't know." Her voice gets all reserved. "I have some study-ing to do."

I laugh. "Girl, you're reading a textbook at lunch. The last thing you need to do is study." She stares at me unconvinced. "Here, just give me your Instagram or something and I'll hit you up with the details. Cool?"

Her eyes slant and she studies me more intently. I can tell she's skeptical. Part of me hopes she just moves back to wherever she's from so Britt won't be able to murder her.

She scribbles in her notebook, then rips out the page and hands it to me.

"Cool. Maybe I'll see you tonight."

She shrugs and goes back to reading.

I'm sitting in front of my locker, headphones blaring while Drake gets me hyped for the game. I nod to the beat, consuming the rhymes, and imagine the work I'm about to put in on the court. I see myself nailing A'ja Wilson–esque pull-ups and crossing my defender over and taking her to the rack. I'm hitting step-backs like Maya Moore and finding Candice on the backdoor cut when they start to overplay her because she's our best three-point shooter.

In other words, I'm about to dominate like prime Diana Taurasi.

Coach tosses a balled-up paper at my head to get my attention, completely ruining my pregame vibes. I pause Drake, which is blasphemy, but whatever.

"Let's go. Game time."

I didn't even notice I was the last one in the locker room.

I place my phone in my locker, then hurry to the locker room doors where my teammates are waiting.

When Candice sees me she says, "What, you meditating or some shit?"

A few of them laugh. I'd smile, but when my game face is on the only face I'm capable of making is a snarl.

They huddle around me. I look around the circle. Their eyes are locked on me like I'm Jon Snow about to lead them into The Battle of the Bastards.

I summon the husky part of my voice that's buried deep in the pit of my chest.

"Y'all already know what it is!" They go quiet. "They not about to come up in here and get a dub in our home!"

Kaleen and a few others nod intensely and shout, "Let's get it!"

It goes quiet in anticipation. They're waiting for me to shout the battle cry. The cry we stole from Michael Jordan and *The Last Dance*. I yell with gravitas so everyone in the gym can hear me. *"Hargrove, what time is it?!"*

In unison the team calls back, *"Game time! Woo!"*

We sprint out of the locker room into the gym. There's not many people here because they all usually start piling in before the boys' game. But sitting in the front bleacher with her maroon South Carolina Gamecocks polo on is Head Coach Dawn Staley.

This is the night I seal my fate and do something Nassir and so many people on my block before me tried and failed: get a scholarship and make it out alive.

CHAPTER 2

I really don't want to be at this fake-ass party. I mean, how can everyone be so damn happy after both the girls' and boys' teams lost tonight? Plus everyone dresses so bougie and overcompensates at these things. The girls with their fake designer handbags, and the guys smell like Axe Body Spray and weed.

Maybe I'm bitchin', but so many people in one house fronting would bother you too.

The bass thumps from the dining room, some new Kendrick Lamar song. Kyle removed all the furniture so there can be a giant twerk orgy. The twerking runs from the dining room into the kitchen, where people twerk in between hits of their beers, and continues into the basement.

Thankfully, I claimed the far corner of the living room next to the dead plant early on, and anyone who dares venture over here I mean-mug, as if to say: *I'm not in the mood, so keep it movin'.* The one downside to my corner is it's right by the wall with all Kyle's family pictures on it, so I've literally been staring at Kyle's bare baby ass in the bath for the past hour. I guess there are worse things to spend an hour staring at, like people dancing, or whatever it is Britt is doing on Jordan's lap in the other room. I'm going to call it grinding. Mikayla and Krystal are in there with the rest of the party. A room full of boners and weaves.

I'm good here just sipping my Gatorade and being mad as hell my twenty-four points and eleven dimes wasn't enough to get us the win.

A few people who were smoking weed and blowing it out the window leave for Twerk City in the other room. It's just me and some guy sitting in the armchair with the plastic slipcover. He looks over to my corner and licks his lips.

I mean-mug him.

"Ay-yo, ma?"

He licks his lips again. Nothing about his crusty, LL Cool J lip licking is sexy.

"Can I help you? You need some Chapstick for those ashy-ass lips?"

He scoffs and subconsciously wets his lips again. "Oh, it's like that, huh?"

"Yeah, it's like that," I mimic.

"Whatever," he says, getting up. "I was trying to give your ugly-ass a compliment. But be that way—lookin' like a trans Steph Curry."

"Oh no. How am I going to survive without your compliment and ashy lips to know when it's cold outside?"

He leaves. Me and Kyle's bare ass are the last ones standing. I have full living room supremacy.

Seriously, the hell with this party. The only reason I'm here is to play wingman to Britt, who, based on her current ass-to-dick position, is doing just fine without me. Oh, and I guess I'm also here to find some way to get Aamani off Britt's shit list. That's another thing. Aamani's not even here.

I gulp down the remaining Gatorade and place the empty bottle under my chair. Trust me, Kyle's house wouldn't be the same without all the empty bottles and rolling papers everywhere. I'm doing my part to keep up appearances.

"I just walked past a guy whose lips look like he ate an entire box of powdered donuts," I hear a soft voice say from the entranceway. It's Aamani. About damn time she showed up.

I don't even recognize her at first. Gone is her Muslim dress-thingy, and in its place is a T-shirt that reads *I lost an electron! Are you positive?*, a red-and-teal scarf that looks like peacock feathers, jeans, and a pair of white Chucks. She's also wearing her hair down. It's somehow longer than earlier and wavy.

"Aamani?" I try to confirm.

She furrows her brow, like, *duh.* "Uh . . . yeah. It's okay that I'm here, right?"

"Nah, yeah, I mean it's cool," I stammer, suddenly losing the ability of language. "I just . . . where's all the Muslim gear you were wearing earlier?"

"What, my churidar? My mom makes me wear it for special occasions, which according to her falls under the first day at a new school." Aamani swings her backpack around and unzips it. She tilts it toward me. Inside are her churidar from earlier and our science and math textbooks. "I told my mom I was going to a friend's house to study."

"Let me guess—special occasion?"

"Special occasion," she confirms with a soft smile. "At least it's not a sari. Those I have to wear on the special-est of occasions. You have no idea how hard it is to put one of those on. They're like the Rubik's Cube of clothes. Like, I feel like I'm solving every variation of string theory when I put one on. I'll have to change back before I go home. I kinda feel like Ms. Marvel when I have to switch outfits in a Wawa bathroom." Ms. Marvel. String theory. I have no idea what she's talking about. So I just nod and go with it. Plus, my eyes are already on the prowl for Britt. If she sees Aamani here, that's her ass. I really didn't think this whole party invite through. "If my parents ever caught me breaking tradition they'd literally pray for a week straight and disown me."

"Damn. Muslims don't play."

She zips up her backpack and tosses it back around her shoulders. "Okay, can we just get something straight right off the bat? Contrary to what you and your friends may believe, I'm not part of ISIS or BFFs with Osama bin Laden's niece. I don't own a cobra that can hypnotize you. I love bacon. My favorite movie isn't *Slumdog Millionaire.* And yeah, while I technically know how to make a bomb, it's only because it's just basic science and knowing your chemical compounds, which is easy-peasy. Also, I'm not Muslim. I'm Hindu. There's a HUGE difference. In fact, there was essentially a civil war fought over it back in 1946 called Direct Action Day. Over two thousand Hindus were killed. So yeah. There's a difference. And I'd appreciate it if you respected that."

The corners of my mouth pull back with guilt. "My bad. I just assumed since you dressed like you did earlier that you were . . . you know—"

"I know," she finishes, rolling her eyes violently. "Every American I encounter thinks the same thing. It's kinda annoying. I mean, don't you think it's a bit elitist to group a culture and religion together based solely on the way someone looks? That's the very definition of discrimination. I thought people would be different here since it's predominantly Black, unlike my previous school. Like, you wouldn't call Eminem Black just because he wears baggy jeans and a do-rag, would you?"

"I mean, dude did spit, like, eight freestyles dissin' Trump."

"Okay, bad example." We chuckle. "What I'm getting at is it's not politically correct to judge solely on appearance. Also, we all don't look alike."

I feel like shit.

She's right. I should've known better than to judge. Martin Luther King Jr. is rolling over in his grave right now.

"I feel ya on that one. Every time we have an away game at one of those fancy white schools in the suburbs, as soon as we get off the bus people start clutching their purses and children like we're there to steal some shit." I curl my lip in disgust.

"Yeah, except you totally did 'steal some shit' from me earlier," Aamani points out in her best "with all due respect" voice.

I chuckle. "Why you bringing up old shit?"

"Hey, I'm not judging," she defends, tossing her hands up in surrender. "I'm just saying if you want to be looked at differently, you may want to try and not feed into the stereotypes."

"Says the girl who knows how to build a bomb. Not a good look, by the way."

"Because of *science*! Science! It's not a crime to love science. It's part of the reason my parents came here from India to give me the opportunity to follow and explore my passions. Also . . . why you bringing up old shit?"

Her smile latches on to mine and before we know it, we're cheesing like we've been friends our whole life.

"A'ight, not to sound ignorant, but I could have sworn it's against your culture to eat pork. So how do you love bacon? Again, not stereotyping here. Just asking a legit question."

She shakes her head. "Okay, one more time, you're thinking of Muslims. Yes, Muslims don't eat pork. They think it's sacred. But I'm Hindu, and there is no rule in Hinduism that forbids pork or any other meat. That being said, some Hindus are vegetarians, including my parents."

"Got ya," I say, nodding like *ohhh*. "So why do I get the sense that your parents don't know about you being BFFs with bacon?"

"Because they don't. There's no way I could be a vegetarian. I have a steaming hot love affair with BLTs and Popeyes chicken."

I cock my face to the side. "What you know about some Popeyes?!"

Aamani cracks a cocky grin. "What do you want to know?"

How the hell am I enjoying myself right now?

"A'ight, answer me this then. It's clear you're not down with all this Hindu shit your parents make you do and wear, so why do it? If it were me, I'd tell them to fuck off."

"Man, so hostile," she says, a smile in her voice. "And we're the ones labeled as terrorists." She shakes her head. I cock my head in contempt. "Look, do I hate wearing saris? Yeah, they bring way too much attention, and in a post-9/11 world scream 'random bag check.' And do I love all kinds of meat? Hell yeah I do. But I play the game for my parents' sake. They sacrificed so much to give me the life I have. Like, I can't even imagine the shit they had to put up with during 9/11. My dad was an engineer in India. Now, after being forced to go to night school to earn a degree he already had, he owns an old, run-down convenience store. It's the least I can do to humor them and suck it up. Repping my culture won't kill me. Well, as long as I stay away from the more southern states," she says with a chortle.

I can't explain it, but talking to her just feels natural. It's really messing with my head. I completely forget that Britt still wants to beat her ass all over Hargrove.

Speaking of Ol' Klepto (apparently, if you say "steal" three times she'll magically appear), Britt pops her head in the living room. Jordan's attached to her hip. Their bodies probably fused together from all the intense bumping and grinding.

"Ay, Lex!" Britt shouts over the Timbaland beat thumping in the background. They're playing old school Missy Elliott. "What the hell you doing in here with Mindy Kaling?" I apologize with my eyes to Aamani, and pray to sweet Jesus that Britt doesn't make me stomp her. But, to my surprise, Britt doesn't try to roll on her. "Y'all look like y'all up to some lesbo shit."

I make some ugly scrunched-up defensive face. I'm not exactly sure how to describe it besides disgustingly offended. "We're not! I'm not a fag!"

Aamani gives me a disappointed look, as if I told her she can never read another textbook again.

"Mhm. We're going upstairs. Holla at your girl if you need me!"

I don't even get a chance to reply because she's already dragging Jordan upstairs to follow through on her Fuck, Marry, Kill promise.

Yep. Just how I drew it up. Britt's too drunk and far too concerned with playing naked post defense on Jordan to remember her beef with Aamani. I'm not saying I'm a genius, but if the shoe fits . . .

Okay, so I totally got lucky as fuck.

"Really?" Aamani asks, dispirited.

"What?" I snap, clenching my jaw. "Facts. I'm not a fag."

"Do you have to use that word? It's unbecoming of you, not to mention terribly offensive. Like, how would you like it if I said I'm not an N-word?"

Just her suggesting such a thing makes me want to go upstairs and remind Britt that she owes Aamani an ass whooping.

I take a step into her atmosphere. We're almost chest-to-chest. "Go ahead and say it and see what happens."

She shakes her head. "You're completely missing the point. No one should ever say either word. Unless it's in a Tarantino movie. And he only gets away with it because he's won an Oscar and made *Pulp Fiction*."

I back down, taking a breath.

"A'ight, a'ight, I see your point. I'm not *gay*. Is that better?"

"Much." She smiles. "And your friend does raise a good point. Why are you sitting in here all alone?"

"Because that"—I point to all the dancing in the other room—"is not my style."

Her mouth falls into her high cheekbones. "You don't like to dance? But I thought all Black people danced."

I smile without teeth. "Now who's stereotyping? No, not all Black people dance," I educate. "Wait, don't tell me *you* dance." It comes out more disrespectful than I intended it to.

If she's offended, she doesn't show it.

Aamani giggles. It's kinda adorable. "Okay, so not to contradict my previous argument on stereotypes, but I'm from the home of Bollywood. Dancing is a part of life."

"You're from LA! You ever meet Kobe?"

She giggles again. It's just as adorable. Wait, what the hell am I saying?

"No. *Bolly-wood*," she sounds out. "It's a form of Hindi cinema. Some of my all-time favorite Bollywood films, like *Pram Ratan Dhan Payo* and *Kuch Kuch Hota Hai* and *Dilwale Dulhania Le Jayenge*, all have epic dance scenes."

I nod politely, even though the movies sound terrible. I don't want any flash mobs popping up in my movies. If anything pops up to sing and dance it better start with a B and end with an -eyoncé.

"What's your favorite musical?" she adds.

"My what? Do I look like a theater nerd?"

She flashes a light smile. "Indulge me."

"The closest I've come to watching a musical is a Beyoncé video."

"Okay, I can work with that." She nods and pinches her chin. "So think 'Single Ladies,' but an actual full-length movie with characters, a story, and even bigger dance scenes. Now tell me that wouldn't blow your mind."

I'd totally be down for a "Single Ladies" movie. Now I'm mad it doesn't exist.

"Maybe it does sound kinda dope."

Her face lifts with excitement. "It is! Bollywood and the food are the best parts of home."

I don't know why, but for some reason her enthusiasm for home makes me sad. I wish I had a home, parents to defy. My mom's been strung out for so long now, I can't even remember a time when things were normal. Aamani has so much family history. She knows where and who she comes from. She has traditions. Me, I just have my mom. So unless I want to continue the tradition of shooting heroin and smoking crack, I've got fuck-all.

My head drops, knowing I'll never have any of it.

"There's that look again," Aamani observes.

"What look?"

"The one where you look like someone just murdered your dog. The first thing I saw when I walked in was Powdered Lip Boy and you sulking in the corner."

"What?! I was not sulking."

She tilts her head. "You definitely were-slash-are."

I sigh. "A'ight, maybe I was a little pissed because we lost tonight and no one seems to give a shit."

"What did you lose?"

I look at her like she just sprouted tentacles. "Basketball. I'm on the ball team."

"Oh, that makes sense. That's why you made, like, every shot in gym today. You're really good at scoring touchdowns or getting home runs or whatever."

I chuckle. "Thanks."

"I can totally relate."

I squint incredulously. "You can? I've seen you hoop, and don't take this the wrong way, but you're so bad that I could actually feel myself getting worse watching you."

Aamani laughs it off. "Yeah, I'm no LeBron Jordan"—there's so much wrong with that sentence, I have to bite my tongue to keep from correcting her—"but I'm on the STEM team, and got pretty bummed when we lost a match at my old school."

"You're on the what now? Is STEM one of those white people sports like lacrosse or hacky sack?"

"No." She cracks up. For the first time, I notice an assortment of perfectly placed freckles below her eyes. They accentuate her high cheekbones and delicate features. Her skin looks like caramel chocolate.

The fuck am I talking about? Snap out of it, Lex. For real. Getting all weird about a *girl*. Do you want to get clowned like Jacob did when he got caught wearing fake Js? Think about all the fine-ass guys at school who can get it—Calvin, Rodney, Leon, that ESL teacher who looks like that fine light-skin dude from the State Farm commercials.

"STEM's not a sport. It's an academic decathlon." Until now I had no idea two words could induce instant boredom. "It stands for science, technology, engineering, and math. Think Quizzo, but no pop culture stuff. Teams are made up of four students and at least one reserve. We don't have any reserves, though. Before I joined today, there were only three members. I played anchor at my old school, which means I'm the last one to answer every round. It's a lot of fun."

Forget Britt. If Aamani is this much of a nerd, she's going to get clowned every day.

"We actually have one of these . . . *STEM* teams?"

"Yep. We practice in Mrs. Hall's room. She's the coach."

"There's a coach," I say in utter disbelief.

Aamani just smiles in reply.

How did I not know this? And why wasn't I invited to the clowning of said team? I can think of at least seven disses off the top of my head. Like, *Do you have to be a virgin to join?*

"Aamani, with all due respect—and I'm only telling you this because I'm trying to help—that's some straight nerd shit that you should not brag about, and in no way counts as a sport."

"I beg to differ. Let me ask you this. Does your *basketball* team have a season?" She puts basketball in air quotes.

"Everyone knows that. It's an actual *sport*." Two can play the air quotes game.

"Is a National Champion crowned at the end of it?"

I roll my eyes. "State Champion, but yes."

"Do schools give out scholarships based on high performance?"

"Yeah. Ever heard of Geno Auriemma? Taurasi, Bird, Moore, Stewart . . . "

"Are you having a minor stroke?" she asks. I shoot her an unimpressed look. "Okay, to my point. So all of said attributes would qualify basketball as a sport?"

I sigh, pinching the bridge of my nose. "Obviously."

The corners of her lips arch smugly. "Well, STEM team has all of the above."

If I was still drinking my Gatorade, I'd spit it out all over her.

"Bullshit," I say. Aamani's grin expands like *checkmate*. "Okay, if this team is a *real* team, and I'm still not convinced it is, then how come I've never heard of it, and where do y'all play?"

Let's see her get out of that. Gonna try and play me.

"Maybe you haven't heard of it because you're too busy sulking in corners and planning your next convenience store heist," she says. "As far as matches go, they're on Saturdays, usually in the opposing team's auditorium."

"Fuck outta here. You're telling me people voluntarily come in to school on a Saturday to talk school shit with other nerds *and* they give out scholarships for it?"

"I find that rather minimizing, but yes."

I size her up, trying to read her and call her bluff. She's loving this. With each unsure look I give, her grin expands. "A full scholarship to a, like, legit college? None of that Trump University or University of Phoenix shit?"

A smile cracks her grin. "Yep. Not so nerdy now, is it, basketball star?"

"No," I quickly dismiss, "it's still nerdy as fuck. But I'll admit the whole scholarship thing is pretty dope. Who knew?"

"Only every school board in America. You do know that academic scholarships are the norm and athletic scholarships the exception?"

"I do now."

We laugh. As I look into her light-brown eyes, I think maybe she doesn't need my protection after all.

The front door opens, and in walks a group of South Philly

Crew (The Crew for short). I know this because they have blue bandanas dangling from their pockets, repping their set. One of them even has on matching Jordans—the blue and white 11s. Usually The Crew showing up would be cause for concern. The battle for Hargrove has claimed so many innocent lives. But Kyle and Trey are Black Mafia (BM), so this is West Side turf. Starting shit on BM turf would be suicide even for The Crew.

"Is everything okay? You look like Liv from *iZombie* when she's having a vision," Aamani says, placing her hand on my shoulder to break my trance. For some reason nerves shoot through my veins and I get the bubble guts like I do before big games.

"Oh, uh, yeah. I just saw some not so cool people. But we're a'ight. What were we talking about again? And I know it didn't have anything to do with whatever nerd, zombie thing you just said."

"*iZombie* is this awesome show based off the Vertigo comics of the same name. It's about this zombie murder detective that eats the brains of the victims and uses their memories to solve their murder . . . "

"Aamani."

She looks at me.

"I. Don't. Care."

"Oh, right." She giggles. "Sorry. I believe you were in the middle of using poor grammar to give me shit for being on the STEM team, and reprimanding me for being a nerd. You really should watch *iZombie* though. Just saying."

"Right," I say, remembering. "You're a nerd."

"And yet part of you is jealous about the scholarship, so what does that say about you?"

Touché.

We trade smiles.

"Speaking of which, we need to talk about your Instagram."

"What about it?"

"Why are you dressed like a cartoon character in every picture?"

She shrugs as if she doesn't know. "I like to cosplay. Sue me."

"And I'm the one using poor grammar? I swear you're not even speaking English."

Frustration floods her voice. "Have you ever experienced anything outside of basketball and robbing new business owners? Cosplay is a well-known thing in today's pop culture."

I suck my teeth. "Well, I've never heard of it." I sound like I just swallowed a petulant pill.

"It just means dressing up like pop culture characters and attending stuff like Comic-Con and PAX East."

I scrunch my face like I just bit into a lemon. "And you do this because...?"

"Because it's super fun. Don't hate on it until you try it."

I chuckle. "I'm good. I'll stick to dressing like a real person."

J. Cole fades out to the snare drum in the other room. Before Drake can start the dancing back up with a beat, people start jawing. There's a bunch of "What's good, nigga? I'm right here!" and "We can settle this shit now, bruh! Fuck The Crew! BM for life!"

There are two kinds of trash talking. The school kind that's funny and usually leads to a standard ass whooping that ends up on World Star. And then there's the out-of-school beef that usually leads to a closed casket. Those aren't funny.

My first instinct would usually be to get the fuck out of Dodge. But for some reason the first thing that goes through my mind is to keep Aamani safe. After all, I got her into this mess. If it weren't for me, she wouldn't be at this party.

I pop my head in the dining room, where all the dancing is

taking place. I see the Crew guys from earlier chest-to-chest with Kyle and some BMs. The Crew guy with the fresh Js lifts his shirt to flash his piece, his boxers cushioning the steel from resting against his skin.

"You feelin' froggy, then leap, bruh!"

It doesn't take a rocket scientist to know where this is going.

I take out my phone and text Britt.

> **Me: Shit's about to pop off down here. GTFO** 🏃🏃🏃

Hopefully the triple emojis will relay I'm not playing.

My phone vibrates.

> **Britt: Good look! Meet us down the block behind old man Hubbard's**

Emojis FTW!

I return to the living room. Aamani's scrolling through her phone and looks up at me when she hears me walk in. "Is everything okay?"

I shrug off the question. "Yeah, but maybe we should get out of—"

Pop! Pop! interrupts me. The gunshots drown out everything but the screams of people fleeing in terror. Aamani drops her phone, covers her ears, and drops to the floor cowering. She's going to get us both killed.

Trained in the art of gunshot-ending parties, I sprint over to Aamani and pull her up. "Come on! We gotta get the fuck out of here!"

The front door is out of the question because everyone and their mom race toward it. I spot a quicker escape route at the open window in the far corner. If being witness to all of Britt's stealing and crime scene fleeing has taught me anything, it's to always be aware of your surroundings and always have an escape plan.

Two more *pops* echo through the now half-empty house. My ears are ringing and I can smell the burnt steel lingering in the air.

Aamani's eyes grow two sizes. I can see the adrenaline and realization that we might die kick in, and before I know it she leaps into action and is pulling me to the window the smokers were using. I guess great minds do think alike.

She steps aside. "Go!"

I snarl. "You go!"

"Are you freakin' kidding me right now?!" With her newfound adrenaline strength, she shoves me through the open window. I nearly face-plant on the concrete and come up spitting gravel.

Aamani follows. But since she wasn't, what's the word I'm looking for, uh, *pushed*, she lands on her feet.

Pop!

Pop!

Two cars screech to a halt out front. Reinforcements no doubt. For which side, I don't know. One thing's for sure, my light-skin ass isn't sticking around to find out.

We hop the fence to Mr. Crawford's backyard. Aamani surprises me with how easily she accomplishes this, especially with that encyclopedia-size textbook in her backpack. The girl has serious hops. But then again, we're literally running for our lives at this point. That kind of adrenaline can turn anyone into a Hindu LeBron.

We run several blocks until we finally reach Old Man Hubbard's house. There's no sign of Britt. Aamani slows to catch her breath. There are no more gunshots, and there are also no sirens. They'll take their sweet-ass time showing up. If we lived in Lower Merion or another part of the suburbs where they have places that sell kale, like Trader Joe's and Whole Foods, then they'd have arrived shortly after the first shot with a SWAT team and Channel 3's Ukee Washington. Shit, knowing white folks and the suburbs, they probably have some kind of *Black Mirror* device they use to stop crimes before they happen. So it's like fuck us, right? Black-on-Black crime ... what else is new?

Aamani grabs at her knees, taking deep, long breaths like she's giving birth. Her long black hair reaches for the cement. I can make out how smooth her skin is, the hairs on the back of her neck standing at attention. I have to force myself to stop looking.

She pants. "Do all the parties around here end like that?"

"Actually, not as many as you'd think." I survey the block to make sure we're in the clear. "It usually ends one of three ways: people arguing about who's the G.O.A.T, Jordan or LeBron; someone getting caught cheating, which ends up with a World Star fight in the street; or the cops showing up."

Aamani and I jump as the bushes rustle behind us. I instinctively throw up my hands, ready to two-piece anything that walks through those bushes.

I start swinging—jab, jab, right hook. The combo's served me well in playground fights and Wii boxing. I catch 'em with the right hook.

"Ah, what the fuck, Lex?!" Kyle says, bobbing and weaving. "Chill the fuck out."

Jordan and Britt come stumbling through the bushes after him. I almost laugh because Britt's hair is all kinds of messed up. There are twigs and leaves sticking out of it, and she's got that frizzy sex hair.

"My bad," I chuckle, dropping my hands.

Jordan nods, impressed. "Damn, Lex. I didn't know you had hands like that."

I grin like *you better ask somebody.*

Britt pulls an Aamani and bends over, searching for air. "I taught her everything she knows," she states proudly.

I nod. "Damn right. Hargrove for life." Then we bump fists.

"Now, what the fuck happened back there?" Britt asks.

Kyle rubs the side of his head as though it's a magic lamp. "Some Crew niggas thought they could start some shit on our turf, so I had to give 'em the business. You know how we do."

Jordan sucks his teeth. "Man, as soon as boul pulled out that strap, you were out like Usain Bolt."

Kyle boasts. "Shit, I bust back."

"Bruh, you were out the back door before we were. You ain't bust shit."

Britt and I laugh. Her laugh turns into an out-of-shape cough.

"Man, whatever, bruh," Kyle says, curling the right side of his lip and turning his head. "If I didn't leave my gun at Sam's, I would've bust back. You can believe that. Fo' real."

"Yeah, and I'm fucking Ariana Grande," says Jordan.

This time even Aamani joins in on the laughter.

"The fuck you laughin' at with your Gandhi-lookin' ass? Like, who is this?" Kyle asks, pointing at Aamani.

Aamani takes the slander in stride. She waves. "Hi! I'm Aamani. Will someone please tell me my ass is at least a size bigger than Gandhi's? Dude literally didn't eat for twenty-one days." She looks in search of validation.

Kyle raises an eyebrow, looking at her like she's an alien coming to colonize our planet.

I step between her and everyone on the sidewalk. "She's cool," I vouch.

"Oh, so y'all cool now, huh?" Britt grunts. "I'm still going to whoop her ass like we planned."

Aamani turns to me quizzically. "Wait. What?"

Before I can bullshit my way out of this, Jordan puts his hand out. "Shut up, y'all. How long's that car been posted on the corner?"

We all turn and look at the same time. There's a silver Impala with tinted windows and chrome rims parked next to the stop sign with the engine running.

I twist my face, thinking. "It must've just pulled up, because it wasn't there a minute ago."

The tires crinkle over the pavement and the car starts creeping forward toward us. As it passes under the streetlight we see the driver's side window descend into the door.

We've lived in Hargrove Projects long enough to know that when a car creeps down a street with its windows down and it's not to bump the music, it can only mean one thing—and Jordan shouts it out at the top of his lungs to alert anyone that may be nearby: "Drive-by!"

Again Aamani freezes, new to the projects and the laws of these streets. Our crime is we're standing next to Kyle. So by association, we're BMs.

I grab Aamani and we all disperse like roaches when the lights come on. Jordan and Britt sprint up the sidewalk and around the corner. Kyle darts across the street and over the chain-link fence. I use my survival instincts and take the scenic route and duck back through the bushes behind us and to the fence. They can't shoot what they can't see.

Aamani shimmies up the fence beside me. Then I hear it.

Pop!

Pop! Pop!

I have half my body over the fence when I feel an explosion of pain shoot through my lower back. The pain travels through my entire body. It feels like someone took the sharpest knife in the world and is digging it into my skin like they're carving a jack-o'-lantern. I lose my footing and go crashing into the ground like a meteor hurling from space. My phone in my back pocket breaks my fall. I hear it shatter. I go to get up, but can't and collapse back down on the cold ground, every part of my body in agony.

I had to have pulled something in my back. Hopefully Michael, our athletic trainer, will have me ready for the game next week.

Tears well in my eyes. I blink and send two drops down my cheeks.

What the fuck is wrong with me? Why can't I move?

Aamani sees I'm down for the count and races to my side. Somehow through all of this, she's managed to keep her fly-ass scarf wrapped around her neck.

Her hazelnut skin almost goes pale, and she tosses her hand over her mouth as she gasps. "Shit."

It suddenly gets hard for me to breathe. "What . . .? W-what's wrong?"

She puts her hands out to steady me. "Nothing's wrong. I just need you to, shit, um, remain calm, okay. Can you do that for me, Lex?" she coaches.

"Why . . ."—I search for my breath—"are you talking to me like I'm a baby?"

"Listen, you were shot. But it's just a flesh wound. You're going to be fine."

"What the fuck are you talking about?! I-I'm not shot! I-I can't be shot! I have a game Tuesday!"

I place my hand over the pain to assess the damage, and feel something slimy and wet. When I pull my hand back to look at it, I see it's coated in blood. My heart starts racing even faster, like it's about to rip through my chest, and my breath flees completely. I can barely make out Aamani through all my tears.

I try to get up, but the pain multiplies and pins me back down. "Don't move!" Aamani instructs. She unzips her backpack and pulls out her dress. She balls it up and presses it against my wound. I cry out in pain because it hurts like a bitch and because my blood has ruined her beautiful Hindu dress. "Sorry, but I need to keep pressure on it."

"What's happening? Why can't I move?" I say, crying my eyes out.

My eyes dry up for a split second, enough for me to see Aamani clearly. "I'm scared, Aamani. I'm sorry for bringing you here."

"Don't go all soft on me. We're not BFFs, remember? I don't even like you," she says with an echo of a smile. "You're going to be fine. I promise." For some reason, I believe her. "I need you to listen carefully. I have to leave you here—"

I jerk my head forward with the remaining strength I have. "No! Do ... don't leave me. Please. I don't want to die. Not h-here. Not alone. Not like Nassir."

She looks me dead in my tear-filled eyes, probing my soul. "I promise, no one's dying tonight, except my willingness to ever go to another party. I need you to hold my churidar and keep pressure on the wound, okay? Unfortunately, your phone is shattered and I left mine at the party. So I'm going to have to go get help."

I grab her. More of my blood smears her arm. "You can't go out there. The block is hot."

"I have to," she announces, standing. "Don't worry. I got this." She adjusts my hand on the churidar. "Now keep it steady. I'll be back before you can say, '*I'm Batman*'," she says in a deep, brooding voice.

Are you fucking kidding me with this, God? I've survived seventeen years fighting the foster system and the projects, only to die from a stray bullet at Kyle Reese's shitty-ass house party. He didn't even have any finger foods. I'm about to be up in Heaven mad as fuck.

I can't feel the pain anymore, which is good. On the other hand, that's because my whole right side is numb, which is bad.

I'm trying my hardest not to pass out. I mean, that would make two blackouts in one day.

I can hear the sirens off in the distance. I just hope it's an ambulance and not the cops. They may see a wounded Black girl and want to finish the job.

CHAPTER 3

He breaks the situation down for me again, making it five times in less than three minutes.

Lies.

It's all fucking lies.

"Nah, that's bullshit!" I snap. "I can still play. I got a game Tuesday!" Why is he lying to my face? "You don't get it. I *have* to fucking play."

"Again, I'm very sorry, Alexis . . ." the generic white male doctor repeats for now a sixth time. He's got one more time to lie to me, then I'm putting my fist through his *Grey's Anatomy* face. "But I'm afraid you'll never play basketball again. Or at least not in the way you did before. The bullet severed a major nerve in your leg. There's nothing more we can do. Our hope is that with some physical therapy you'll be able to walk without the assistance of a cane. I'm sorry, but barring a miracle, you will be walking with a severe limp for the rest of your life, which I'm afraid means no extensive running or jumping."

"But . . . p-please . . ." I beg with wide eyes. "Please don't take this from me. It's all I know how to do——" I nearly choke on the realization of my circumstance. That growing up in the hood, I've only ever been told I can be one thing to make it out——an athlete. So I beg for my life. "Please, yo, don't do this."

"I'm terribly sorry..."

There's a ringing that fills in the rest of his words. It's like someone fired a Glock directly into my eardrums. All I can do is stare at this rich-ass white man and try to comprehend his words. "You'll never play basketball again." That's what he said. The words rolled off his tongue with the same certainty as when he stated his fucking name.

Rage clutches my throat tight.

This can't be real.

I can't speak.

I can't breathe.

I dig my nails into my forehead and try to peel my skin away as if it's hoarding all the air.

I want to scream. I want to cry so hard my eyes feel like they're on fire. I want to put my fist through his stupid I-used-to-be-in-a-frat face.

The doctor puts his hands up, trying to calm me.

"I know it's quite a lot to take in. But I assure you, you'll be able to live your life like you otherwise normally would, just without the ability to run or jump like you did prior to the accident."

I hate this bitch-ass doctor.

I hate his perfect teeth. That chiseled jawline. I hate his white skin filled with so much fucking privilege. I hate that he could probably buy Hargrove and gentrify it. But most of all, I hate his two functioning legs. That he can put all his weight on either and run and dribble and shoot; I hate that he can play basketball and I can't.

The ringing subsides. Now all I can think about is that shitty court on Baltimore Ave.

I used to go there before and after school, and I'd stay until the sun went down. The lines on the court were faded, and even if they had replaced the net that morning, by the time they'd cut the lights off (they'd cut them at nine, because it was prime drug real estate and the city didn't want kids there while people were slinging) it would be hanging on the hoop by a thread. I'd just hoop. It was like nothing else existed when I was on that concrete. The cops didn't bother us. The dealers weren't offering. We didn't worry about getting shot. The only thing I was concerned about was putting in work, which I always did. No one on the court wanted this smoke. That court—really, any place with a hoop is my sanctuary. If I wasn't playing ball, I would have been posted on the corner slinging like Nassir. Or worse: dead.

And here's this rich white man with movie-star hair telling me I'll never be able to play again.

A hot tear crests over my right eye and tumbles. I wipe it away. Then another one follows, and another one. Now they're streaming down my face like raindrops on a windowpane.

I look up at him and dig into the back of my throat to pull up the words. My voice is defeated and shattered, just like the nerves in my leg.

"Just fucking kill me, yo."

CHAPTER 4

I start to lose my balance as I take another step toward the kitchen. The added weight I'm forced to put on my left leg has all but fucked up my equilibrium. It also doesn't help that there are LEGOS scattered around the crumb-covered floor like landmines. Thankfully, the arm on Marcus's crusty-ass couch, which has more stains than a bed at Motel 6, helps me regain my balance. I caught him beating off on it one night when I came down for a glass of water. Since then I've tried to avoid all contact with the Cum Couch. If we watch a movie or a basketball game, I sit on the floor and pray a roach doesn't crawl up my ass. It's the lesser of two evils.

"You need to stop being so damn stubborn and use the cane the doctors gave you," suggests Britt. She's already in the kitchen, unpacking the McDonald's bag and setting aside the Dollar Menu burgers for the kids.

I flash her the stank-eye and go back to focusing on walking twenty feet in under an hour.

I know she's only trying to look out for me. But, justifiably, for the past few weeks I've been in a shitty mood since being shot in the ass. So fuck her suggestions.

Once word got out that my playing days were over, all the scouts stopped recruiting me. No more letters or school visits from

Coach Staley. I was lucky to get a clichéd Instagram post of some BS Tupac line like "*Keep your head up.*"

I take two more long and excruciatingly slow steps toward the kitchen. I'm almost there. Kinda. Not really. Also, every time my right foot touches the ground without the support of my cane, my leg feels like it's being dipped into the deepest pits of hell.

"Yo!" Britt shouts past me. Her voice reverberates upstairs through the tiny row home. "Come and get y'all's food!"

Less than ten seconds later the kids come storming past me like that wild herd of wildebeests that killed Mufasa in *The Lion King*. Rashard makes up the rear and almost sacks me. The boy's nine and already pushing 150 pounds. He's a tank.

"Don't worry about me. I'm only walking here," I say to Cum Couch, because no one's listening.

Claudia, Miles, and Keyshawn race out in front and grab their Dollar Menu burgers. Then they sprint back upstairs. No hellos. No thank-yous. Just food. Room. Toys.

I don't even bother asking Britt how she could afford all of this. I know she's selling drugs again for Devon. She spent the whole lunch period "in the bathroom," or more accurately, at the drop.

She's already digging into her burger. Her hair's tied up and a few strands poke out the sides behind her ears. "Hurry up before your burger gets cold. Over here limping like Peeta in that cave scene."

After a long-winded journey through LEGO pieces and cum-stained couches, I finally reach the kitchen table. I grip the back of the chair and gingerly take a seat, squatting on the cushion like I'm about to take a shit.

Britt snorts. "I'm sorry," she lies, breaking into full laughter. "Not funny. My bad." Then she snorts again.

"You're right. It's not funny." A part of me actually wants to laugh though. I guess I've done enough crying for a lifetime. Crying over it isn't going to change shit. My leg still won't work right.

Peeta is just one of the names I get clowned with now. I've also been called an extra in *Thriller*, been told I walk like a pimp, and that it looks like I'm constantly doing the Stanky Leg.

"It's cool. Peeta's a real G in *Catching Fire*. Remember when he volunteered as tribute for Haymitch? Boy got heart," I educate.

We're closet Tributes. People and businesses would always donate the books to the foster home for Christmas. So for, like, four years all we got for Christmas were Hunger Games books and socks. The crazy thing is we actually had the attention span to read them. That's because Katniss is one of us: a badass bitch from the projects who's down to ride-or-die for her block.

"I'm telling you. You need to put that pimp cane to use. Remember when Trayvon sprained his ankle and didn't want to wear the boot because then he could only wear one pair of Jordans? Then his clumsy ass tripped and fell down the staircase by the gym and actually broke his ankle. He had to get that cast that smelled like ass, and was forced to wear one Jordan anyway for, like, a year. Don't pull a Trayvon."

What she left out was Trayvon's not the smartest. I told him it was chilly outside once and he asked how much for a bowl.

"Girl, I gave that cane to Old Man Grady. What I look like using a cane?"

"Like someone who can walk ten feet without the seasons changing."

I laugh. She got me on that one.

I unwrap my burger and finally take a bite, savoring every chew with an orgasmic eye-roll. When you live on corner-store frozen pizza, Pop-Tarts, and stolen Hot Cheetos, McDonald's suddenly becomes a meal cooked by Gordon Ramsay.

Britt smiles as she watches me devour my burger. She takes a sip of Sprite and burps. "What your mom say about you giving away your cane?"

"Nothin'." I swallow. "I haven't seen her since I got out of the hospital."

She takes another bite of her burger, not at all surprised. She knows the Felicia Duncan drill. The one that goes something like: new guy, massive bender, missing-persons case. "You think you're going to end up back in here?"

"I doubt it. She's been gone longer than this before. Difference is I'm older now, so no one's going to snitch to social services about it."

Britt follows up her bite with another swig of Sprite. "I still can't believe she was mad though. It's not your fault you got shot."

"You should've seen her. She was mad as fuck. I don't even want to know how she got the money for the medical bills."

"You know. The whole damn block knows."

I shiver, trying to get the image of her sleeping with the whole block to raise the funds out of my head.

Mom's a shade lighter than me. Or as Britt clowns, "Light, bright, damn near white." Guys have always gone crazy over her like she's J.Lo or something. When I was too young to know what was going on, right before child services scooped me up the first time, she would have random guys over every night. She'd leave me in the dining room and tell me to watch TV while she helped her "friend" with something in her room. I always thought *she sure has a lot of friends.* Turns out not one of them were actually her friend. Then she'd blast some R&B and fifteen-ish minutes later said *friend* would leave. I'd walk in the room, the bed sheets ruffled and half-tossed off the bed, and she'd be lying there passed out with a rubber tube strapped to her arm. The first time I found her, I thought she was dead. I'd soon realize these D.A.R.E. people that come to our school and drone on about the dangers of drugs were on to something.

Mom's skinny as a rail, and her bones look like they could snap if she were to trip. I'll give her this, though. She somehow managed to keep her ass. I know this because boys at my school love to point it out. They say things like, "Daammnn, your mom got a fat ass!" And once when she had to come to school to meet with Principal Garrett, I received a text from Dwayne that simply said: *Dat ass tho.*

"At least she got the money. It kept you alive, didn't it?"

"If she'd signed up for that insurance, she wouldn't have had to pay out of pocket. She didn't do shit. If it weren't for Aamani—"

"Who?"

I tilt my head, like *come on.* It's her fault Aamani hasn't spoken to me since that night. The least she could do is remember the girl. "You know damn well who I'm talking about. The Indian girl that went and got help."

"I don't know that bitch's life!" Her voice rises an octave in disgust.

"Whatever. If Aamani wasn't there, they'd have never gotten to me in time to rush me to the hospital."

"Yeah, but your mom paid for those doctors. Rushing you to the hospital don't mean shit. They rushed Pac to the hospital, too, and look how that turned out."

"With seventeen new albums," I state, obviously.

"Bitch, you know he's dead."

A loud thump crashes over our heads. Britt looks to the ceiling as though it's the culprit. "Y'all better knock off all that noise before Marcus gets home!" She keeps her eyes locked on the ceiling, daring it to make another sound. When silence once again reigns throughout the house, she returns her attention to me. "At least your mom gave a shit to get the money. If I got shot you can bet your ass Marcus ain't doing shit."

We both laugh because it's true.

"You're right. Truth be told it's nice having the house to myself. I don't have to hear her and Randy going at it."

Britt's eyes grow two sizes. "She's still getting with that broke-ass, Bobby Brown, pitbull-looking motha fucka?"

I picture Randy's pitbull-esque nose and his played out New Edition fade, and start to crack up. It feels good to laugh.

"For real, though. They're so loud. It's disgusting. When I do eventually have sex, I won't do it with a megaphone."

"Ha," Britt scoffs. "You need to find a man first. You're the only light-skin girl I know that can't get one. What, you got a diseased cooch or somethin'? Maybe you need to find a guy with a handicap fetish. There's got to be an app for that."

"I'm not handicapped. I just walk with a limp," I protest.

"A limp that's turned you into a grandma with your should-be-cane-using ass. Bitch, you handicapped. Shit, you should take advantage of it. See if Make-a-Wish Foundation will let you meet Drake."

"I'm pretty sure that's not how Make-a-Wish works."

We share another mood-cleansing laugh.

Keys jingle in the front door. We both tense up out of habit. I can still recall the unadulterated dread that would engulf me every time he walked through that door. It was like being stranded in a field with a tornado headed right for you.

Britt smacks her teeth. "I really don't feel like hearing his mouth." Then she shoves the rest of her burger into her mouth as if she's competing in a burger-eating contest.

Marcus tosses his keys on the Cum Couch and shuts the door behind him. You can hear the scattering of tiny feet upstairs as the kids make a desperate last-second attempt at cleaning their room. He glances our way and spots the McDonald's bag on the table. He beelines it for us.

"Son of a bitch!" he shouts, clutching his right foot. He picks up the LEGO he stepped on and throws it against the wall behind the staircase. "Miles! Keyshawn! Get your asses down here and pick up these toys!"

The boys come racing downstairs faster than they did when they heard there was McDonald's. Rashard hangs back at the top of the stairs, too scared. They drop to their knees and frantically begin picking up all the LEGO land mines. The entire time they look up at Marcus with watery, puppy dog eyes.

"Don't give me that look. I told y'all yesterday to stop leaving your toys all over the goddamn house. Next time I see 'em not in their box, I'm throwing 'em in the trash."

The boys nod and retreat back upstairs.

I know I should be concerned with the kids not losing what little toys they have, but all I can think about is how nappy Keyshawn's braids are. I'm going to have to redo them tomorrow. I'd do them tonight, but I'm not trying to be here when Marcus is home.

Marcus makes his way into the kitchen, carrying a brown grocery bag. He sets it on the counter, then turns his attention toward us.

"I see you got money to eat out now, huh."

"So? It's my money," Britt replies with a roll of her head.

"Oh, so you think you're grown now. Get smart again and see what happens." Britt sucks her teeth and looks away. "You sellin' that shit again?"

"No, sir." Britt says this to her chest, still avoiding eye contact. It's like looking into his dickheaded eyes will send her to the Sunken Place.

He digs into the grocery bag and pulls out a bottle of Henny, some bread, lunch meat, and a pack of cigarettes. "You're full of shit." He takes out a cigarette and places it between his teeth.

Thankfully my presence has yet to be acknowledged, so I start to creep from my seat and go for a smooth escape. Only, my ability to creep is gone now that it takes me a year to get the strength to stand, and it hurts like a bitch.

"Nah, don't let me break up y'all's little spending spree. Sit your ass back down, Alexis."

I do as instructed. Not because he told me to, but because I want to. Okay, and maybe a little because he told me to.

He lights the cigarette and blows a cloud of smoke our way.

"Did you fill out those lunch forms for the kids like I asked you to?"

Britt remains silent. I can see her anger boiling as she stares coldly at the table.

"I know you hear me talkin' to you."

"No," she answers dryly.

"No what?"

"No, sir," Britt revises. "I forgot. Too busy trying to feed everyone."

Marcus smirks, then calmly walks up behind her. With a cock of his hand, he smacks her upside the head. I know it stings because

(1) I've been on the receiving end of one of his slaps, and (2) he's got that old man strength.

"What the fuck I tell you about following directions? Now I'm going to have to go down to the school and fix this shit. Your brothers and sister need their free lunch. Unless you plan on using your drug money to buy McDonald's for them every day since you got it like that now."

Britt balls her fists and clenches her teeth. I give her three taps under the table with my foot. It's a code we developed when I lived here to tell the other to calm down.

But the next thing I know, he's cracking her upside the head again. This time he curls his knuckles into a half fist. The half punch rings out through the kitchen and I hear Britt grunt, the pain catching her off guard.

She's burying all her anger and trying her damnedest not to go off on him. A tear of frustration rolls down her cheek. I give her three more soft taps to let her know it's going to be all right. Seeing someone as tough as Britt cry and be beaten down makes me squirm.

"If you ignore me one more time . . . so help me Jesus."

"Man, you didn't even ask me"—I quickly tap her again, this time harder so she checks herself—"I mean, yes, sir. I fucked up," she admits through gritted teeth.

He takes another pull of his cigarette and again blows the smoke in our faces. He touches the ashes in the sink and grabs the bottle of Henny off the counter.

"Don't worry. I'll go down and fix your mess. Story of my life."

God, I want to raise the point that he's the adult here and it's not her job to do his errands. But I bite my tongue because I know it won't help matters, and I'm really not in the mood to get bitch-slapped.

"Make me a sandwich and bring it to my room," he commands, leaving.

As I watch Britt begrudgingly get up and start on the sandwich like his fucking slave, I'm reminded I don't want this life. The drive-bys. The foster homes. The drugs on every corner. My mom doing those drugs and every guy on those corners. I have to get out, scholarship or not. I don't care if I have to crawl. I'll find a way.

CHAPTER 5

I t's been weeks since I've been back to Super Mart, since the day I had to outrun the fattest cop of all time. But after Devon denied me my last chance of making enough money to get out of here—he said, "Can't no cripple work the corner. How you going to run from the cops or catch some nigga tryin' to jack your shit?"—I figured I need to suck up my pride and go back. Because I really need a win right now. Or better yet, I need to binge the shit out of some Kit Kats to drown my sorrows. Also, Super Mart's the only store in Hargrove that has the king-size Kit Kats for under a dollar-fifty. And without king-size Kit Kats, I'm not sure there's a point to life.

The store's empty and no one's manning the register, which seems like a terrible way to run a business in the hood. But then again, what do I know about business and making money? I can't even push drugs on the corner, and they let idiots like Kyle do that.

The top of my right Nike scrapes the linoleum as I approach the glorious candy section. It looks like Willy Wonka and the West Philly Chocolate Factory. My few physical therapy sessions have marginally increased my walking pace. Though it's done fuck-all for the pain. The one downside is I now walk like a zombie, hence the shredded tongue of my right Nike. Even with all the noise the dragging of my foot makes, no one comes to check it out. No sign of Aamani or her pops. Maybe me, Britt, and Tubs are the only ones that shop here. It's legit weird that this place always looks like it's been hit by the rapture.

I put my hand in my pocket and run it over the ten dollars I stole from Mom's drug stash. For some reason, she thinks I don't know about it. I mean, she hides it in the most cliché place: under the mattress. What, she thinks I've never seen a movie? I'm good as long as I stick to taking a dollar here and there. Mattress banking isn't the most efficient way of keeping track of your funds. Not to mention, it's not like she'll be auditing anyone anytime soon. Shit, she's so strung-out that half the time she thinks Obama's still president.

Now, normally I would just jack these Kit Kats and call it a day, especially since no one's here. They're pretty much asking to get got. But I'm trying to turn over a new leaf. And with my shitty luck someone would come out the back room right as I'm leaving, and except for a hundred-year-old woman on her deathbed, I'm not outrunning shit.

So I wait at the counter, money in hand, a perturbed look on my face. I sigh loudly every couple of seconds. When that doesn't work I go, "Ay, anyone back there? Hell-o?"

I hear some movement in the back followed by a faint voice. "One second . . ."

Five long, impatient seconds later, Aamani comes stumbling out the back room. She has on the same pair of dark jeans from school today, except instead of the Iron Man T-shirt she was wearing, she has on a kurta and her hair is pulled back with a scarf hair tie. I only know this because I went on a Hindu Google binge the other day out of boredom. It's what my life has come to now that

I can't play ball—Googling pointless shit and stalking celebrities on Instagram.

"Sorry," she apologizes, tying her blue apron around her back and hurrying to the counter. "I had a serious Doctor Who emergency. The new Doctor regenerated tonight."

"A doctor what now?"

Aamani looks up from her apron tying. When she realizes it's me, her face folds into itself. "Oh, it's you." Her voice is coated with attitude. I almost go *well, fuck you too*, but refrain. "Can I help you?" She follows this up with a little eye-roll.

She clearly doesn't want the ten dollars in my pocket. Whatever happened to service with a smile?

"I want to buy these Kit Kats." Then I toss in a dose of attitude. "*Obviously*."

Aamani grabs the candy, scans them with her pricing gun, and then points to the green lights displaying the price on the register.

I cock my face to the side. "Really? Are you that petty that you can't even tell me how much they cost? Or are you still trippin' about your doctor emergency? You get knocked up or something?"

"Doctor Who's a Time Lord. Not an actual doctor."

"I'm going to assume you're speaking nerd."

"Do you have the money or not?" she bites.

And to think I once saw her as this sweet little Muslim nerd with a transforming lunchbox.

I basically shove the money down her throat. "Fine. Be that way. I can barely walk because of what happened, but you go ahead and be all bitchy because I tried to be nice and introduce you to some new people."

"Yeah, new people who want to *exterminate* me like the Daleks.

Or did you forget about that?" She says *exterminate* in this robotic British voice.

"Okay, real talk. You have to chill with all the nerd shit."

"Your friends want to kick my ass," she translates sheepishly.

I give her a fed-up eye-roll. "For the hundredth time, I wasn't going to let anyone kick your ass. I mean, yeah, they were about to beat your ass in the caf, so maybe I suggested they wait to do it at the party when there would be no adults around." As soon as the words leave my mouth I want to take them back. "Okay, that sounds fucked up when I put it like that. What I'm getting at is my plan was to get you to the party and buy some time to think of a way to get you off my friend's shit list. I mean, I'm kind of, like, a hero in all this. Just sayin'."

Her eyes tighten, aloof. "Well, you did a poor job. Because correct me if I'm wrong, but I believe your BFF's exact words were, and I quote, 'I'm still going to whoop her ass like we planned.' Keywords 'still' and 'like *we* planned.' I know I'm new here, but that sounds to me like you guys are still very much planning to kick my ass."

Yeah, I got nothin'.

"And one more thing. Who makes an elaborate plan with their friends to lure someone to a party with a fake invite? Who are you people, George Clooney and Brad Pitt?"

"What's rich white people have to do with it?"

"They're the stars of *Ocean's Eleven*. It's a movie."

"I know what it is. I watch movies."

"I'm trying to say you guys seem to like planning ways to steal things."

I think for a second. "Isn't there an all-women Ocean's movie with Rihanna? That would've been a better comparison."

"Yeah, except no one saw that movie. I was trying to give you a reference you'd actually get." She smirks. "We see how well that worked out."

"Look, yo. I'm trying to be nice here. But your little attitude is starting to get on my nerves."

She stares in reply.

I gaze into her light-brown eyes. I don't like this scarf hair tie. Hiding her long wavy hair is like hiding a shooting star. It's selfish not to show anyone.

I stare.

She stares.

It's getting weird.

I'm not entirely sure what she's trying to accomplish, but I'm too invested in the staring contest to back out. Plus, I hate to lose.

Aamani blinks (*Yeah! In your face, Aamani!*) and shakes her head like I'm the childish one who initiated the staring contest. "Um . . . sixty-seven cents."

"What?" The corners of my mouth pinch in confusion.

"You're short sixty-seven cents."

The green lights on the register display $10.67. I look down at my lonely $10, then take sixty-seven cents from the ashtray full of nickels and pennies by the cheap phone chargers on the counter.

She takes the change and drops it back in the ashtray. "You can't use this. It's for when you're, like, five cents short. Not almost a dollar." She hesitates. "Do you really not have sixty-seven cents?"

I can't afford eight fucking Kit Kat bars. Of course I can put one back, but it's the principle of the matter. Not to mention it's a well-known fact that eight Kit Kats are better than seven.

Pressure starts to build in my chest and expands in the back of my throat like a balloon. I swallow, pushing the lump back down.

No basketball. No money. No future. No eight Kit Kats. Sweet baby Jesus, are you even up there?

Stop being a little bitch. Don't you cry in front of this girl again, you hear me? Don't!

Aamani stares at me with these big, sympathetic eyes as if I'm one of those starving African kids rich white people sponsor to make themselves feel better.

Two tears spill down my cheeks. I turn and quickly wipe them away.

"Are you okay?" Aamani asks, her voice softer and less confrontational.

The lump I've been suppressing uppercuts through my throat and more tears escape.

"I can't even afford a few fucking Kit Kats," I rant, picking one up and slamming it down on the counter. "And since I lost my only chance at a scholarship, I won't be going to college and I'll never play in the WNBA. Shit, I can't even get a regular job. You know I tried to slang heroin and they wouldn't even let me do that. Like, how fucking pathetic am I for them to tell me I'm too worthless to work a corner? Like, what the fuck?! I shouldn't be surprised. My mom's life's always been shit. I'm going to turn out just like her. I'm going to be messing around with broke-ass niggas like Randy. People will look at me and go, 'There goes that crackhead Alexis. She was supposed to be the one to make it out. Now she ain't shit.'"

The self-pity and anger engulf me. Now I don't even give a shit that I'm crying.

"Let me ask you something. Do you have any idea what it's like to be me? To have the only thing you've ever loved taken from you because you went to some corny-ass party you ain't even want to go to?" I look at her. She deflects and looks down at her shoes. "No?

I didn't think so. I'm going to be stuck in the hood the rest of my life, struggling to feed myself every day. So no, Aamani, clearly I'm not fucking okay."

Annnd my life just got more pathetic. I'm having a mental breakdown and acting crazier than Kanye at an awards show.

Aamani's eyes dart everywhere except at me.

"Sooo . . ." she lingers awkwardly. "You don't have the sixty-seven cents?"

Her delivery is dry and I can't tell if she's messing with me, trying to defuse the situation with humor. At this point I just want to leave while I still have a shred of soldier left in me.

I take back my money and reach over the counter. Aamani flinches and jumps back, crashing against the cigarettes. I take a plastic bag and toss all eight Kit Kats in.

"You know what—fuck it. The system's rigged for me to end up a criminal, a product of my environment, so I might as well embrace the inevitable. I'm going full Jada in *Set It Off*." Aamani's still cautiously leaning against the cigarettes, keeping her distance out of fear. I reach over the counter and snag a plastic bag. "Yeah, I watch movies too."

I zombie-walk out, money and candy in hand. Aamani doesn't even try to stop me.

I stick my key in the door. I can hear Mom and who I assume to be Randy on the other side. You never know with my mom. She goes through guys like Taylor Swift. God, I hope I'm not about to walk in on her giving him head on the couch again. I was going to watch the Sixers game on that couch. And what is it with adults and sexual acts on couches? Are pleather and armrests aphrodisiacs?

Much to my relief, Mom's not even in the living room. Randy's posted up on the couch, unpacking his drug travel kit, which is fully equipped with needles, a plastic tube strap, dime bags, and little vials of heroin.

"What's good wit' you, Lex?" Randy says, up-nodding that pitbull-esque nose of his. He doesn't even attempt to hide the drugs. "Me and your mom are about to chill and watch some TV. You might not want to be in here for this grownup shit."

Is that what adults call *getting high off your ass* these days?

"Yeah, I bet," I say, dripping sarcasm.

Then I hear drawers slamming and Mom cursing like she's on a diss track. That's when I realize she's in my (!!!) room. I power walk to the back. Well, I power zombie walk, anyway. The shit hurts. But what the fuck is Mom doing in my room?!

Randy chuckles. "Ay, Felicia? Your girl seems pissed. If I were you I'd hurry up and find my shit before she gets back there. She's got that look in her eyes."

Mom almost runs me over when she comes storming out of my room. Her forehead is damp with sweat, and her eyes are buggy. She keeps scratching her inner forearm as though she's trying to subdue a mosquito bite.

I'm all too familiar with this look. She's feigning hard.

I try to walk past her to see what the hell she's doing in my room, but she slides to the left like she's Kawhi Leonard and grabs my arm. I manage to get a glimpse of my room over her shoulder. It's a complete mess. My drawers have been pulled out and tossed on the floor, and my mattress is flipped and dangling halfway off the frame. Boxes of my ball shoes have been yanked out the closet and thrown open. The only pair of Jordans I own (I stole them from some white girl at an away game) lay next to a pile of my sports bras.

"Where's my money, Alexis?" she demands. Her eyes go twice as buggy and her arm starts shaking. Her once-luscious hair is dry as beef jerky. I wonder when's the last time she washed it.

"No one's got your money," I answer, turning up my nose.

"Don't fuckin' play with me. I *need* that money." She practically begs.

I suck my teeth and try to pull away, but she tightens her grip. I double down. "I'm not playing."

Her breathing intensifies as her chest starts to expand and deflate like she's out of breath. Her buggy eyes dart around the hall in search of answers.

"What's in the bag?" she queries, steadying her voice.

Shit.

"Uh, what bag?"

Real smooth, Lex.

She yanks the bag from my hand. Before she can look inside I go, "I stole them."

"Bullshit!" she says, digging through the bag. Beads of sweat glisten on her forehead. "Why you have a bag then?" That's actually a good observation. I'm not sure how she managed to sober up enough to deduce that. "I know you're lying to me. And after all I've done for you. I brought you into this world. I put a roof over your head. I paid your expensive-ass bills with money I don't have . . . and you go and . . . and steal my shit to buy fucking candy?!"

She chucks the bag in the living room, and then grips me up from my front collar.

I wrestle to break free. "What the fuck, Mom!" I fail. She has that crackhead strength.

"I-I need that money," she pleads. "Give me my shit!" Her breath smells like ass from all the cigarettes and sexual favors she hands out like party flyers.

I'm losing my balance and can feel my right leg giving out as Mom applies more crackhead strength. Eventually she overpowers me and we both go tumbling to the floor.

Mom takes the opportunity with me pinned against the floor to loot my pockets. She finds the ten dollars stuffed in my back pocket, and shoots up off of me. Then she runs to Randy to present her findings like a cat bringing its owner a mouse for praise.

"I got the rest of the money!" she announces proudly, and hands it to Randy. "Now let me hit that needle." She reaches over him for the travel kit.

"The fuck is this? Ten dollars?" Randy chuckles. "You ain't hittin' shit with this."

"Come on, baby . . ." Mom's draped all over him like white on rice. "I just need a couple of hits. That's it. I-I need 'em to make me feel good."

He shrugs her off. "What you need is to get me the rest of my damn money."

Randy picks up his travel kit and heads for the door.

Mom makes a final attempt at stopping him, groveling at his feet as though she's one of those Victorian peasants we read about in English class. "Baby . . . don't do me like that."

"Bitch, get the fuck off me." He kicks her away like a stray. "You didn't put in on this."

As soon as the door shuts, Mom collapses against it, weltering into a fetal position. She increases the scratching. I fear she's about to scratch her arm off. Two generations of Duncan women now lay on the floor adjacent to each other.

She looks over at me, swallowing her sweat-filled tears. "You fuckin' bitch," she sneers, her voice saturated in loathing. "You and your goddamn bills. It's not fair. That was my money." Then she retreats back into her fetal ball and rocks herself in torment, the whole time muttering, "Fuckin' bitch . . . You fuckin' bitch . . ."

With the help of the wall, I pull myself up through the pain, retrieve the candy, and then escape into my newly dismantled room. I'm not sure I can survive another day in this life. This living hell.

I do my best Mom impression and curl up on my bed. The moon spills in through the pried-open blinds, illuminating the mess. A gunshot followed shortly by sirens echoes in the distance. The hood's symphony, conducted by murderers and dream slayers.

I open a Kit Kat and take a bite. It tastes of comfort and processed sugar. As I turn to look out the window, my view of the sky and our back alley, my cracked phone lights up with a new DM. I slide it open. A smile comes to my face when I see it's from Aamani.

> Sorry about basketball and the way I acted earlier. I'm still pissed about that night. I thought you were different. But I can't even begin to imagine what you're going through. Come to Mrs. Hall's class tomorrow at 3:15. I think I can help with everything.

CHAPTER 6

Mr. Hilbert drones on about Russian history. Everyone except Aamani and white Lindsay is nodding off. They're actually taking notes. I keep going over Aamani's DM. I mean, unless she has some spare robot legs hidden under her kurta, how does she plan to help?

Then, I don't know why, maybe I'm having a stroke, but something inside of me clicks and I decide to follow Aamani's lead and actually pay attention.

It feels mad weird.

Mikayla, who's skillfully texting under her desk, looks up from her phone and leans across the aisle. "Yo, what are you doing?" she whispers.

"Taking notes," I whisper back, trying my damndest not to lose focus. Too late. Lost it.

"Ew, gross," she says, twisting her face. Then she goes back to texting under her desk.

"So the Russian Revolution, people," Mr. Hilbert educates, pacing the aisles. I write down *Russian Revolution* in my notebook, because I'm studious like that. "Does anyone want to be brave and tell me when it was and what triggered it? There's a big '*good job*' in it for you if you do."

I get a huge whiff of his old man cologne as he walks past. I hope he doesn't wear this much cologne on his Tinder dates. He glances down at my notebook and I give him a proud smirk like, *yeah, that's right, I'm taking notes, and what?!* Mr. Hilbert is one of those uppity, intellectual Ivy school brothas. Like, no matter the weather he always wears a tie and cardigan like he's freakin' Mr. Rogers. And I'm pretty sure he only wears glasses to complete the "intellectual" look, because even when he's not wearing them he catches me when I'm not paying attention. So I call BS on him not having 20:20 vision.

Shawn Stevens raises his hand. Mr. Hilbert sees him out of the corner of his fake this-motherfucker-can-see glasses, and dismisses him. "Yes, Mr. Stevens, it will be on the test," he confirms in a monotone voice. "Now . . . any takers?"

Crickets.

"Come on . . ." Mr. Hilbert implores. "It was in the readings, people. If you don't do the readings, how do you expect to pass the test?" More crickets. "Anyone? Bueller? . . . Bueller?" We all stare at him as if he just sprouted a unicorn horn. "Your generation has no taste in movies," he complains, and then settles at the head of the room. He surveys the class until he stops at Jordan, who's goofing off with Trey in the corner. "How about you, Mr. Clark? You seem very chatty today. Care to enlighten us about the Russian Revolution?" Jordan shakes his head vehemently. "That was rhetorical, Mr. Clark. Time and what triggered it—go!"

Jordan coolly leans back and sighs through his nostrils. "I don't know, man"—Mr. Hilbert gives him a death stare—"Mr. Hilbert . . . I mean, Mr. Hilbert," Jordan quickly corrects. "Did it happen back in, like, the eighties when Ivan Drago dropped Apollo Creed?"

Light chuckles fill the room.

Mr. Hilbert removes his glasses and pinches the bridge of

his nose. "I suppose I only have myself to blame. No, Mr. Clark, the Russian Revolution did not begin because of incidents that transpired in the, and let's be clear, worst *Rocky* movie." Then he turns to Aamani and deploys her like a relief pitcher. "Miss Chakrabarti, please save us."

All eyes are on Aamani. Her cheeks are flushed, and she sinks into her seat as if trying to hide. Her long, wavy hair spills over the back of her chair. It all makes her kinda adorable.

"The Russian Revolution," Aamani commences, "began in 1917 and was triggered by a combo of economic breakdowns, the disconnect with the autocratic system of the government, and the willingness for the war. It first brought a coalition of liberals and moderate socialists to power, but their failed policies led to the seizure of power by the communist Bolsheviks in October . . . uh, twenty-fifth, I believe."

Wow.

"Fucking nerd!" Trina Cho shout-whispers.

"Thanks, Wikipedia," Malcolm teases.

Victoria adds, "Yeah, ain't nobody ask you all that."

Everyone laughs, including me. Because seriously, how the hell does she know all that?

If Aamani sinks any farther into her chair, she'll be sitting on the floor.

"You'd all do well to take after Miss Chakrabarti." He eyes Jordan. "At least *someone* bothered doing the readings."

Jordan smirks with his lone dimple as if to plead, *Give a brotha some credit for sitting through the worst* Rocky *movie.*

I'm not sure how she plans to help me, but if she can decipher the density of a molecule and recite Russian history like Biggie lyrics, then maybe, just maybe, she knows a thing or two about helping out a crippled athlete with no future.

The final bell rings. It marks the sound of sweet freedom.

Britt and Krystal follow me to my locker under the impression I'm about to kick it with them, which is the norm when Britt's not slanging and I don't have practice. Krystal never has shit going on, so we don't take her plans into account. We never do anything worthwhile. We usually end up chillin' on Krystal's steps, blasting Spotify with all of those annoying ads. And sometimes we go to the court and I play pickup with the guys while Britt and Krystal flirt with all the guys waiting for next. But the basketball thing is no longer an option for obvious reasons.

"Ay, y'all want to switch it up and do my place today? Marcus works until eight," Britt informs, stopping mid-stride to lean against the locker next to mine. Ah, leaning. I remember when I could do that. I look down at my leg and throw some serious shade at it. Krystal, forever on Instagram, nearly walks into her. I don't know why she spends so much time on the 'gram. She only has, like, sixty followers.

Shit. I have to meet Aamani. I have to figure out a way to bail.

"Yeah, I'm down," Krystal says, glancing up from her phone and settling at the locker behind Britt. "My dad said if we want to chill on our steps we have to turn the music down. Like, a lot. So it's probably better if we go to your house."

Britt does a one-eighty and turns to Krystal. "I know this is messed up to say since your pops is a man of God and shit. But he gets on my damn nerves. Why is he so scary all the time? He doesn't let you do shit but attend prayer circles."

"You tellin' me," Krystal agrees, her face dropping from the memories.

They trade more Reverend Mayfield anal parenting stories. I remain quiet, thinking if I don't make a sound they'll forget I'm here. Standing next to them. Right in front of my locker.

Okay, so it's not the greatest plan.

"You cool to come through, Lex?" Britt asks.

Yeah, definitely not the greatest plan.

I panic and stick half my body into my locker to avoid the question. I pretend to search for our math textbook. I rummage around the back of my locker for a minute, prolonging my answer, pulling out everything but a textbook—an empty Hot Cheetos bag, my practice shorts, a hoodie, my copy of *To Kill a Mockingbird* (so that's where that thing went).

Britt says, "What you need that for? You know you can't read." Krystal thinks this is Kevin Hart levels of funny, knowing damn well my vocab is better than hers.

I just give Britt the most blasé look ever.

"So you coming or not?" Britt repeats.

"Yeah," Krystal adds, not bothered to look up from her screen.

I can't be honest and tell them about my plans with Aamani. Because (1) they'll roast me until the end of time for being a nerd, and (2) they might accuse me of being gay again, and I'm not trying to put out that social fire. High school's already hard enough without having to withstand a constant stream of public scrutiny.

I freeze and run my finger along the spine of *To Kill a Mockingbird*.

The moment of truth, or rather the moment of lies.

"Ladies!" Trey interrupts out of nowhere. I've never been so happy to see his fake Nick Cannon ass. He tosses his left arm over Britt's shoulder and his right over Krystal's, pulling them in to make a Trey sandwich. "Y'all going to wish Big Daddy luck for the game tonight?" The thought that there's a game tonight without me is like a punch in the stomach. "Yo, Lex, what you got that textbook for? Your ass can't read."

Apparently everyone's got jokes today. Let's all just shit on the cripple.

Krystal and Trey laugh.

Britt elbows Trey in the ribs and shrugs off his arm. Krystal, on the other hand, embraces his touch and snuggles into Trey's shoulder for several seconds before he pulls away in pain, clutching his ribs.

"Touch me again and I'ma break my foot up in your ass," Britt threatens.

"I was just tryin' to give you some TLC. You didn't have to go all Ronda Rousey on my ass."

Jordan strolls up behind us, a smug grin and solo dimple on his face. "Britt, chill. We need Trey for Chester tonight."

Bullshit they need him. Trey barely gets any playing time.

"Thank you!" Trey seconds, wide-eyeing Britt. "Get your girl, bruh."

Wait. Britt and Jordan are a thing? How'd I miss that? Oh, right, too busy dealing with my life falling apart.

"I mean, who else is going to bring me water," Jordan says, expanding his grin.

We all laugh.

"See, that's fucked up. Y'all outta pocket for that," Trey says shaking his head.

Jordan looks at me. "Looks like that physical therapy is workin' for you, Lex."

It's the strangest thing. Ever since I was shot, Jordan's been super nice to me. He even texted me some of those Tupac lines when I was in the hospital.

Keep your head up.

Bow down and pray.

How do you want it?

Actually, that last one he meant to send to Britt. I guess that should've tipped me off to this whole couple thing.

"Thanks," I reply dryly.

For some reason, Jordan's eyes linger on me. So what do I do? I toss half of my body back into my locker in search of another textbook I don't plan on using.

Clarence Shaw slows down in the hallway to shout at Jordan. "Yo, J?! The bus just pulled up. Coach wants everyone in the locker room to go over the scouting report one last time."

Jordan nods. "A'ight." Then he starts making out with Britt, their tongues wrestling.

After an awkward ten seconds, the kiss ends. Britt is euphoric.

Trey leans in to do the same to me. I pull a ninja move and quickly *Matrix*-bend out the way, sending his crusty lips into the locker. I feel bad for Krystal, because I know how much she likes him, yet he gives her no play.

Trey rubs the side of his face. "Damn! You girls take that Me Too shit too damn seriously. A little TLC ain't never hurt no body. Ask MJ."

"Come on, Bill Cosby," Jordan says, draping his arm around Trey's shoulder. "Let's get you outta here before you catch a case. We'll holla at y'all."

I give him a nonchalant wave, like *cool story, bro.*

As soon as the boys leave, Britt gives me a fed-up stank-eye.

"I'm not about to miss the bus because you can't make up your damn mind. You coming or not?"

Britt's stank-eye intensifies, and Krystal looks up from her phone long enough to add her own.

Think. Think. Or better yet, keep it real.

"Uh . . . Mr. Jones actually gave me detention . . . so, uh, I can't."

The corners of Britt's eyes crinkle. "For what?"

I loosen my tone to really sell it. "Some bullshit I didn't do. You know how he is."

I await judgment, nervously eyeing Britt. She has a long French braid in her weave.

"Shit, you know I *know* how he is. We'll link up later then."

"For sure."

Krystal looks up from her screen to give me a goodbye up-nod.

I look at my phone. It's 3:18. Let's go see what this Hindu girl has up her kurta.

Aamani's waiting outside Mrs. Hall's room. Seriously, the girl's actually waiting for me. She's sitting cross-legged under one of the hundred D.A.R.E. posters that litter our walls (someone's written *drugs are really educational* in black Sharpie under the acronym), flipping through a comic book. She's leaning against her backpack, which is three times the size of mine. I guess it's what a backpack looks like when it's actually filled with books.

Looking at Aamani, sitting there like a nine-year-old, cross-legged and reading a comic, I consider bailing. This is all probably going to come back and kick me in the ass.

But Aamani spots me out of the corner of her eye as she turns the page. She closes the comic, tucks it in her hiker's backpack, and stands to greet me.

"I'm glad you decided to show," Aamani says with a warm smile. She has this way of always looking like she doesn't have a care in the world. I don't get it. "You just won me ten bucks."

I shrug in defeat. "Yeah, well, I got shit else to do. And I'll be expecting a cut."

"That's the spirit," she says, sarcastically chipper.

I raise the left corner of my lip. "So what's this master plan of yours? It better not involve whoring me out. Because I don't get down like that."

"Oh my God, no!" she gasps. "The fact that that's where your brain goes to solve a problem only further solidifies you needing my help."

"Uh-huh. Let's just get whatever it is over with."

"Okay, but first you have to promise not to freak and keep an open mind."

I raise an eyebrow like The Rock. "Why?"

"Just promise, or I can't help."

The last time I promised someone I wouldn't freak was when I was living with Marcus, and Britt had hidden two bags of Devon's drugs under my bed without me knowing. Of course she told me this as Marcus was stomping up the stairs to come and sweep our room for narcotics. When he found it, he assumed I was the one slanging and beat my light-skin ass. For a month I had to wear more makeup than someone trying to cover up bad Botox.

Something tells me comic-book-reading Aamani hasn't hidden a pound of heroin in my locker.

I sigh. "Fine. I promise."

She raises a pinkie.

"What are you, seven?" I deadpan.

"Pinkie promise or no deal."

We lock pinkies, binding our agreement in a blood oath.

"Now, follow me. And remember, keep an open mind."

"Wait," I stop her before she opens the back door to Mrs. Hall's class. "Why are we going through the back door? You're already off to a shady start."

"Because you're late and they've probably already started."

"Why don't I like the sound of any of this?"

"Because you like being difficult. Now just come on and be quiet."

She carefully opens the door, considerate to not disturb the nerds inside. There's a long table with four chairs in front of the whiteboard. Lindsay Ross and two other nerds I've only seen in the caf are seated at the table. A portable red button sits in front of each of them, including the empty seat. One of the boys is white with shaggy brown hair and glasses. He's wearing a graphic T-shirt with a tree with arms and a face that says "I am Groot" in a word bubble beside it. He could be Lindsay's brother for all I know. And the other boy is this lanky Asian with spiked hair, high-water jeans, and a white polo shirt, looking like the *High School Musical* version of Jet Li.

Sitting in the front row is Mrs. Hall, a thick textbook sprawled out on the desk in front of her. I've always been cool with Mrs. H. I mean, I never pay attention in her class, because science is all kinds of boring, but she's always cool about it. She never calls me out like Mr. Hilbert. Also, she played Division III basketball back in the day, so she would often talk ball with me before class.

"All right, gang. Time for the dreaded lightning round," Mrs. H says malevolently. The nerds hunch over their buttons. Mrs. H looks down at her Bible-sized textbook. "It'll be judge's choice. Ready?" She clicks the stopwatch in her hand. "Begin! First question: Twenty percent of two is equal to?"

Lindsay slams on her buzzer. "Zero point four."

"Correct!" acknowledges Mrs. H. "Next question. Which one of the four basic forces of the universe is most directly involved with maintaining the planets in their orbit?"

Lindsay, without hesitation, rings her buzzer again with a cocky grin, looking like a brunette version of me when I know a defender can't guard me. "Gravity. Give us some hard ones."

"Right again, Lindsay. Okay, what is the most common source of energy for brain cells in humans?"

Lindsay buzzes again. Glasses groans.

Aamani leans over to me and whispers, "Glucose."

Lindsay, still wearing her I'm-the-shit grin, answers, "Glucose."

"Told ya," Aamani whispers, a smile in her voice.

"Bingo!" Mrs. H stops the timer. "Great job, Lindsay, but let's give the rest of the team a chance to answer a few." Lindsay falls back in her chair and folds her arms. "Okay, boys. Annnd . . ." She restarts the stopwatch. "Begin! What is the year of a person's death who was born in the year five hundred and eighty BC and lived sixty-three years?"

Glasses hits the buzzer and speaks up. His voice is kind of nasally, as if he just swallowed air from a balloon. "Five hundred and seventeen BC."

"Way to go, Matthew! You remembered our lesson on time and its intervals during the BC era. Next question: True or False. Impetigo can sometimes result after a moderate to severe blow to the head?"

Matthew buzzes again, beaming with confidence. "False. The

correct answer is concussion. Impetigo is a skin infection that is most prevalent in children."

"Correct! All right, final question before we move on to some keyword practicing. Brian, I want you to answer this one." Brian's eyes grow two sizes in preparation. "What is the most common term for the ratio of the output force to the input force of a simple machine?"

Brian sits on the answer, stumped. A blood vessel pulsates on the side of his head in thought.

"Oh my God," Lindsay exacerbates, "It's sooo easy."

Aamani seconds this with a whisper. "It *is* pretty easy."

Easy my light-skin ass. All of these questions sound like problems only a rocket scientist could solve.

"Remember what we talked about, Lindsay—champion your teammates."

Lindsay frowns.

"But unfortunately I am going to insist you quickly come to an answer, Brian. It is the lightning round. You're not going to be allotted this much time in the match."

"Come on, B-rye, you got this," he mumbles to himself.

Brian thinks for another minute, then squints. "Is it mechanical advantage?"

"Hell yeah it is!" Aamani shouts in celebration. Heads turn to look at us. "Oops, my bad."

"Aamani's correct. I knew you could do it, Brian! You just have to remember to keep your composure. You know the answers."

I have a huge, satisfied grin plastered on my face. This whole thing is freakin' hysterical. These nerds really get off on answering questions only people like Neil deGrasse Tyson give a shit about. It's adorable. They actually think nerd Quizzo is a sport. It's like watching high school *Jeopardy!* without the money. And if there's no money involved, then really, what's the point?

"Before we move on to keywords, I think we have a new recruit in our midst. I'm so glad you decided to join our team, Alexis. I think this will be really good for you."

I do a three-sixty, looking around for this Alexis person of whom she speaks. Because I know damn well she's not referring to *me* joining the nerd *Jeopardy!* team.

When I turn back around, everyone's staring at me like I'm Jesus resurrected.

"Oh no no no, *hell* no. Not happening," I ramble, backing up toward the back door from whence I came.

Aamani grabs my arm and shepherds me to the back door with a big, fake smile. "If you'd excuse us for just one sec."

If anyone else would've grabbed me like that, they would've caught a right hook.

"What happened to keeping an open mind?" she asks, irritated.

"You said for me to keep an *open mind*. Not for me to lose my goddamn mind, which you clearly think has happened if you think I'm going to willingly join a team that makes me do even more schoolwork. Are you crazy?! I can't join that shit in there."

Aamani puts up her hands in defense. "Okay, simmer down. I'm not asking you to join a cult, or Tom Cruise you into Scientology. Just prove everyone wrong."

"What's that supposed to mean?"

"I haven't been here long, but we do have three classes together and lunch. I see how you follow Britt around and the way the whole school has written you off because of the shooting. You're not just some stupid basketball player. You want a scholarship? You want to get out of this town so you can walk, or in your case, hobble down the street and not worry about being shot? You want to silence all the haters?"

"Well, when you put it like that," I say, guiltily frustrated. I release a sigh that comes from the deepest pit of my lungs. "You know I want all of that."

"Okay then. Joining the STEM team is your best and only chance."

"Fine. I'll join. Just stop trying to sell me on it." She smiles, satisfied. "Fuck me, I'm going to get clowned so hard for this. Sweet baby Jesus, please help me," I say, looking to the heavens.

"Then we'll get clowned together."

"Yeah, somehow that doesn't make me feel any better."

I follow her back into the classroom.

"Welcome back," greets Mrs. H. "So have you decided to join us? We really need you."

The nerds need *me*? I don't know shit about equations, glucose, or mechanical advantages.

"You do?" My voice drips skepticism.

Lindsay chimes in, turning her upper lip. "Unfortunately, we do. We're not allowed to compete in competitions without at least one reserve. Even if said reserve is dead weight."

I lean over and whisper to Aamani. "If I join, will it really piss her off?"

"Yeah, she's not too thrilled about the whole thing," Aamani whispers out the side of her mouth.

"In that case . . ." I announce loudly, "I am so hyped to be part of the team! When do we start busting some nerd ass in trivia?!"

Aamani interjects. "We try to refrain from using the N-word around here."

"It's cool. I'm Black. I'm allowed to say it. Just don't let me catch any of y'all saying it."

Aamani's face jumps back defensively. "Not *that* N-word—*nerds.*"

I laugh. "Oh, my bad."

I stay for the remainder of practice to get a feel for how this stupid game is played. Spoiler alert, it's boring as fuck.

What's kinda dope, though, is witnessing Aamani in her nerd habitat. She runs shit. The girl's only been here for, like, a month and she's already team captain.

But about STEM, none of the questions make any goddamn sense. Like, I don't know shit about some titanium dioxide. And how the hell am I, or any normal person who doesn't devote their life to memorizing the periodic table, supposed to know how to best describe a streak of a mineral?

The game may be stupid and the questions impossible, but the rules are easy enough. Let me break it down.

As Lindsay so piously pointed out, teams require at least five players—four "in game" players and at least one alternate. Alternates can sub in between games. I'm not too concerned with subbing, though, because I'm cool with being a bench rider. Also, Lindsay made it clear that the only way my dumbass would get to sub in is if some *Independence Day* shit goes down and aliens abduct one of our teammates, requiring Will Smith to save them.

The game is split up into four phases, each fifteen minutes long. Phase one is the "warm-up" phase and consists of short tossup questions worth ten points each. Phase two is made up of longer toss-ups which, if answered correctly, earn the team a chance of a bonus question. The longer toss-ups are worth fifteen points and the bonus questions are worth thirty. Teams are allowed to consult on bonus questions, leaving the captain to answer on behalf of the team. The third phase is what Aamani and I walked in on—the lightning round. Here the team with the lowest score chooses from three topics and has a minute to answer as many questions as they can. Each question is worth ten points and if a team answers every question correctly they are awarded an additional twenty points. And the final phase, which is very anticlimactic, is a retread of phase two.

Mrs. H puts me out of my misery and ends practice a few minutes early.

My head is spinning from having just sat through two-and-a-half hours of straight knowledge. My sanity is short-lived, as Mrs. H swings by each desk and drops a thick packet of papers off. It's the new practice questions, which I'm told she hands out every week. This thing's a monster. I instantly regret agreeing to any of this.

"Do not fret," Matthew says, scoping the look on my face as I curl the packet like a pair of dumbbells. For some reason, he doesn't look me in the eyes as he talks. "The size isn't correlated to the difficulty. It ranges from easy to moderately challenging. For example, topics can consist of extended variables, Mercator projection, all the way to commensalism."

I force a toothless smile. "Thanks . . . I think."

"You're welcome," he says, still staring off into the distance. "If you should need any further assistance, we'd be happy to help."

"Speak for yourself," Lindsay scoffs as she walks by us and out the door.

"Everyone except her," Matthew corrects.

Brian interjects. "Ignore her. She'll come around."

"I don't think that's accurate," states Matthew.

"Dude, I'm trying to make her feel better."

"Oh," Matthew says, catching up to the subtlety. "Yes, she will grow to be more tolerant of your presence over time. But not really."

"Again, thanks . . . I think."

Brian brushes Matthew to the side. "Lindsay's just salty because you're, like, a hundred times cooler than all of us, and she's no longer top of the social pyramid with you here."

"Hey, I resent that," Aamani says. "She's, like, so not cooler than me." She does a little hair flip and throws her voice up a California octave to mimic a valley girl.

"Sorry, Aamani, you're cool and all, *buuut*"—Brian lingers, setting up the punch line—"you've never hit six threes in a game."

"Hold up. You saw me play against West Catholic last year?"

"I've seen you play a bunch of times."

"*You have*?!" Aamani and I say in unison.

"I didn't even know you liked basketball, or sports for that matter," Aamani says, shocked.

"What?! I love basketball! You know, my older brother plays for Drexel. You were on fire that night! Swishing every shot like Steph Curry."

"Thanks for the love. Everyone usually only watches the boys."

"No way," Brian dismisses. "You guys have better fundamentals."

"Damn right we do. Jordan struggles finishing with his left. I saw him miss two wide open reverses one game."

Brian and I share a laugh at Jordan's expense. He's pretty cool for a nerdy Asian.

Aamani bows out. "Ugh, get a room, sports nerds."

"Oooh, you said a bad language word?" I tease.

"It's okay. I am one, so I can say it."

"You don't like basketball, Aamani?" Brian asks.

"You lost me at threes, brought me back at curry food, and lost me again at reverses."

I shake my head. "You're just not as cool as me and my new Asian friend here." I go in for a fist bump, but Brian awkwardly goes for a handshake. We meet halfway and high-five.

Aamani chortles. "Case in point that you two need a room."

Matthew's phone rings. He looks at it, then sends it to voice-mail. "My mom has arrived. We must make haste, Brian."

"I'm not trying to be rude or anything, but why do you talk like you're from Middle-earth?"

Matthew looks away and tilts his head in curiosity. "I don't. I sound nothing like a hobbit, elf, orc, troll, Nazgûl, or any other habitant of Middle-earth."

"You know what," I backtrack. "Forget I asked."

"I'm autistic, and tend to speak and think differently from most people. Perhaps that's what you're referring to. Also, I have an affinity for words. Did you know there are over two hundred and seventy-three thousand words in the Oxford dictionary?" he asks, his inflection spiking with excitement.

I cut him off before he recites all of them. "That's cool, bruh. I don't even know what Middle-earth is. I just heard that joke in a movie once."

Matthew's eyes expand like an owl's. "Middle-earth is a fictional realm in J. R. R. Tolkien's *Lord of the Rings*. It was first establish—"

Brian swoops in and grabs Matthew, ushering him to the door. "Okkaayy . . . let's not get him started on *Lord of the Rings*."

"But she inquired, Brian. It would be rude of us not to inform her."

"I know, buddy, but your mom's waiting for us."

"Oh, right. Yes, then let us make haste."

"Yes, let's," Brian agrees, giving us an apologetic look. "Glad you're on our team, Alexis."

"Call me Lex."

His eyes light up as if I just promised to take his virginity. (I think it's safe to assume everyone in this room is a virgin. I mean, a guy just referenced orcs and trolls.) "Cool! See ya tomorrow, Lex!"

Matthew waves, and then they exit through the front of the room.

"So you think your mixed-race babies will be good at sports, or does that not work when only one of the parents is athletic?" Aamani asks. A smile teases at her lips.

"Ew!"

We laugh.

Aamani and I gather our stuff and say goodbye to Mrs. H. We take the same bus on account of Aamani living above the corner store. Her stop's three before mine, so no one will see us together.

Mrs. H stops us. "Aamani, would you mind waiting in the hall for Alexis while we have a little chat?"

"Sorry, Mrs. Hall, but I *have* to catch the 6:15. I work tonight."

I suck my teeth. "You mean you have to catch that Doctor Hoover tonight."

"First off, it's *Doctor Who*. And secondly, one day I'm going to *Clockwork Orange* you and make you watch an episode. Only then will you truly understand the sheer beauty and significance of the Doctor regenerating."

"Doubt it. And joke's on you. I don't know what a *Clockwork Orange* is."

"Okay, that's fine, Aamani. You can head home. If needed I can give Alexis a ride if that's okay with her?"

Give me a ride?! Has she lost her damn mind? How long does she plan on pep-talking me?

Aamani anxiously shifts her weight from left to right, itching to get out of here.

Then I shrug, yeah. Because on second thought, if I get a ride I won't have to waste money on my bus pass.

"Cool. Cool. Have a good night!" Then Aamani hurries to the hall.

I sit back down because my leg's starting to do that thing that makes me want to saw it off. Mrs. H comes over and sits in the desk beside me. I swear she's mixed, because she's as light as Paula Patton, and has that good white girl hair to boot. It's even straighter than mine.

"How are you feeling after your first practice?"

You mean besides feeling like all of this is a colossal waste of my time? Oh, I'm mad hyped.

"Honestly? Not great. I mean, come on, Mrs. H, you've seen my grades—good lookin' out with that C, by the way—I'm not cut out for this nerd shit. I mean nerd *stuff*," I quickly revise.

"I'm not going to lie to you, Alexis. It's going to be difficult for you to catch up. It's going to be a challenge unlike anything you've ever had to face. All the kids in STEM take this team very seriously and have been training for years. No one expects you to turn up and be the smartest person on the team. But with practice and a lot of extra hours studying, you can become a valuable team member. You're also going to have to have a significant amount of patience and self-belief. You're going to actually have to put forth an effort and apply yourself on the team and in the classroom. Can you do that?"

She's dropping that Rocky on Michael B. Jordan knowledge. And if there's one thing I love, it's a challenge.

I nod. "Yes, ma'am."

"Good," she says, smiling, her wrinkles forming below her eyes. "Because Lindsay was right. I only allowed you on the team because there was no other option if I wanted to give these kids a chance of competing and getting the college exposure that comes along with it. We've already had to forfeit the first couple of matches."

So much for that "self-belief" she was talking about.

"It wouldn't have been fair to deny them the chance at doing something they worked so hard for, all because the majority of your peers don't care about education, or value themselves enough to know they too have a brain. But with that said, let me be clear. If I didn't believe in you, then I wouldn't have insisted Aamani bring you. You can do this, Alexis. You're capable of greatness outside of basketball. You just have to give a damn. Remember that science test you had to take last year before States? The one if you didn't ace you wouldn't have been eligible?"

"Yeah, it was the only A I ever got. It was on our refrigerator at home, before my mom wrote a grocery list over it."

"Exactly. That's what you can do when you put your mind to it. You slacked off all semester, and yet still managed to condense and grasp a whole semester of concepts in three days. So I think you very much belong here. I just need you to be *that* Alexis Duncan. Clear?"

"Crystal."

"Good." She smiles. Then she stands and adds, "And who knows. You may end up liking this nerd *shit*."

CHAPTER 7

STEM practice hasn't gotten any easier. And I really have been trying to study. But how am I supposed to read a new packet every week that's the size of our history textbook in addition to the schoolwork I already have? Not to mention it's impossible to study in my house. Between the sirens, gunshots, and Mom's shitty nineties R&B sex music, it constantly sounds like an episode of *The Wire* scored by Jodeci.

It's not just the added schoolwork that's kicking my ass. I'm getting it from all angles—Britt, Krystal, Trey, Mikayla. People are quick to turn on you.

I know what you're thinking. Why did I tell them about STEM? I had to. See, the problem with lying about having detention every day is Mikayla actually does have detention nearly every damn day.

Nowhere in school is safe.

A prime example is right now. I look across the caf at the same table Britt and I have sat at for the past four years, only to see her grilling me. I start limping toward them. Britt leans in and whispers some shit I know is about me to everyone at the table. They all look at me, now standing in the middle of the caf, and start snickering. All this because I joined a quiz team and don't want to waste my afternoons doing fuck-all on Krystal's stoop.

It's cool. I stroll-slash-limp right past them and head for the one table in the caf that I can still sit at—Aamani's.

"Come on, yo. We're just playin'. Stop being so damn sensitive," Britt says as I pass. She can't even control her laughter.

Trey, heaving, adds, "Ay, she probably about to go play Dungeons & Dragons or some shit."

The table erupts.

He goes in for an encore. "Yo . . . yo," he calls out, using all his stomach muscles to suppress his laugh, "ask your girl if she can throw one of those seventy-two virgins my way."

Britt falls out her chair laughing.

It's really not funny, but whatever. Fuck me, I guess.

I'm so pissed that when I sit down I throw my bag of Cheetos against the wall and almost nail Aamani in the face.

"New rule. If you're going to sit with me because you're too chicken to stand up to your so-called friends over there, then there's no decapitating me with junk food. At least do it with something healthy, like a carrot."

She picks the bag off the floor and hands it to me. "My bad. They just get on my damn nerves," I say through gritted teeth.

"For what it's worth," she says, opening one of her tiffin compartments. The smell of curry consumes the table. "Your friends are stereotypical A-holes. All nerds don't play Dungeons & Dragons. Like, our lives aren't episodes of *The Big Bang Theory*." She takes a huge bite of curry and rice.

"Right?! Thank you. I wish someone would tell them *that*!" I say loud enough to carry.

"Wait," Aamani stops mid-swallow. "I think Matthew plays Dungeons & Dragons. So scratch that. You totally hang with full-on nerds. And I do read a lot of comics. Dang . . ." she thinks aloud, "our lives really are episodes of *Big Bang*. Huh, wild."

I open the bag of Cheetos and toss a few chips in my mouth, binge eating through my new depressed life as an outcast.

Aamani shakes her head in disappointment. She takes apart a container of her tiffin and fills it with rice and what looks like tofu curry, and then slides it across the table to me. I don't know if I'm warming up to the idea of curry, or if I'm just hella hangry, but it looks good as fuck.

"I can't in good conscience stand by and watch you eat chips every day."

"They're not chips. They're Hot Cheetos."

"What's the difference? Neither is a proper meal."

"Cheetos are high in cheese, and since cheese is part of the dairy family, it makes it part of the food pyramid. So they're basically healthy."

"Yeeaahh, that's not at all how nutrients or the food pyramid work."

I suck my teeth. Her knowing everything is getting annoying. "Well, it's all I've got. And I don't need your charity."

"It's not charity," she argues. "Tiffins are meant to be shared. Why do you think they have so many compartments?" She nods to the compartment in front of me. "So by all means."

Damn. It does smell good. And I am starving.

I stand up.

"Where are you going? I'm telling you, you're going to like it."

"I'm getting a fork."

"Lex, Lex, Lex. You don't eat saag paneer with a *fork*. You have to get all up in there with your hands. Make love to it. Watch." She takes a piece of the flat, charred bread and demonstrates. I look at her like she's a cave woman. "Eat it like, um, like, a chicken wing. I know you know how to eat them." She drops the bread and looks at me in horror. "Ooh, that came out super racist. I'm sooo sorry. I just meant both of our cultures eat with their hands."

"Uh-huh, just finish your demonstration."

"Okay, but it would be better if you tried it. Here, let me help."

She reaches over and takes my hand. I freeze. It's as if I've been shot all over again, and my whole right side goes numb. Everyone at Britt's table is watching Aamani and me essentially holding hands.

I push her hand away, nearly knocking her off her seat.

"What the fuck are you doing?!"

"What? I'm trying to show you how we eat in India with chapati," she says, her voice innocent.

I look back at Britt's table to see if they're clowning me yet. They're not even paying attention. Shawn, using the table, dropped a beat and Trey's freestyling. "Don't ever try any gay shit like that again. I don't know how y'all do it in India, but like I told you, I don't get down like that."

"Okay, sheesh," she says, retreating back to her side of the table. "Talk about being hangry . . ."

Her hand was warm and soft. I feel bad for snapping on her, and even worse that I'm too much of a pussy to apologize.

She finishes her demonstration, using her own limbs. I'm still hesitant though. "It just looks so nasty."

"Just try something new for once."

I take the chapati and pinch the saag paneer like it's a taco, and take a bite. Half the rice falls out the back. They may have us beat on fancy lunchboxes, but we still have them in the utensils department.

A collection of foreign spices floods my taste buds and throws a spice party in my mouth.

"Iwt's gwood," I mumble through my mouthful.

"I'm sorry. I couldn't hear you over the sound of you admitting you were wrong."

I swallow. "You heard me. It's good, okay. Real good."

She struggles to hold in a smile.

"What?" I sigh.

"Nothin'. Just don't want to say I told you so, but—I told you so."

I take another bite. I don't say this lightly, but Indian food is crack.

We share the rest of the tiffin, and honestly I don't care who's watching because it's that damn good.

After I swallow my last piece of chapati, we start studying this week's packet. The embarrassment of studying during lunch only dwells on me for a few minutes. By then I'm too busy trying to figure out what any of this shit means.

A shadow casts over my question on equilateral triangles. I'm not even mad someone's blocking my light, because I wasn't going to figure out the answer anyway. I turn and look. Britt's standing over me with Mikayla and Krystal by her side, looking like a rundown TLC. Krystal has even put her phone away, so you know shit's about to get real.

"You can't kick it with your girls no more because you're all Ivy League and shit?"

I attempt to laugh it off. "Nah, it's not even like that." Britt's not trying to hear it, though. "Come on, y'all. I told you. I'm just trying to do something good with my life." I regret the words as soon as they leave my mouth.

"And I'm not doing something good with my life—out here grinding every day? You used to be about that life. But I guess since you joined whatever nerd shit this is, you're too good for the Grove, huh? You think you're better than us because you walk around with big-ass books and ISIS over there."

Aamani takes no offense. She just sits there. Cooler than the other side of the pillow.

"Are you serious right now?" I ask, trying to hide my I-have-better-things-to-do tone. "Do you have any idea how hard this shit is? I have to learn, like, a million definitions by our game tomorrow. And you know how many I've learned? Two."

"I don't give a fuck about what you have to learn. You actin' ocky as fuck out here."

All right. I'm starting to lose my shit now. "After everything we've been through—watching each other's back while we stole to eat, putting up with Marcus's shit for all those years, almost getting booked for you—you're going to try and tell me I'm not down for the Grove...? Fuck outta here with that," I say, sucking my teeth.

Britt takes a step into me, her knee brushing up against my back. Krystal's phone comes out real quick. She's ready to get her World Star on. I bite my bottom lip and look away, begging Jesus to give me the strength to not fight this girl.

"You ain't shit, and ain't ever gonna be shit. You might as well cut all this fake-ass studying out and start ho'ing like your mom."

"*Oh shit*!" Some kids instigate from the table next to us.

"Aren't," I answer calmly.

"What?"

"You said 'ain't.' The word you're looking for is *aren't*. *Ain't* isn't a word. Just so when you try and talk shit in the future you won't sound ignorant as fuck."

The surrounding tables go silent. Everyone's on edge, waiting for what we all know is coming—Britt taking a swing at me. I don't want to get dropped sitting down. Like, I at least want to give myself a chance. So I go to stand, but as soon as I push off of the seat, I feel a sharp pinch in my leg. I got up too fast. I can't let her know I'm wounded. So I bite my bottom lip and suck up the pain. We stand, grill-to-grill.

"What your crippled ass gonna do?"

My leg feels like it's been dipped in acid. Sure wish that physical therapy was good for something other than how to be an extra on *The Walking Dead*.

"I'm not trying to fight you over some stupid shit. We're supposed to be homegirls," I say, pleading for her to repurpose her anger elsewhere.

She fake smiles and looks away at Krystal. This is her move. She looks away to get your guard down, then sucker punches you with a nasty right hook. It's classic Britt.

Her balled fist moves in my direction, so I start to bob to the right when all of the sudden I get pushed on my ass from the side. Now I'm looking up from the dirty caf floor as Aamani takes the punch meant for me.

"*Oooh!*" echoes from the surrounding tables.

Seconds later, Aamani is lying beside me.

She's. A. Total. Badass.

Mr. Pryor races over and breaks it up before Britt can get another swing in. Aamani is clutching the left side of her face. When she removes her hand, I wince. Her eye is already slightly discolored.

"Yeah," she says in clear pain. "That really hurt. Movies make taking a punch look so easy."

"What were you thinking? Britt's knocked out dudes twice your size . . . and *American*."

"I'm not sure what their nationality has to do with anything, but, uh, okay. Thanks for the belief in my fighting skills." She tries to smile, but quits halfway through because of the pain. "You took a bullet for me. The least I can do is take a punch for you."

"I . . ." I start to tell her I didn't take a bullet for anyone, and would've gladly preferred anyone else had gotten shot in my stead. "Thank you."

I help her back to her feet. My leg still hurts. But fuck it. I can suck it up.

She's still protecting that left eye with her hand. "Now if you'd excuse me, I have to go see a nurse about my chances of being cast as the next Nick Fury."

CHAPTER 8

Today's our first match. I mean, it's really the third match, but it's the first we don't have to forfeit because they now have me, bench-riding extraordinaire.

We play Rider, which is in white suburbia about an hour from Hargrove in Delaware County. We have to be at school by ten a.m., which means I had to wake up at eight a.m. on a *Saturday*. So they'll be getting tired, don't-give-a-fuck Lex.

I hobble into Mrs. H's class. Thankfully, the pain's only a four out of ten this morning. Otherwise I'd have stayed in bed. I threw on my dingy, ripped sweats, and put up my hood in an attempt to hide my bed-head from the world this morning. But I quickly realize everyone is dressed in matching maroon blazers with our school mascot, Bucky the Lion, stitched on the breast pocket.

Of course on game day these nerds dress like a glee club cult.

Lindsay and Aamani take it a step further and are wearing matching plaid skirts, high socks, and nice shoes, looking like extras in a Japanese anime. Matthew even has on a black tie and gray dress pants.

Compared to them I look like a homeless janitor.

"Why are y'all dressed like that?" I ask mid-yawn.

Lindsay's face goes peach-red. "I'm curious. Do you blatantly disregard every rule, or do you not know how to read?"

She must've lost her damn mind. I wake up real quick.

I lunge at her, ready to knock her perfect, extra-on-*Riverdale* teeth into her throat.

Aamani steps in before I can rip Lindsay's head off.

"Hey, hey, hey! Knock it off!" Mrs. H instructs, raising her voice. "You're teammates. Start acting like it." Our heads dip in shame. "I'm sorry, Alexis. It didn't dawn on me until last night that I forgot to inform you of the competition's dress code that's highlighted in the back of your packet. I take sole responsibility for that. I have your blazer right here, and I believe Aamani was kind enough to bring you a skirt and a dress shirt." She takes a peek at my beat-up Js. "Your sneakers will be okay for today, but you'll need some dress shoes for future matches."

I cut my eyes at Aamani. "You brought me what now?"

"I always bring a spare just in case."

She's clearly lying. I've seen Aamani's wardrobe that she stashes in her backpack— shalwar kameez by day, nerd tees by night. Neither involves skirts ripped from the set of a Britney Spears music video.

"Lindsay," Mrs. H calls to her, "this is your final warning. If you disrespect a teammate again you'll be demoted to reserve indefinitely. Are we clear?"

"Yes," Lindsay acknowledges through gritted teeth.

"Good. Now apologize to Alexis."

Lindsay saunters over and sticks her hand out. "Sorry," she says, not at all meaning it.

"It's cool. But say some shit like that again and I'm gonna straight drop you, no questions asked."

"*Alexis* . . ." scorns Mrs. H, cutting her eyes at me.

"I'm just playing, Mrs. H." I give Lindsay a bear hug to demonstrate our new friendship. Lindsay stands there stiff with her arms firmly latched to her sides. I whisper in her ear. "But for real, though. Say I can't read one more time . . . "

I release her, and go to the bathroom to change.

I can't even look at myself. I look like my parents have a 401(k) and a good marriage. I resemble one of those sell-out Black kids that takes the bus two hours to go to a white school.

This isn't me. What if someone from the block sees me? Or worse, what if someone sees my pale thighs? Because this skirt is hella short. I'd get roasted.

The mood's changed when I get back to the room. Everyone is mournfully quiet, and Lindsay is now an apple-red. (And they have the nerve to call us "colored.")

"What?" I say, going straight for my skirt. I tug at the sides, trying to stretch it out. "It's the skirt, isn't it? This thing's riding up my ass-crack."

Aamani cringes. "So, uh, the thing is, Brian kinda has mono. So . . ." I look at her like *please, God, no*! "You're going to have to fill in."

First thought: Who the hell is making out with Brian Chang?!

Second thought, which I say aloud: "Fuck my life."

Like I said, Rider is about an hour away from Hargrove. So you can imagine the torture it is to have to sit through a whole trip of Aamani, Lindsay, Matthew, and even Mrs. H singing memorization songs for the periodic table, the square root of pi, and the Pythagorean Theorem. By the time we arrive I can name seven elements, rattle off the first five digits of pi (3.1415), and tell you anything you could ever want to know about a right triangle. Also, thanks to this uncomfortable skirt, I have the world's deepest wedgie.

We walk into Rider's auditorium with no swag, looking like a team ready to get their ass beat. The place is two times bigger than our auditorium, which isn't an auditorium at all, just a stage and fold-out chairs in the caf. Their seats actually have cushioning and are bolted to the floor. The place also smells of money, of trust funds and privilege.

I gulp down a sob when I see the steep staircase leading up to the stage. All this money and they're not accessible? Um, #CrippleLivesMatter. I've been making minor strides rehabbing with our athletic trainer before school. But I know these stairs are going to make the pain flare up. They look like Mount-fucking-Everest.

Aamani, as if reading my mind, comes up behind me and helps me up the stairs. For some reason the embarrassment is lessened by her being by my side.

On stage are two long tables on opposing sides with a wooden podium in between at center stage. There's a mic and buzzer in front of each seat. I feel like we're at a presidential debate. Like someone's about to be called a "nasty woman."

A banner hangs from the rafter above the stage that reads **STEM Quiz Bowl.**

A quarter of the auditorium is full. Are people so bored in Delaware County that they choose to spend their Saturday afternoons watching kids answer quiz questions? Have they ever heard of Netflix or South Street?

The Rider team emerges from backstage and takes their seats at their designated table. They're our opposite: three guys and a girl. All white. One guy is actually wearing a bow tie. A bow tie, though? You know he's smart as fuck.

Butterflies riot in my stomach as we take our seats. A few adults in the front row start whispering when they see me. They're probably thinking *Black people like STEM now?*

Aamani leans over and whispers, "Your skirt."

"I know," I whisper back. "It's too damn small. Where'd you get this thing—Baby Gap?"

She flicks her eyebrows down toward the table.

I look at the table, stumped, not expecting to have to solve a riddle before the match even starts. Table. Skirt. Skirt. Table. Then it clicks. I'm sitting like I'm on the bench during a timeout. My panties are on display like the American flag. I embarrassedly cross my legs, which feels weird in itself, and go back to wishing I was anywhere but here.

Once my public exposure is under control, Aamani huddles us up.

"Okay, Rider is a good team, but we can take 'em if we stick together. Remember what Mrs. H taught us: trust each other, always go with your gut, and never rush your answer."

"Or in Lex's case . . . don't answer," Lindsay snarks.

"So not helping," Aamani chimes.

I just grin and say, "Man, you must really want that ass whooping, huh?"

The huddle disperses. I look down at the red buzzer in front of me. And even if by some miracle I do know an answer, my hand is shaking too much to press it.

There's a light applause as a baldheaded white guy with a gray goatee and thin-rimmed glasses approaches the podium.

"Good afternoon and welcome to match day three of the

Delaware County School District STEM Quiz Bowl. My name is Donald Sutter, and I'll be today's moderator for the zero wins Hargrove Lions and the undefeated Rider Appleknockers—"

I snort. Loudly. "The fuck?"

Awkward chuckles sweep the auditorium.

Lindsay shushes me. Everyone in the front row, including and especially Mrs. H, gives me a death stare.

"Excuse me, Miss . . ." the moderator stops to check his notes— "Duncan. I'd ask that you please remain silent until the start of the round. Thank you."

"My bad." He frowns and Aamani nudges me under the table. "I mean, uh, sorry."

"That's quite all right. Now, as I was—"

"Sorry," I interrupt, "but can I just say one last thing?"

"If you must."

"There's no way that's their real name. What even is an Appleknocker?"

"Appleknocker originates from farm laborers who developed the technique of knocking apples off trees to maximize the apple-picking process. And I can assure you, Miss Duncan, that it is indeed their real name."

"Okay," I incredulously concede. "Whatever you say, Monopoly guy."

Our table snorts.

I manage to make it through the match without answering a single question. Coach Stevens used to tell all the bench players that every player, from the starters to the bench riders, has a role to play in the team's success. My role for STEM is to shut up, make being a nerd look dope, and let all the smart kids do the work. They don't need me anyway. Aamani and Lindsay carry the team like Shaq and Kobe. Which I guess would make me, what, Tyronn Lue? Ew. Dude got put on his ass by AI, then stepped over.

We're ahead fifteen points. All we have to do is answer the final question right and we make hood history and become the first inner-city school to beat a suburban school in something that doesn't require a ball.

I can't even front. The last two rounds were brutal. It's so. Damn. Boring. In fact, if it weren't for the annoying sound the buzzers make, I'd have passed out drooling on my blazer two hours ago.

Mr. Monopoly, whose monotone voice doesn't help, announces, "The final question of phase four . . ." As soon as he starts rambling, my eyelids start to feel like they're doing bench presses to stay open. He gets halfway through the question when I give in and nod off. "The greatest geophysical impacts from the movement of Earth's . . ."

Snooze.

My big-ass head becomes too heavy and rolls off my hand, plummeting toward the table. I jolt awake, trying to avoid an impending concussion. In doing this, I accidentally press the buzzer.

Shit.

"Miss Duncan for Hargrove," Mr. Monopoly acknowledges.

I look up in horror.

Aamani looks on, proud, under the stupid assumption that I buzzed in on purpose. A twitch of skepticism curls Lindsay's lips. And Matthew looks like he just won front row tickets to Beyoncé; he probably thinks I somehow possess the winning answer.

"Do you have an answer for us, Miss Duncan?"

I've never been called "miss" so much. I feel like Meghan Markle.

"Um . . ." I try to buy time. For some reason my tits are sweating. "What's the question again?"

A collection of groans echo off the walls. Lindsay facepalms with a shake of her head. Matthew's magical Beyoncé tickets turn into Dave Matthews tickets and his face flips over.

"The greatest geophysical impacts from the movement of Earth's lithospheric plates are most often seen and felt in which area?"

Seriously, like, what the fuck? Is he for real with this question? I can't even pronounce lith-o-spher-ic, let alone define it.

Mr. Monopoly leans into his mic. "Five seconds, Miss Duncan."

I think.

I think some more, milking every second.

Then I think why the hell am I thinking? I know damn well I don't know the answer.

Here goes nothing. "What is the first six numbers of pi, 3.14159?"

The groans from the audience turn to chuckles. Lindsay almost knocks herself out with how hard she facepalms.

"It's not *Jeopardy!*, Miss Duncan. You do not have to answer in the form of a question. And as far as said answer, I'm afraid that is incorrect. The question will now go to Rider High with a chance to steal."

Bow Tie wastes no time and cockily leans into the mic like he's Kanye or something. "The greatest geophysical impact of Earth's lithospheric plates is most felt at the plate boundaries."

"Correct! Fifteen points, Rider. And that final question marks the end of the match, leaving the game tied at 130 points. We will now commence the overtime phase where I will pose three toss-up questions. The first team to answer two questions correctly wins the match. Captains, are you ready?" Aamani nods. Bow Tie gives a corny thumbs-up. "First question: In what structure of a nucleated cell are ribosomes assembled into their subunits?"

Lindsay uses her hand like a gavel and slams the buzzer. "Nucleus," she answers confidently.

"I'm sorry, but that is incorrect."

"What?! B-but," Lindsay pleads.

The sole girl on Rider buzzes in. She's less sure of her answer. "Nucleolus?"

"Correct!" Monopoly's a little too hype with his *correct*. "Rider wins the first point. Question two: if Rider answers correctly, they win the match. Regarding computer technology, which of the following best describes the bit: (A) an analogue magnetic storage sequence, (B) a computer processor, (C) a memory value of one through eight, or (D) a binary that stores information?"

Aamani's first to the buzzer. "D, a binary that stores information."

"Correct. Second point goes to Hargrove. Final question: consider a lever with an ideal mechanical advantage of eight. What will its mechanical advantage be if the effort arm length is reduced by half?"

Aamani pounces on her buzzer, but is beaten by Bow Tie by a fraction of a second.

I had one job—to do nothing. Now we're about to miss out on making history because of me.

Bow Tie leans into his mic, already celebrating with a smug grin. "I believe the answer you're looking for is six."

What a douche.

Aamani's face looks like she just hit the lottery.

"I'm sorry, but that is incorr—"

Aamani's already buzzing in before he can finish "Four!" She can hardly contain herself.

We look over at Monopoly, awaiting his confirmation. He takes a calculated, reality TV show host pause, then says, "Correct! And the match goes to Hargrove High School. Well done to both our teams today for a competitive match."

Matthew, Aamani, Lindsay, and Mrs. H shoot up from their chairs like rockets. They start hugging each other like they just won the championship. I remain seated. The only joy I get is from watching the Appleknockers' bitter faces as they come over and congratulate us for kicking their ass, which means they have to admit defeat to me, a hood girl who can't even pronounce lith-o-spher-ic.

The celebration continues on the ride back to Hargrove, filled with Snapchat hashtags—#CalTechBound (Lindsay's), #WinningLikeTheAvengers (Aamani's)—and more memorization songs. I ignore the celebrations. I didn't earn it. Instead I stare out the window, watching the white lines on the road whizz by. It kinda feels like my future whizzing by and fading into the rearview.

Who am I kidding? I'm not cut out for this shit. My future ended with that bullet.

By the time we get back to school I've about had it with their corny-ass educational songs. Like, if I hear "*There's . . . Hydrogen and Helium, then Lithium, Beryllium / Boron, Carbon everywhere, Nitrogen all through the air . . .*" one more damn time, I'm going to snap.

The parking lot is parent central. Lindsay's mom is waiting in her rundown Toyota. Matthew's Hallmark Channel–looking parents are anxiously waiting for him with welcoming smiles from the front seats of their green minivan. On top of that, as soon as he gets in they smother him with hugs and kisses like he just came back from war. It's a bit creepy if you ask me, but then again what the fuck do I know about being loved? The closest I've come to a kiss from my mom is that time she sneezed on me when she had the flu. Or maybe it was hepatitis. I don't know. Anyway, even Aamani's dad made the trip from the store, waiting with a change of clothes.

No one's waiting for me.

No parent kissing booth.

No minivan.

No change of clothes to get out of this toddler-sized skirt.

"You want to walk to the bus with us? You know, like, after I change," Aamani offers. I look over at her father, who's grilling me like I owe him money. "Yeah, he's still not over the whole *you trying to rob us* thing."

"I'm good. I'm gonna walk."

"Is that wise with your leg?" she asks.

"Probably not. But I need to do some thinking."

"Some thinking you say? Don't hurt yourself," she teases, a smile in her voice.

"You got jokes?"

"Maybe a few." Her dad yells something in Hindi to her. "Okaaay!" she replies, annoyed. "I have to go. Mom's watching the store and she always screws up people's change. Can I say one thing really quick?"

"I feel like I'm going to regret this, but yeah. Go ahead."

"Okay, well, the thing is you sucked today. Like, hard. If you're going to be on the team, then you need to take it seriously, because no one's going to grant you a scholarship with an abysmal performance like that. You may not care about your future anymore, but we do. Like, I asked you to join the team to help us and yourself. But today you helped no one. So if you don't want to be here, quit and we'll find someone else. Sorry . . . don't be mad?"

What she doesn't know is, being a former team captain, I respect her leadership and dedication.

"I'm not mad."

"Really?" She crinkles her eyes quizzically.

"Nah, 'is cool."

"Okay, because I was lying about the whole finding someone else thing. You're all we've got. But, next time we need you to actually contribute something. You know, like, score us a touchdown or whatever it is you do in basketball."

I smile pretty hard at this. "Even after gym you still have no clue how to play basketball, do you?"

She starts backpedaling toward the building. "Nope. That's why I have you."

On the trek home I replay Aamani's and Mrs. H's pep talks. I'm not sure if I can do this. I'm not smart. My whole life I've been told by my mom that I'm not shit. But I hate to lose. And I really hate letting my team down. Last year, I missed a game-winning free throw against Frankford. So I stayed up to one a.m. at the park practicing. I almost got jumped by two crackheads, but that's beside the point. The point is I stayed out there until I made two hundred free throws.

Mom's not home. She's probably off somewhere with Randy doing something that would make addicts everywhere proud. I'm not complaining though. I'm not trying to see her anyway. Also, since it's the weekend and still light out, no one on the block is acting a fool—no gunshots or sirens—so I might actually get some studying done.

I pull out my textbooks and lay them out on the bed next to my packet. Then I just stare at them mocking me. The fuck was I thinking? I have no idea what I'm doing.

So I DM Aamani.

> **Me: Question**

A minute later my phone pings.

> **RealFanGirl_18: Answer ☺**

> **Me: You really think I can get a scholarship?**

I wait a couple of minutes. No reply. Then I make a peanut butter sandwich (because we're Craig's house in *Friday*—we never have anything that matches).

> **RealFanGirl_18: Sorry. I had to help my dad with something downstairs. But yeah. You can totally do it if you don't suck like you did today. Because you suuuccckkkeeeddd! Don't @ me.**

> **Me: Alright I get it. You think maybe you can tutor me? I'm trying to become the GOAT**

RealFanGirl_18: I knew it! My basketball reference earlier totally got to you. My knowledge for America's pastime is unparalleled.

Me: Sure. If you say so. So are you going to help?

RealFanGirl_18: Of course! First session tomorrow at the store.

Me: Tomorrow's Sunday

RealFanGirl_18: I know. I'm going to pirate this new sci-fi show on HBO. What's your point? Do you want to learn this stuff or not?

Before I can reply, Aamani responds.

RealFanGirl_18: That was rhetorical. See you tomorrow at 4 sharp.

CHAPTER 9

"**S**ay one more word, bitch, and I'll beat the shit out of you!" I roll over and look at my phone. The bright screen nearly blinds me. It's two twenty a.m. I wish Mom would've stayed wherever the hell she was. Life's much quieter when she's off on a bender.

"Why can't you ever keep your fuckin' mouth shut?!" Randy continues.

That whole *quieter* thing goes double for Randy's loud ass.

I roll back over and bury my head in my pillow, numb to their arguing.

"Fuck you, you limp-dick motha fucka!" Mom retaliates.

I snort into my pillow.

Looks like I have no choice but to listen to Ike and Tina out there.

Seconds later I hear a loud crack, like the sound of a whip, followed by the vibrations of a body hitting the floor. I toss off the covers and scramble to my feet, careful not to put all my weight on my bad side. It's one thing to have to tolerate Marcus's abuse, because it was either putting up with that or living in the streets. But I'll be damned if Randy's bitch-ass is going to come up in my house and lay a finger on me or Mom.

Mom's curled up into a ball on the floor, seeking protection against the couch. He's really going to town on her with his belt, beating her like she stole something; her face bloody with lash marks. "Stupid . . . Bitch . . . Why . . . You . . . Make . . . Me . . . Shout . . . At . . . You . . ." he grunts in between each crack of the belt.

Randy's back is to me, so he doesn't see me coming. And thanks to his play-by-play of Mom's beating, he doesn't hear me either. This is going to hurt like a bitch. But fuck it. It'll be worth it. I dip my shoulder like J. J. Watt and drive it through Randy's lower back, sending his belt skidding across the floor and landing under the couch. I sack him into the coffee table, then the floor for a five-yard loss. I straddle him to keep him from getting up. He uses his adrenaline to free his arms and throw two jabs from his back. I dodge the first, but he catches me with the left. I eat it, though, and follow up with a two piece of my own, catching him with both punches and splitting his bottom lip.

He squirms beneath me trying to break free. It's taking strength I didn't even know I had to keep him pinned down. I have to bombard him with a constant flurry of combos to keep him off balance and make up for my inferior strength. Luckily for me he only shoots heroin and smokes weed. He doesn't have that superhuman crackhead strength.

I connect with eighteen of my thirty-two punches. I have him beat, that is until he gathers his old man strength and half flips me. Now I'm pinned between his knee, which is stabbing my pelvis, and the floor, which is squishing my face. And to make matters worse, Randy finds a loose heroin needle under the couch and digs it into my bullet wound.

I feel my scar rip. It burns like someone stabbed me with a cigarette lighter.

I scream in unadulterated agony. I don't care if I wake the block.

My skin's on fire.

Mom doesn't do shit. It's like don't worry, Mom. I clearly have the situation under control. Your only daughter is throwing down with your drug-dealing boyfriend-slash-pimp and crying out for help. But you just sit there and watch. No need to get up.

By the time the pain is so excruciating that everything goes numb, the fight's damn near over and I've lost. He's landing punch after punch with no resistance from me. But despite how all of this looks, I'll still be telling people I won this fight, because I definitely did. Dude took advantage of a cripple's wound. That's some Tyson-biting-Holyfield's-ear cheating shit right there.

Luckily for my face, Randy's pathetically out of shape, so he eventually tires himself out and puts an end to the ass whooping. No one offers to take me to the hospital. Or even some ibuprofen and a Band-Aid. Mom doesn't even tell Randy to leave. Shit, she doesn't even help me up. Instead she looks over at me and says through tear-filled eyes, "Get the fuck out," and points to the door.

So I bounce. Who needs them?

I hobble to the curb outside our apartment, my face and T-shirt coated in dry blood. It takes a moment for my eyes to adjust, as everything initially is a blurry haze mixed with the early morning darkness.

At a loss of what to do and only partially feeling my face, I walk to the one place I know I can crash for the night.

Britt meets me at the downstairs window, the one we've used countless times to sneak in and out after Marcus falls asleep. I still remember the first time we snuck boys in. Marcus made a midnight refrigerator run, so we all hid in the closet. I had an umbrella digging into my right ass cheek, while Chris's hand was on the other.

"Damn! The fuck happened to you?" Britt asks, half laughing and half sympathetic. Spoken like a true friend.

"I whooped Randy's ass. What's it look like?"

Facts.

"Bitch, please. You look like Martin in that boxing episode."

I sigh. It hurts. "Can you please move out the way so I can get in? She kicked me out."

For some reason she remains blocking the window. "Nah. You ain't staying here. You was outta pocket with that shit you pulled."

"What are you talking about?!" I snap. "Why are you being so petty? Like, all I did was join a math and science team. Like, what the fuck?"

"Girl, nobody cares about you joining some team. There are rules to this shit, and you broke 'em. Ol' girl snitched and got us shot at. Yet you ridin' with her and her crew now, eating lunch and shit. You don't text us no more; kick it with us—bottom line, you don't fuck with us."

"Do you hear yourself? Her *crew*? Have you seen the STEM team? They are in no way a *crew*. One of them uses a freakin' inhaler."

I mean, while she has a point, now's not the time to be petty. Not when I'm out here bleeding from thirty percent of my body.

"You know what? This is fucking stupid. Be that way then."

Britt doesn't try to stop me. She doesn't ask me where I'm going or what I'm going to do. She just shuts the window and fades into the house.

I walk a few blocks to the vacant crack house where addicts, home-less, and the like go to prove that no one listened to D.A.R.E. when they were in school. I've only ever stepped foot in here once, when I went looking for Mom after the first time she was gone for more than a week. Most of the windows have been shattered and boarded up. Cops act like it doesn't exist because it's in a Black neighbor-hood. They couldn't care less if we poison our bodies and kill our-selves. Just one less nigger to worry about.

The inside of this place looks to be all kinds of haunted with ghosts of crackheads past. I hear a crunch under my feet. I assume it's just some broken glass from one of the six shattered windows in this place, but it's the remains of a shattered syringe. I search for the needle to make sure I don't step on it, and find three of them scattered at the bottom of the stairs. My mind races back to earlier, and I say a quick prayer that Randy didn't infect me with whatever disease Mom may or may not have . . . give me this one dub, Jesus! I step over the needles and head upstairs away from the loose needle graveyard. There's the overwhelming aroma of fresh piss in the air, as if someone sprayed piss-scented Febreze. Each room is dark and filled with people passed out with tubes laced around their arms, their chests inflating and falling in unconscious breathing patterns. A rat the size of an iPhone Plus darts from the shadows into the room across the hall. I'd rather chill with Ratatouille than risk stepping on a used needle, so I continue my search.

I spend another two minutes searching before I find a room with a somewhat clean mattress and less than ten occupants. I claim the spot in the back corner next to the world's skinniest man. His hair is peppered with gray and matted. He's missing the majority of his yellow, stained teeth, and he smells like the inside of a leg cast. His ripped thermal shirt is more of a rusty brown than it is its original white, and he has no shoes and only one sock that's ripped at the big toe. He leans forward and flashes a big gap-tooth smile. I ball my fists in case I need to fight my way out of here with the little strength I have left from my rumble with Randy. But the man hands me an itchy wool blanket like the free ones they give out at the shelter on Broad Street.

"Here," the toothless man says. "I have two for when it's really cold."

Everything inside me is telling me not to take it, especially since it smells like he wiped his ass with it. But it is chilly in here and I'm not about that hypothermia life, nor do I think getting sick in a crack house is a wise health decision. So I take it.

"Thank you."

The man sees my busted face. "Ya got to learn to bob and weave, kid. Bob and weave." He demonstrates with a horror movie cackle. Then he retreats to his disease-infested mattress, talking to himself as he lies down. "Ali, Frazier, Joe Lewis. She didn't bob and weave, Jim . . ."

I curl up into a tight ball, wrapping my arms around my knees, sure that no parts of my body touch the floor or wall, trying not to gag from the smell. Closing my eyes, the last thing that goes through my mind is the memorization song for pi: "*They said would you like some pie, I said yes I would / I forgot they majored in math, I would undo it if I could / They said: 3.14159, 2653 . . .*"

The next morning I creep back into my house to get my books for my study session with Aamani and to wash the crack house and blood off my body. I put a Band-Aid over the bloody hole in my skin where my bullet scar used to be. It'll have to do. The good news is Mom and Randy won't be awake anytime soon, as their days usually start around two p.m. I guess it takes a lot out of you doing nothing all day.

My phone's dead—crack houses aren't exactly mobile hotspots. I plug it in before hopping into the shower. As soon as it registers service, it erupts with texts from Britt.

> **Britt:** I still don't fuck with you but you ok?

> **Britt:** WTF

> **Britt:** You for real ignoring me right now?

> **Britt:** Yo forget I ever text you. I hope that nigga kicks your ass again

I roll my eyes. This is too much damn drama for me, especially since odds are I have internal bleeding.

> **Me:**

I do my best to dress up my wounds, but it doesn't matter. No amount of makeup can hide a stone-cold beat down. My face looks like I was jumped by a gang of cats. This is one of the downsides of being light skin.

I'm not even going to front. Seeing Aamani's dad manning the register with his resting bitch face has me shook. I mean, last time we were in his store together he almost had me shot. That doesn't exactly say *come on in and study with my daughter.*

So I wait outside.

Aamani comes trotting out the same back room she did the night she abandoned her post to watch *Doctor Who*. Her eyes water and grow a size when she sees the state of my face through the window.

As soon as she opens the door she gasps and throws her hands over her mouth. "Whoa . . . what happened?! Are you—"

I cut her off before she can finish. "I don't want to talk about it. Can we please just go study?"

She curls the left corner of her lips and blinks away her watery eyes. "Come on then, Okoye."

I follow her inside. As soon as her dad realizes it's me beneath the battered face, he starts yelling at Aamani in Hindi. Aamani doesn't back down, retaliating with a fiery mouth of Hindi. They're talking over one another like some Black folks at a barbershop arguing over LeBron or Kobe.

Her dad lands the final word. "Izzat!"

"Ugh . . . okay. I heard you." Aamani sighs, nodding for me to ignore him and follow her to the back.

"Izzat, beta. Izzat," he reiterates, staring me down as I pass.

We walk through the back, past the freezers and stockroom full of merchandise, everything from boxes of chips to cheap hair products. There's a compact office with a tiny TV, dingy couch, and a desk full of envelopes and papers. At the end of the corridor is a loading door that leads to the back alley. Next to it is a narrow staircase leading to Aamani's apartment. Fuck. Me. After last night, I'm not sure my leg can make the climb.

I grab the railing, and with Aamani's help, slowly make my way upstairs, each step a conquering triumph.

"What was your dad saying—or do I even want to know?"

"You really don't. My parents are stuck in their ways," Aamani says, her hand cradling the small of my back as she helps me navigate up the mountain.

The first thing that hits me when she opens the door is the sharp aroma of fresh spices. It's her tiffin times a thousand. I can even hear the sizzle of spices leaping from a pot in the kitchen.

"Please take your shoes off," Aamani instructs.

I do as she says and place my beat up Js next to the other pair of shoes.

Aamani's apartment is slightly larger and quieter than mine. She lives a few blocks over, the opposite direction of Devon's and the crack house, so there aren't as many sirens and gunshots. It's also cleaner, with less drug money stuffed under mattresses and weed butts overfilling ashtrays. I also peep an elephant sitting cross-legged tucked away in the corner of the living room, surrounded by candles and a multicolored altar no bigger than a Connect 4 board.

"Can I get you something to drink before we start? Maybe some chai?"

"Chai?"

"Yeah. It's actually really good when my mom makes it. When I make it, it's just okay."

I shrug. "I mean, I guess. Do you have anything else?"

"Let's go find out," she says, turning and walking into the kitchen.

I follow.

An old woman with wrinkles like a bulldog is dressed in a long red shalwar kameez and singing to herself in Hindi as she stirs the crackling pot that smells as if a group of spices were having an orgy.

Aamani sways her hips and joins in, planting a kiss on the

old woman's cheek as she harmonizes. She leans over and gets a good whiff of the pot. "Mmm, smells good, Aunty. What are you making?"

"Your mother is making coconut curry. I'm just watching it for her while she goes to the store for more coconut cream."

Unlike Aamani, the old woman's accent is thick.

Aamani looks back at me. "Two things Super Mart doesn't carry: coconut cream and, weirdly enough, butter," she says, shrugging. I'm awkwardly lingering in the doorway. "Aunty, this is my friend from school."

The old woman nods, churning her wrinkles into a smile. I panic and bow like she's the Queen of Wakanda.

When I look up from my hopefully inoffensive gesture, the old woman's wrinkled face droops in horror. She looks at Aamani, then back at me. Then she says something in Hindi, gesturing to the refrigerator. She walks to the freezer and pulls out a family-size pack of peas and hands it to Aamani with instructions in Hindi.

Aamani passes the peas to me. "She said put this on your face. It will bring down the swelling. She also said you need to go to hospital."

I place the peas over my right eye, which caught the brunt of Randy's beatdown. "Thank you," I say to the old woman, and for some reason I bow again.

She says something else in Hindi. Aamani translates. "She says less talking and more peas." This translation is followed by a bag of green beans from the freezer.

Fair enough, I think.

"And, dude, you really have to stop bowing," Aamani informs, a light chuckle in her voice.

"If my mom asks, please tell her we're in my room studying."

The old woman replies with a courteous nod and smile.

Aamani opens the fridge and rummages around the Tupperware of leftovers until she locates a six-pack in the back. "Is Mountain Dew okay?"

"Do you have Sprite?" I ask.

"Sorry, we're a Dew family."

Words I never thought I'd hear her say.

"Mountain Dew's fine then."

She grabs two sodas, then closes the fridge.

While my room is a barren wasteland that resembles the aftermath of an apocalypse, Aamani's room is decorated with colorful posters of nerd shit, most of which are comic book characters I don't know, and a few I do, like the Avengers. She also has a scattered collection of these bobblehead things called Funko Pop! Figures. Next to her desk, which is covered with textbooks and an old laptop, is a bookcase filled with more comics than I can count. Her closet is open, and I can see some of the elaborate cosplay costumes she posted on Instagram. One of them being the photo she took in a suit and brown trench coat, holding a screwdriver-looking thing that lights up blue at the tip. She captioned it with #TheTenthDoctor.

I'm looking around her room like I'm in a museum.

In front of her bed is the one thing I can actually relate to: a PlayStation connected to a tiny TV.

"What games do you have?" I ask.

Aamani takes a seat at her desk and opens a draw filled with games and an extra controller. "I have a bunch of games— *Overwatch, Horizon Zero Dawn, The Last of Us, Fortnite, Dark Souls*, and *Spider-Man*, which is my favorite. I want to get the new *Final Fantasy*, but have no money and don't want to trade in any of my old games for it. Are you a gamer?" Her voice spikes with an inflection of hope.

"I mean, I play *2K* at Krystal's house sometimes," I answer, doing my best to brace her for disappointment.

"I don't have that." Her voice sulks. "Maybe I'll give it a try and we can play sometime."

"It's a basketball game."

"Oh," she retracts, "then maybe I won't."

I hobble around her room and examine every poster and Pop! Figure carefully.

"You're really into comics, huh?" I stop and look at a character, one she has four posters of. She actually resembles Aamani, if Aamani knew how to pose like a badass. "Who the hell is this"—I tread carefully—"Hindu or Muslim Girl?"

"That's Kamala Khan, a.k.a. Ms. Marvel!" she says excitedly. "She's by far my favorite character. She's awesome!"

"You do know the Avengers and all of this comic shit isn't real, right?" I say, entertained by her levels of excitement.

Aamani gives me a look like she's ready to turn into the Hulk. "Have you ever even read a comic?"

"Nope. And don't intend to. Nobody's got time for that."

She Draymond-Greens me and goes into full defensive mode.

"You shouldn't shit on something you've never tried. Or do I have to remind you of what you said the first time I told you about STEM? Comics have changed my life."

I cock my head to the side. "Really? How?"

"I don't know if you've realized this, but my skin color, my clothing . . . I kinda stick out."

"I've noticed. How do you think I feel whenever I'm around white people?"

"Yeah, but the difference is you're at least accepted by your friends and family. Like, my parents want me to be this perfect little Hindu girl who does her pujas every day and wears a sari for every occasion. That's not me. And on the other hand, the world I want to be accepted in won't have me because they think I should fit the female stereotype of chasing boys and posting selfies. All I want to do is study, watch the Doctor and his companion save the galaxy, read the new issue of *Captain Marvel*, stay up twenty-four hours trying to beat *Dark Souls* in one day, and maybe go to some conventions rather than worship. Like, is that too much to ask? I'm constantly walking on eggshells, trying to please everyone by being someone I'm not. But then I was introduced to Ms. Marvel. For the first time I saw someone like me, but with, you know, like, badass superpowers and stuff. She's a huge gamer, super nerd, loves movies and pop culture, and she's just as obsessed with the Avengers as I am. Not to mention she's Pakistani and has to deal with balancing her parents' cultural expectations with her contemporary American ones. Every time I read anything with Kamala in it, I'm reminded that I'm not alone; that it's okay to like what I like, while at the same time being proud of my heritage."

I look back up at the Ms. Marvel poster. She's dressed in her costume of red tights, a blue kurta with a yellow lightning bolt down the center, and a red scarf, posing heroically with her fists on her hips while she looks off stoically into the distance. Her red scarf's flopping in the wind. She does look like a total badass, and I understand the social importance of representation (she's talking to the girl who saw *Black Panther* three times), but I just can't understand how she treats a fictional character like a god.

"Ms. Marvel does look pretty dope. But have you ever heard of Diana Taurasi? Now, she's a badass."

"Uh-uh," Aamani says, shaking her head curiously. "Is she DC or Marvel?"

"Neither. She's real. She's the starting shooting guard for the Phoenix Mercury. She's, like, the LeBron of the WNBA."

The sting of cringe warps her face. "Can you put her badassery in comic terms? You lost me at shooting guard."

"The only comic stuff I know are *The Avengers* and *Black Panther*. And that's only because Machone's in it and Michael B. Jordan can get it." I smile to sell it.

Aamani's face lights up like Times Square. "Ooh . . .! *Black Panther* was sooo good! I love Shuri! Have you seen *Infinity War*?"

For some reason, despite already knowing the answer, I contemplate this for a second. "That's the one with Thanos, right?"

She nods enthusiastically, like a bobblehead. I can't help but crack a smile at how hype she gets over this shit.

"Nah," I answer, crushing her spirits. "I only know about Thanos because there are, like, a million Thanos-LeBron memes."

"What?!" Aamani shouts, standing. "You have to see it! Greatest. Movie. Ever."

"Uh-huh, sure," I dismiss, looking at her like she's crazy. Because this reaction pretty much confirms it.

"Seriously . . . "

The old woman comes barreling in, panting as though she just ran five suicides. "I heard screaming."

"Oh, sorry, Aunty. Everything's okay. I was just yelling at Lex because she's the only person on Earth who has yet to see *Infinity War*."

"Oh. That is unacceptable. It is a very good film. Almost as good as *Dilwale Dulhania Le Jayenge*."

"Told ya," Aamani boasts.

"And I love that Iron Man. He's so funny." With the danger passed, the old woman retreats back to the kitchen.

"How has she seen it?" I inquire, partly jealous.

"We have movie night once a week. Last month when it was my turn, I chose *Infinity War*."

Shit. Is a hundred-year-old woman more comic woke than me?

"You know, you keep adding to this 'watch' list and I won't have any time to study," I point out. "And how old is your aunt, anyway?"

Aamani chuckles. "Bharti is not my actual aunt. She's just a friend of the family who lives down the street and loves mooching off us. Aunty is just a formal way of addressing our elders," she educates. "And I tell you about these things because I care. It's my duty as a nerd to educate all the nonbelievers. Plus, they're both on Netflix."

I sit on the edge of her bed and take out my notebook and packets. Then I notice the giant blue telephone booth blanket.

"Um, what the hell am I sitting on?"

She shakes her head. "See, this is why you need to start watching *Doctor Who*. Then you'd know it's bigger on the inside."

I'm trying my best to follow along. Maybe by the end of all of this I'll be the G.O.A.T. of STEM, which derails our studying several minutes when I have to explain to Aamani what G.O.A.T. stands for (Greatest Of All Time). I even write down everything she says, including "I'm so hungry, I could eat my arm!" which again derails us another ten minutes, as she proceeds to explain how it's scientifically impossible to do so. After she realizes I have no intention of ever eating my arm, we go back to studying.

We study as much as we can, everything from tetrapods to

phototropism to why atoms can bond together to make molecules. She even has me download this free STEM app that has all kinds of study materials—flash cards, crossword puzzles, practice exams, a matchmaking game. According to their slogan, it's the perfect way to "prep on the go."

A few hours into our session Aamani's mom pops in to check on us. She's short and dressed in a brownish shalwar kameez. It's not nearly as colorful as the ones they make Aamani wear. She has a stern, accented, I-run-this-family voice that demands respect.

I'm pretty sure she knows of my heist attempt, because she gives me the biggest stank-eye ever. Aamani tries to play it off like it's no big deal, as if her mom tries to strangle everyone with her eyes. But I know her parents hate me. Honestly, I don't blame them, or Mrs. Chakrabarti for leaving the door propped open when she leaves.

We go back to studying and before we know it, it's dark outside. I've consumed more useless math and science knowledge in one day than I have my entire life. I'm surprised my brain doesn't explode.

Her mom appears in the doorway, a drill sergeant scowl on her face.

"Beta, dinner is almost ready. It's time for your friend to go."

I take my cue and start packing, because Mrs. Chakrabarti scares the living shit out of me.

Aamani with a caress of my arm stops me. It catches me off guard and sends euphoric chills up my arm. "Can Alexis stay for dinner?"

I'm not going to lie. A free meal would be clutch as fuck right now, especially with how good that coconut curry smells.

Her mom throws extra stank on her stank-eye and goes apeshit on Aamani in Hindi so I can't tell it's about me. Which, come on, you saw that stank-eye; it undoubtedly is about me. "Patel will be here in ten minutes for dinner, so you need to change out of those boy clothes—*now*. Let's go!" she finishes in English, clapping at Aamani to get a move on.

Aamani protests in Hindi, but is ignored as her mom falls back to the kitchen.

She turns to me with apologetic eyes. "Sorry my mom's being such a pain."

I shrug and go back to stuffing my backpack. "I'm not trippin'. I should probably get home, anyway. It's a school night." I pause. "The fuck did I just say?"

Aamani accepts this with a long face, as though her happiness depends on me staying. I zip up my bag and sling it over my left shoulder. "Ay, not that I care, but who's Patel?"

"Some guy my parents are trying to set me up with."

"For real?" I flick the corner of my mouth incredulously. "Like, as in an arranged marriage? Y'all actually do that?"

"I mean, it's technically still a thing, but it's also kinda not. Most Hindus nowadays have stopped practicing arranged marriages, but there are still a handful of O.G. Hindus like my parents who still believe in it."

My lips curl with a pinch of skepticism. "Since when do you know what an O.G. is?"

"Hey, I'm from Jersey, remember? I know a lot about a lot. Just not what the G.O.A.T is," she answers sheepishly. "So in other words, I'm pretty much engaged. Would you like to RSVP to the wedding now? Please don't get us a bread maker or crystal stemware."

"Shit. That sucks. How many guys have they tried to set you up with?"

"Only three," she says, relieved. "My parents started their arrangements when they were my age, so as soon as I turned seventeen last summer they began turning my life into *The Bachelorette*."

I hesitate. Dread infiltrates my voice. "Do you like this guy like that?" I ask, my eyebrows reaching for my hairline, aggravating my bruises.

Her face clenches as if she swallowed a whole lemon. "Ew! No! First off, dude's more O.G. Hindu than my parents. The guy prays, like, thirty times a day. And most importantly he's a Trekkie. And I could *never, ever* marry a Trekkie. I'm a *Star Wars* girl all the way. I'm straight-up one with the Force."

A sense of relief washes over me.

CHAPTER 10

STEM practice begins with Matthew asking if he can address the group.

He approaches the whiteboard, turns to us, and starts pacing. In typical Matthew fashion, he does all he can to avoid eye contact. He's standing there in a *Return of the King* T-shirt, his glasses inching down the bridge of his nose because he's staring at his laces.

"You are all cordially"—yes, Matthew just said "cordially"; I freakin' love this kid—"invited to my birthday party sleepover this Saturday. My mom thinks I should've sent out actual invitations, but I think this will suffice because the other way involves too much writing and I get carpal tunnel easily due to my calcium deficiency. There will be chicken fingers and French fries for dinner with three dipping sauces. If you would like something other than Szechuan, honey mustard, or barbecue, or have any food allergies, please inform my mom via Facebook. Her name is Elizabeth Miller. She created a Facebook group titled Matthew's Seventeenth Birthday that all of you are welcome to join. Also, I was instructed to think of a game everyone would enjoy, so we will be playing D & D. Lucky for you, I'm a great and fair dungeon master, so everyone will have fun."

He stops pacing and briefly looks up. Then puts his head back down and heads for his seat. He gets halfway before remembering something important, and returns to the whiteboard.

"Oh, and sorry, Mrs. Hall, but it would be inappropriate for you to attend this party."

"I'm in," Brian says, digging the idea.

Aamani, and to my surprise Lindsay, accept.

Everyone's awaiting my response.

I mull it over for a second. Do I really want to be trapped with these nerds all night, playing Dungeons & Dragons? Trey would have a field day with that information. I can hear them clowning me now.

"Come on, Lex," Aamani insists, "we'll stick Brian's hand in water while he sleeps to make him pee his pants."

"You do know I can hear you," Brian declares, frightened for the dryness of his sleeping bag.

"It'll be fun," she encourages.

I highly doubt that. And why would I want to sleep next to some dude we're apparently going to make pee himself? It all sounds boring and unhygienic as fuck. But then I look over at Matthew, who's still awaiting my answer. I can't say no to that face. He looks like a lost puppy, begging for a home before Cruella de Vil makes him into a coat.

"Fine. I'll go. But I would like to request hot sauce as my dipping sauce."

"That can be arranged if you query my mom, Elizabeth Miller, on the Facebook group," Matthew says dryly.

"Seriously? You can't just tell her for me? I don't even think I have a Facebook account anymore. Like, Mrs. Baxter uses Facebook and she's got to be knocking on a hundred and five."

"I'm afraid I can't give you any special treatment. The request is too crucial. I hate when I get the wrong sauce. Also, I don't know the level of hotness you like or what brand you prefer or—"

"Okay," I stop him before he goes on for the next hour about hot sauce, "what's the Facebook group called again?"

When I was little, I believed only Black people were poor. I know, I was an idiot and so very gullible. Some would argue I still am. But every time I stepped out of the house, I bore witness to the poverty of Hargrove, populated with people who look like me. Even when I turned on the TV it was always white people in the nice neighborhoods and Blacks in the hood being represented in shows like *The Wire* and *Atlanta*. I mean, I didn't even see a nice neighborhood in person until we played Lower Merion freshman year, and everyone there was extra white—we're talking nanny-having and *Friends*-rerun-watching. I've always assumed Lindsay's parents drive that shitty Toyota with the mismatched doors as a front, because they really live in the suburbs and drive Lindsay to Hargrove so she can secure an easy valedictorian for her college applications.

Call me paranoid if you want. But I call it K.Y.W.P.—Know Your White People.

All of this is to say that I was not expecting Matthew to live a block from the foster home. Like, I've never seen him, or any other white person who wasn't a cop, in Hargrove.

Matthew's house is a small row home similar to Marcus's.

His dad answers the door dressed like what I imagine all white dads to dress like—accountants. He has a tight buzz-cut and is about six-two. I swear he looks like a poor man's Steve Kerr.

"Hi! You must be Alexis. It's a pleasure to meet you. Matthew is so thrilled all of you could join us to celebrate his birthday," he says with the most welcoming of smiles. "Please, come in. Can I take your hoodie?"

He's so nice. I feel like he's treating me like I'm white. I'm not buying it, though. K.Y.W.P.

"I'm okay, thanks," I say, guarding my hoodie like it's Jordan brand and not a hand-me-down from the church clothing bank.

"All right then," he says, widening his smile. "The kids are in the den."

This throws me at first, until I see where he's pointing. It turns out "den" is just what white people call a basement.

I follow him through the clean living room to the basement door by the kitchen. Mrs. Miller says hi from the counter, where she's hard at work prepping the chicken fingers and dipping sauces. She has a blond pixie cut and tired eyes behind her glasses, and is just as tall as Mr. Miller. I see where Matthew gets his eyesight and height from. She's actually wearing an apron. Where I'm from, you just cook in whatever you're wearing, and if you spill anything on it, then it shows you're putting your foot in it.

I grip the railing. Embarrassed, I wait for Mr. Miller to look away before beginning my long and painful trek down the staircase.

The basement is not even close to being finished. There are a bunch of moving boxes stacked against the insulated walls, cobwebs in the corners of the ceiling, and a giant beige rug sat beneath the TV stand and the couch.

Everyone's heavily engaged in an intense game of *Mario Kart*. Matthew is crouched on his knees directly in front of the TV. Everyone else is tilted on the couch, trying their best to lean whichever way their racing kart is moving on the screen.

"Aamani," Matthew calls to her. She's hunched for extra focus.

"My apologies, but you are about to face the wrath of the O.P. blue shell."

"What?!" Aamani slams on the joystick to avoid the impending turtle shell. As it appears in her frame, she goes, "Son of a Dalek…"

Her character, Yoshi, whines as the blue shell torpedoes into the back of its kart, knocking the fat-nosed green dinosaur out of first place.

Toad, Brian's character, in the left corner of the screen, runs over a power-up.

"I hope you're enjoying your time in first, Mattie," Brian says.

"I am."

"Good, because I've got one word for ya: Suck on some lightning!"

"That was four words," Matthew points out.

With a press of a button Brian sends a lightning bolt to each corner of the screen, shocking each character and turning them into miniature versions of themselves. This allows Brian to overtake Aamani and Matthew in the standings.

If you haven't guessed, Lindsay's slow-ass is dead last; no power-ups, no chance of gaining. She bumps into every wall and keeps driving off the track, only to be saved by the magic of video game logic and the Koopas.

"Oh, what's good, Lex!" Brian says, looking over at me as his character nearly loses his lead and drives into a tree. "You're just in time to watch me pwn these noobs."

Finally, someone acknowledges me. I get mumbled "heys" from Aamani (too focused on regaining the lead) and Lindsay (too busy hating the fact that we inhabit the same planet).

Matthew leans in closer to the TV. If he reached out he could touch it. "I'm going to win!"

"Sorry, Mattie, but that's not happening," Brian counters.

"Ha! You boys are adorable," Aamani says, her voice dripping with sarcasm. "None of you noobs are a match for Yoshi."

Brian scoffs. "Get real. There's no freakin' way you're catching up after that—"

With the added speed boost of a mushroom power-up, Aamani burns Matthew and Brian to reclaim first place.

"Um, you were saying?" Aamani says, grinning from cheek to cheek.

There's a sliver of space on the couch between Lindsay and the armrest. I look down, giving Lindsay the universal look for *can you scoot over*? She looks at me, then back at the screen and spreads her legs to gobble up the remaining couch space.

"Really?" I deadpan.

The bitch doesn't move. She just sits there pretending she doesn't suck ass at *Mario Kart*.

"A'ight then. That's how you want to play it," I say, nodding. Then I cop a squat right on her lap so she can't see or do shit. Thanks to my physical therapy, this doesn't hurt nearly as bad as it would have a month ago.

"Get off of me!" She struggles, her face turning Kool-Aid Man red.

"Make me," I reply, putting on more weight as she squirms beneath me.

She wrestles with my ass for a few more seconds before summoning some hidden white girl strength and pushing me off of her. See, this is why you have to K.Y.W.P. My foot gets tangled in her controller cord. I go to grab the armrest to regain my balance, but the cord yanks and pulls the console off the TV stand, rendering the screen black.

"I win! I win!" Aamani announces. "Let the record note that I win. I was in the lead," she justifies.

From his knees Matthew looks over the fallen console as if it's been murdered in cold blood. He raises his fists to the heavens. "Nooo!"

"Shit. Uh—my bad. I didn't break it, did I?" If I did, then he's shit out of luck, because I can't afford a video game system. Not even an old-ass Wii.

Aamani snorts. "You didn't break anything. He's just doing his best *Revenge of the Sith* Darth Vader impression and being overdramatic. Right, Matthew?"

Matthew picks up the console, cradling it in his arms, and returns it to the TV stand next to his PlayStation. "Don't underestimate the power of the dark side."

"*That's a yes,*" Aamani and Brian say in harmony.

"It was Lindsay's fault. She started it by not moving." I sound like a petulant five-year-old.

"It wasn't my fault," Lindsay protests. "It was that big ass of yours and those gigantic Sasquatch feet."

"You say that like it's a bad thing. People like big asses. Remind me, when's the last time your pancake-ass went on a date?"

Matthew, extra worked up, interrupts. "No more talk of butts and mythical creatures, unless said creatures happen to appear in *Star Wars* or *Lord of the Rings*. Now, if you all will kindly take out your party schedule, I'd like to bring your attention to subsection D"—yeah, there are actually subsections in this thing—"where due to our abrupt end to the video game phase, we shall proceed to the D & D portion of the festivities."

For some dumbass reason, I raise my hand. Matthew has that teacher-like effect on people. He comes off like a wise old man.

"Yes, Alexis," he says, making brief eye contact.

"Um, I don't have one of these schedule things."

"Of course you don't. I threw yours away," Matthew replies bluntly.

"Uh, why?"

"Because you were thirty-four minutes late. So I marked you as being absent."

The right corner of my mouth arches. "That doesn't sound very practical. But okay."

"You can share with Lindsay if you'd like."

Lindsay and I look at each other with disgust, and then retreat into our personal space.

"You know, I'm cool. I'll just listen and follow whatever y'all do."

The door to the basement opens, and down comes Mrs. Miller with a tray of neatly laid-out chicken fingers and sauces. My stomach growls like a T-Rex. Food has been kind of hard to come by in the crack house. I'm usually forced to rely on half-eaten hoagies my roommate, Crackhead Marvin (that's not me clowning him; he introduced himself that way), gets when he asks for loose change outside of Wawa.

"Who's ready for chicken fingers?" she announces, a joy in her voice that my mom's never possessed.

"*Mom* . . ." Matthew groans, stopping her halfway down the stairs. He looks down at his phone. "You're twenty-seven minutes and forty-two seconds ahead of schedule. Did anyone bother to read the subsections?"

"Sorry, honey. I just thought your friends might be getting hungry. Not everyone eats dinner as late as we do."

"I don't think anyone's hungry yet," Matthew answers.

I almost mimic Matthew's Darth Vader scream of *noooo*! I need those chicken fingers.

"Um, I am," Brian says timidly, raising his hand to make sure he's heard.

Aamani elbows Brian in the rib. "Dude, don't freak him out. You know how Mattie gets about change."

"I lied, Mrs. Miller. I'm totally not hungry. I'm still full from a bagel I had earlier. If I even look at a chicken finger I'm gonna throw up."

Mrs. Miller smiles. "Okay, well I'll just come back in twenty-seven minutes."

I take a step toward the tray. If my legs worked properly, I'd snatch it and run.

"Are you hungry, Alexis?" asks Matthew.

For my stomach's sake, I speak up. "I mean . . . I could eat."

Matthew plays around with the idea for several seconds. "Well, your butt did ruin *Mario Kart*, so we are moving up D & D on the schedule anyway. Okay. If people are hungry, I think it's a good idea to have an appetizer before we begin D & D."

Mrs. Miller gives me a smile to let me know my big ass hasn't ruined the party. "I think that's a very thoughtful and fair compromise, honey."

We get off the couch and go grab a chicken finger. Brian practically sprints over. There's a special serving dish marked *Alexis's Sauce*. They sure do know how to make a girl feel special. I take four.

After a bite, Matthew turns to his mom. "Thank you for the appetizer. Can you bring the food back down when we start D & D?"

"Of course," she replies with another warm smile. "If anyone needs anything, Mr. Miller and I are right upstairs."

As soon as the door shuts, Matthew scarfs down the rest of his chicken finger. "Back to subsection D . . ."

Aamani stops him. "Um, before we do that. I feel it's my duty as team captain to disclose Lex's big secret that she has been hiding from the team."

This captures everyone's attention, especially mine. I start racking my brain in search of what she could know. Shit. I hope she's not referring to my crack-house sleepovers. Lindsay would just love to know about those. She probably lives in a castle where animals help her get dressed in the morning.

Aamani flashes a smile to calm me. "Guys, I'm afraid to inform you that our new teammate here has yet to see the mind-blowing epicness that is *Infinity War*."

Gasps.

I roll my eyes.

"What . . .?" Brian chokes. "For the love of Iron Man, please tell me you're joking."

Matthew starts pacing. "No no no no no . . ." Then he beelines it to a moving box and starts digging through the slush of forgotten movies.

"Is he okay?"

"Ah, he's fine," Brian says, uncertain.

"Y'all need to for real chill on this movie. It can't be that damn good," I state as fact. "And I'm sure Lindsay hasn't seen it either. And you guys aren't giving her shit for it."

"Don't drag me into this. I'm woke on Marvel movies," Lindsay retaliates.

Matthew emerges holding a copy of *Infinity War*. "It's okay, people. I have secured the package. We can now rectify this terrible, terrible injustice."

He sprints up the stairs to the kitchen. The kid may be mad weird, but he sure can run his ass off. Who knew? If I wasn't sure he'd get murdered or try to turn the team into *Lord of the Rings* enthusiasts, I'd suggest he try out for football.

Aamani comes and sits beside me, cheesing extra hard. "So, are you pumped to pop your *Infinity War* cherry?"

We hear the patter of Matthew's footsteps upstairs followed by the door shooting open and Matthew sprinting back down, movie in one hand, tray of chicken fingers in the other. He sets the tray on the coffee table, then pops the movie in.

Matthew pauses and turns to me. "Before we begin, have you seen every MCU film leading up to *Infinity War*?"

As I open my mouth to say no, Aamani fake coughs: "*Ah-say-yes!*"

"Um, yeah?" I reply unconvincingly.

"Good," Matthew accepts, then returns to setting up the movie. "Because we were going to have to start from the beginning of the Infinity Saga if you hadn't."

I lean over to Aamani. "This better be good. Because y'all are mad hype. I won't ever get this hour and a half back."

Everyone except Matthew bursts out laughing.

"You really have no idea what you've gotten yourself into, do you?" Brian warns.

I'm slowly becoming terrified. "What?"

Aamani enlightens me. "*Infinity War* is, like, three hours long. You can't fit so much awesome, *and* ten years of universe building, into ninety minutes."

"Three fuckin' hours?!" I say. "We better actually be going to space."

She nods.

I shake my head.

"Language," Matthew censors. Then he takes a bite of a Szechuan-dipped chicken finger and hits play.

I gargle Matthew's fancy, name-brand toothpaste that tastes of cool mint, and then spit it in the sink. Aamani's simultaneously brushing her teeth and grilling me in the mirror, awaiting my movie review.

I'm not sure what she wants from me. I need some time to digest the past five hours—three watching the movie, and two watching Matthew replay scenes with director commentary while pointing out Easter eggs.

I dab the corners of my mouth with the red hand towel latched around a ring by the sink.

"A'ight, let me be clear." I pause for dramatic effect. "Black Panther *dies*! Like, are you shitting me?! The movie was straight-up trash."

Aamani cracks a grin, which is mad impressive-slash-weird since she's currently brushing her teeth like she's scrubbing floors.

"For real, though. I'm serious. It's all kinds of trash."

Her grin spills into a full smile. My face spills over into full-on irked mode. Why isn't she listening?

"Me thinks the lady doth protest too much," she mumbles through a mouthful of blue toothpaste.

"Me thinks y'all like shitty movies. I for real need therapy after watching that. Whose idea was it to kill off every major character? They even killed my boy Groot. Why would you make me watch that?"

She does a quick rinse and spit, then reverts her mouth back to cheesy smile.

"It's not funny, Aamani. You have legit scarred me for life. And that's saying something, because I've seen some shit. But nothing compares to watching a Black icon and a teenage tree die. And then Matthew telling me that Groot's last word was 'Dad . . .' That's savage."

She spits one more time, then runs her toothbrush under the water. "You do realize that by forming such a strong opinion, you're essentially admitting you love the movie and are slowly but surely becoming one of us."

"Uh, no, I'm not. We finally get a badass Black hero and they kill him off like the shit's *Game of Thrones*. This movie's some straight-up bullshit. I hate Thanos. Looking like a purple Deebo."

"Just admit it . . ."

Her whole face implores me to give in. I hate when she looks at me like this. With the same look she used to get me to join STEM. That innocent grin and doe eyes aren't fair.

"If it makes you feel better, people die and come back to life in comics all the time. Wolverine's been dead, like, twenty times. And Goku dies, like, every other day on that show."

We finish in the first-floor bathroom, and then return to the basement. I again rely on the banister to help me down each step. But the pain is nothing compared to going up. That's what really sucks.

"Is there a sequel?" I inquire.

"Aha! See, I knew you loved it. You want to marry it you love it so much."

"No. I'm just too invested now and scarred to ignore it."

"Suuurrre, whatever you have to tell yourself to suppress your inner nerd. Give in to the power of the dark side."

I shake my head. It's all I can do to keep myself from admitting she's right.

Of course Lindsay claimed the couch all to herself. She's already passed out, all cozy with her head tucked beneath the armrest and her sleeping bag unzipped and draped over her. Matthew removed the coffee table to make room on the rug for me, Brian, and Aamani. I'd never waste money on a sleeping bag, so I'm using some old sheets Matthew's mom provided.

Matthew's asleep on his mattress in the corner. The three of them helped him carry it down the stairs, along with a pillow he's had since he was a child. The thing looks like it survived its own infinity war, but he was adamant he couldn't sleep without it. I can't say I blame him. He has us sleeping in this cold-ass dungeon. I just saw a spider the size of a watch craw up the wall.

Brian's knocked out and snoring in his sleeping bag in front of the TV. I'm lying in my makeshift sleeping bag, the rug doing very little to keep the coarse edges of concrete from shanking me in the ass. Why'd I agree to this sleepover again? Oh, right, because free food and the simple fact that this place isn't a crack house. You know, the little things.

"You have to admit tonight's been fun."

Even though Aamani's in the sleeping bag next to me, it's too dark to see her face.

I think back on a night of video games, movie watching, and chicken tenders. "Yeah, it was pretty dope."

"Pretty dope indeed . . . pretty dope indeed," she says, fading into sleep.

I can hear the space heater buzz in between Brian's snoring. For such a thin guy, he sounds like an asthmatic polar bear. Honestly, it's not even his snoring or the creepy space heater that's keeping me up, it's the lack of all the noise—the sirens, people pushing weight on the corner. You can't hear Hargrove in this dungeon.

I stare at the dark ceiling, held hostage by my thoughts. I start to wonder what my mom's doing, because I know she's not asleep. Don't ask me why I care. I just do. Then I start to worry about Britt. She's come into some money and I hope for her sake she's not in too deep. Because once you're in the game, you're in it for life.

"Psst . . ."

I look over, despite not being able to see shit in this dungeon. "Aamani?"

"Yeah, homie. You up?"

"Obviously. I'm talking to you."

"True. True. Can't sleep?"

"No," I whisper back, although I'm not sure why we're whispering. You can hear Brian's snoring from space. "It's too quiet. And please don't ever say 'homie' again. The only people who say that are from the nineties or cholos."

"Sorry. I was trying something new," she says, going silent. "I feel like I should give you a nickname or something. Something to solidify our friendship so people know we're tight."

I turn to her and tighten my face. Then I realize I'm doing this for nothing because she can't see me. "Uh, that's a'ight. I'm good."

"Hmm . . ." she contemplates aloud, completely ignoring my request to squash the idea. I guess "friends" don't listen to one another in her world. "What about Lex Luthor? You know, because you like to steal things."

"I don't like to steal things," I say, resenting the conversation.

"Oh, or Alexis-ander Hamilton?!" Silence cuts through the air. "*My name is Alexis-ander Hamilton / And there's a million things I haven't done / But just you wait, just you wait,*" she sings. I can't even begin to reply to that. "You're right, that's a bit of a stretch. Admittedly, not my finest work. I'll come up with something."

I huff. "Aamani?"

"Yes, Ex-Lax?"

"I know you can't see my face right now, but I promise I'm not playing when I tell you that if you ever call me any of those names, I'll disown you as a teammate and friend."

"Ooh, I got one!" It's like I'm not even here. "How about Sirius A? Like, *you're my girl, Sirius A*. Or *pass the ketchup, Sirius A*."

"Sirius what now?"

"*Sirius A . . .*" she repeats, as if saying it again will magically make me know what the hell she's talking about. "Sirius A is the brightest star in Earth's sky. With a visual magnitude of negative one point forty-six, the star's outshone by only several planets and the International Space Station."

I pause to consider it. Not that she'll listen either way. She seems to be lost in her own world where science beakers fill automatically with the proper solution of compounds, and math is the national language. "So when you look at me, you think of a star?"

"Is that weird?"

There's an inclination of hope to her question.

"It's not normal," I reply sharply. "But 'is cool. Just don't call me that in public. That shit will get me clowned for sure. I also have a rep to keep."

"Do you, though? I feel like your rep should be the least of your worries."

She has a point. I should be more concerned with what I'm going to eat tomorrow night.

Apart from Brian's snoring, it goes quiet again. Somehow, I can sense a smile on her face. How is it she's able to see through me, able to weed out all my bullshit?

"Sooo, too quiet to sleep, huh?" Aamani asks, doing her best at making conversation. "I can't sleep either. There's a group of women, uh, let's just call them women of the night, who work at that strip club down the street. And every night around two a.m. I hear them walking home and trading stories. Now I can't sleep without them."

"What do they say?" I inquire curiously. I'm a little too invested in this story if I'm being honest.

"Stuff like, 'Girl, you know I asked Jerome for a cat for all them damn mice in my house, and this dummy brought me some fat stray with glaucoma. Thing's running into walls and shit.'" I snort. "And yeah, some of the club stuff too," she admits, embarrassed. "Like, 'I ain't suckin' that?!' and 'He tried to put his finger where?!' It's impossible not to eavesdrop. They literally walk right below my window. I just find it super interesting that even though their lives take place at different hours and they've seen and done things I never will, we're all so connected. The world's just one big cesspool of connecting neurons."

"Trust me, Aamani, strippers are in no way connected to you. Their tips, yes. But you, *definitely* not. I doubt any of them watch *Doctor Who* or can do math better than a calculator. There's no philosophical meaning behind what they do. They just really like dancing and making money."

"I mean, well, yeah, I assume they enjoy twerking," she giggles. What the hell is wrong with me? Why does her giggle melt my heart like a newborn puppy sneezing? "I'm just referring to the scientific fact that we are all connected to each other and, as such, one with the universe."

I give her an incredulous smirk, despite knowing she can't see it.

"No lie. You sound dumb high."

"Would you like me to break it down for you?" she asks buoyantly.

"Sure. Either that or pass the blunt you're hiding."

"Okay, but it's about to get real nerdy up in here," she warns.

"Aamani, my Hindu friend, with you guys, when is it ever not nerdy?"

Again, I can feel her smiling hard.

"All right," she says, bottling her excitement. "So the beginning of this universe was marked by rapid expansion and cooling—"

"I'm going to stop you right there," I interject. "You're really about to go in hard, aren't you?"

"If you don't want to hear it, all you have to do is say so. Last chance. Speak now or forever hold your astronomy-ignorant peace," she teases.

I can sense the excitement oozing from her. She has this high-pitched inflection as though she's a kid waking up her parents on Christmas morning to come downstairs and see what Santa brought. It would be a crime to deprive her of her nerdy moment. I'd feel like the dick telling said kid that Santa isn't real and Christmas is a bullshit holiday manufactured by the toy industry.

"Go ahead," I say with a light smile. "Hit me with all your nerdiness. I want it all up in my face."

EVERY VARIABLE OF US

She ruffles her sleeping bag as she sits up, ready to leap into nerd action.

"So, as I was saying, as the infant universe expanded and cooled, different windows opened for the formation of subatomic particles—these babies are the building blocks of matter; we're talking quarks and electrons."

I give a fake gasp. "*Nooo* . . . not quarks and electrons." I put a smile on my voice to let her know I'm only teasing. She thinks I'm totally serious though.

"Oh yeah, quarks and some coldblooded electrons. Crazy shit, right? Anyway, further expansional cooling allowed the quarks to embrace one another and form longer subatomic particles, like protons and neutrons. More cooling allowed the positively charged protons and negatively charged electrons to slow enough to a point where they could no longer resist that sweet, sweet electrostatic attraction, and with such, hydrogen atoms were born!"

"Cool story. That's it, right?"

"Ha, you're funny. Not even close."

God, help me.

"As the universe continued to expand and cool, that hydrogen I told you about began to clump and the first stars were born. Stars are the ultimate alchemists. Like, the thermonuclear fusion in the core of stars takes hydrogen and creates larger elements. The death of the largest of stars is a violent explosion known as a supernova, which is when a star shines its brightness because of said catastrophic explosion that ejects most of its mass. Anyway, when stars die they leave behind a mix of elements. This mix will then combine to create another star and possibly a planetary system. How cool is that?!"

"Not to be *that* girl, but let's wrap this up."

"Okay, okay, almost there. So about four-point-six billion years ago, give or take, a planetary system formed in a sparsely populated region of the galaxy known as the Milky Way. Which reminds me, I have to tell Dad to restock the candy aisle."

"Aamani?! Please, while I'm young."

"Sorry, my bad. So one of the planets in said system had the right conditions for the perfect elements and molecules to form water and amino acids, and those amino acids reacted to form proteins. And those proteins became DNA. And I don't need to tell you, but your body is made of cells that contain those molecules."

"So...?"

"*So...*" she mimics, dumbfounded as to how I'm not getting this "...approximately half of your body is made of hydrogen atoms. All those hydrogen atoms were formed in the infant universe. The rest of the atoms in your body were formed in the cores of stars that died billions of years ago—hello, supernovas, anyone?! All of this further confirms you're so a Sirius A. Now come on, you just found out that we're all made from supernovas... how badass is that?"

I don't know if badass is the right word, but it is pretty dope to know I come from a star. It blows my mind that she can remember all of that. I struggle to remember what I ate for breakfast, despite it usually being a stolen Pop-Tart. This universe is so expansive and never-ending, and I'm nothing but a speck in it. I guess we're all just specks when you stop to think about it. Tiny fish swimming in a universe-sized fish bowl. Jesus, now Aamani has me sounding like I should be wearing a hemp beanie and listening to the Spin Doctors.

"How do you remember all of that?" I ask, cocking my head quizzically. "Matthew I get, because he's wired that way; Lindsay's an attention whore who likes to show off; and Brian's my young boul, but he's not on y'all's level. But you being able to recite all that blows my mind."

Aamani tilts her head in thought. "That's one thing I'll never fully grasp, why no one around here can pronounce *boy* right?"

"It's a Philly thing," I answer. "You wouldn't understand."

"You have no idea why everyone says it that way, do you?" Aamani deadpans.

"Not a clue."

"Let me ask you something," Aamani says, her voice now sounding fed up. "Who would you consider to be the G.O.A.T. of basketball? I am using that correctly, right?" she checks.

"You are. Good job. And the G.O.A.T. is MJ. No debate. If anyone tries to say LeBron, you just hold up six fingers and walk away."

"Okay, and why is this MJ character the G.O.A.T.?"

"I keep forgetting how little you know about my world," I say, taking a moment to bring up his Airness's résumé. "He was Rookie of the Year, bruh, the man averaged damn near thirty as a rookie—unreal; made fourteen All-Star teams; was eleven times All-NBA; was the Defensive Player of the Year; five MVPs; ten-time scoring champ; two-time Gold medal winner; won seventy-two games in ninety-five; was the star of the OG *Space Jam,* the greatest cartoon movie ever made—"

"Every Pixar movie ever says hi, but continue."

"And the mic drop—the man has six championship rings. Tell LeBron fans to suck on that."

"Ladies and gentlemen of the jury, I rest my case," she announces proudly. "No further questions, Your Honor."

"Did I miss something? What exactly is your point? MJ's a beast. That's nothing new to anyone who's ever had a pulse."

"Once again my point is you're more than capable of retaining just as much information as me and the rest of the team. You've fed into the stereotype of dumb jock for so long that you haven't a clue how smart you truly are. You knowing every basketball stat is no different than me knowing astronomy or what issue Spidey gets his symbiote suit. He gets it in *Amazing Spider-Man* two-fifty-two, bt-dubs."

My mind goes blank. What do you say to someone who believes in you with so much vigor when you know for a fact that you're not shit?

"Give me your hand," she requests. I assume she's holding her hand out. I feel like we've been buried alive with how dark it is. "Don't worry. I'm not about to put it down my pants or anything if that's what you're worried about."

I hesitate, not summoning the courage to trust her. But then my nerves wash over me and I find my hand creeping toward her until I feel the plastic zipper of her sleeping bag, then her soft palm kissing mine.

"Can you feel how quickly a simple touch raises our body heat? That's because every time we touch, a chemical called oxytocin explodes inside us like tiny supernovas. It's just science. And science says you're a supernova. Remember that."

I don't care about why our hands are touching, or how oxytocin works. I don't even care that there are some serious gay vibes floating around right now. All I care about is figuring out a way to make her never let go.

CHAPTER 11

You want to know the worst part of it being winter? Basketball season is in full swing and I'm not part of it. Every morning I show up for physical therapy and go through Michael's routine—I squat to pick up tennis balls, stretch out my leg with the elastic band, and practice balancing on my damaged leg like I'm a goddamn flamingo—all while the players from the team ice their sprained ankles and brag about their stats and the recruitment letters they've received.

It's been two months of that shit.

Well, not today. I skip rehab and track down Janitor Mike. He feels so sorry for me, I don't even have to bribe him to let me into the gym an hour before school starts. I pick up a basketball and dribble a few times. I go between my legs and around my back, all stationary. Each move quick and precise. My handles are still there. I can do this. I can still hoop. I go to explode like I used to. I'm not even a centimeter into my movement before a seething pain shoots from my upper thigh down to my ankle. My brief explosion turns into a heavy limp, and I quickly throw all my weight onto my left leg and hit the hardwood.

I'm pathetic. Why did I think I could do this?

I gulp down the tears building in the back of my throat.

It's really over.

Physical therapy may have turned my zombie walk into a limp, but I'll never turn it into a sprint or even a jog.

I gaze at the bright lights. The only sound is the buzzing that emanates from their high-wattage bulbs.

"Finished already," Mike says, standing over me.

I sigh and close my eyes. "Yeah, Mike. It was a good run. Just leave me here to die on the court."

He chuckles.

I was serious.

"You remember when I said you're going places?"

I open one eye and look up at him. "Uh, yeah. What about it?"

"I didn't say that because I just watched you cook Malcolm." My other eye shoots open, because now I am thoroughly confused and remotely curious. "I've been working here for twenty-seven years. I've seen kids come and go. Some of them amazing ballplayers. But none of them worked as hard as you. In the past four years, you've been in this gym more than me. So I told you that because I know that no matter what you do, if you put that amount of effort into it, you'll be great."

Huh. I never thought of it that way.

I roll over on my left side and look at Mike. His beard graying, catching up with his hair. And he has an assortment of freckles that look like chocolate chips under his eyes.

"Has anyone ever told you you look like Morgan Freeman?"

He laughs. I put my flamingo exercises to good use and pick myself up.

I toss him the basketball.

"Where are you going?" he asks.

"You cool with Mrs. Francis?"

"The librarian? Yeah, I've run into her a few times in the hall. Why?"

"You think I can bribe her to open the library early?"

"Hmm," he says, stroking his beard in thought. "That depends. Do you know how to stack books?"

"Like a true G."

"Okay then. Follow me."

Three weeks after Mrs. Francis and I become BFFs, weird shit starts happening.

The first thing I notice is I'm missing two sports bras and my only underwire bra. That's weird enough in itself. But perhaps even weirder is the other two women at the crack house both have chests bigger than me. So my 32Bs aren't going to do them any good. Which leaves my roommate, good ol' Crackhead Marvin, who I know is an A-cup at best. The crazy thing is I'm not even mad that someone stole them, because it gives me an excuse to sneak back into Mom's place to grab my remaining sports bras and to get a shower. There's only so many times I can shower in the locker room, before people start asking questions. Like, no one has gym that often.

The crack house isn't all that bad when you get used to it. Imagine the nicest Airbnb you can think of. You know, the kind that comes up when you Google "Airbnb"—clean sheets, fast Wi-Fi, one of those nice welcome baskets with fucking Fiji Water and an assortment of fruit. A real five-star establishment. Now take the opposite of that, sprinkle in some crackheads who are apparently into drag, and you too know how it feels to live in a crack house. In all seriousness, when I close my eyes at night, it almost feels like home. The sirens, gunshots, and sounds of people blissfully succumbing to their high puts me right to sleep. It's my hood's lullaby.

Then yesterday I get called into Principal Garrett's office. That's not the weird part. I used to get called into his office damn near every day because of something Britt and I did. I would even skip homeroom on occasion and go straight there to save him the trouble of having to summon me. But this time he and Mr. Jones interrogated me on my recent increase in GPA. Mr. Jones implored me to "Tell the truth!" like he's Will Smith and I'm some corrupt NFL rep. He said lying will only cause more problems for me. It took Mrs. H to come to my defense before they released me with the stern warning of "I have my eye on you." I wanted to tell Garrett and his lazy-eye that I don't care.

And I thought Mr. Jones believed in me. It's like, jeez, thanks for the vote of confidence.

And today I get this weird text from Aamani as I'm walking out of second period.

Aamani: So how sick are you? Walter White Breaking Bad sick, or Tom Hanks Philadelphia sick?

I Google "Tom Hanks Philadelphia." He looks really pale in this picture. I mean, Tom Hanks is as white as they come, but in this picture he's Casper white.

Me: Are you calling me a cancer-having ghost?

Aamani: No. Brian said he saw you every day this week leaving the library before homeroom. I figured

> you must be sick or Brian is
> smoking crack.

I smile, because Aamani just has that effect on me. I almost tell her this. That every time I see her name pop up on my phone I smile. But I don't. I banish the feeling.

> Me: Not sick. Just studying 📚 👍

A moment passes, then my phone pings.

> Aamani: 🤔 🤔

We're inside for PE today because of the snow. Not that it matters. It's not like I can participate. So I use the time to study on the bleachers.

Coach Jackson tells everyone to hit the showers. This includes me even though I didn't sweat. I still had to change into my gym clothes for some reason. Something about school policy. I think they just get off on making me tardy for next period.

Anyway, as soon as we get back to the locker room, I swap out my science textbook for last week's STEM packet, just to make sure I fully grasped the chapter I was reading. This is the problem with reading ahead. You're basically teaching yourself until the rest of the class catches up.

Aamani reaches into her locker and removes her jeans and a T-shirt with Albert Einstein sticking his tongue out.

"Someone looks ready for Radnor."

I don't know why she's asking about our next STEM match.

Unless Brian miraculously catfishes another girl into making out with him and giving him mono, I'll be riding the bench per usual.

"Yeah," I reply. "I was just talking to Brian about that last period. I told him he needs to watch out for those astronomy questions. He missed a bunch last practice. Radnor's going to be on point."

She nods in agreement.

"I told him to go over last week's packet," I continue. "Mrs. H loaded that with astronomy questions. Like, did you know space is not a complete vacuum? There are about three atoms per cubic meter of space."

"I did not know that," Aamani says with a heavy grin.

I'm too in the astronomy zone right now to acknowledge how weird she's being.

"And that neutron stars are so dense that a teaspoon of them would be equal to the weight of the entire Earth's population. I swear, yo, this astronomy shit is wild. The universe is one dope place."

I know what you're thinking. *She wasn't playin' about taking this STEM shit seriously.* Finding out you're made from an exploding star and not just your dad's jizz can have that effect on a person.

"Hmm . . . interesting," Aamani mumbles, as if developing a diabolical plan.

"What?"

"Nothing. Just—interesting. Very interesting."

"Aamani, what? And I swear, you better not say 'interesting.'"

The bell rings. Because of course it does. I haven't even begun getting changed.

Amy Grant, sitting beside me, panics and hurries off the bench. There's a huge sweat stain where her ass used to be. Ironically enough it kind of resembles Pluto, which is no longer a planet,

FYI. Apparently it couldn't clear the neighborhood around its orbit, among other things. We have that it common, Pluto and I. Because at this rate, I'll never clear Hargrove.

CHAPTER 12

I've never liked Christmas. I mean, what's to like? People are fake nice to each other; radio stations play Christmas music on a loop (if I have to hear "Jingle Bell Rock" one more time, I'm going to Jingle-Bell-blow-my-brains-out); it's cold as fuck outside; some fat guy supposedly breaks into your house, drinks all your milk and eats all your junk food (where I'm from that's called having a crackhead problem); and furthermore, said jolly fat guy's GPS doesn't just avoid tolls, it also avoids the hood. So I may be in the minority here, but Santa can die from a diabetic coma, for all I care. The only thing Christmas has going for it are the NBA games and winter break. But now, ironically, I actually want to go to school. So it doesn't even have that going for it.

School is now the only place in my life that I can count on heat, electricity, free food, and internet. Some nights, when my boy Tom (everyone on the block calls him Scooter) in 1A below Mom's apartment tells me he hasn't seen her for days (because she's on one of her missing-persons benders), I'm able to sneak in, shower, and steal some supplies—mainly bread and old-ass leftovers she's forgotten in the back of the fridge. A girl can only live off those half-eaten sandwiches Crackhead Marvin gets for so long. And on nights when I can't raid Mom's, and Marvin's got nothing for me, I go to the shelter on North Broad. I try to only go there a couple times a month, when things get really dire. Otherwise, Child Protective Services starts asking questions. I've dropped a few pounds, but nothing noticeable. I'm surviving.

What really has me in a mood is my whole *friends* situation. Everyone thinks I've sold out because I'm not on the block kicking it with them anymore. When the reality of the situation is half the time I can't go home even if I wanted to. Also, if I'm not searching for my next meal, I'm at the library with Mrs. Francis, studying until it closes, or at Aamani's studying until her mom kicks me out for one of her Hindu Tinder dates. But I'm really not trying to do fuck-all on a stoop for the rest of my life. At least with STEM, it feels like I'm working toward something, toward a future.

It's our last day before break, hence my beef with Christmas. It's crazy to think that we're halfway through the season, and since I joined we have yet to lose a match. Not that I have anything to do with our success. I've yet to participate in a match since the infamous mono incident. I swear, I'll find out who was making out with Brian if it's the last thing I do.

Mrs. H is delivering her end-of-practice speech, which involves handing out the extra-thick packets and pointing out what sections each of us has to focus on. This is also the time when she preps us for the end-of-practice questions. She informs me that I need to focus on the algebra II section, specifically the questions on linear equations. She's not lying. My math skills are still mad suspect. A B- is good and all, but that's not going to put me in the running for any scholarships. And it's definitely not going to help me on my quest to become the G.O.A.T.

Mrs. H flips to the final page in her lesson plan. She reads half the page, then looks up at us capriciously from her desk. "Is everyone ready for their question?"

I'm her first victim.

"Alexis," she says, looking back down at the page, "what is the most well-known asterism in Ursa Major?"

Without hesitation, because my astronomy game is on point, I answer, "Big Dipper."

She smiles. "You got it! Okay, something a little more challenging. What nucleon balances the charge of electrons to give an atom a neutral state?"

That *Jeopardy!* music starts playing in my head, *du-nu-nu-nu-nu-nu-nu/Alexis, why-are-you...so-fucking-dumb*? I think back to me and Aamani's last study session, the one where she had to leave in the middle to play Hindu Bachelorette for her parents. I didn't trust him from the jump. Dude's name was Aadavan. No one has that many As in their first name. Anyway, I remember before fake-name boy showed up, we were going over nucleons. Aamani even used a pack of Starburst to represent the different types of nucleons. That's when we argued which was the best flavor. The clear answer being red, even though Aamani argued orange. She put extra emphasis on electrons needing to link up with this one specific nucleon to achieve "perfect" balance. What makes the word *perfect* so special? Why does she like orange Starburst? Why isn't there, like, a turquoise Starburst? Why do I all of the sudden really want Starburst?

I nearly leap from my chair when the answer hits me like that delicious explosion of cherry flavor from the red ones. "The pink Starburst!"

Lindsay snorts.

Matthew looks more confused than that time I tried to convince him that *Uncle Drew* is a better movie than *Return of the King*.

Aamani nods with pride.

"I'm not saying I know the answer, because I totally don't," says Brian cautiously. "But something tells me that *pink Starburst* is not it."

"I mean—proton. The answer's proton," I elaborate, filling them in on me and Aamani's candy study code.

"Right again," Mrs. H congratulates. "Pink—I mean, proton is correct."

I do the Running Man in my mind. Then I concede I can't dance in reality or fiction. But the fact that I'm even fictional dancing over STEM means I'm doing something right.

Mrs. H ends practice early so we all have time to exchange Secret Santa gifts. Well, her version is actually called Winter Break Exchange. There was a lot of pushback on the title because Aamani's Hindu, but believes in Time Lords more than she does Krishna; Matthew's a firm believer in the big bang (he even keeps a PowerPoint on his phone to sway any nonbelievers); Brian's family does celebrate Christmas, he just likes to regift, which Lindsay complains is not Santa-like; and you already know my stance on Santa's breaking-and-entering-ass (you sneak down a chimney in West Philly and you're getting rolled on).

Two weeks ago each of us received a slip with the name of our recipient. I got Lindsay, because of course I did. The universe hates me. I couldn't afford a Coach bag, or Coldplay tickets, or whatever else white girls like. (This is what happens when you don't K.Y.W.P.) So I wrote her an honest letter, thanking her for accepting me on the team despite my checkered past of sucking at all things academic.

I stand up. I figure I may as well get the embarrassment of being nice to her over with. "Here, Lindsay," I announce, handing her the sealed envelope with her name on it.

She unfolds her arms and receives it. "What's this?"

"You *don't* have to open it now," I say, stressing the *don't*. She opens it anyway.

"Is there money in it?" Brian asks.

"Cards are about the sentiment of being thought of. Not the money," Aamani scolds. "But, between us girls, Lindsay, is there money in it?" she whispers.

Lindsay finishes reading it, and then looks up at me. Her resting bitch face softens, and for a second I think she's going to smile, but she doesn't.

"Thanks, Lex," she says, a solemn tug to her voice. "Really."

We share a cognizant and allied look of approval, bordering on friendly.

Brian stands. "All right, enough with the feels. This isn't the end of *Endgame*." He digs into his pocket and retrieves a small jewelry box. Aamani and I look mortified, praying Brian's not about to declare his love for one of us. "I had you, Mattie." Thank baby Jesus. "I hope it fits. The ad said one size fits all."

Matthew opens the box. His face erupts in a huge smile. He doesn't even look down at his shoes, he's so happy. "A replica of the Ring of Power," he informs us. "*One ring to rule them all*," he says in a deep, movie trailer narrator voice. "Thank you, Brian. This is the best gift ever!" He slings the necklace with the gold ring around his neck. "Do I look like Frodo?"

"Totally, dude," Brian confirms with an approving head nod.

Matthew one-ups his smile. And seeing Matthew smile this hard makes everyone else smile.

"I was also assigned you, Brian," Matthew says. He fixes his glasses, then dives into his backpack, pulling out an Avengers gift bag. He's still riding his emotional high and doesn't break eye contact.

Brian pulls out a pack of Listerine Strips, a bottle of blue mouthwash, a stick of unscented Chapstick, and a Halloween's-worth of gum.

"Uh, are you trying to tell me something?" Brian asks, cupping his hand to his mouth and inhaling a whiff of his breath.

Matthew's joyful demeanor fades. He looks like one of those abandoned puppies in the PETA commercials. "You don't like it."

"No, I do. It's just, uh, I . . . uh—" Brian takes a breath. "I don't know why you got me a *your breath's kickin' like Bruce Lee* kit."

"Is it not obvious?" Matthew asks.

"I'm going to have to go with a hard no on this one, dude."

"Whenever we see an attractive woman, be it TV or real life, you always comment on her looks and tell me how you'd like the chance to make out with her. You even said as much about Gamora and Nebula the first time we watched *Guardians of the Galaxy*."

"Ew, Harvey Weinstein much?" Lindsay says, turning up her nose.

"You'd really bang an alien?" Aamani adds.

"What? No. I never said that!" he refutes.

"Yes, you did. You said, and I quote, 'I'd like to show them my infinity stones.' You followed this with a wink that made me mildly uncomfortable. Please refrain from doing that in the future."

"*Gross*!" Aamani and Lindsay say in unison, and start laughing.

"Who knew Brian was a little closet freak," I add.

"Well, yeah, but . . ." Brian stammers, searching for a way out. "That was one time."

"No, it was on multiple occasions," Matthew rallies.

"Um, no it wasn't," Brian defends with the most OJ of looks.

"Yes, it was."

"Can we just move on please, and leave past alien interactions that may or may not have happened out of it?"

"Certainly," Matthew says, accommodating. "After you confided in me that Katrina Morales gave you mono—"

Lindsay and I lose our shit!

"Katrina 'More Head' Morales?!" I repeat in disbelief.

Brian drops his head. "Someone kill me."

"*Dude*!" I say, shaking my head. "You're better than that."

Lindsay is beside herself with laughter. I don't think I've ever seen her smile so much.

Matthew continues, unfazed by the reveal. "So, based off your devout love for women of *all* species, and your diseased experiences in the art of making out, I decided the best gift would be products that will heed you in your quest to obtain the perfect make-out experience."

"He means *one* make-out experience," Lindsay corrects. "Katrina Morales. I can't believe you made out with a girl who was caught giving head in the Checkers bathroom."

"Well . . ." Brian lingers, "obviously I didn't know that at the time."

"Suuureee you didn't." I drag the word out as if it has ten syllables.

"Man, whatever," Brian dismisses. "Y'all obviously don't know how hard it is out here for a hot Asian like me. After *Shang-Chi*, everyone wants a piece of this." The three of us roll our eyes. "Thanks for the make-out merch, Mattie. I'll put it to good use."

"Yeah, with Katrina *Moráles*," I say, tossing some Latin flair on her last name.

Lindsay and I chuckle, before Aamani puts an end to it. "All right, seriously . . . let's cool it with the slut shaming."

Lindsay volunteers to go next. She hands Aamani a rectangle-shaped gift wrapped in Christmas tree wrapping paper.

"For *moi*?" Aamani asks, gesturing to herself in fake disbelief.

She tears off the neatly wrapped paper to reveal an unusually thick comic book titled *Champions*.

"I hope you don't already have it," Lindsay says. "The guy at the comic store said it's perfect for Ms. Marvel fans. I put the gift receipt in the first page if you want to take it back."

"No way!" Aamani says, excitedly flipping through the book, her face lighting up every time she sees Kamala kick some ass. "I've been dying to get into *Champions*. This is awesome! There's also Ironheart, Spider-Man, and my girl Viv—Vision's daughter."

Aamani closes the book, using her ring finger to keep her page, then gives Lindsay a bear hug. Lindsay accepts the hug with a smile. "Thank you. This is so awesome! I'm going to stay up all night reading this."

As soon as the hug is over, Aamani goes back to flipping through the book, ignoring the outside world. It reminds me of when I used to hoop. When I was out there on the court, everything around me stopped, and there was only the ball, the defender, and the basket.

Brian clears his throat. "I think someone is forgetting their Winter Break gift buddy."

"Oh, my bad," Aamani chuckles. "Kamala and Miles together are so adorable it makes me want to die." She looks up from the book. "What'd I miss?"

"Your gift," Brian assists.

"Oh, right." She reaches into her pocket and fishes out two NJ Transit bus passes and hands one to me.

"Um, thanks? I don't really want to go to Jersey, though, if that's all right," I say, cocking my head in confusion. "In fact, no one should ever have to go to Jersey."

"Going to Jersey isn't the gift. It's what's in Jersey that should get you excited."

"What? Shitty sports teams and a crap ton of *no left turn* signs?"

"No," she says, furrowing her brow. "Trust me, you'll like it."

"I'll go to Jersey with you," Brian says.

"No. Lex is my Winter Gratitude buddy, not yours. I'm going with her."

Brian sucks his teeth.

"You're coming?" I ask.

"Uh, yeah. How else are you going to know where to go?"

"She has a phone," Lindsay points out.

"Will everyone stop critiquing my gift?" Aamani says. "We're going to Jersey, and I promise you're going to love it."

Considering I'd planned on teaching Crackhead Marvin how to change Instagram filters, Jersey doesn't sound half bad right now.

"When is this planned trip to the Dirty Jers?" I ask.

"Tonight," Aamani informs. "There's no time like the present."

Mrs. H comes back in after Winter Exchange. She asks me to stay behind for a minute. What's her deal with making me late for things? She never makes anyone else stay after for pep talks and reminders that it's not okay to kill Lindsay, no matter how annoying she's being.

"I'll be quick," she says, crossing her legs behind the desk. "I just wanted to give you some extra incentive to keep up with your studies over break. I'd hate to see you lose all the headway you've made this semester. You've made some incredible strides, Alexis. I knew you had it in you."

"Thanks, Mrs. H."

"Don't thank me yet. It's only going to get more challenging from here. I've decided you will start subbing in for Brian between rounds at STEM matches."

Did I hear her right?

I'm finally getting playing time?

A smile starts to creep across my face. I should be overjoyed. I should be twerking in celebration. But I'm not. As soon as the realization hits me that I'll be participating in competitions, I think of what this must mean for Brian and the team.

"Does Brian know?"

Mrs. H smiles. "Yes. I informed him this morning during home-room. He was very excited for his friend."

"For real?"

"For real," she repeats.

This makes me let out that big-ass smile I was holding.

"Wait," I say, again retracting my smile. "What about Lindsay? There's no way she's cool with this."

"You let me worry about her, okay? All you need to do is study hard over break and come back ready to go."

I nod. "I got you, Mrs. H."

"I know you do, Alexis."

I hobble out of her room with a smile. Maybe Christmas doesn't suck after all.

I can't hide my bubbly smirk, looking like Thanos. I'm going to finally get a chance to impress some college recruiters. This is what Aamani and I have been working for since I joined STEM. I might actually have a chance at getting out of this town.

The woman sitting across from us grips her daughter close. It's like, *Don't look at the crazy grinning lady, sweetie*. It's at this moment that I realize Aamani's been oddly silent about the serial killer grin on my face.

She's staring out the window. I tap her on the shoulder to get her attention. "Hey, how come you haven't asked why I'm so happy?"

"Because I assume it's about you subbing in after break. Old news."

My grin fades, and in its place is an incredulous stare. "Did Brian tell you?"

"No. Who do you think suggested the idea?" she answers, smiling with the right side of her face. "It's time to cut off that pigtail, young Padawan."

The bus rolls to a stop, stuck in Jersey Turnpike traffic.

"Why do you believe in me so much?"

She gives a whimsical look, half smirk, half smile. "Because you're a supernova, remember."

The bus drops us off in Collingwood, New Jersey, on the corner of Hick Valley. Sounds super racist-slash-marry your cousin to me. But whatever. We're here now.

There's a parking lot in front of us with only one car parked, a VW coupe. Next to the lot is an old masonry brick building with an enormous gold-plated dome peeking out the top. On the corner, next to the surely racist street sign, is a steel sign that reads *Mount Haddon Astronomical Observatory*.

"Not to sound ungrateful, but please tell me there are Sixers season tickets inside with my name on them," I say, staring up at the large dome-shaped building. It's almost dark out, so the sky's a russet golden brown, fading into the dusk.

Aamani adjusts her backpack straps. "Just come on," she says, stepping into the parking lot.

"Can you at least tell me why Jersey?" I ask, doing a hobble power walk through the minor pain, trying to catch up. "Like, they don't have observatories in Philly? Jersey's the worst. They steal our radio stations and sports teams. You know how many Eagles bandwagon riders there are here?"

She continues on to the observatory with no answer. I suck it up and follow her blindly into the possibly racist New Jersey night.

There's a lobby with linoleum tile floors, two rosewood benches, and a receptionist desk beside a turnstile. On the wall beside a certificate from NASA is a laminated poster advertising tour hours and group rates. At the bottom of the poster it reads *Gift cards available. Give the gift of the stars!*

Sitting behind the desk is a middle-aged white guy with a scruffy professor-esque beard, receding hairline, and glasses twice as thick as Matthew's. The guy can probably see into space with them. His name tag reads *Walter*.

Walter looks up from his computer when he hears the squeaks of our shoes on the polished linoleum. "Welcome to the Haddon Observatory," Walter recites. "How can I help you?"

Aamani flashes a polite smile, the same one she uses on customers at the Super Mart. "Two tickets, please."

"Do you have a reservation or Groupon?"

We look at him like he's on something. This place is as dead as my basketball career.

"Do we need one?" I ask, twisting my face.

"Nope," Walter replies. "Just following protocol." He starts typing. "Would you like to add an additional fifteen minutes of telescope time for five dollars? It's our twilight special."

Aamani looks to me for confirmation. What the hell is she looking at me for? This wasn't my idea. And I know she doesn't expect me to come off five bucks to look into an overgrown contact lens.

"We'll take it!" Aamani replies excitedly. You'd think he just offered her a new car.

Walter goes back to slamming on the keys. Seconds later out print two tickets. "It's twenty-five dollars, please."

Aamani pulls out her TARDIS wallet and hands him a crisp twenty. She flashes big Bambi eyes. "I only have a twenty," she confesses.

Walter studies her as though they're locked in a heated game of poker and he's conflicted about whether or not to fold. "I'll tell you what," he says. "Since we're closing soon, the fifteen minutes are on the house. Enjoy."

"*Thanks*!" Aamani and I say in harmony, jinxing each other.

"After you," Aamani says, shepherding me through the turnstile and into the first exhibit hall.

The walls in the first room are painted black. There's a mural of all the constellations and planets painted on the walls in glow-in-the-dark paint, and beneath each constellation is a plastic plaque with its name.

The next few exhibits are similar. The difference being each one focuses on a different constellation. One of the rooms even focuses on the International Space Station and the moon landing.

There's an obnoxiously large portrait of Neil Armstrong in this one, posted beside a miniature one of Katherine Johnson. (I knew this town was racist.) There's also some cheesy patriotic music playing on loop in the background. In the middle exhibit, there's a Tesla coil that resembles a giant snow globe with reoccurring lightning storms. Aamani reaches for my hand and places it on the electric-inducing sphere, as lightning bolts attack my fingertips and mimic their movements. She then goes on to explain how Tesla coils work, followed by a TED Talk on the fierce rivalry of Nikola Tesla and Thomas Edison. After she finishes her TED Talk, she places her hand on the sphere opposite of mine. It's not lost on me that there is literally electricity between us.

We make our way up to the observatory room located in the dome. The ceiling is made up of thousands of gold-plated windows, which Aamani informs me is to keep the light out. It looks like a cathedral. In the center of the room, so large there's a set of metal stairs to reach it, is a telescope as big as a submarine. Clearly this thing's on a strict diet of steroids and creatine shakes.

Aamani doesn't offer any more facts before hurrying up the metal stairs.

I stand, wide-eyed, gaping up at the technological wonder in front of us, like it's a dinosaur.

Aamani tosses me an up-nod, inviting me to join her on the telescope platform. When I finally make my way up the stairs and onto the platform, Aamani hits me with a goofy smile. "Check this out," she says, pushing a button on the console in front of the telescope.

Next thing I know, the room starts to rumble and the dome contracts like a convertible, folding in on itself and revealing a sky full of stars. The russet glow of the evening's leftover colors has been swallowed by the dark of night. A soft chill sweeps in and pinches the tip of my nose. The head of Breanna (I decided to name it) reaches out into the infinite universe.

Now I know how that curly-haired white boy in *Transformers* felt the first time he saw Bumblebee transform.

I take a nervous step back as the dome finishes transforming, careful not to fall down the stairs and mess up my other leg, which would totally be my luck. After the final clang of metal, a silence echoes through the observatory and there's only stillness.

"*Come. On.*" Aamani says, her soft voice vexed. "There's no freakin' way you can honestly stand there, look me in the eyes, and say that wasn't one of the coolest things ever. I'm pretty sure I just won Winter Exchange opening the roof alone."

I'm still paralyzed from the miniature earthquake we just survived.

Aamani shakes her head in disappointment, and then looks into the lens. "It's a twelve-inch Zeiss refracting telescope, the same size and model as the one in the Griffith Observatory in California. It's standing on an equatorial mount that's aligned with the Earth's axis. *I* think it's pretty cool. But apparently you're only impressed if basketball is involved."

After all the years of hating school with the burning fire of a million suns, roasting every nerd Britt and I came across, always equipped with infinite excuses to get out of doing schoolwork (my already-dead grandma has died, like, fifty times), I can't believe the words are leaving my mouth: "This jawn's dope as fuck."

She pulls away from the telescope to look at me. Her light-brown eyes flicker, mimicking tiny supernovas. She can barely contain herself and lets out an adorable squeal. "I knew you'd like it! If I could, I'd live in this place." She goes back to looking through

Breanna. "Plus, all the best people are in space—the Guardians, Rey, Yoda, Thanos, the Doctor, Captain Marvel, Lockjaw. It's also where the Fantastic Four got their powers," she educates. She pries her eye away from the scope and looks at me. "Go on. Have a look. It won't bite."

I approach Breanna, cautiously, as though it's a wild animal. I feel like I should let it sniff my hand first. I close an eye, and then lean forward and peer into the twelve-inch lens that's no doubt worth more than my apartment building.

Millions of stars congregate before my eye, reflecting with a luminous, golden glow like tiny prisms in a black abyss. I had no idea so many stars were visible to the human eye. The Milky Way swirls like age rings on a tree stump; the Big Dipper sparkles an outline of a giant ladle; and Orion's Belt reflects the bent angles of an obtuse triangle. Each star harmonizes with its neighbor, a controlled chaos of random beauty. It puts in perspective how insignificant this world is. I used to believe that making it out of Hargrove, going pro, and getting Candace Parker money was all this life could offer. But now I see there's a universe of untapped possibilities.

Another thing I notice is the stars don't so much twinkle as they spark, igniting the eternal flames of the universe. So I'm going to have to call bullshit on "Twinkle, Twinkle, Little Star."

My eye remains glued to Breanna. If Aamani tries to detach it, I'll treat her hand like a Chipotle burrito.

She interrupts my slice of heaven with some random facts. It's like, *WTF? Trying to examine the cosmos here.* "Did you know that every star you're looking at is brighter than the sun?"

"Wait, what? Was that in last week's packet?" I ask, freaking out that I might've missed a section. That is not how one goes about becoming the G.O.A.T.

She giggles. "No. You're good. I'm just dropping some knowledge about the stars."

I exhale. Operation STEM G.O.A.T. is still on. "A'ight then, if they're so hot, how come they're not melting my face like Anakin on Mustafar?"

Her face is taken aback, impressed. "Nice pull. Terrible movie, but nice pull."

I perform a little curtsy with my lower half. "Thanks. You guys talk about *Star Wars* so much, I figured I should watch the damn things. I found them online for free. The OG trilogy was all that. Han was a straight up G."

"You should see him in the comics and extended universe. He's so cool. He even gets married to Sana Starros, this badass smuggler who's Black."

"Damn, even in a galaxy far, far away Black folks got to be criminals."

"She's more of a reluctant hero like Han. She even goes on to team up with the rebels and Leia. But I digress. Back to the stars."

"Yeah, back to the stars," I repeat.

"Not to get too nerdy with it—" She pauses to see if I've reconsidered my interest in the conversation. What she doesn't know, and never will, is that my favorite part of the day is watching Aamani's face flood with a tidal wave of happiness when she explains anything nerdy—the Pythagorean Theorem or the pathos of the thirteenth Doctor.

She smiles when I don't object. "Okay, so, like even though the sun's ninety-three million miles away, we can't look at it. Everyone knows that. But why? It's because of all the radiation it gives off.

That's why we have special glasses to watch things like the eclipse, so our eyes won't turn to oatmeal."

"And why P. Diddy wears glasses inside."

"That too," she laughs. "But with the stars you're looking at now it's a little different. These stars are what are known as black bodies."

"That's super racist, bt-dubs," I say, looking extra hard into Breanna, trying to see if I can see any black on the stars.

"I can say it. My skin's darker than yours."

"Barely," I protest. "If I'm caramel, then you're hazelnut."

"An-ee-way," she continues, rolling her eyes, "they're called black bodies for a non-racial reason. Basically it's an object that absorbs a hundred percent of all electromagnetic radiation. Stuff like radio waves and light." She pauses. "What? Why are you looking at me like that?"

"Has anyone ever told you that you're a huge nerd?" I ask with admiration in my voice.

"Yeah, *you*," she deadpans. "Like three times a day."

"Good. Just checking."

"Whatever," she fires back. "You so love it."

I curl my lips in thought. "What's today?"

"Friday."

"Only on Fridays," I tease with a half smile.

"Moving on," she continues, returning my half smile with a full one, "a star absorbs all radiation that falls on it, but it also radiates into space much more than it absorbs. That's why you can look at the stars above and not directly at the sun. Think of black body stars like a sponge, soaking up all the bad radiation so you can look at them. And the sun, not so much."

"Nice." I'm playing it cool. I've fallen in love with this shit. There are constant and infinite variables at play in the universe. And I want to learn them all. And better yet, I want Aamani to teach me.

"You don't even know the half of it." She takes a deep, calculated breath and goes back in. "Stars are among the most fascinating things in the universe. Just think about it. They've seen it all—the dinosaurs, Jesus, Rome falling, Pompeii, *Empire Strikes Back* opening night, both World Wars, Destiny's Child form and then break up. The Milky Way alone is an estimated three-point-two billion years old. That's insane!"

"Okay, okay, simmer down, Aamani deGrasse Tyson," I say, nudging her with my shoulder.

"My bad," she apologizes with a giggle. "I really like stars."

There's something infectious and inherently beautiful about how passionate she gets about things. I hope someday someone is that passionate about me.

I pry myself away from Breanna so I can look at Aamani. Our eyes hold each other's. This only lasts a second, though, because I go back to Breanna, back to the stars.

"I didn't just bring you here for the telescope," Aamani says. She sounds jelly of what Breanna and I have. "I mean, I did because it's awesome, but I also wanted to tell you something. I'm not sure how you're going to take it."

It kills me to pull away from Breanna, but I do.

"Make it quick. I'm wasting quality time with Breanna."

"Who?"

"Nothing. Go on."

"Well, um . . ." She tucks a runaway hair behind her ear. "I'm not really good at this kind of stuff."

"You're cool. Just say what's on your mind," I encourage, trying to hurry this up. Mama needs her Breanna time.

She takes a deep breath, as though she's about to jump off the Titanic. "The color of a star is a fraction of its temperature, which is a fraction of its mass and composition." She stops. "Too nerdy?"

"You have no idea," I say, a smile in my voice. "But stars, temperatures, mass, African American bodies—I'm with you."

"They're *black bodies*," she corrects. "Not racist. There's a reason I'm telling you all of this. It's the only way I know how to, like, get it out."

I straighten up. "For real, I'm listening."

"At the coolest end of the stellar colors are red stars. These stars are mostly red giants that have evolved off the main sequence. They are the coolest temperature-wise, by far. Their surfaces can get up to about two thousand degrees. But as stars get hotter and shine brighter their colors change from red to orange to yellow to white, and eventually blue. Blue stars are the most beautiful, in my opinion, and they're factually the hottest. We're talking Ghost Rider, Human Torch levels of heat. They have a surface of anything between twenty-five thousand to fifty thousand degrees. So what I'm trying so scientifically to say, and I already know I may get killed for this, is you, Alexis Duncan, are the brightest of all the blue stars."

Did she just say I'm hot on a cosmic scale? I'm pretty sure she did.

That's the most romantic thing anyone's ever said to me. And I once had a guy say I'm hotter than Beyoncé. He only said it because he was trying to talk me into giving him head (I didn't, because ew!), but still it was nice to hear.

Why am I not creeped out by this?

Why do I want her to say more nice things?

Why do I want to tell her that with her hazelnut skin, long wavy hair, and hypnotic smile, her star's bluer than mine?

Why do I want to tell her that I love her imperfections, like the assortment of freckles under her high cheekbones?

What's happening to me?

What is it about her dropping science facts that makes me get all weird inside?

Noticing my dumbfounded expression, she takes a step into my atmosphere, the tips of our noses almost touching and our breaths colliding.

Okay. What. The. Fuck. Is. Happening?

There's a knot the size of Brittney Griner's shoes in my chest. The air has been sucked out of the room. I think I want her to come closer. No—I *know* I do.

A smile creeps down her right side. A smile uncontrollably creeps down my left. She leans in, eyes closed, lips pursed. I've lost all control and start to lean in. This is happening, and there's nothing I can do to stop it. For some reason, as our lips are about to meet, I think back on Mrs. H's lesson on magnets. A permanent magnet is an object that produces a magnetic field around itself. It's that field that enables magnets to stick to each other. Aamani is my magnetic field. Her lips the Earth to my orbiting moon.

I give in.

Because what's happening between us is science. And there's no refuting science.

Our lips brush, and as they do a loud crack of mechanisms and metal start moving and the lights cut on. The room rumbles as Breanna retreats back inside the observatory. Walter comes across the PA system. "The observatory will be closing in five minutes.

All guests please make your way to the lobby. And no making out in the exhibits. There are cameras. I can see you."

Aamani snorts.

I frown.

A New Jersey clam-jam. I knew there was a reason I hated this place.

CHAPTER 13

We returned back to school in the second week of January, and things have been weird.

Today at practice, I noticed Aamani looking like someone had set her comics collection on fire. She was so out of it she didn't even buzz in once during the lightning round. And the lightning round is her jam. Like, we all call it "the dreaded lightning round." Aamani just calls it "easy-peasy." Then I go on the streak of my life and Aamani doesn't give me the slightest smile or a "good job." I mean, I'm droppin' right answers like Sue Bird drops dimes—flagella, deoxyribonucleic acid, a hectogram. I was straight ballin' and she gave me nothing.

For a second I thought it was because of me, because we hadn't really spoken since break, apart from a few random texts of some dank memes she just had to see. You'd think I'd have had the courage to bring up the observatory at least once to clarify what that was, but every time there was a chance I'd get scared of my feelings, scared of getting an answer I don't want, or worse, getting one I do.

Now I'm sitting across from Aamani on the edge of her bed, doing a terrible job at focusing on our homework. She's wearing the same disheveled look she had earlier. She has on dark jeans and a blue kurta with crepe prints. She twirls her pencil between her fingers, and then jots down the answer to the next question on our algebra homework. Now I know something's wrong. She doesn't show her work. She lives to Aamanisplain her work to me. I mean, I know the answer's seventy-five, but that's beside the point.

"Okay," I say, closing our textbook. "What's wrong? And don't say 'nothing' like you did earlier."

She anxiously starts chewing on her pencil, leaving tiny bite marks in the wood. This must really be bad. Aamani's not one for being unsanitary. This is the same girl who once berated me for not showering after gym by reading off an encyclopedia of facts about germs and the ways they interact with our cells, possibly leading to cancer, which will lead to my body rotting away for two years until the chemo fails and I die tragically at nineteen like the white boy in *The Fault in Our Stars*. You know, as you do when someone's late for fourth period and doesn't have time to shower.

"I'm fi—"

"Ah, don't say it," I stop her. "I know you. Everything is definitely not fine. You just bit into your pencil like it's a cheesesteak."

You know, now would be the perfect time to clear the air on our near make-out session. I look over at Aamani, her anxiety-filled face still soft with freckles above her cheekbones.

Nah, she's good. I'll bring it up some other time.

She takes out her phone, which she never does when there's schoolwork in front of her, and swipes left through her photos until stopping on some Indian dude with thick Anthony Davis eyebrows, parted prep-boy hair, and an awkward smile that says *It's picture day; they're making me do this.*

"This is Rajeev," she informs, handing me the phone so I can pinch and zoom for a better look. His eyebrows look like untrimmed hedges. "We've been on ten dates and no matter what I say or do my parents won't let me drop him. The first time I tried ghosting him he actually called the house phone and talked to my mom. Like, who does that?"

"Okay, first off, you have a house phone? And secondly, they don't seriously expect you to marry this guy, do they? His eyebrows look like they're about to cocoon and hatch into butterflies."

She almost cracks a smile, but the burden of Rajeev and his caterpillar eyebrows weighs on her.

"Mom swears by Shiva that our families are perfect for each other and will only help strengthen our union," she says, taking back her phone. I can't unsee those eyebrows. "It's total bullshit, though. They only like him because his family has money. I think his dad's a doctor or something. I don't know. When he talks all I can do is stare at his eyebrows and think about the size of lawn mower I'd need to trim them. Mom's throwing a dinner tonight for both families to meet. My cousins are even coming down from New York for this. I haven't seen my parents this excited since the last Shah Rukh Khan movie."

"Sounds like you don't have much of a choice," I say, not help- ing. "And you're sure you don't like him?" She shows me his picture again in reply. "I mean, he's no Hemsworth, but if you squint real hard and turn off the lights, he kinda looks like Kumail Nanjiani if he had eyebrows the size of socks." She cuts her eyes at me. "A'ight, just asking."

"And, uh, like, you do know I'm gay, right?"

Nah, I've seen too many hashtags and protests on Capitol Hill to fall for this trap. I must proceed with caution. "You are? That's cool."

"Uh-huh," she says, squinting incredulously. "Didn't realize I needed your approval."

"You don't," I reply, almost too defensively. "It's just cool that you are." That's my story and I'm sticking to it.

194

Her face softens and a wave of vulnerability washes over it. She tucks a loose strand of hair behind both ears, then rubs the back of her neck. "And I don't know, I was, like, kind of hoping *you* liked me or whatever. You know, after the whole observatory, blue-star thing. We haven't really talked about it."

There's that Brittney Griner–sized lump in my throat again. I have to look away at one of her Ms. Marvel posters to keep from giving her a look that might offend. How do you tell someone you're not who they think you are? That you can't be what they want you to be?

"Ay, I——I don't know," I stumble, falling over my words. "I'm sorry, but like I told you, I'm not gay. Not that there's anything wrong with that, because there's not," I'm quick to add. "Be as gay as you want to be. That's cool. Just not for me. Like, if Jordan didn't think his shit don't stink, I'd probably be on his dick like everyone else. I do think you're cool people, though," I say as consolation. "Keeping it hundred, you make me feel——" I choke on the word. "Loved. No one has ever made me feel like that before."

If she's let down by any of this, she doesn't show it. "You do realize it's possible to like women and men? It's called being bi-sexual. Sexuality, like life, isn't black and white."

"Yeah, but——" I have no idea where I'm going with this. The first time I touched myself was to a Drake video. I don't care how smart she is, or how cute she looks when a piece of her long hair falls in her face and she has to tuck it behind her ear, or how said ear (the left one) has a tiny mole on top that looks like a heart. "I——I don't know."

Smooth, Lex.

"What's to know?" Aamani shuffles over to my side of the bed, closing the space between us. "Here," she says. Then she takes my palm and places it on her cheek, leaning in so our foreheads are touching. "In this fixed moment of the universe, without any outside variables, how do you feel?"

My body goes numb. I feel like my whole body's made of funny bones and I just hit them all at the same time. I know how I feel. I just can't bring myself to say it. She has no idea what it's like to feel things you shouldn't be feeling.

"Aamani, I—you just don't understand. How can you?" She pulls away, our foreheads separating. "You're not Black. Being bi, gay, whatever; it doesn't matter. The Black people I know aren't very progressive. We like to front like we are, but trust me, we're not. My homegirl's mom told us that 'Jesus didn't give us vaginas to rub it up against another one, or dicks to stick up another man's ass.' Like, she actually said that shit. Is it right that that's the way people around here think? Nah, it's not. Do I agree with them? Hell no. But it is what it is. I have it hard enough being Black in America, let alone Black *and* bi. People around here clown queer people because they don't understand it—shit like *pause* and having to say *no homo* after everything. It's all a fucking joke to them. I don't wanna be a joke."

She cocks her head, finally exhibiting some frustration. I knew it was coming. I'm about to get hash-tagged. "Okay, so I Googled that player you're always talking about—Diana Tyrannosaurus."

"Taurasi . . ." I correct.

"Whatever. And I found she's queer and happily married. So if your favorite player can be queer, why can't you? Why do you care so much what your friends think?"

Rage clutches my throat tight. "Because I'm not her. She's not Black. She's not from my hood. See, that's what you don't get. It's not just about my friends. It's about being Black. Everywhere I go, everything I do; I don't care if it's STEM or basketball, all these white people see is a thug. A drug dealer. A threat. Being queer only adds another target to my back."

"I may not be Black or from the hood, but if you think I don't have to live my life ostracized by one of society's vices, homophobic or otherwise, then you're severely mistaken. Half of the people I come across think I'm a terrorist. Even you thought that."

"No, I didn't," I defend.

"You might as well have, assuming I was Muslim because of my skin tone and attire. I'm not blaming you, just pointing out our situations are not so different when you really look at it. And that level of ignorance is doubled by my family and their beliefs. I can't even come out to my parents because they think being a lesbian is sacrilegious and would bring eternal shame on the family. As if me liking women magically casts some kind of Scarlet Witch hex on us. I live my life trapped; I'm constantly looking over my shoulder to make sure no one's noticed me."

I never considered how much our cultures have in common. I've only ever noticed our differences. I was only ever given one point of view—the world according to Hargrove.

"We deserve happiness too," Aamani says, trying to tilt me to her side of the debate.

"It's not—" I have to check my volume because her parents are in the living room. The last thing I need is for them to think I'm in here yelling at their daughter as though we're in a heated lover's quarrel. (I can't believe I just used the word "quarrel." Damn you, Matthew.) "It's not that easy."

Aamani leans forward. There's no reserve or hesitation, only the assuredness of what she wants. "It is," she states, blitzing my lips before I can scramble out of the pocket.

A hurricane of relief sweeps through me. This is not the emotion I thought I'd have. Kissing a girl is different from kissing a boy. With her, it's like she's kissing me for who I am—not just because I have breasts and a vagina, or because they want to get in a few dry humps before rolling over satisfied. If this is what it's like kissing a girl, I don't know why anyone would ever kiss a boy. Or maybe it has nothing to do with her gender. Maybe it's simply the fact that I'm lost in Aamani and have no desire to ever be found.

The door pops open. We jolt apart, retreating to our corners of the bed as if being caught in the act of murder. Me, holding the knife, and Aamani with bloody hands.

My breathing races as though I'm in labor. I'm so nervous, the pain in my leg from jolting apart doesn't even register.

Her dad stands in the doorway, a heartbroken expression skewered on his face. Then all hell breaks loose and he starts shouting at Aamani in Hindi—"Kya tumhaara dimaag phir gaya hai!!!"—fully consumed by a fiery ball of rage, his mustache flailing. He grips Aamani by the arm and drags her from the bed to the door. She's almost in tears.

Seeing Aamani unhappy is like drowning. It's like being awake for open heart surgery. And it begs the question: Why do I care so much?

He tosses her into the hallway like a rag doll, handing her off to her mom. Mr. Chakrabarti snitches and fills her in on what Aamani and I were just doing.

"Jo aap soch rahe ho, yeh voh nahi hai. Mujhe maaf karo," Aamani says through tears.

Aamani's words are met with a swift Serena Williams backhand to the face from her mom that echoes through the hall. I wince, as I can feel the slap reverberate from over here.

Mr. Chakrabarti turns his rage on me, sizing me up as though we're about to go twelve rounds.

I forget to breathe.

He says in the most crystal-clear English I've ever heard him speak: "Get out of my house. And stay away from my daughter."

CHAPTER 14

After the kiss, I started doing a lot of thinking. And a lot of Googling—"What it means if you kiss a girl and like it?" After I sift through all the Katy Perry search results, I come across a few articles. But no one in the articles looks like me. They all look like their mom's name is Karen. And when I add "Black" to the search, I get a few hits of celebrities, Tessa Thompson and Janelle Monáe. But they're rich with millions of followers. Their Insta pages are flooded with support. I'm not them. They're not from Hargrove. Then I Google "Black queer hate" and am bombarded with articles and statistics of how LGBTQ people of color face "compounded violence." And that article came from NBCNews.com, so you know it's legit—white people read that shit. And yeah there are articles about people organizing to raise awareness and end the hate. But is that enough?

Because it's not the articles or statistics that shake me to my core. It's the names. The names of Black LGBTQ people who have been beaten within an inch of their lives; Black trans women who have been slain for being who they are. Names no one walks in protest of. Names I didn't know until today. Names of people from Philly, right down the block.

Google's no help. There's no "hood" filter.

Which leaves me with the thought ... who can I be?

Aamani's parents have forbidden her from seeing me. They make her go to Mandir (the Hindu temple) with them every day and pray for two hours to whatever gods they pray to, asking them to forgive her for her family betrayal and to remove the gayness—whatever the hell that means—from her body.

I didn't think I'd actually care that I'd been banished from Aamani's life. But not being able to have our study sessions affects how I do on the team. Which affects my chances of getting out of here. She was supposed to help me start applying to schools this week.

Not only can she break stuff down for me so I can understand it better, but even after our textbooks are closed and we couldn't possibly look at another equation or scientific theory, she still wanted to talk to me. She's my friend. The only one I have at the moment if you don't count Crackhead Marvin, and he only considers me a friend because I share my Hot Cheetos with him every now and then.

That's not entirely true. I never share. Marvin just eats them when I'm not looking. Crackheads are sneaky like that.

Now the only time Aamani and I can talk is during school and at practice, which means no more binging shows together for my "Pop Culture Studies" as Aamani calls it, no more of those mouthwatering samosas Bharti brings over to make sure I eat, and no more losing to her at video games. The girl's seriously good at every video game. In her former life, I think she *was* a video game.

Bottom line, even though I see her at school, it's not nearly enough. I miss having full Aamani access. I miss spending time in her atmosphere. But most of all, I miss seeing her happy.

Next week's the first STEM match I'll actually be competing in. Only two weeks back from break and already the grind of trying to keep up with all this schoolwork is slowly suffocating me. Life's become a corset I can never take off. I'm not ready to be on that stage. To go up against teens who have been training for STEM their whole lives. I'm screwed without Aamani's tutoring sessions.

Why did Aamani have to kiss me? Why was I born with a wicked crossover instead of reading comprehension skills?

So yeah, I'm panicking. And yeah, I may have spazzed out during Mr. Jones's class when he assigned us *War and Peace*. "Bruh, a fucking Russian?!" Admittedly, not the most woke statement I've ever made. "Tolstoy writes more than Krystal texts. Like, do you see this jawn?" I said, thinking I could do a better job of getting my point across if I stood up. You can tell I was wildin', ranting about Russian authors as though I'm MLK delivering his "I Have a Dream" speech. "It would need its own seat on an airplane. I have term papers, STEM packets, and college essays coming out my ass! And you want me to read fucking Tolstoy on top of it. I can't read this shit." Everyone was staring at me like I just told them aliens exist and they beat me in *2K*. "What? Should I have raised my hand? Yeah, definitely should've raised my hand."

I was sent to Principal Garrett's office shortly thereafter.

I've even considered calling Aamani's parents and telling them, "Hey, I'm not gay, fuckers. So you don't have to worry about me lesbian-ing up your Hindu daughter. Now give me back my tutor or face the wrath of a Negro with one-and-a-half functioning legs." But everything about that seemed like a terrible idea.

I'm at a major impasse here. You'd think after raising my GPA to damn near a 3.5 and getting more answers right at practice than Brian, I'd be more confident in my ability to compete. But as I look down at this week's packet and imagine how the opposition is going to eat me alive, I know I'm fucked. Also, Mrs. H is giving me a look like I should be participating in practice, not daydreaming about how much I suck.

Practice ends.

I toss my textbooks in my bag and hobble toward the door. I don't even want to stay and talk to anyone about lightning round strategies or that crazy fight at lunch where Tasha pulled out Mariah's weave while managing to hold up her ripped shirt with her other hand to keep her boobs from popping out. It was truly unbeweavible. I just want to find the nearest bridge and jump off it so I won't have to compete on Saturday and watch my future disintegrate like Thanos's snap.

Matthew scurries to the doorway and blocks my exit.

I stop and huff, my nostrils flaring.

"Sorry, they're making me do this," he says, looking at the tops of his shoes. "Also"—he raises his head and sticks out his chest for this part—"*you shall not pass!*"

Brian jumps in to clarify, "We *offered* him the chance to be door guard because we know he always wanted a legit reason to say that. Worth it, Mattie?"

Matthew nods profusely.

"What are you guys doing?" I ask, trying to remain calm, because I'm really not in the mood right now. Not when I have a million things racing through my mind, like STEM, where my next meal is coming from, and how can I spruce up my corner in the crack house. The U-Haul box with my clothes in it hardly counts.

Aamani looks at Lindsay. "Do you want to take this?" she asks. "It was your idea."

Lindsay sighs. "I'd rather not."

"You don't have to," Aamani says. "I'm sure Brian would love to break it down for us."

"Facts," Brian agrees. "It was Lindsay's idea, but my dope title."

Lindsay takes her previous sigh and amplifies it by two. "Fine." She rolls her eyes, turning to me. "Aamani told us about how you're shitting the bed over Saturday's match."

"Told you?" Aamani repeats, nearly breaking into laughter. "After her Kanye breakdown in Jones's class last week, I think the whole world knows she's shitting the bed."

"Oh, I almost forgot to tell you, Alexis. Your observation was very entertaining," Matthew says. "Russian authors are indeed known for their heavy word count, among other things. Did you know *War and Peace* is over 500,000 words long?"

"Doesn't surprise me," I acknowledge.

"And did you know Tolstoy's wife copied the book as he wrote it? She wrote eight complete copies by hand."

"That's wild," I say to be polite. I really want to leave. I've got some moping to do, bridges to jump from. And my leg's starting to hurt from all this standing.

"Okay," Lindsay jumps back in, "Aamani brought it to our *attention* that you've been stressing out. And before I move on, let me be clear that I developed this plan solely for the good of the team. Your stress levels and lack of academic knowledge are the least of my concerns."

"The feeling's mutual," I assure her.

She continues, "Now that you've become a valuable part of the team—"

"Wait," I interject. "Did she just admit that I'm a valuable part of the team?"

"Why, my dear Lex, I believe she did," Aamani says, using her Doctor idiosyncrasies.

I tilt my head to the side. "Don't call me 'dear.'"

"Right. My bad."

"That's what I heard," Brian confirms.

"I too must concur," adds Matthew.

Lindsay deadpans. "I'm already regretting this. As I was saying, we can't have you stressing out and missing questions and messing up our chances to go to Nationals. So I kind of came up with a plan to make sure that our winning streak remains intact."

I raise my right eyebrow like The Rock. "What kind of *plan*?"

Brian can't contain himself and jumps in. "Using study buddies! Again, I'd like to point out I came up with that name. Pretty dope, huh?"

"No. It's really not," Lindsay answers.

"Study buddies?" I repeat dryly.

"Yeah, well, we're still workshopping it," Brian says, his enthusiasm faltering.

"No we're not. There is no name. We're just going to help her out so we don't lose, go to Nationals, win, and call it a day. End of story," Lindsay reiterates.

"We should name it The Legion of Saur—"

Brian interjects. "Dude, we are not naming it after *The Lord of the Rings*."

Matthew shrugs it off. "It's a better name than 'study buddies.'"

Aamani snorts.

Aamani's kicked back on Mrs. H's desk. Her face tilts with a smile. She must love all this team camaraderie bullshit. She's wearing ripped skinny jeans and a Ms. Marvel T-shirt that she bought herself for Christmas. For her, being on lockdown with her parents is just a return to the status quo. Back to having to lie to have a social life. So she's been pretty chill for the most part, since her parents don't think she's actually gay, just bewitched by me. Nothing a little prayer can't cleanse. Still, watching her tuck a runaway hair behind her ear, I wonder if she ever thinks about the kiss, about the electricity that exploded between our lips. Not that I'm saying I want to kiss her again. I'm just saying I didn't altogether hate the moment. It was a'ight.

Lindsay lays out her idea, which is for me to have a new Legion of Sauron partner (Matthew's right, much catchier than *study buddy*) each day this week—Matthew tomorrow, Wednesday Brian, Thursday Lindsay, and they'll all stay after practice Friday to help with any subject I'm still struggling with. They're also going to help me fill out applications for schools, since the deadline for getting them in is the end of January. One less stressful thing to worry about.

Why do they care so much? Their futures are already set. Matthew's already gotten into three schools, including Penn, and Lindsay and Brian have a few schools they're choosing from. Even Aamani has a handful of schools fighting over her. Part of me dies with the thought that I won't be able to kick it with her when she goes to some out-of-state school halfway across the country.

"You guys would do that . . . for me?"

"Of course," Brian says without hesitation.

"Yes," Matthew says. "We are a team, and teammates stick together. And if we can't protect you, you can be damn sure we'll avenge you . . . and other Avengers quotes that apply to this situation."

Aamani nods to Matthew. "What he said. Dibs on Iron Man, bt-dubs."

Lindsay looks to the ceiling, then to every corner of the room, anywhere but at us. I'll admit. I get a tiny sense of joy watching her squirm to be nice. "What? I already told you guys. I'm only doing this because I plan on going to Nationals and Lex is not about to mess that up."

Aamani sneezes, "Ah-bullshit!"

Brian laughs.

"Bless you," Matthew says considerately.

A lump travels from my throat to the pit of my stomach. A warm, unfamiliar feeling washes over me. Besides Britt, none of my other friends had my back beyond the odd fight. And that's just because they *really* love to fight.

I want to smile, but I don't want to get too hyped over something that in the end might not even matter. We can't afford to lose any of our remaining matches if we want to go to Nationals. Since I've joined, we've gone unbeaten and now have by far the best record of any team in school. So I still may very well cost us a shot at Nationals.

Tuesday arrives and I do my first Legion of Sauron session at Matthew's house. You know what's funny? In all the years I've run with my crew, I've only ever been inside Britt's and Krystal's houses. Why is that? I've known my STEM peeps for three months and by the end of this week I'll have been to all of their homes. I'm not sure what that signifies, but I feel like it signifies something.

Anyway, Matthew meets me at my locker two minutes after

the final bell, upon which time he hurries me to get my stuff so we don't make his mom wait.

Before we study, he helps me apply to a few scholarship programs at some local community colleges, and revise some outlines for the essay portion of the applications. Earlier in the week, before STEM practice, Aamani tried to talk me into applying for this astronomy scholarship at UConn. Fucking UConn! Alma mater of the G.O.A.T. Diana Taurasi. I nearly laughed so hard I peed myself. I put an end to that idea quick. I'm trying to be real with this shit. I know where I'm gonna end up. With my grades and lack of STEM exposure at competitions, there's no way I'd get into a big program like that. So why put myself through the embarrassment? So I told Matthew the same thing I told her: "Only schools with really, and I mean *really*, low standards."

Studying with him is like you'd expect. Every question is broken down to the minutest detail.

We come to a math problem: Screen-printing a batch of shirts requires one minute per shirt in addition to twenty-one minutes of initial set-up time. If it takes thirty-five minutes to screen-print a batch of shirts, how many shirts are in the batch?

I make the mistake of bringing up my ol' head Rodney, who sells fake Polo shirts out of the back of his truck on 69th Street. Matthew is not a fan of this business model at all. He veers off on a tangent, questioning the validity and accuracy of Rodney's books. Fair. Matthew even offers to give Rodney a free audit.

It takes twenty minutes of him explaining to me what an audit even is and why Rodney desperately needs one before we get back to studying.

Studying at Brian's house is all that.

His mom, who happens to be shorter than him (we're talking she can't ride certain rides at Six Flags), keeps us stocked with brain food like Hot Pockets and grilled cheese. And considering my mom hasn't been on one of her benders for a few weeks, it's much appreciated to have a meal that doesn't consist of a half-eaten sandwich and a bag of Hot Cheetos. Having some warm food does remind me of all the amazing study food Bharti used to hook me and Aamani up with. It's weird. Literally every time we studied, it was as if Bharti was on a mission to fill my belly. I remember this one time, after praising her for this bomb-ass aloo gobi, I said, "Bharti, you're the G.O.A.T.!" I'm pretty sure she had no idea what I was talking about, just that I wanted to marry her aloo gobi, and even still, she smiled, fucking *hugged* me, and in her thick accent said, "Call me Aunty." I looked over her shoulder at Aamani, and she looked at us hugging like we were the most adorable meme she'd ever seen.

Brian doesn't help me study in the same way that Matthew does. He doesn't even help me fill out an application to a school— said his Mom filled out all of his. So I do it myself using his computer and Wi-Fi. I'm more or less tutoring him since it appears I know more about science than he does, especially astronomy. It's still beneficial though, me having to break down equations for him and demonstrating how to show our work. It actually gives me a firmer grasp on the material.

Was this Lindsay's plan all along? Some sort of Jedi mind trick where the Padawan becomes the master?

Lindsay lives in the apartments over on Diamond Street across from the Hank Gathers rec center. My levels of respect go up two notches for her. Diamond is one of the roughest parts of Hargrove. It's known as the murder capital of Hargrove, but we try to keep that quiet to not scare off the white folks and their businesses. Rumor has it that the city's thinking of building a Chick-fil-A there. So the fact that the whitest person I know has survived this long here blows my mind. She doesn't have a Barbie Dream house she commutes to like I originally believed. She's slumming it like the rest of us.

One of her hallway lights is out and the other is flickering like a horror movie. I check my back to make sure no one's about to run up on me from the shadows. There's shouting coming from the other side of the door and I don't think it's the TV. I knock. The arguing escalates. I hear someone shout Lindsay's name. Definitely not the TV. I ball my fist and knock like I'm the FBI. It goes quiet and I hear the locks unlatch and the door pops open.

Lindsay opens it and steps aside. "Hey," she says, inviting me in with an up-nod.

She looks to have aged in the two hours since I saw her in school. She looks tired. Her hair is tied up in a messy knot at the nape of her neck, and she's wearing a gray sweatshirt that's two sizes too big for her. Usually Lindsay's so well put together. She has that perfect I-should-be-on-a-CW-show face and luscious Dove model hair. The only CW show she should be on now is *Riverdale* in a guest appearance as High School Dropout, Sleep-Deprived Hobo #1.

"Hey," I reply. I take a step in the house, checking my back one last time as the light flickers in the hall illuminating the white masonry for a quick second before coating it in darkness.

Her parents are in the kitchen. This is the first time I'm seeing them together. Usually it's one or the other that picks Lindsay up from school after our away matches. Her dad, who looks nothing like the accountant Matthew's dad looks like, is scrubbing dishes. He has a scratchy five o'clock shadow that's peppered with gray and long washed-out-rocker hair with a receding hairline. He has on a dingy wife-beater and jeans, and sports a tattoo of a cross on his right shoulder.

Her mom looks even more battle worn than Lindsay. There are dark bags beneath both her eyes and her hair is frizzy and dry, and not as brown as Lindsay's. She's more of a dirty-blonde, emphasis on the dirty. She stands in front of the refrigerator, giving Lindsay's dad a death stare. The kind of stare a teacher gives when they want to let you know you fucked up.

"Are you going to stand there and watch me do the dishes all night? Because I gotta tell ya, that's really fucking annoying, Virginia," Lindsay's dad says. His voice is deep and agitated.

"I have to make sure you don't fuck this up too," she informs.

He slams a plate in the soapy water. Suds spill on the dirty counter, which is stacked with more dirty plates waiting their turn. "What's that supposed to mean? You bitch about me cleaning, so I'm fucking cleaning."

"You know damn well what it means."

"No, I fucking don't. That's why I asked."

I give Lindsay a look: *Sooo…library then?*

She just looks down at the floor in defeat.

"I asked you to do one goddamn thing. One. The only time I get a second to relax is when I have my coffee in the morning. And not only did you use all the filters, but your lazy ass can't be bothered to replace them. I bet you'd have replaced them for that whore over in 7C."

I so don't want to be in the middle of this domestic Royal Rumble.

"Oh, here we go. You always have to bring up Melanie. It was one fucking time, Virginia. It meant nothing. Why do we have to go over this every goddamn day? Maybe if you'd get off my fucking back I could actually remember shit."

"Maybe if you had a job and didn't stick your dick in anything that moves I wouldn't have to be on your back."

I swear they should be charging pay-per-view for this.

"Please, for the love of God. Take your ass down the street and get your own damn filters. I'm going to fucking slit my wrists if I have to listen to your voice for one more second. Lindsay's not trying to hear it either."

"Oh, I could be so lucky," says Lindsay's mom. "You'd be doing the world a favor."

He gives her a sturdy middle finger. They couldn't care less that we're standing here.

She reaches for a mug from the cabinet, then slings it at his head. He ducks. The mug shatters against the wall above the sink. Lindsay doesn't even flinch.

"What the hell, Virginia?! You almost hit me!"

"I wish it did." She turns and grabs her pocketbook off the counter and heads out the kitchen. "Fuck you, Jason!"

"Yeah, yeah, fuck you too."

She finally notices Lindsay and me standing in the hallway. She gives a faint smile. Her eyes are the same shade of ocean blue as Lindsay's. "I'm sorry, sweetie," she apologies, sucking in the tears that sound like they're coming. "I have to run to the store. Do you girls need anything?"

"We're fine, Mom. Thanks."

"Okay. Be good," she says, kissing Lindsay on the forehead. Ah, the old forehead kiss. Has there ever been a deeper way of symbolizing a parent's love? I wonder what that feels like.

As soon as the door shuts, her dad shuts off the water, dries his hands, and goes to the bedroom, slamming the door behind him.

Well, it's nice to meet you too.

Lindsay doesn't say anything. She just leads me to the kitchen table, where she has her books laid out in preparation of our session. There are a couple of empty plates beside her textbooks. A few flies hover around the rims.

Lindsay doesn't seem the least bit bothered by what just went down. She flips open her workbook and looks at me with her mom's death stare to do the same.

I look around. The house is pretty dirty. There's empty TV dinner containers stacked on the coffee table in front of the TV and an ashtray overflowing with cigarette butts. There's also a tangy stench that I can't put my finger on that's masked by the lemony scent of the dishwashing detergent in the sink. It doesn't look like a family lives here.

Her dad doesn't come out of the bedroom to offer us a snack or something to drink. Not that I'd risk swallowing a fly. Is it possible that even though Lindsay has both of her parents in her life she's just as alone and isolated as someone like me or Britt? Maybe she's even more so. I mean, at least Britt and I have been on our own for the majority of our lives. We have grown calloused to the notion of loneliness. It all still seems so new to Lindsay.

"Do they fight a lot?" I ask.

"We're here to study. Not become BFFs."

I suck my teeth. "A'ight, simmer down. Nobody's trying to

be BFFs. I'm just saying that if you want to, like, talk about it or whatever..."

"I don't want to talk about anything. I just want to study."

"Fine," I concede. "Forget I said anything."

She flips vigorously to the first assignment. I open my workbook and do the same. Two can play the *take out your anger on the inanimate object* game.

"Let's start."

I glance down at the first question: *What is the limit as x approaches infinity of 1/x?* "There's going to be riddles on Saturday? See, they want me to fail. The whole system's rigged, yo."

"They fight all the time now," Lindsay adds out of nowhere, her voice hollow.

"What?"

"My parents. They fight all the time now. And always over something stupid."

I exhale in relief. "I'm glad you said something, because fighting over some damn coffee filters is the whitest shit I've ever heard. Y'all ever hear of a Keurig?"

She almost cracks a smile. "They're not really fighting over the filters. The stem of the problem is my dad has cheated on her, like, a billion times. Which, while it's totally fucked up, I can't put all the blame on him. He cheated on his last wife with my mom and they had me. Like, once a cheater, always a cheater. What did she think was going to happen? That he'd renounce his cheating ways and we'd be one big happy family like we're on fucking *Full House*?" She slams the workbook. I hope this doesn't mean I won't be learning anything today, because I really do need to learn something. "I mean, what's the point of bringing up him not having a job every five minutes? My dad lived in a trailer park before he met my mom. Like, no shit he doesn't have a job. It wasn't even his trailer. It was his ex-wife's."

I just nod to let her know I'm listening. Her blue eyes are glazed over and her voice isn't so much solemn as it is irritated. I can tell she's had it with her parents' shit.

Boy, do I know the feeling.

"What really pisses me off is that I overheard them one night talking about how they have to stay together for me. Like I'm a fucking kid that doesn't know that ninety percent of marriages end in divorce." I don't think that number's accurate, but I keep it to myself. "I wish they'd just get one already so we can all have some peace and quiet."

I feel like I've freed a bunch of worms that I now can't get back in the can. I have to say something. Anything to tame the mood.

"Not that it's a contest"—not a good start, Lex, abort, abort—"but my dad's dead—I think—and my mom is the biggest drug addict on the Eastern Seaboard. You know, my mom has literally traded our food stamps for crack. What a terrible trade that is. Some of these drug dealers are fucking dumb. Like, *you want some discount milk for a dime bag? Sure, don't mind if I do. That seems like a fair trade.*" I really want to laugh out loud. Because you have to laugh at the batshit insane decisions my mom makes. Otherwise you'd go mad. "The woman's resourceful as fuck, though. I'll give her that."

"Dang. Really?" Lindsay asks.

"Yeah. My mom's like the Willy Wonka of Hargrove. She somehow manages to get her hands on all kinds of shit. I've even seen her mix whatever she has lying around to make up her own drug of *pure imagination*. The woman will snort, hit, and shoot anything. Shit, I remember this one time," I reminisce chuckling, "she was so fucked up she tried to snort the marshmallow powder at the bottom of the Marshmallow Magic bag."

She cocks her head, confused. "*You* like Marshmallow Magic?"

"Best generic brand cereal there is," I state as fact. "You?"

"I like Honey Ohs."

"Ugh. I'm not eating anything that's sole ingredient is made up of what horses eat."

"There are oats in Marshmallow Magic, too, you know?"

"Yeah, and *marshmallows*," I say. She smiles in defeat. "You know I had actual Lucky Charms once back when I was, like, six. A social worker gave me some. They were fucking magically delicious."

"I've never had name-brand cereal," she admits.

"Never? Not even the Cap'n?"

"Nope."

I pull back as if a wider view will grant me a better perspective of her. I can't believe I'm here discussing generic cereal with Lindsay-fucking-Ross. Fifteen minutes ago I thought she ate caviar for breakfast. Talk about K.Y.W.P.

"Don't look at me like I'm that white girl. I'm just as Grove as you."

I test her, tossing up a G symbol with my fingers. "Grove for life . . ."

"Grove for life," she recites, dapping me up the proper way, and with some soul.

"Fuck me. Maybe you really are Grove."

She smiles bashfully.

"Hey, I'm sorry about your mom," she says, reopening the workbook. This time she doesn't treat it like it owes her money.

"Thanks. I'm sorry about your parents."

She snorts, then tries to contain herself, but fails and her snort spills into laughter.

"What's so funny?"

"I can't believe your mom tried to snort Marshmallow Magic."

"Man, whatever," I say, chuckling. "Your mom over here mad about some damn coffee filters. First-world problems much?"

We laugh.

We go on to study. Her mom doesn't come home for another two hours, and when she does she smells like a brewery.

The first thing I do when we finish is text Aamani.

Me: Can you hook us up with some Honey Nut Cheerios?

Aamani: Us?!?! 🤭

Me: Are you going to help a girl out or not?

Aamani: What do you know? A box just went missing from inventory.

CHAPTER 15

It's the day of the match.

I say ten Hail Marys before I leave the crack house. Nine to give me strength to not fuck up, and one asking God to protect my last sports bra. Maybe I should've reversed that order. I really need that bra to last. They don't grow on trees.

I'm running late, so I power limp to the caf. Thanks to months of physical therapy, this doesn't make me want to chop my leg off.

I stop in front of the barren trophy case and the water fountain. Above the water fountain is an overly glittered pep rally sign, advertising the basketball game tonight.

I shake my head.

They're unbelievable.

The whole STEM team is standing in front of the caf doors waiting for me. Brian holds up a poster board sign when he sees me. It says **The Legion of Sauron Assemble!** in big Sharpie letters.

I gasp at them.

Un-fucking-believable.

"See, she likes it," Brian says, nodding. "I told you she was going to like it."

"What is this?" I ask, unable to contain my smile.

"We wanted you to know that we're here for you. No matter what happens in there today," Aamani says.

"I talked Brian into changing the name," Matthew says, claiming credit.

"For the hundredth time, there's no name. Just helping her to help us," Lindsay states. "This is all for Nationals. If it takes showing up before the match like a bunch of butt-hurt protesters carrying poster boards, then that's what we've got to do."

Lindsay folds her arms and doubles down on her resting bitch face. I walk over to her and put my arm around her, pulling her in for a half hug.

"Aw, you really do care, Lindsay. And your frown is as bright as the sun. Speaking of the sun, it's four-point-six billion years old and accounts for ninety-nine-point-eighty-six percent of mass in the solar system."

"Someone's ready for the match," Aamani says. Her face tilts with a smile. She has her hair pulled back. It opens her face so I can make out every freckle and blemish, all working in perfect harmony to make her inexpressibly beautiful.

"Yeah, yeah," Lindsay dismisses, trying to shrug me off. I tighten my grip. She's not getting out of this PDA. "After all the time I've wasted helping you study, your ass better be ready."

I look down at Lindsay. "See, you say mean things, but I know you don't mean them," I say, playfully grinning. "I bet this send-off was your idea."

Brian lowers the poster as if it weighs a hundred pounds. "What the hell is this thing made of?"

Aamani's mouth presses into a tight line. "Um, I'm going to go with cardboard. My grandma can lift that thing."

"Well, if you want to get technical," Matthew starts, "the cardboard itself is composed of layers of paper that have been compressed together."

Brian huffs. "Then this is the heaviest paper ever." He takes another gasp of air. "Oh, also this was all Aamani," he says, gesturing to the Legion of Sauron.

"Yeah, thanks again for this idea. I had to get up at seven thirty on a Saturday to help make this damn thing."

I hush Lindsay, giving her shoulder a squeeze. "Shh! Mama knows, child. Mama knows." I look at Aamani. "So you did this?"

She shrugs. "Ah, it was nothin'."

But it most certainly is something. Every decrepit limp I take these days she's there, watching my back.

I shake my head. "You guys are such nerds." I look right at Aamani as I say it. I want her to know I'm grateful for everything she's done.

"WHOA!!!" they say in unison. "HEY!"

"We do not use the N-word," Aamani reminds me.

I roll my eyes and shake my head. My cheeks are hurting from smiling so much. "My bad. What I mean is thanks for this. For real. I don't know how I can ever repay you guys."

"You can repay us by not screwing up our chances at Nationals," Lindsay states.

"Don't worry. I got you."

I look across at Aamani in our pre-match huddle; she's careful not to get too close since her parents are in the audience today (they're usually too busy with the store to attend matches). She can't even find her voice to deliver our pre-match pep talk. She shakes her head, forfeiting the duty.

"Uh-um," Brian says, clearing his throat. "It looks like Big Daddy Brian is going to have to inspire us to victory. Okay, team.

We're not goons, we're not bullies. No matter what people say or do we have to be ourselves. Because we're Team USA, gathered from all across America, and we're going to stick together because that's what ducks do..."

"Bruh," I interrupt, deadpanned. "Are you quoting the *Mighty Ducks*?" He must think we don't have Disney+ in the hood.

"Pfft! No," he says offended. "Anyways, say it with me: quack... quack... quack..."

Matthew raises his hand. "I don't know what is happening, but I'm uncomfortable. And would very much like it to stop."

"Me too," Aamani says, finally breaking from her parents' trance.

"You want a speech? I have a speech," Lindsay says, irritated. "Everyone answer the questions right. And, Lex? Try not to mess up. Speech over."

"I do not feel very confident in our ability to win this match after either of those speeches," Matthew states as we disperse the huddle.

"Me either," I second, taking my seat on the substitute's chair behind our table.

The opening round flies by. Lindsay and Matthew carry us to a ten-point lead.

It is finally my turn to sub in.

I nervously approach the table. Looking out into our run-down caf/auditorium, I see Mrs. H in the front row looking on proudly, Aamani's parents cursing me with their eyes, the judges studying their thick answer books, and a bunch of empty chairs. Next thing I know, I'm sweating my tits off.

Why is it so damn hot in here?

It's the same feeling I had before my first varsity game. It's only when I think of this whole thing in the context of basketball that it hits me. STEM. Basketball. It's all the same. Us versus them. The buzzer's the ball, the other team my defenders, a right answer is a made shot, and the moderator is the ref. And looking over at our competition, I know for a fact that before the injury, none of them could stick me in ball.

I got this.

The ref tosses the ball in the air: "Identify the noble gas discovered in 1898 from the residue of liquid air that has an atomic number of fifty-four."

I smack my buzzer and coolly state, "Xenon."

"That is correct," says the ref.

Swish. Nothing but the bottom of the net.

I crossover my defender, then spin around him like a ballerina: "Chondrichthyes." I score again. Then I take the ball coast-to-coast, weaving in and out of the defense, making a reverse layup: "Forty decibels." And in the final quarter I make a deep step-back three right in their captain's face: "The correct answer is standard deviation, sir."

Brian doesn't even sub back in. We win the match by sixty-three points.

As soon as the match ends, Aamani's parents escort her off stage and out the doors. The rest of us celebrate in Mrs. H's room. I even give Brian a few quacks.

I text Aamani.

Me: Where u at?

The message fails to send two, three, four times. It's finally happened. Mom either realized that rent is more important than the phone bill, or she finally got the patience to sit through all of those automated operators to remove me from her plan.

Then I nearly slap my face with my phone. Because, duh. It's still on airplane mode. What was I thinking? Mom will never get her priorities straight, and she damn sure won't stop being lazy. She's so good at it.

My phone pings.

Aamani: New phone. Who dis? 😁

Me: Girl, stop playing

Aamani: My parents thought if I
went back to the classroom with
you guys I'd shove my tongue
down yours or Lindsay's throat
#LGBTQIAPeopleProblems

Me:

Aamani: I'll be at the party tho

Aamani: Lied and told my parents I'm
going to a college prep seminar in
King of Prussia so won't be back
until late 🎉 🥳

I pull away from the phone. My cheeks pinch in confusion. "What party?" I say aloud.

Matthew overhears. "I believe you're referring to the party at my house. We will have cheese pizza from my favorite pizza place. No chicken fingers this time. This is what happens when you throw a party last minute and don't use the proper Facebook channels to do so."

"A party for what?"

"To celebrate our conquest of Cheltenham High School," he replies as a matter of fact.

"Listen, guys, I'm grateful for all the love, and no disrespect to your favorite pizza, Matthew, but I have a better idea of what we can do tonight."

"That's what people say when they definitely don't have a better idea," Lindsay says.

"Trust me."

"I definitely don't trust you," Lindsay counters.

"I'm down," Brian says. "As long as whatever this idea is doesn't require sign holding."

> **Me:** Change of plans. I'm taking you guys to a basketball game.

> **Aamani:** I think Siri just autocorrected your text wrong. It says you're taking us to a basketball game.

> **Me:** One basketball game won't kill you

> **Aamani:** There's no way you can scientifically know that for sure.

> **Me:** STFU you're coming

> **Aamani:** Fine. I guess I'll watch some sweaty people make some touchdowns.

> **Me:**

✳ ✳ ✳

The boys' team is in fifth place with only four games left. Fifth place doesn't sound that bad, right? There are only six teams in the conference. Do with that what you will. It's funny; one of my goals at the start of this year was to be on the best team in school. I just never thought it would be STEM. With the win today, we now have one of the best STEM records in the state.

But you wouldn't know it. No one shows up to our matches. We don't get pep rallies with posters that look like a Michaels barfed on them or letterman jackets. Nobody wishes us "good luck" when they pass us in the halls. There are no groupies with our team jersey number painted on their cheeks with gold glitter. We're the misfits. The wallflowers.

But I like it. I look down the bleacher and see our team of misfits and know they'd do anything for each other. They're the ultimate ride-or-die clique. The Crew and BMs don't have shit on STEM.

The game is sold out, despite the team's 8–15 record. Overbrook is first in the conference and their fans love to come out and rub it in. The opposite bleacher is populated with Overbrook fans, repping their school colors dressed down in black and orange. Their step squad is in full *You Got Served* mode and is tossing some serious dance shade at our cheerleaders, who've got nothing in reply but some corny-ass "We've got spirit, yes we do!" cheer.

Overbrook's center is seven foot. He towers over every player on Hargrove, making Jordan look like a Minion.

"How come all of our players look like hobbits?" Matthew asks me.

"Yeah, it's what we call *about to get that ass whooped*," I tell him.

Our side of the bleachers starts stomping their feet, turning our section into hundreds of tiny jackhammers. They break into our pregame chant: "*Oooooooh...!*"

They hold the note as the starting five takes the court.

Brian knows the drill and joins in. I would, but I'm working with one good leg here. Then Max Richardson, the head of our student cheer section, who's shirtless and has his whole body painted Hargrove red, yells at the top of his lungs: "*HAR-GROVE!*"

Our side of the gym answers: "*YOU KNOW!*"

I notice Lindsay is not altogether hating this. There's, dare I say it, an echo of a smile on her face. Or maybe she just secretly ripped one and is waiting for the smell to kick in. I follow her line of vision, which brings me right to Jordan's sweaty ass cheeks. Wait. Lindsay has a thing for Jordan? I almost burst out laughing. If Britt only knew. And can I just say, Jordan's cheeks? Not that impressive. Someone's been skipping leg day.

The ref tosses the ball in the air and Overbrook's giant center wins the tip easy.

Aamani leans over. "When do they start scoring touchdowns?"

"Will you stop acting like you don't know what basketball is?" I snap.

"Why?" A smile teases at her lips. "Trolling you is so much fun. Look at your face." She chortles and pokes my cheek. I swat her finger away and pull back smiling.

Overbrook's shooting guard drains a deep three. Their fans go apeshit, drowning out our poor excuse for a cheer section. Their step squad does a little *in your face!* dance to rub it in. Our cheerleaders pathetically sit on their pom-poms like chickens trying to hatch an egg.

"We're allowed to yell ... on school premises?" Matthew asks, anticipation on the tip of his voice.

"Oh yeah," I answer. "You can cheer and yell as loud as you want. Go crazy, bruh."

"But that's in direct violation of the Student Code of Conduct subsection 7A."

"Well, not here it's not."

His face lights up.

"YAY, TEAM! GREAT SHOT! DO MOVES AND MAKE MORE BASKETS! SPORTS ARE VERY EXHILARATING! SPOOORRRTTS!"

The Hargrove fans surrounding us look at Matthew like they're ready to pounce.

"Um, Mattie," Brian says, scared for all of our lives now, "only cheer when *we* score. Not the other team."

"Sorry," Matthew apologizes, not losing an ounce of excitement. "This is very exhilarating."

Brian looks around our section. "White people. Amirite?"

Jordan hits an Overbrook player with a smooth in-and-out crossover followed by a nice Kyrie-like scoop layup. Our section erupts. Matthew looks over at me for the okay. I nod. He starts wildin' and even high-fives some guy in a do-rag next to him.

Lindsay shouts, "Yay, Jordan!"

This girl's mad thirsty for that Jordan D.

Britt's sitting on the bottom bleacher. She looks up with Krystal, Mikayla, and Brianna and tosses some serious shade Lindsay's way. Between Lindsay throwing googly-eyes at Jordan and Matthew rooting for the wrong team, we're definitely going to get jumped by someone after the game.

I toss Britt an up-nod. She rolls her eyes and looks away. I'm going to take that as our beef is still very much cooking. It's probably well done at this point.

Overbrook comes down the court and drops the ball into

their big man in the post. He fakes left, then puts up a nice little Embiid sky-hook. It's nothing but net. The guy can ball. We brick two straight possessions and Overbrook runs the same down screen to get their big man open. He gives Jacob the same move on the block. Jacob doesn't fall for it this time, but he's too small to contest the shot and ends up slapping big guy's elbow. Swish. The ref blows his whistle for an and-one.

Do-rag guy next to Matthew erupts.

"What the fuck you lookin' at, ref?!"

"That ain't no foul!" another guy shouts from behind us.

"You suck, ref!" another voice adds closer to the benches.

"Yeah, get your eyes checked, ol' head!" a woman yells.

Matthew's eyes grow two sizes. He looks like an anime character.

"We can yell at the authorities, as well?" he asks, hopeful. "Even though it's in direct violation of subsection 7B?" We look at him blankly. "Has anyone bothered to actually read their Student Handbook?"

"I didn't even know we had a Student Handbook," Brian admits. "Is there an audio book?"

"Yeah, I'm going to go with a big no," Lindsay says.

"We're not supposed to yell at the ref——" I start.

Do-rag cuts me off. "Yeah, you can yell at them. Go on and let that bitch-ass ref know how you feel, young boul."

Oh, God. I can't watch. Who knew Matthew had so much pent-up rage and school spirit in that pale, overly allergic body of his?

"I'm not sure why that language is necessary, but here it goes," Matthew says. Do-rag looks at him like, *the fuck?* "Hey you, in the zebra-print shirt!" The ref standing at half court actually turns and looks up to our section. This isn't happening. "My name is

Matthew Miller and I'd like to file a complaint that you, sir, are very, very"—everyone is waiting for the punch line—"bad at your job! I hope someone contacts HR so your error is accurately documented in your next performance review!"

Matthew looks down the row at us with a huge smile to weigh our reactions. Aamani gives him two thumbs up; Brian facepalms; and Lindsay is too busy eye-banging Jordan up and down the court to care.

I pat him on the back. "Good job, Mattie, that'll teach 'em."

Matthew nods like, *you're damn right it will*. Although, I can say with a hundred percent certainty that is not what he's thinking.

We're behind 30–48 at halftime. The cheer team trots out to center court, waving their pom-poms like they're trying to land a plane. Each one is wearing a fake smile and too much makeup. Like, we're down eighteen points. What is there to smile about? I'll never understand the point of cheerleaders. The play on the court is supposed to get you hyped, not a group of identically dressed PG-13 strippers.

Aamani goes, "Do they take requests? It'd be dope if they could recreate that scene from *Bring It On* when Gabrielle Union caught the white girls stealing their cheers."

I shake my head.

This girl, man. How come every time she opens her mouth I end up smiling?

We make it through the third quarter before getting kicked out. We were down by thirty with no chance of coming back, so obviously everyone stopped cheering for what few points we did manage to score. They also stopped yelling at the refs every time they blew the whistle in Overbrook's favor. Everyone except Matthew, that is, who was too busy having the time of his life to consider the score and circumstance. So after our hundredth *if you don't shut that white boy up* look, I stood and declared it was time to go.

"That. Was. Awesome!" Matthew declares as soon as we step foot outside.

The late February night is brisk and nips at my ears.

"So that was basketball, huh?" Aamani says, as we walk toward the SEPTA stop on the corner. "Thought there'd be more home runs. Also, there needs to be more math and science questions. Now that would make it fun."

"Then it'd be STEM," I reply, not impressed by her trolling skills.

"My point exactly. A *real* sport."

"Well, I had fun," Brian says. "You know, minus the whole us sucking part."

"There were definitely a lot of good-looking guys out there, that's for sure," Lindsay adds, probably still daydreaming about Jordan's ass in those shorts.

"I can't wait for the next one!" Matthew says.

Brian tosses his hoodie over his head, then sticks his hands in his pockets. "How about we wait until we play the worst team in the conference? Then you'll be able to cheer all game."

"I think we *are* the worst team in the conference," I state.

"Never mind then. We're never going to a game again."

Aamani cocks her head. "Hey, Matthew, you think your mom can still hook us up with that pizza?"

"I believe so."

"So . . . *Mario Kart* and pizza, anyone?" Aamani offers, flexing her eyebrows.

The consensus is an overwhelming hell yes!

If I play my cards right maybe I can sleep over again and avoid the Russian roulette of seeing if Mom is missing on a bender.

Friends FTW!

CHAPTER 16

Okay, I realize that by me saying this, it almost certainly guarantees some bad shit's about to happen. I mean, it's rule number one of jinxing. But I can't front like things aren't going well for me. This is pretty much the best stretch of my life, hands down.

We're one match away from finishing the season on the longest win streak in Pennsylvania history. I even secured us fifteen points last match against Lower Merion. We won by one. One could argue it was my mad STEM skills that made the difference. Not bragging here, just stating facts. Anyway, spanking Lower Merion means with one match left, if we win, we qualify for Nationals. But if we lose and Germantown Academy wins, then they're in. So, yeah, no pressure, right?

I'm not even sweating it, though. Between the five of us, no one in the state can beat us.

What can go wrong?

For the first time in three weeks I was able to sleep in my own bed. Last Tuesday I got so hungry I risked it and stuck my head in the front door to see if anyone was home. I was met by Randy, who told me I can leave peacefully or we can square up. I didn't really feel like getting my face caved in again, so I left. I'm not mad at Mom for choosing Randy over me. Sex, free drugs, someone else paying your rent; I'd have chosen him too.

It's nine twenty a.m. I cup my ear to the still air, listening for any signs of Mom and Randy. It's hood quiet: the sounds of oppression and public transportation. I should have the place to myself for at least a couple of hours, giving me time to eat breakfast and get some last-minute studying in before I have to squeeze into Aamani's plaid skirt and switch over to White Girl Lex for the match.

I check the cupboards to find them surprisingly stocked. And with Cinnamon Toast Crunch! Not the fake-ass knockoff brand, Cinnamon Squares. *The* Cinnamon Toast Crunch. I guess Randy's not completely worthless after all. I make the clear decision to go ham on a bowl of CT Crunch, careful to not be heavy-handed with my pouring. I don't want to set Randy off. The last time he found his box of cereal half-empty (how he considered the cereal to be his when it was in *our* cabinet is another rant for another day) he almost put Mom through a wall. Addicts don't fuck around with their cereal.

I have a bite, savoring the taste of name-brand food. Then I review my packet again for a final time. I've managed to nail most of the sections. I only missed two flash cards last night, and got ninety-four percent on the STEM practice exam study app.

I'm ready for today. I know the packet like I do Diana Taurasi's MVP winning stats (20 points, 4 assist, and 6 rebounds per game) and I'll have a stomach full of name-brand cereal fueling us to a win.

A loud, cop-esque knock interrupts my peaceful and well-nourished morning. I shove a giant bite of CT Crunch in my mouth in case it is the cops and I don't get to finish it, and then I do a quick sweep of the premises to make sure none of Mom's needles or narcotics are visible. The place is actually clean for once, which can only mean they're off buying more. It's the circle of a drug addict's life, where they hold the new eight-ball up like baby Simba like *Nants igonyama bagithi Baba / Sithi uhm I-need-another-hit-gonyama.*

I clear my throat. "Who is it?" I ask, putting some bass in my voice. First rule of addressing the cops: Show them you aren't scared. They can sense the fear, and it makes them jumpy as fuck.

"Open the door, bitch."

A muscle feathers in my jaw. It's Britt. Figures. She doesn't talk to me for months and the first thing she does is call me a bitch. Ladies and gentlemen, my so-called ex-best friend.

I slide the bolt lock, then the chain one. Britt storms in, out of breath and sweating. Her hair is pulled back in cornrows.

"Can I help you?" I didn't mean to come off so bitchy, but I want to get back to that CT Crunch before the milk makes it soggy and it's CT without the crunch.

She acts like she has a warrant and barrels past me in search of something. I notice she's wearing the same clothes she wore in school yesterday.

"Are we alone?" she asks, grabbing at her knees to catch her breath.

"Yeah," I reply, cocking my face to the side in confusion. "Why are you acting like a fugitive?" I suck my teeth. "You steal another weave?"

She double- and triple-checks the room. "I'ma keep it real. No bullshit. I need your help."

"You've gotta be shitting me," I say, taking the opportunity to throw her pettiness back in her petty face. "I thought we weren't cool anymore, and you wanted to beat my ass for no reason? I believe you called me, and correct me if I'm wrong here, ocky.'"

She answers quickly to clear up any confusion. "Oh, I still don't fuck with you. But if you help me out, we can squash all of that."

Can you believe this girl? She wants *my* help. Where was she when I got my ass beat and had no place to sleep? Or when I had to dumpster dive a Taco Bell for a half-eaten Locos Taco? Or when I spent Christmas morning freezing my tits off in a crack house? Or when the new Drake album dropped and I had no one to analyze it with?

Britt scratches one of her cornrows. "A'ight, look, shit's been fucked up. *I* fucked up," she admits, leveling with me. "I lost a shit ton of Devon's supply last night in Newport."

My eyes grow two sizes. "*Newport*?! That's, like, the damn capital of Crew territory. Do you want to die?!"

"You think I don't know that?! Why do you think I'm here talking to your sellout ass?"

"What the hell were you even doing out there?"

She rakes her hand along her face and sighs. "I've been skimming some of Devon's supply and selling it for myself."

"You haven't!" Even for Britt, this is crazy. Ripping off a drug lord is a one-way ticket to the afterlife. One that will involve a whole lot of slow singing and flower bringing.

"He's got no idea I'm doing it," she says, trying to reassure me. It doesn't. "It's easy dough. I had a connect over in Newport that was hooking me up so I wouldn't be selling around the way. I'm not stupid. You don't shit where you eat. He hit me up last night saying he'd only be at the spot for an hour, so if I wanted to move some product I had to do it now. I was in the middle of working the spot for Devon over on 52nd, so I just took the whole stash Devon had me pushin' and rolled out. Long story short, my guy set me up. I had to ditch the whole stash in the trap house. I spent the whole night runnin' from them niggas."

I feel for her. If I'd lost a dime bag of Devon's, I'd move to Mexico, invest in a fake mustache and Spanish lessons, and change my name to Pedro. But there's nothing I can do beyond pointing her in the direction of the dollar store for those fake mustaches. Unless she just needs to vent. In which case, venting over. So bye, Felicia.

"Ay, I feel ya. But what do you expect me to do about it? I can write you a bomb-ass eulogy," I say, trying to lighten the mood. I'm partly serious, though.

"Come on, Lex. How many times have we run up in someone's house and stolen their shit?"

I shake my head. My moral Spider-Sense is tingling. Everything about this feels bad. "Too many."

"You and me," she says, pointing to the both of us, "we're like Queen Latifah and Jada. Ain't no place we can't set off."

She's referring to this old bank-robbing movie with Queen Latifah and Jada Smith that they used to show on TNT all the time.

I crinkle my nose. "You do know Queen Latifah dies in that movie, right? And I'm not trying to die because you did some stupid shit like stealing from Devon."

"Nah, Queen Latifah doesn't die. Vivica and the light-skin bitch dies."

"First off, so not the point. And secondly, everyone except for Jada dies."

"If you say so," she concedes apprehensively. "But I think you're thinking of another movie."

"Oh my God!" I explode. "I've seen *Set It Off*, like, twelve times on TNT."

"Damn, chill," she says, cracking a grin. "We'll be in and out. Nobody will know we were even there. I promise. And after that, I'll never ask you for shit again." She gives me that persuasive Britt look; the one that peer-pressured me into taking my first hit, downing ten shots of vodka one New Years, and listening to Lil Yachty. I regret that last one the most. "*We ride together, we die together—*"

The fact that I'm even considering this means I need all kinds of therapy.

"*—Bad girls for life,*" I say, finishing the quote. "So when are you talking about doing this?"

"Bet!" she says, excitedly pumping her fist like Tiger Woods nailing a putt on Sunday. "We gotta hit 'em up, like, now. The block is too hot at night. Someone's going to find the stash. It's not exactly in the best hiding place. It's under a pile of clothes."

"What?! I can't go now. Our last STEM match of the season is today. If I don't play, we're going to have to forfeit and won't go to Nationals."

"For real?" she deadpans. "We're talking about some serious life or death shit right now, and you're over here girlin' about some nerd competition. Are we doing this or not?"

She's right about one thing. If she doesn't get the drugs back, Devon's going to kill her. And if I miss the match and ruin our season, Aamani's going to kill me.

The choice is simple.

"A'ight, let me finish my cereal first. It's probably going to be my last meal."

We take the L-train to South Philly. The entire ride I can't shake the sinking feeling that I should pull the emergency brake and bail. Go to the match instead. My conscience is eating me alive. I imagine the heartbroken looks Aamani, Brian, Matthew, and Lindsay give Mrs. H when they realize I'm not coming. Then it kills me to consider the possibility of Aamani vouching for me, doing her best to convince them that I'll show up, I won't let them down. And what hurts the most is the thought that they might actually believe her.

The fact of the matter is I've let the only person who ever believed in me down. There's no getting around that. And you know what, even though I might be essentially saving Britt's life, I still feel like shit because of it. I can't even summon the courage to text her. The fuck is wrong with me? Why can't I ever make a good decision? Why can't the universe ever be on my fucking side for once?

Well, it's too late now. Even if I wanted to bail on Britt for the match, there's no way I'm making it to Ridley in an hour, nor can I afford the seven transfers to get there.

We post up across the street, next to the abandoned house, to scope the situation. Britt was right. The block is a ghost town at this time of day. A few guys with blue bandanas tucked in their back pockets get out of a navy Impala and head into the house. I squint. Wait. That looks like the Impala that shot me. Motherfucker! Now I'm for sure ready to fuck up their day. One of the guys has a high-top fade and the new Jordans, which are fire. But that's beside the point. The other is Latino and is wearing a fitted Sixers hat cocked to the side.

A few minutes pass and another guy in ripped jeans and an extra-snug white T comes out of the house and takes a seat on the porch in a green-and-white lawn chair. He leans back and starts swiping through his phone, looking bored as fuck.

"A'ight, what's the plan?" I ask, securing my hood in place so that I remain inconspicuous.

"You go over there, tell him you want an eighth"—I nod, following along—"and when they take you inside, I'll create a diversion so you can grab the backpack from the room upstairs."

"Wait. What?" I shout-whisper. "Why do I have to go in? You go. I'll create the diversion."

"Because I'm Jada and you're Queen Latifah." Um, if anyone's Jada, it's me. But okay. "And they already know what I look like, genius. I thought that nerd team made you smart."

"What if I get caught and have to run? Didn't think of that did you, Jada?"

She crinkles her eyebrows. "Don't get caught then," she deadpans.

It's clear she already had her mind made up before we arrived, so there's no use fighting her over it. It would just be a waste of precious heist time. "Tell me you have money for this. They're not going to sell me anything without showing them something."

She digs in her pocket and pulls out seven twenties. I nod, impressed, but also terrified as to how she got it. After flaunting her stack, she tells me the plan. The backpack is in the room next to the upstairs bathroom, buried under a mound of clothes. I am to take it during the commotion caused by her diversion, and then meet her at the Orange Line. Sounds easy enough.

Britt looks at me. Her face is at the same time kind and filled with concern, like it used to be before things got so fucked up between us. Part of me misses those days at Marcus's, back when our only worry was how we were going to get our hands on the next *Hunger Games* book. Back when we really would ride together or die together.

"Don't worry," she encourages with a nod. "You got this."

I take a deep breath, then step into the street, putting an extra limp in my walk to look harder than I am. Putting the extra weight on my leg hurts, but it's time to soldier-up.

I got this.

I think.

I focus on selling my gangsta limp. In the end, I probably come off looking like I'm in serious need of Brian's dad's chiropractor.

"You lost, Shorty?" Baby-T asks as I approach the porch.

"Nah," I answer. "I need to get an eighth."

"An eighth, huh?" He straightens up in his chair. His biceps contract as he pushes down on the armrests. He looks pretty swole in that extra-smedium T-shirt. "And what *you* gonna do with an eighth?"

I bite back with, "I'ma make it do what it do." I have no idea what that means. I think I just quoted the movie *Ray*. Clearly, I'm out of practice.

The left side of his mouth curls devilishly. "Is that right? A'ight then, you got eighth money?"

I take a quick look at my surroundings, checking both shoulders to make sure no one's about to run up on me. Then I flash him the dead presidents.

He reaches for the stack. I pull away and tuck the money back in my pocket. "Uh-uh. Same time, bruh. I don't know you."

"A'ight," he surrenders, raising his hands. "Hold up." Then he disappears into the house without me. This was not the plan. He was supposed to take me in with him. I pivot back to the street only to see Britt has vanished. Because of course she has.

Baby-T guy returns with the eighth; it looks like a tiny eight ball in his hand.

"It's a hundred and forty," he requests.

Shit.

Think.

Think.

"I'm short," I say, leaving a dub in my pocket and counting the rest.

He closes his palm. "Can't help you then, Shorty."

"Wait, maybe there's another way I can repay you," I suggest, twisting my face into what I hope is a promiscuous look. I probably just look constipated, though.

His right eyebrow flicks with curiosity. "How old are you?"

"Eighteen," I reply, even though my birthday isn't until June.

Once he knows I'm legal, fucking creeper, his eyes make a beeline for my chest. I arch my back to make my 32Bs look bigger, then I remove my hood and toss my hair like I'm on a shampoo commercial.

"How short we talkin'?"

"A dub," I lie, failing miserably to sound sexy. In my defense, I don't even think Beyoncé can make *dub* sound sexy.

He nods and licks his lips. "I can work with that. Follow me."

Now it's up to Britt to do her part before I have to actually do something with a guy wearing one of Tyrion Lannister's T-shirts.

The house is musty, with cracks in the walls and a mountain of unopened envelopes by the mail slot. It smells of weed mixed with the boys' locker room. I can see the room by the bathroom at the top of the stairs. The two guys we saw come in are sitting on the couch in the living room watching *SportsCenter*.

High-Top Fade goes on a rant about how Ben Simmons is better than Steph Curry because he's a walking triple-double. The Latino boul is rolling a blunt, and licking the paper replies, "Bruh, Curry's got two MVPs. Fuck outta here."

I follow smedium-T up the old wooden staircase. Each step croaks like a dying frog. High-Top Fade turns around when he hears us creeping.

"Okay, Malik! I see you!" he cheers. I nearly pop a blood vessel rolling my eyes. Fucking men.

We disappear into the room next to the one with the backpack. Baby-T (I know his name is Malik, but his tight-ass T-shirt is too ridiculous not to clown) shuts and then locks the door behind us, because that's not Cosby levels of creepy or anything. If Britt's going to do something she needs to do it now, or else he's going to try and take my Jell-O pudding.

There are clothes and weed butts on the floor. It doesn't smell nearly as musty as the rest of the house. And it may just be my current situation, but it feels kinda rapey in here. He takes a seat on the twin bed and unzips his jeans.

"Come here," he says, patting the space beside him. "I ain't gonna bite."

I don't want to blow my cover—on second thought, maybe blow's a bad choice of word—so I do as instructed. "Sooo . . ." I say, awkwardly searching for something to stall the Jell-O pudding shenanigans. "How about them Sixers?"

Yeah, that's all I got. Don't judge me. My heart's about to beat out of my chest, I'm so fucking nervous.

He moves my hair out the way and starts kissing my neck. All I can think about is how much I hate Britt right now. If Devon doesn't kill her, I will. I need to get out of here. He needs to back the fuck up.

"Embiid needs to stay healthy," I continue, awkward and

tensing up, "and Simmons needs to act like he's actually shot a basketball before, but if we can do that, I think we have a good shot at the chip." Then I jump when he places my hand around his dick. I drop it and ball my fists.

I want to Floyd Mayweather the shit out of his jaw right now.

"What?!" he asks, irritated. "I didn't bring you up here to talk about ball. You know what this is."

He closes the gap between us again, and this time takes the initiative and forces his hand down my jeans. Right when I'm about to right hook him, a boom reverberates through the house and every car alarm on the block goes off.

Someone outside shouts, "WHAT THE FUCK?! MY CAR!"

Tyrion Lannister-T and I hurry to the window and look outside. The Latino's Impala is up in flames like a damn Michael Bay movie.

"Oh shit!" Tyrion Lannister-T says, scurrying to hide his boner and zip his jeans. Then he sprints down the stairs and out the front door.

I waste no time and go look for the backpack. There's another unmade twin bed and an old desktop computer. Thing probably runs on dial-up. It's only a fraction smaller and dirtier than the Cosby room. I dive into the closet headfirst and start tossing clothes onto the hardwood floor behind me. My leg's hurting like a bitch from being on this ancient hardwood floor, but I don't have time to dwell on it. When I get to the bottom there's a mountain of clothes piled in the middle of the floor. Then I see the backpack. I unzip it to check the contraband. It's stuffed to the brim with bricks of heroin.

Got 'em!

The guys are still trying to contain the fire. We're in the hood. Fire trucks and police cars take their sweet ass time. As a last resort

High-Top Fade dumps a pitcher of lemonade on the flames, which of course does fuck-all. These guys are idiots. Don't they know the reason *water* works is because it displaces the free oxygen molecules so that it isn't available to participate in the burning process? It also turns into steam, which carries the heat away from the fire, cooling it to the point where it can no longer burn.

Damn, I would've killed it at the match today.

I'm not complaining, though. These dumbasses make my job easy, and I limp right into the kitchen unnoticed. My escape route is a few feet in front of me, unmanned. That's when I see it, a pile of money spread out on the kitchen table. I know this is just the astonishment of seeing so much money in one place playing tricks on my mind, but I swear there's a golden halo hovering above it and a gospel choir singing "Hallelujah! Hallelujah!" I should go. Don't push my luck. But come on. There has to be at least a couple thousand dollars over there. It would be a crime *not* to take it. I'd be able to eat for months. Also, fuck these guys! They shot me. In the *ass*.

Yeah, fuck that.

I raid the table, stuffing all the cash I can grab into my pockets, bra, then when I run out of space, jeans. I'm not telling Britt shit. We'll call it compensation for putting my ass on the line to save her.

Britt's waiting for me at the Orange Line when I arrive. She runs over when she sees me.

"Did you get it?"

I turn around to show her the backpack I'm carrying. I hear the cash in my bra crinkle as I do, and I look up hoping she didn't hear it.

"What'd I tell you?!" she says, dapping me up. "Jada and Queen Latifah! Fuckin' right!"

"Yeah, and I was nearly Cosbied," I say, seething. "What took you so long?"

"What?" she replies innocently. "I had to run to the liquor store to get some alcohol to set on fire. Can't blow up a car without a bomb."

I shake my head and hand her the bag. "So, are we cool now?" I ask, holding out my fist for confirmation.

She pulls me in for a hug. The money crunches as our chests connect.

Shit. Play it cool. "New bra," I say, shrugging it off with my eyebrows.

She squints, trying to read me. "We're cool," she says. I sigh, in the clear. Then she pulls away. "And what I tell you about stuffing your bra? Own them small titties."

Britt hasn't said much on the trip back. She dozed off a few times, then scrolled through the Gram and liked a few posts. I think she even commented on the photo I posted with the team after I went MVP on Lower Merion: #STEMGOAT 🐐 . I only know this because I get an Instagram notification. I quickly swipe it away. I'm too concerned with how I let the team down today to give an ounce of my time to Instagram #EXSTEMGOAT 🙁 🐐 .

I resort to staring out the window aimlessly, watching the run-down brick houses of South Philly fade into West Philly. I try to read the graffiti written on the sides of the abandoned houses and beneath each overpass. Anything to take my mind off of how

I ruined our season. The longest winning streak in school history down the drain.

I don't think it's working.

The train sways from left to right like a boat on steady tide. It would be soothing if I wasn't having a minor panic attack. I know Aamani probably hates me now. I can imagine the look on her face. A seething stare as she gives me a disappointed frown; her eyebrows crinkling her hazelnut skin. What really has me feeling guilty is imagining her soft brown eyes and the way they're judging me like Jesus on the cross. That's some scary shit.

Yeah, this whole window-looking thing definitely isn't working.

"Yo, Lex?"

I look away from the window.

"Huh?" I say, clearly distracted.

"I've been calling you for, like, two minutes. You deaf now?"

"My bad. I just have a lot on my mind."

"Girl, are you still tripping over that game you had today?" I don't say anything. I just look down at the dirty floor. SEPTA is about as clean as the crack house. I feel like I'd get every letter of hepatitis if I touched the pole you have to use when the train car is full. "Why do you care so much about this nut-ass team?"

"The fuck if I know," I say, frustrated at how much I care. "I guess because they really do care about me. They were the only ones that believed in me after the shooting. They believed I could still be somebody. And they believed I didn't need a basketball to do it. They showed me I have potential, I guess. It's fucking weird having people who care for you."

"That's it? Bitch, I could've told you that. You've always been the smart one."

"Um, have you seen my grades prior to joining STEM?"

"I don't give a fuck about school. Since when has school ever helped anyone from Hargrove out? I'm talking about what's up here," she says, tapping my temple with her index finger. "I'm talking about your street smarts. You remember that time we hadn't eaten for, like, three days and were like 'fuck it, we're just going to rob a bank'? What did I say?"

"You came up with the worst plan ever. Didn't you suggest robbing some dude working the late shift at the McDonald's in Olney? You do know that guy probably only had, like, fifteen dollars on him, right? I mean, he worked at McDonald's."

"Not my best idea, a'ight. The point is you didn't let me do it. Instead you came up with that dope plan to sneak into ol' man Grady's crib and steal his annoying-ass dog. Then when he offered a reward we gave it back. We made two hundred real quick. You're always thinking of clever shit like that to get us out of a problem."

"I don't think that makes me smart. It just means I'm good at ripping off old people, which is not what I want written on my tombstone."

Her face drops with a hint of sorrow. I don't think I've ever seen Britt this empathetic. "I guess when we stopped talking I didn't have you there to talk me out of doing dumb shit."

"Like stealing from Devon?" I hope she hears the disappointment in my voice. Because that really was dumb as fuck.

"Like stealing from Devon," she confirms. "That's cool they got your back like that, though. It still sounds nerdy as fuck and I'll never understand why anyone would ever volunteer to do *more* schoolwork, but I'm happy you found something outside of ball. You're my girl, Lex. I want you to blow up. Like, one of us should get the fuck out of here. And let's just be real, we both know it was always going to be you. My ass ain't ever leaving Hargrove."

"That's not true," I reply. Although part of me knows that it probably is. If Britt's selling in Crew territory and skimming Devon's supply, then she's already in too deep. People don't come back from that. But this isn't the life I want for her. For my friend. "You can leave too. It's not too late to stop working for Devon and get your grades up. You'll probably have to go to summer school and repeat again, but I can help you. Aamani can help too. She's an amazing tutor. The girl's like a Hindu Stephen Hawking."

"Do you hear yourself? Me going to summer school, studying and shit. Nah, I'm good. I'll leave that nerd shit to you and your nerdy-ass friends."

It pains me to concede, but I get it. College isn't for everyone. And you can't just stop going to school for months and then decide to become a Rhodes scholar. It doesn't work like that. If Aamani and STEM have taught me anything this year, it's that school is like everything else in life. It requires hard work and dedication to succeed. You can't half-ass it. I just wish we never fell out of touch. I wish I didn't act so petty. Maybe I could have steered her down the STEM path like Aamani did me. Maybe I could have saved her from a life of Molotov cocktails and stealing backpacks of drugs from rival gang members. Yeah, Britt was out of pocket for the way she treated Aamani and how she turned on me for joining STEM. But maybe that was just her way of admitting she needed me more than ever. Maybe the only one who failed here is me.

"No matter what, you're always going to be my girl." It's the only way I know how to say *I love you*. "Bad girls for life?"

She daps me up. "Bad girls for life." Then she tosses in, "You fucking nerd."

We trade smiles.

Her smile folds over. "And who the fuck is Stephen Hawking?"

CHAPTER 17

I'm in no mood to sleep on a mattress that smells like burnt bacon that was marinated in spoiled milk, or to listen to Crackhead Marvin hold a full-blown conversation with himself about how the system's rigged to keep a Black man down as he takes another hit from his crack pipe. So I pray to Jesus that Mom and Randy are out making terrible life choices.

Please, universe. Just let me have this one thing.

I have seventeen missed calls and texts from the team when I turn my phone back on. I had purposely turned it off so I wouldn't have been tempted to ditch Britt. The majority of them are from Aamani, and a few from Brian and Mrs. H. I even have a missed call from Lindsay. She was the only one to leave a message.

I feel like such a dick for failing them.

Lindsay's message is a good minute and a half long. I hesitate, thinking maybe I shouldn't listen to it. I mean, what good is going to come from it? I doubt she's about to sing my praise for a minute and a half or be like, "So the team pooled our money and entered you in a raffle that you won. You are now the owner of a new Ferrari!"

I take a breath and press play.

"I fucking knew it. I knew something like this was going to happen," Lindsay starts, sounding ten notches beyond enraged. "I know we haven't always seen eye to eye, but let me be clear when I say that you let everyone down today, including me. This is exactly why I didn't want you joining the team. I don't think you understand that STEM is all I have. Because unlike you with all your basketball friends, Brian, Aamani, and Matthew are the only friends I have around here. Nobody wants to talk to the supposedly rich and stuck-up white girl. Both of which I'm not, as you now know. The world might be a terrible place for people with your skin tone, but Hargrove is a terrible place for people with mine. So it really pisses me off when you pull the shit you pulled today. You hurt my only friends and put the one thing that gives me peace, where I feel safe, at risk. I hate you for that." Static of dead air comes over the line. For a second I think she hung up, but then she starts back up with a vengeance. "Everything just comes so goddamn easy for you. You stroll into STEM, take Brian's spot, and everyone falls in love with you despite you not knowing shit about science, technology, engineering, or math. You already had a shitload of friends and a life. Why'd you have to come along and take mine? You don't even care about them. They deserve better. *We* deserve better. And you made Matthew cry. I hope you're fucking happy about that."

Well, shit. That hurt.

Is it me or is there a pattern here that I'm missing? Like maybe, just maybe, I've been so programmed by society to accept being a stereotype that I'd begun to stereotype everyone around me. Am I really a narcissistic asshole? I don't know. Maybe I am. But who is she to judge? She doesn't know half of the shit I've been through this year.

It turns out life doesn't see race or creed. It's content to fuck everyone over equally.

Now that's equality for your ass.

The sad part is I don't know if I'm even capable of changing.

I don't know how to be anything but what society has built me up to be. I'm drowning in Hargrove. Every time I try to move beyond it, it pulls me back in like quicksand. The harder I pull away, the harder it tightens its grip. And the decision I made today may have just sealed my fate.

When I turn onto my block, the first thing I see is Aamani in her STEM uniform, arms crossed, pacing in front of my stoop. And she. Looks. Pissed.

And I thought Lindsay hated me.

Aamani doesn't wait for me to reach the stoop. As soon as she sees me she starts marching toward me like a battalion heading for enemy lines. She stares me down. We meet in the middle of the block across the street from Mr. Edmore's Deli. Kalhil and a few others are smoking a blunt on Mr. Grave's stoop. They puff then pass, and look up to us for entertainment.

Staring down a heated Aamani is kind of terrifying. I now know how the US Army felt staring down the beaches of Normandy on D-Day.

Sorry for all the war similes. We're studying WWII in Mr. Hilbert's class. This is the kind of thing that happens when you actually pay attention.

"Let me see your phone," she demands, holding out her hand.

"Why?" There's no way I'm handing over my phone—the one bill Mom always finds a way to pay—to a pissed-off girl who's staring at me like she wants to use me as a human sacrifice.

"Give me the damn phone," she doubles down.

I stand corrected and hand over the phone.

She presses the home button and my wallpaper ignites the screen. "So it does work."

"I can explain," I begin, trying to deescalate the situation before she spikes my phone like Odell Beckham Jr. in the end zone. "See, what had happened was . . ."

She gives me the hand. My eyebrows shoot to the top of my forehead. Surprised. I know she did not just do that. "I don't want to hear it. I'm here because I wanted to look you in the eye when I say you and me are *done*. After all me and the team did for you—we accepted you, helped you apply for scholarships, invited you into our lives—and this is how you repay us, by screwing us over the first chance you get?"

"I-I had to help Britt," I eventually spit out. As soon as her name leaves my mouth I realize it's not going to help my case. I probably should have thought that one out a little more. But she's put on the full court press. I'm trying not to turn the ball over here.

"Wow." She turns and starts to walk away. "Bye, Felicia."

I look on, gasp. Did I just get *bye, Felicia-ed*?

Kalhil and the rest of the high stoop burst out laughing.

I grab her arm and spin her back around. "I had to help her. It was a matter of life or death. No lie."

She shakes her head in disbelief. "How long are you going to keep blaming everyone else for every mistake *you* make? It's getting old. Britt's always in trouble. There's always something to run from when it comes to her and you. Let me guess, she did something illegal and turned to you to bail her out?" My mouth opens, but words don't come out. "Thought so. Do you seriously not see that she's using you? That just because her life is messed up and she has chosen a different path that it doesn't mean you have to go down it too. You don't owe her anything, Lex. But you do owe it to yourself to not screw up what can be your only chance of getting out of here."

I shake my head. Bitter. "You don't get it."

She huffs. "I'm so sick of you saying that. 'You don't get my life.' 'You don't know what it's like to be Black.' As if microaggressions aren't the story of my life too. We're living in a post-9/11, post-Trump world, where people with my skin tone and last name get labeled a terrorist or an illegal alien. You know, despite the little fact that I was *born* here. So don't talk to me about not *getting it*. I fucking get it. I get that you're too scared to stand up to Britt out of fear of breaking some unspoken street code, which is by far the dumbest thing I've ever heard."

Maybe it's the shitty day that's put me in a shitty mood, or maybe there's some truth to her words, but I explode.

"You don't know my life! Britt's been there for all of it. She was there to help quiet the nights when my stomach was rumbling; she was the shoulder I cried on when our foster dad beat the living shit out of us. You think dodging a few bullets at a party one night makes you know our struggle? Try dodging bullets your whole life. You're standing here talking to me about your life being hard because of some small-ass microaggressions. Because people occasionally look at you wrong. You have a family that loves you. You have a future. Try not going to school for two weeks because your face looks like you just went twelve rounds with Floyd Mayweather. Or having to steal chips and a pack of gum from a convenience store and calling it dinner. So, no, you have no fucking clue about our struggle."

I pause. Catch my breath. Then go back in.

"And you're such a fucking hypocrite, you know that? Like, for real. You're always on my ass about me being scared of being who I am. Yet here you are still in the closet. I mean, what the fuck? Your parents caught you kissing another girl and you still can't be real with them. You'd rather live a lie and marry some rando with eyebrows the size of loofahs. So fuck outta here with that shit. Take a hard look in the mirror before you come at me about my life. Because I know who I am. I'm just another nigga from the block. Surviving. And you're a fag from India. Deal with it."

Her eyes swallow her face. That once flicker of stars that shone in her eyes full of hope and belief in me, perhaps us, has burnt out, extinguished by my words. Left behind is a corpse of the girl I've come to know and admire.

What have I done?

She brings her heavy eyes to meet mine, and blinking away the tears, says, "Fuck you, Alexis."

I'm paralyzed as she walks away.

I slip under the covers. I don't care if Mom and Randy come back from their bender and catch me here. I want to be safe tonight.

I think about Aamani: how she's feeling, what she's doing. My life's been defined by watching people hurt the ones they're supposed to love. Why do we do that? If this life is an endless pursuit of happiness, why do we induce so much pain? If life were a math problem, pain would be the constant variable and suffering the square root. Maybe happiness is just a myth regurgitated by greeting card companies, religion, and shitty rom-coms. Maybe it doesn't exist.

My phone pings.

Brian: Okay. I get you're avoiding us, but you have to tell me what happened to you today. We're all worried about you. I promise I won't tell anyone.

Brian's chill. There's no reason I should cause him or anyone else on the team further pain.

> Me: had to help a friend. You can tell whoever you want. I don't care

Brian: I'm glad you're okay. And I hope your friend is okay. I'm going to stop using the word "okay" now.

It'd be easier if he hated me like Aamani and Lindsay. Him being so understanding only makes me feel worse about making them miss out on their chance to do something special, to achieve something they worked so hard for.

I wait a minute, looking up at the water stains on the ceiling. It's a miracle this apartment building is still standing. When no new text comes, I reply.

> Me: Did Matthew really cry?

Brian: For like a second. But he also cries at Return of the King and Infinity War when Spider-Man dies. You're in good company.

My hand motions to chuck my phone at the wall in rage of knowing that I made Matthew cry. I consider not being able to afford a replacement phone. I pull my hand back real quick.

> Me: My bad I fucked up and made you guys miss out on Nationals

His speech bubble pops up and the ellipsis flashes.

Brian: No one told you? Germantown
lost! 🎉 😄 🎉 😄

Me: For real? But Ridley sucks.

They really do. They only won two matches all year. Well, I guess three now.

Brian: Yep! Germantown is doneski!
Heard they choked in the speed
round. Noobs 😂 😂

My first thought is the universe is giving me a chance to make amends for today. Because Aamani and Lindsay can have a fit all they want, but there's no way in hell I'm not going to Nationals and putting in work.

Me: So we're in then?

Brian starts typing . . .

Brian: Yes and no. Yes because we now
have identical records but own the
tiebreaker. And no because Mrs.
Hall told us there's not enough in
the school budget to send us to DC
😭 You wouldn't happen to have
any get-rich-quick schemes would
you? Lol

I look over at the money I stole earlier. The corner of my mouth rises.

CHAPTER 18

The Crew's stash practically covered the cost of the trip. Thank you, Crew, for being the most incompetent gang members ever. It also helps that Nationals are in DC, which is only two-and-a-half hours away. I sent the money to Mrs. H, marking the envelope as *Anonymous*. If I showed up making it rain it would've raised more questions than I was willing to answer. In the end, we only had to come up with a couple hundred dollars. Lindsay's parents, being the Caucasians they are, came up with the idea to do a bake sale. I was quick to point out that unless there's weed in the brownies, nobody from Hargrove is going to buy them. Thankfully they took my suggestion to heart and decided to have the bake sale outside a Starbucks in the suburbs. We raised the money in an afternoon. Those hipsters couldn't get enough of Mrs. Ross's brownies and Mr. and Mrs. Miller's chocolate chip cookies. K.Y.W.P, people. K.Y.W.P.

So we're going to Nationals. I'm a goddamn hero.

Okay, maybe that's not entirely accurate. I'm, like, an unsung hero to half the team. The half that's not Hindu or a white female. Both of whom are still not talking to me. Not even in practice, which is impressive since we literally have to converse during team questions. There has been a lot of middlemanning: "Matthew, tell Alexis this" and "Brian, tell the traitor who shouldn't be here that." That second one is Lindsay in case you couldn't tell from the overdramatic teen angst.

Warranted? Yeah. Beyond petty? No doubt.

I do feel some kinda way for disappointing Lindsay. But Aamani? Well, she can be mad at me all she wants, because I'm still pissed at her for how she came at me. She was outta pocket for that. I don't care how many matches I miss, I'm not about to let anyone talk to me like that. But the one thing that does bother me is how Aamani's been acting toward the rest of the team. She's been uncharacteristically standoffish and sullen. She even snapped on Matthew last practice when he quoted *Lord of the Rings* for the tenth time in five minutes: "Oh my God, Matthew! Just talk like a normal person for once! Please!" Something's clearly bothering her beyond our fight. She wouldn't just go off on Matthew like that because of me.

I know one thing, though. I don't particularly care for this alternate universe Aamani. She should leave the bitchiness to the pros.

I've never been out of Pennsylvania. I'm not counting New Jersey. It's not a real state, just crumbs of Pennsylvania and New York mashed into a dirty peninsula. There's not even a toll to get into Jersey because they're pretty much begging people at this point to visit.

Anyway, I had to forge Mom's signature on the permission slip, which was easy considering her signature resembles an infant scribbling with crayon on a kids' menu. The school provided us with one of the small buses, the kind the kindergartners ride. Our bus driver is an old Black man with curly white hair, who goes solely by Alan, as if he's Prince. If his life were a movie, Danny Glover would definitely play him. Alan seems nice enough. He spends the whole ride down to DC talking to Mrs. H. Everyone else elects to brush up on any STEM questions they're unsure of. I go over the past three packets. By the time we reach Maryland, Brian has given up on studying and has pulled out his Nintendo Switch, talking Matthew into a game of *Super Smash Brothers*. I hold out for about five minutes before the sound of Pikachu zapping fools is too much and I have to join. Lindsay remains committed and keeps studying, while Aamani throws on extra sulk and blocks her face with a textbook. Disapproving of video games? Now I know for sure some serious shit is going on with her.

Nationals are being held on George Washington University's main campus, so Alan takes the scenic route through downtown DC. We see the White House and the Lincoln Memorial and the Washington Monument, which nearly scrapes the clouds.

Everything is just so clean here. Every monument and building, even a McDonald's, all looks like it just received a fresh coat of paint. I mean, the Kennedy Center looks like a damn palace. I nearly broke my neck trying to see if Meghan Markle was up in there. If nothing else, this trip is showing me this: if this is what the rest of the world has to offer, then I have to get my ass out of Hargrove ASAP.

We're staying in this run-down motel twenty-five minutes outside of Georgetown. Somehow, they managed to find the one place in DC that vaguely resembles Hargrove. Gone are all the freshly painted buildings, and in their stead are garbage-littered streets and homeless people asking for loose change outside a Dunkin' Donuts.

We're greeted by a drunk concierge who slurs "wel-come" and spits chewing tobacco in a Coke can. He's wearing a flannel shirt in the middle of spring and a—I wish I was making this up—*Make America Great Again* hat. He keeps eyeballing Aamani in her kurta like she masterminded 9/11. She's still balls deep in her textbook, so she's oblivious to Country Joe over here. No doubt this is a shitty, B-horror-movie, racist-ass motel. But compared to how I'd been living this past year, this place is Buckingham Palace. Plus, they advertise free cable. So there's that.

Mrs. H rooms me with Aamani and Lindsay.

None of us are cool with this.

When Lindsay goes to complain, Mrs. H cuts her off, "I don't want to hear it, girls. You're teammates. Whatever it is that's going on between you three, you need to figure it out and fast." She passes out the key cards. "Everyone head to your rooms and settle in. We'll meet back here in the lobby in an hour to head over to the opening banquet dinner. Remember to dress nice, please," she urges. "Let's act like we have some home training, yes?"

We take our keys and sulk to the room.

We're on the second floor. The boys' room is next to ours, and Alan's and Mrs. H's rooms are on the first floor by the vending machines, where I'm pretty sure the guy standing next to it isn't waiting for a Sprite but selling something. There's an old TV with an antenna (so much for my dream of watching free HBO) and two twin-size beds with crusty, stained covers. If we put a black light to the room it'd look worse than Marcus's Cum Couch. I volunteer for the portable cot in the corner. They don't object. What they don't realize is this thing's a therapeutic mattress compared to my bed at the crack house. I bet my leg's going to feel good as hell snuggled up on that thing.

Lindsay rips off the sheets and replaces them with ones she brought in her duffle bag. Aamani ignores us and sits cross-legged on the bed, laying out her textbooks and packets to study all simultaneously.

I venture into the bathroom. The first thing I see is a dead cockroach curled on its back beside the toilet. Next to him is a nice-sized shower that's clean enough to use—barely. Probably not. I look back down at the cockroach. Definitely not. But whatever. I haven't showered since gym earlier this week. I turn it on and run my hand under the water. The water pressure is just right, like a refreshing waterfall, and the water is actually hot, unlike our shower, whose temperature maxes out at *frozen-tundra*.

I pop my head back into the room. "This thing actually gets hot!" I announce, overzealous.

Aamani doesn't bother to look up and Lindsay answers with, "No shit, Sherlock. That's how showers work."

Whatever. They're not about to ruin this for me. I slip out of my clothes and into the shower. I don't get out until my fingers are pruning.

Around ten p.m. I go to the vending machine for a soda.

I see creepy concierge guy from the lobby window. He watches me like a hawk as I limp up the staircase. Lindsay goes straight to bed with the caveat of needing her "beauty sleep," and Aamani cuts on the lamp by the bed, pops in her headphones, and starts studying. She has barely said two words all night. When I asked her what was wrong, she just sighed and said, "I'm fine." Lies. She looked like someone told her they've decided to cancel all Marvel movies until the end of time, like she had given up all hope in this world. If she would talk to me, I'd tell her to join the club. We have T-shirts.

I snuggle into my cot and stare up at the ceiling. I'd study, but I'm afraid of overdoing it. I got this. After all the packets, mornings at the library, raising my GPA two whole points, if I don't know my STEM shit now, I never will. Plus, the significance of the moment isn't lost on me. Tomorrow can be the day I rewrite my life. Some admissions person can be in the crowd. I could impress these white folks. Tomorrow's my chance to best fate, to navigate around the collision course I have of becoming my mom.

Just five wins and we're National champs. Five wins and I might just get out of Hargrove alive.

We got this.

CHAPTER 19

Each round is held on a different part of campus in some old hall or meeting room. Our first match is against Millard West High School in the Jack Morton Auditorium, which smells of leather-bound books and rich mahogany. Not that it matters, but Millard's team captain is a light-skinned brotha with a tight fade. I only bring this up because who knew that not only do they have Black people in Omaha, Nebraska, but they have sharp barbers too.

Anyway, there's an extra set of butterflies holding a rave in my stomach, and I keep picking at my cuticles like I'm digging for gold. Similar to March Madness, if we lose, we're eliminated. Back to Hargrove. Back to the crack house. Back to not having a future.

Due to me missing our last match, I've been demoted back to subbing. Banished to the team dog house. I do all I can and cheer on the team from the substitute bench. No use bitching about something I can't change.

We begin the match fairly well. Aamani wins us a bunch of points and Matthew nails the final question in phase one on engineering, which he actually answers while making eye contact. I was very proud of him for this. Seeing him become more comfortable in his skin makes me happy, and we exchange an awkward fist bump between phases. I say awkward, but it's typical white people shit. I go in for a fist bump, he goes in with a high five. In the end we meet in the middle and he slaps my fist.

But Millard's no joke, and even with our decent start we're losing 30–45 after phase one. No one's panicking though. The majority of our matches are won in the lightning round, where between Aamani, Lindsay, and Matthew, no one can keep up.

"What is the most common term for the energy an object has because of its position or configuration?" the moderator asks, opening the lightning round.

I do a fist pump in my lap. There's no way we don't get this right. It's the easiest question in the history of STEM. Any person with a brain knows the answer is *potential*. Easy-peasy.

Brian confidently slams on the buzzer, beating out the other players.

"Exploitative," Brian answers.

Never mind. We're fucked.

Crack house, here I come.

In our lightning round minute, we manage three correct answers, allowing Millard to steal four of our questions. And when it's their turn, they only miss one, which Lindsay then steals for us.

Going into the final phase, we're losing 115–200.

I'm not mad at Brian for sucking hard today (my guy's only answered one question right all day) or even Aamani for holding a grudge and punishing me and the team by leaving me on the bench to rot. I'm mad at myself. I let the team down when I made that decision to help Britt.

As the moderator leans into his mic to commence the final phase and send us back to Hargrove losers who wasted nearly three thousand Crew dollars, Brian bends over clutching his abdominal.

The sudden thrust of his weight against the table knocks the buzzer to the floor.

"Uggghhh . . ." Brian cries in agony. Albeit unconvincingly, but still agony nonetheless. "I . . . uggghhh! I think my appendix just burst. I-I can't play anymore."

There's a collective gasp from the small audience of parents and non–Ivy League recruiters and admissions people.

"Really?" Matthew questions, cocking his head. "I would have thought you would be in far greater anguish, considering your appendix is currently spilling infectious materials into your abdominal cavity."

Brian, worried his terrible acting job has exposed his blatant lie, looks around the audience. A few gullible people pull out their phones and dial 9-1-1.

"Thanks, Mattie," Brian says through gritted teeth out of the side of his mouth.

"You're welcome," answers Matthew with a big smile.

Brian pumps the brakes on his death. "Uh, did I say appendix? I meant diarrhea. The Egg McMuffin I had earlier is not sitting well with me." Then he throws in another "Uggghhh . . ." to try and sell it.

I think it's safe to assume Brian won't be challenging Denzel for acting supremacy anytime soon.

The moderator shakes his head in utter disbelief, a look on his face that reads *I fucking hate teenagers*.

He sighs. "Very well. Hargrove High will be allotted an additional two minutes to deal with Mr. Chang's illness—whatever it may be—or to activate their substitute."

We turn away from the mics and huddle at the table. Brian's still half clutching his abdominal muscle and throws in a loud moan every few seconds to keep up the illusion.

"What the hell are you doing?" Lindsay scolds.

"I'm saving our season," Brian retorts. "Uggghhh..."

"Brian, I know your stomach is currently imploding from the inside. But I ask that you do your best to refrain from farting. This huddle would be the ideal vacuum for it," Matthew says, just putting that out there.

"Pray tell, how is your Razzie-winning performance going to save our season?" Aamani asks, her face showing she's completely fed up with Brian's shenanigans.

"I don't know," Brian concedes in frustration. "It was the best I could come up with. All I know is we have to put Lex in."

Lindsay twists her face. "Do we though?"

"If we want to win, yes," Brian says wide-eyed. "I've been *Suicide Squad* levels of bad this game."

"More like *BVS* bad," corrects Aamani. "At least *Suicide Squad* had Margot Robbie in short-shorts."

Brian nods. "Good point. But regardless of what shitty DC movie I'm being today, we all know we'll at least have a shot of coming back if Lex takes over for me."

Lindsay pushes out a heavy sigh. "I hate to admit it, but he's right, Aamani."

Brian and I both go to talk at the same time.

"*He is*?"

"*I am*?" We look at each other across the huddle. "I mean, uh, yeah, I am."

Aamani crinkles her right eyebrow. This means she's thinking. "No," she states firmly. "I stand by me and Mrs. H's decision. We're not about to sacrifice our integrity for a win."

"I would like the record to show that I am not opposed to

sacrificing my integrity for a win," chimes Matthew, using his index finger to push his glasses up the bridge of his nose.

"I second that, Mattie," Brian agrees.

Silence engulfs the huddle. We all look at Aamani, our eyes doelike and pleading.

Surely she has to give in. It's three against one.

Silence continues.

Brian lets out another fake groan.

"If no one is going to talk, can I bring up the point that Brian left me alone in a motel to go get McDonald's, and even worse, he didn't bother to bring me back any?" Matthew says, unintentionally alleviating the mounting tension. And if I know Matthew like I think I do, he's never been more serious about anything in his life.

"Dude, there was never any Egg McMuffins," Brian assures him with a pat on the back. "I just made up the story to call this huddle."

"Oh, okay. Will there be Egg McMuffins at some point in time during this trip?"

"Sure, Mattie. We'll go after Aamani comes to her senses and lets Lex take my spot so we can win."

"Okay. Aamani, come to your senses so I can get an Egg McMuffin."

Aamani frowns.

"Come on, Aamani, you're clearly outnumbered here," Brian points out. "Just let bygones be bygones. You guys are acting like Tony and Cap in *Civil War*."

She shrugs, stubbornly. "No. Now can we please get back to the match? This is so embarrassing."

I don't know how I do it, because I'm mad pissed right now, but I explode without raising my voice beyond our huddle.

"Jesus Christ. I said I'm sorry. What the fuck's your problem?"

"Language," Matthew scolds.

Aamani shakes her head. Her eyes well with tears, but she bites her bottom lip to hold them back. "You make me so angry. You're so smart, but act so stupid about certain things. My problem is I'll never be good enough for you. You'll always choose that part of your life over me, over *us*, even when you know it's the wrong thing to do. So there's no point acting like you're part of the team when we both know good and well you're incapable of committing to anything or anyone but yourself or Britt."

"Hargrove, your time is up. Are you ready to continue?"

Brian pokes his head out of the huddle. "One second, chief. I mean, uggghhh, the pain . . ." He submerges back into the huddle. "All right, I didn't want to have to play this card, but you leave me no choice."

He looks over at me and instantly I know the card he's referring to. "Brian, don't."

"Don't what?" Lindsay asks, her curiosity piqued.

"I'm sorry, Lex. But I have to." There's a dramatic pause. "It's the only way. We're in the endgame now," he finishes with apologetic eyes. It kills me that in the midst of the shit show that is our predicament, I almost crack a smile at Brian's *Infinity War* reference. "Lex is the anonymous donor. So if it wasn't for her we wouldn't be here getting our asses handed to us by a team from fucking Nebraska."

"Language," Matthew reiterates.

"My bad, Mattie. But they're from Ne-bras-ka. Seriously, people, we can't lose to a team that probably rides mountain goats to school."

"Seriously?" Lindsay asks, her jaw nearly hitting the floor.

"I didn't know you were rich, Alexis. Can I borrow five dollars for an Egg McMuffin after the match?"

Aamani's eyes glaze over and she gives me a look that could stop time, I swear. I would sell my soul to know what she's thinking.

"*Whaattt...?! No way.* You've all been Shyamalaned," Brian says sardonically. "And with that I will see myself out stage left." He disbands the huddle and takes a seat in the front row next to Mrs. H.

I guess we're doing this.

I pick up the buzzer and take my seat between Lindsay and Aamani. Aamani's glazed look lingers for a few more seconds before she gathers herself and turns to the moderator. Lindsay scribbles something down on her notepad and slides it in front of me: *Thanks for the money, but don't fuck this up.*

The moderator clears his throat and taps his index cards on the podium. "All right, if there are no further interruptions, then let us begin. Six minutes on the clock, please," he says, nodding to the judges' table. "Contestants, hands on your buzzers. Ready? And . . . begin. Question one: The sum of two numbers is sixteen and their product is fifty-five. What are the numbers?"

My eagerness to prove my worth to the team and to shut Aamani up (I'm capable of caring about things other than myself or Britt . . .) takes control. I even forget to go into basketball mode. The next thing I know I'm watching my hand push down on the buzzer in record-breaking time when I don't have a fucking clue what the answer is (how to juke my defender). I see it and feel it moving, yet there is nothing I can do about it. My body is like *You're going to answer this damn question whether you like it or not.*

The moderator looks to me for the answer.

I start doing the math in my head, calling back on my *Sesame Street* days, anything to help me make an educated guess. The sum has to equal sixteen. The square root of sixteen is four, which is an integer, which is a whole number that can be positive, negative, or zero, which is different from a real number, and, uh, what was I talking about again?

"Hargrove, do you have an answer?"

Fuck it.

"Ten and six," I guess.

Without hesitation he replies, "Incorrect. Millard will now be allotted the chance to steal."

The lone Black kid buzzes in. "Eleven and five," he says knowingly.

"That is correct. Fifteen points, Millard."

What the fuck, bruh? We're, like, the only Black people here. We're supposed to have each other's backs. I can't even be mad at him though, because that question was actually pretty easy. I need to focus and stop overthinking.

"Next question. Which of the following is often the *least* reliable property of a mineral that is used in mineral identification: (A) magnetism, (B) specific gravity, (C) color, (D) cleavage?"

Matthew, like a boss, buzzes in. "Color."

"Correct. Fifteen points, Hargrove. Next question. What layer of Earth's interior contains over sixty percent of the Earth's mass and is composed of iron and magnesium-rich silicates?"

Aamani slaps her buzzer like it stole something. "Mantle," she answers.

"Correct. Another fifteen to Hargrove."

I see the portable scoreboard change to read 145–215. And just like that we shed all the bullshit that has been throwing us off our game. Now we're only focused on answering the questions put forth by the moderator. At least, for the time being, no one's concerned with how much they hate me or comparing me to Judas or the *Game of Thrones* finale. And everyone stops glancing into the audience every couple of seconds to make sure the admissions people are still present and watching.

This is what made us the best team in the region, and why we were able to turn a zero-and-two start of the season into the biggest winning streak the school's ever seen. Because when we're locked in and trust one another, we become the 2018 Golden State Warriors of STEM.

Aamani and I make it four straight baskets. Millard is shook now. After two minutes their one-hundred-point lead has evaporated, and the remaining four minutes becomes a tennis match with us answering correctly, then them answering correctly, so on and so forth. But what they don't understand is we're Serena and they're the field.

The score is tied at 315 with twenty-four seconds remaining on the play clock. We all know this will most likely be the final question of the match. Both teams are hunched over their buzzers, each player's hand only centimeters away from the red button. My knees are weak and my palms sweaty. All this stress has turned me into a damn Eminem song. I don't want to lose. I'm not ready to go back to Hargrove. I want to live in the fantasy of a college campus in another state a little bit longer.

"In astronomy"—my eyes embiggen at the mention of my favorite subject—"what color of star has a luminosity class of three or two and is in many cases considered to be . . ."

I press my buzzer, interrupting him like Kanye at an awards show.

Like Pac, all eyes are on me.

"I must warn you. Being that I wasn't able to finish stating the question, if you have buzzed in prematurely, then I'm afraid I'll have no choice but to dock Hargrove points for stalling."

Lindsay's face looks as though she's plotting to suffocate me with my motel pillow tonight.

"No," I reply. "I know the answer."

An incredulous look sweeps the room, turning everyone's face over in confusion. Everyone except Aamani. She's smiling at me, her freckles bunching at the tops of her cheeks and reaching for her hairline. It's a smile that calms the soul and makes it easier to speak. Oh, how I've longed for this smile. The smile only she can give. The smile that says she believes in me and what I can become. It's not judging, nor envious.

I square my shoulders and follow through, my hand making a goose neck, releasing the perfect jump shot. "The answer's a blue star," I say, not daring to look away from Aamani.

Bewildered, the moderator nods and leans into his mic. "That is correct. Fifteen points, Hargrove. Next quest—"

The timer sounds.

Brian rises to his feet, cheering. "Fuck yeah! Suck on that *Nebraska*!" He freezes up when he realizes all eyes are on him. "Oh, I mean, uggghhh...?"

Mrs. H doesn't reprimand him for cursing or gloating. She just looks up at the stage with joy.

Millard's faces drop into their hands. I feel bad for them. They didn't deserve to lose, not after kicking our ass for seventy-five percent of the match.

The moderator announces our win. We somehow manage to contain our joy as we meet Millard center stage to tell them "Good game." The Black dude shakes my hand and we exchange a little head nod of respect. It's that nod that Black folks everywhere give each other. The one that signifies I've got your back if some shit goes down with these white folks.

One win down. Four to go.

Aamani approaches my booth, looking like she's prepared to be both good cop and bad cop for a murderer interrogation. I'd planned on hashing out our differences on the ride home, preferably after winning Nationals so she'd be in a good mood, unlike the moody and honestly bitchy Aamani we've gotten in the past few weeks. That was the plan, anyway. But it looks like we're about to have it out in a fucking McDonald's with my clothes smelling of fried food and failed dreams mixed with a dash of McFlurry.

She slides into the booth and sets down her tray of Dollar Menu goodness: a chicken sandwich, fries, and McFlurry.

I toss a handful of fries in my mouth. Thank you, Hargrove and petty cash. Funny how they can give us money for meals but not transportation or hotels. Anyway, maybe if my mouth is full she won't ask about the money, because we all know that's the only reason she's civil again. I mean, stuffing your face works in Snickers commercials. Plus, I highly doubt she's about to apologize for overreacting to me missing one match to help a childhood friend or to thank me for saving their ass last match. But, hey, I've been wrong before.

"Be honest," she says, peering through my soul. "Did you steal the money?"

I knew it.

I don't know why she's even asking. We both know she already knows the answer. Apart from me hitting the lottery or inventing the next killer app, there's no way I go from crack house resident to Jay-Z rich.

I shove a few more fries in my mouth. My cheeks expand like a squirrel storing food for winter. Come on, Snickers commercial, don't fail me now.

A muscle feathers in her jaw. "I know you hear me."

So much for thinking I can use fast food for something other than a clogged artery and the runs.

"I mean, technically . . . but hear me out—"

She cuts me off. "Are you shitting me?" she snarls with a shake of her head.

I toss up my hands. "What? I did it for the team. I thought you'd be happy."

"Bullshit."

"I'm sorry, am I missing something here? The fuck do you care what I may or may not have stolen? You've been duckin' me for weeks. Acting like me missing a match is a federal crime."

My mouth curls in disdain. I'm so sick of her holier-than-thou bullshit. She acts as though I need saving. That I need her. I don't need anyone.

Aamani shakes her head. "You really can't grasp the concept of caring for someone, can you?" She pauses a beat. "And the thing about it is I can't figure out if it's because you've been deprived of having been truly loved or you're just that selfish."

Every defensive bone in my body explodes. "You're one to talk. Like, are you capable of going thirty seconds without judging me? You don't know shit about me or my life. Who are you to fucking judge?"

"I'm not judging," she retorts, capping her voice at a decibel that doesn't carry beyond our table. "What I'm saying to you is, yeah, you fucked up and almost cost us a chance at Nationals, and yeah, I'm still thoroughly pissed about that. But that doesn't mean that I stopped caring for you or that I want to sit back and watch you throw your life away over something stupid like stealing. I don't know why you're so incapable of seeing how much you have to offer."

"Why do you keep saying that?"

"Because you do, Lex. Just because society says you're one thing, doesn't mean you have to be that."

"This is me, Aamani. A girl from the streets trying to survive by any means necessary. This is who I am."

"See, I don't believe that. Even if you don't believe in yourself, I do."

I sit back in my booth. The padded cushion feels good against my nerve damage. I don't know why she's saying this. Why she's fucking with my emotions. Why she supposedly believes in someone who's such a colossal fuck-up. The only reasoning I can think of is she's lying. Maybe it's just part of her culture to blow smoke up people's asses. Like, it's their version of doing a good deed.

The others are oblivious to my internal debate. Matthew is going ham on his Egg McMuffin, and Lindsay and Brian are laughing about something. Probably how weird I look right now trying to figure out Aamani's play. And Mrs. H and Alan are chilling at a two-top, chatting about adult shit, I assume.

"That's not what you said the last time we talked," I remind her.

"What did you expect? I was mad. Maybe kinda jealous," she admits, her voice falling with her eyes.

Jealous? What's she have to be jealous about?

Aamani rubs the back of her neck. "I, um, may have said some stuff out of anger. I didn't mean it. Well, I didn't mean most of it, anyway."

I don't know how, maybe it's the solemn tear in her voice that's filled with heavy remorse or her big brown eyes that capture me like sun rays, but I can feel her trepidation.

"Look, Aamani..." My voice trails off in search of the calming words needed. "I said some messed up shit too. I," I sigh. "...I don't think you're just a Hindu fa—"

She puts her hand up, stopping me. "Let's not bring it up. What's done is done. We both said some things we didn't mean. Let's leave it at that."

"Okay."

"I just need you to understand that you stealing and jeopardizing your future trying to live up to someone else's expectations, expectations you're better than, does not make me happy. The shit pisses me off on, like, them making a Venom movie without Spider-Man levels. Look how far you've come: 3.8 GPA and into the second round of Nationals. You're more than a product of your environment. You're a supernova, remember?"

I bite my bottom lip and look away. This girl. Why does she care? My mind is twisting like a pretzel. My heart is telling me to trust her, while my brain tells me to call her on her lies. She doesn't care about me. No one has and never will.

I just want to stop talking about me. About my feelings. So I change the subject. "Maybe stealing the money wasn't the best decision," I admit. "But don't I get some points for not spending it on Jordans or a PlayStation?"

"No," she answers sharply, unwrapping her sandwich. "Maybe a little. And thank you for that, by the way. I may not condone you stealing, but it was nice of you to give it to the team."

"Of course I was going to give you guys the money. That's what friends do." She looks up at me with a warm smile. She reminds me of the cosmos. An uncharted vacuum of space filled with endless possibilities. She's an elusive enigma that I'd love to explore and go where no woman's gone before. "What if I told you I stole it from those dicks who shot me? Would you condone it then?"

"No way. Seriously?"

"Yeah. Britt and I raided their place. We took all their shit. Well, not *all* of it. Just the money and some drugs they stole. You know, the important things in life."

She frowns. "I'm going to act like I didn't hear that last part."

"You can act all you want. It happened though."

She takes a bite of her sandwich. I use the opening to scarf down the rest of my fries, dipping a few in my McFlurry. Then I realize that her mom didn't pack her a tiffin. It didn't even dawn on me until having to watch her sacrifice good Hindu food for a McChicken sandwich, which while edible is in no way up to the standards of her mom's or Bharti's cooking.

"Where's your tiffin?"

She swallows. "Look, I don't want you to get the wrong idea," she deflects, "but just because we're sharing a booth at McDonald's together and you gave us money, doesn't mean we still don't have issues we need to sort out between us. Because we do."

"Oh, I agree. Like, why have you been such a bitch recently? To me, I get. But you freaked out on Matthew. That shit wasn't cool."

Her head drops. She struggles to bring it up to look at me. A strand of her long hair falls in front of her face and she doesn't bother to brush it out the way. Part of me wants to lean over and tuck it behind her ear. But I refrain.

"Yeah, about that . . . now's not the time. Let's stay focused on Nationals and deal with that later."

I don't push her.

The good thing is she's talking to me again. And I can't lie, knowing there's still hope for our friendship brightens my universe.

CHAPTER 20

So we lost.

There wasn't any *Remember the Titans*, Disney bullshit where we made a miraculous comeback sparked by some Oscar-winning speech by Mrs. H, all while learning a valuable life lesson that in the end made us better people. Sorry if that's anticlimactic or bad storytelling. But this is real life. And in real life, the better team always wins. Fact is: we got our asses handed to us by a school from Texas. Fucking *Texas*. I bet they're Cowboys fans too.

FML.

For what it's worth—and to make it more Disney for you—we did manage to reach the semifinals. After beating Nebraska, we were on fire, nailing question after question, making the other teams look stupid in comparison with our efficiency. We were bal-lin'. We strolled up to the Texas match dripping swag. We couldn't lose. A team made up of Einstein, Hawking, deGrasse Tyson, and Bill Nye couldn't beat us. Until they totally did.

Wait. Hold up. Maybe we did end up learning a life lesson after all—*never get too full of yourself*. Huh, what do you know? Disney knows their shit.

In the end, reaching the semifinals impressed some people, including a few colleges who gave me applications for scholarship programs. Everyone on the team, including Mrs. H, lost their shit over all the praise I was getting. I played it cool. I mean, there was no guarantee I'd get into any of the schools—these weren't community colleges. Also, since late registration was quickly approaching, I wasn't even sure I'd be able to fill them out in time. So I was chill all the way back to the motel. But once we got back, I locked myself in the bathroom, cut on the shower so no one could hear me, looked at all the applications, and burst into tears of joy. No one ever thought I was smart enough for college. But these applications . . . well, who's smart enough now?

I filled them out with no help from anyone.

I'm chilling on my cot, laying on my side as I use my elbow to prop up my head so I can see the TV that's bolted to the chipped dresser. As if anyone wants to steal a TV from the Cold War. Lindsay's doing her best to not make contact with the dirty headboard, and Aamani's reading the new issue of *Ms. Marvel*.

Brian and Matthew come barging in. No knock. No callout to see if we are butt naked. Nothing. They just walk in as if cued by a funky bass line.

I cut my eyes at Aamani and Lindsay. "Neither of you bothered to lock the door?"

"I thought Lindsay did."

"What? I told you to lock it."

I shake my head at Aamani. "I can tell you didn't grow up in the hood, leaving doors unlocked."

Brian interrupts the scolding. "Anyone want to get out of here? Mattie and I are sooo bored."

"To clarify," Matthew begins, "Brian is bored. I was quite content rereading *Lord of the Rings* in my room."

"Correction. I am bored. Matthew was just doing something boring."

"Well, count me in," Lindsay says. "I need to get out of this nasty room."

Aamani puts up her index finger, giving everyone the universal sign to *STFU and wait*. "Aaand, done." She closes the comic. "I'm in."

Brian smiles. "Good! Because I want to go swimming. So we're, uh . . . borrowing the bus."

Lindsay considers aloud. "Wait. No. Uh-uh. We are not stealing the bus. Are you insane?!"

"Lindsay, Lindsay, Lindsay," Brian says, patting Lindsay's shoulder. "Who said anything about stealing? We already have the keys." He digs in his pocket and pulls out a silver keychain and dangles it in front of Lindsay like he's teasing a cat.

Aamani grabs them. "What?! How'd you get these?"

"Let's just say I pulled the old *slip-in-your-room-while-you're-at-the-ice-machine* trick. Figured they might come in handy."

Aamani nods in approval. "Usually I don't condone stealing, but I'm all out of comics, and there's no way I'm staying here all night without reading material. I guess the only question is does anyone know how to drive a bus?"

Brian volunteers with a half hand raise. "I think I can."

Lindsay snorts. "I'm sorry, but didn't you fail your driver's test—*twice*?"

"Technically, uh, yes," Brian confirms. "But that's because the first time I thought stop signs were just suggestions. How was I to know the law is you have to come to a complete stop? Rookie mistake. And the second time was only because I ran over a few cones parking. Other than that, I'd have my license."

"Gee, that's a relief," Lindsay says. "Thanks for putting our minds at ease."

"No worries. The kid's like Vin Diesel behind the wheel."

"I was joking. This whole plan is freakin' insane."

I stand. "Shotgun!"

Lindsay's eyebrows pinch and her face twitches. "Am I the only one with any damn sense around here? Matthew, please back me up on this."

"No. I actually sanction this bus-stealing endeavor," he says, to all of our disbelief. Lindsay facepalms so hard. "My mom keeps telling me that I need to venture out of my comfort zone."

Brian starts Flossing like he just had a ten player kill streak. "*Yo, uh, uh, yo . . .*" he starts rapping, "*Look at us / We're stealing a bus / And going downtown / About to clown / With my boy Mattie / He's about to sneeze / Got dem allergies / Making bucks, boy chill / pushing weight like Zyrtec and Benadryl . . .*"

Lindsay's facepalming so hard if she doesn't ease up she's going to pop her head like a pimple. "Huhhh," she sighs deeply. "Fine. But I swear to whatever God you Asians pray to—"

"*We rep the same God, because I'm Catholic / About to drive through traffic, looking for my Chapstick . . .*" Brian spits another bar.

"If I end up in a DC prison, I'm going to kill everyone here except Matthew, and I'm starting with you, Brian."

Brian yanks the keys back from Aamani mid-Floss. The rapping continues. "*That's a risk I'm willing to t-ake / I'm killin' it on the mic like Dr-ake.*"

We eventually make it downtown. I say eventually because Brian overcompensates for his lack of driving skills by driving thirty-five miles per hour under the speed limit. My disabled ass can walk faster than that. It's a miracle we made it here before dawn.

Being that Brian can't really drive this thing, let alone parallel park (think of the Driver's Test Cone Massacre this year), Aamani and I are forced to get out and help guide him into a space the size of the Grand Canyon. I take the front and Aamani takes the rear. We're signaling instructions with our hands like we're trying to land a plane.

Everyone was hooked on the idea of some water-based activity. The only place we can think of that has a "free" pool at two in the morning is the Lincoln Memorial Reflecting Pool.

Not our best idea.

But then again we did just steal a bus and drive it without a license. So maybe "dumbass choices" is tonight's theme. I mean, even if taking a dip in the Lincoln Memorial Pool is somehow not illegal, it's at the very least frowned upon. But whatever. Fuck it. If Drake has taught the world anything, it's YOLO and Canadians can rap.

The streets and sidewalks surrounding the monument and reflecting pool are vacant. There's a stillness to the city as if it's asleep. The temperature is at that perfect spring warmth, the kind that makes you want to live outside. The moon, accompanied by the stars, is sick and pale and reflects off the pool, sticking true to its name. It would all be romantic if we weren't in the midst of committing a felony.

As soon as the brakes hiss and the door folds, Brian races down the metal stairs past us. He beelines it to the Lincoln Memorial steps.

"Where are you going?" I call out. "The Reflecting Pool's that way!"

"I'm going to run the Lincoln steps," he answers. "That's a thing people do in DC, right?"

I lean over to Aamani. "Why is he so hype about running some steps?"

"Honestly," Aamani replies, watching Brian sprint the steps like a professional athlete in training, "I think he's high on field trip."

Brian stops halfway up the stairs and bends over, grabbing at his knees and gasping for air.

"You a'ight, bruh?" I shout.

He sits down on the stair and through gasps calls back, "Too . . . many . . . huh . . . steps. Need . . . oxygen."

Lindsay and Matthew make their way off the bus and head over to the Reflecting Pool, which thanks to Google I now know is 2,029 feet long. Lindsay kicks off her shoes and rolls up her jeans, making capris. The water ripples as she steps in.

Matthew timidly approaches the edge. "Is it cold?"

"It's perfect," Lindsay assures him.

Matthew starts to pace.

Lindsay steps to the edge and cups her hand with water. She looks at Matthew tenderly. "Is this okay?"

He nods.

Then she pours the water over his hand.

Matthew flinches and coils as if its lava. "The water temperature is . . ." He gives it a moment to register as his brain processes. ". . . acceptable."

Matthew kicks off his shoes and gingerly dips a foot into the pool, having a second examination. He lets it linger there for a few seconds before gradually stepping in. After an additional few seconds of getting acclimated to the water, he makes a wall with his hands and pushes a tidal wave of water at Brian, soaking his clothes. Brian quickly kicks off his shoes and runs in after him.

World War III breaks out between the three of them.

"Aaah! Don't touch my hair!" Lindsay shouts, shielding her free-flowing brown hair.

Watching Lindsay protect her hair like a Black woman is comedy gold. Like, who knew she had some Black in her. I'm dying. But when I look over at Aamani, she's not even smiling. She's gazing at the Washington Monument off in the distance. The crescent moon bounces off the ripples of the water and reflects in her light-brown eyes.

I'd trade my other leg to know what she's thinking.

"Hey," I say, breaking the monument's hold on her, "do you want to finish our conversation from earlier?"

She looks down and sighs with a shrug. "Sure. Why not?"

"Don't be so enthused about it."

She gives me nothing in return but a pathetic half smile.

We walk to the bench overlooking the Reflecting Pool and sit down.

"Come on, you two! Get in!" Brian yells as he kicks up another ball of water at Lindsay. "Look, Mattie, I'm water bending!"

"It would be much cooler if you could bend all the elements like the Avatar."

"Yeah, I'm being overwhelmed by Y chromosomes here, ladies," Lindsay shouts, doing her best to dodge the onslaught of water being kicked at her. I still don't know why she's drawlin'. She has that good white girl hair. Her hair probably gets wet and turns her into a Dove commercial.

Aamani's still comatose, so I guess I'm taking this one. "In a minute!" I turn to Aamani with a smile. "White folks, am I right? Can't take them anywhere."

She gives me another half, disinterested smile and nods like *STFU.*

"A'ight. That's it. What's been up with you lately? Why are you acting like Jada when Will gets snubbed for awards?"

"I don't really want to talk about it."

"Then what the fuck did we come over here for? Speak now or forever hold your peace."

"I'm just . . ." She pauses and lets out a sharp breath through her nostrils. "I'm just not ready to go home."

She can't even look me in the eyes as she says it. She veers away, back to the monument, back to the skyline that's engulfed in stars.

"I feel ya. I don't really want to go home either. But then again I also live in a crack house most nights, so there's that."

"Wait. What?"

"Nothing. Why don't you want to go home?"

"Because my parents kinda, like, really hate me right now."

"Are they still mad about the, you know"—I look around to make sure no one's eavesdropping—"kiss? You told them they can ask anyone on the block and they'll tell you I'm straight, right?"

"Yeah, but not in the way you might think."

I cock my head to the side, confused. "Explain."

"It's not so much about the kiss or you not being bi. It's just that I came out to them a few days ago and now they really freakin' hate me."

"Shit," I say, sitting back to take it in. "Did you tell them about your love affair with Popeyes too?"

She nods.

"Damn. I didn't think you'd actually listen to me and do it."

She straightens up.

"I didn't do it because of you or anyone else," she says in disgust. "It was my secret to tell. The world doesn't get to dictate when and where I come out. *I* do that. And I felt the time was right."

I want to cheer because I'm so proud of her. But that look of *insinuate you played a part in my choice again and I'll fucking kill you* says I should hold it in. My joy quickly turns to envy, though. I wonder what it feels like to be out. To be free.

"Did your parents really take it that bad?"

"Let me put it this way. My dad has literally not said a word to me for four days, and my mom hasn't left the prayer mat for two of them."

"Fuck. That's some cold shit."

"Yeah, I know." She slouches down on the bench.

I smirk. "I mean, yeah, they definitely sound mad pissed. But you're fine. They still love you."

"I don't think you heard me. My mom hasn't eaten for two days. All she does is pray for the shame I brought on our family to be washed away. Two freakin' days. As in forty-eight hours. 172,800 seconds."

"I heard you. I just think you're being a bit dramatic."

She smacks her teeth with her lips. "Fuck you, I'm being dramatic. You don't know my parents. Their religion, our bloodline, this is a big deal to them."

I shrug. "Maybe not. But you know what I do fucking know? I know what it means to really not be wanted. To not be loved. I was kicked out of my first foster home when I was four. Did you know that? Fucking four. Now you tell me why someone would take in a four-year-old, beat the living shit out of them for two months, then ship them back a month later. And my Marcus Foster Home years were even worse. It was basically wake up (get beat), sneeze (get beat), forget to wash your dish (get beat), wipe your ass wrong (get beat), miss the bus home (get beat), eat the last Hot Pocket (get beat), wake him up in the middle of the night because you have to flush the toilet (get beat). Not to mention my current trip on the Beatdown Express, where my mom watched her drug dealing boyfriend beat me within an inch of my life and then kicked *me* out the fucking house. It's like, *yeah, you're my only daughter and I know you just got beat by a grown-ass man, but can you get the fuck out before you get your blood on my carpet?* So the fact that you have no bruises, and still have a home to go to, tells me your parents love the fuck out of you. Enjoy being wanted. It must be real fucking nice."

My anger is boiling. I can't believe I just told her all of that. Britt doesn't even know about my first foster home. I've learned to live with it. It has all become so matter-of-fact at this point. As if it comes down to the simple fact that I have shit luck with foster homes and life.

Aamani catches me off guard and swipes her index finger across my cheekbone, wiping away a tear.

I'm crying? Don't tell me I'm fucking tearing up.

"Lex?"

My eyes well and I blink away another tear.

"You may think I'm full of shit," she says. "But none of that is your fault."

I shake it off with a snicker, trying to soldier up. "Yeah, I know. I can't kick my own ass."

"No. It's really not your fault," she repeats, dead serious.

"Uh, yeah, I know. I just said that."

She takes my hand. It's warm and smells of her vanilla lotion. Nerves flood my body.

"The fuck are you doing? For real, yo. Let go."

I go to pull away, but she tightens her grip, staring at me. Her eyes are wide and bathed in sincerity. A part of me gets lost in her heavenly spheres.

"Alexis Duncan, I'm sorry that stuff happened to you. But I promise there's nothing a four-year-old, or teenager for that matter, can do to warrant so much pain. It's not. Your. Fault." We trade stares. "You're wanted. I want you."

Her hand in mine. The stars above. The monument piercing the skyline. Our friends splashing and laughing, having the time of their lives. The sincerity in her eyes, in her voice. Mr. Ferguson hitting me with a closed fist. I was four. I was sorry. I didn't know I wasn't allowed to do that. She wants me? Someone wants me?

It's all too fucking much and my body reacts before I can soldier up. I fall into Aamani's embrace and cry my eyes out.

She wraps me up like a mother consoling a child, which is appropriate because I have that deep hiccup cry that you get when you're a kid. No one has ever held me like this before. With such care. With such respect.

The only words that come to my lips are "I'm sorry . . . I'm so fucking sorry."

She strokes my hair and rests her chin on the top of my head. "There's nothing to be sorry about," she whispers. "I still want you. I will always want you."

I cry some more, because fuck it. I'm gone at this point.

After I soak her shoulder with tears, I get my shit together enough to pull away. I sniff and dry my eyes. "I probably look like a straight up bitch, crying like a white girl at the end of *The Notebook*."

She chuckles. "And you've never looked more beautiful."

I laugh it off. "Stop fucking with me."

"Deadass." She weighs the expression on my face. "Am I using that correctly?"

"Yeah. You are."

There's a scream from the Reflecting Pool. It appears Lindsay's attempts to keep her hair dry have failed. And just as I thought, it falls down her shoulders perfectly. There should be a caption under her that reads *Easy, breezy, beautiful Covergirl.*

"So, you're officially out of the closet for all to see, huh? No more hiding?"

"Yep," she says confidently. "I can finally express my undying love for Emma Watson and Popeyes and not care what my parents or anyone else thinks."

I stare at her.

"What?" she asks bashfully.

"And you've never looked more beautiful."

She smiles as big as the Kool-Aid Man. "Deadass?"

"Deadass."

And I lean in and steal a kiss.

CHAPTER 21

I still don't know how to define my queerness. How to navigate being Black in society's labyrinth. The thought of all of it scares me to fucking death. Aamani came out to her parents. She looked that fear in the eyes and told it to fuck off. But I keep seeing those articles in my head. All the documentation of "Black queer hate"—the trans women of color murdered in cold blood for being queer—all because some people fear what they don't understand. My friends don't understand. I must've heard "no homo" said at least a million times in my life. As if being homo is some disease you don't want to catch, a disease that makes you less, the butt of every joke.

What if I come out and end up another name in an article? What if Hargrove isn't ready for someone Black and queer? What if I become the punchline? Like, every time someone from the block says something that can be misconstrued as homocentric, they follow it up with: *Whoa, chill! I'm not gay. I said "no Alexis."*

My sexuality. My emotions. They're a billion puzzle pieces scattered on the floor and I don't know where any of them fit.

The one piece that snaps together is Aamani. There's no experience as euphoric as kissing her. When our lips meet, it's as if we disappear into our own singularity.

I want to finish what we started on that bench.

But Lindsay won't take her ass to sleep. She's in bed, eyes closed, headphones on, tapping her finger on her phone to the beat of "Going Bad." Okay, that's it. The girl's bumpin' Meek Mill. I'm officially bestowing her with an honorary Black card. Good at cookouts and barbershops and corner stores everywhere.

I look over at Aamani and mouth, "*Why won't she go to sleep?*"

Aamani, who's nestled comfortably in her bed, shrugs it off. She lets out a long yawn. Her eyelids flutter like tiny butterflies. "So . . . tired," she whispers, nodding off peacefully.

No, no, no.

"Psst!" I shout-whisper. "Wake up!"

She snuggles, going balls deep into her pillow, and closes her eyes.

Why does the universe hate me?

It's four a.m. An hour has passed. I'm lying on my side, staring out the bent blinds that look to have been chewed. If it weren't for Lindsay's headphones, it would be serial killer, jump-scare quiet up in here.

My eyelids are heavy. I feel like I'm lifting weights trying to keep them open. Between me not really having a place to live and Aamani's parents treating me like Netflix named a season of *Making a Murderer* after me, we're never going to get another chance like this again. Alone. Well, mostly alone. Thanks to Lindsay and "Going Bad." Wait. I sit up and turn my ear to the beds. Why is she listening to the same song? I quickly look at her. She's passed out and drooling on her pillow as though she'd just taken twelve horse tranquilizers to the ass.

Now's our chance to take the four-a.m. train to Singularity Town.

I ease out of my cot and over to Lindsay's bed. I snap a quick pic because something tells me a picture of Lindsay looking like a coma patient will come in handy someday. I put my phone back on the cot, and then through the pinch of pain that erupts as I lift my leg, crawl into bed next to Aamani.

I spoon her and kiss the back of her neck.

"Mmm . . . that feels nice," she says with wonder, as if lost in a dream.

I whisper in her ear, then kiss the top of it. "Wake up."

"Can't. Aamani tired. Need sleep."

Apparently she turns into a cavewoman when tired.

"Come on," I plead, planting a kiss on her shoulder. "I want you."

She quickly rolls over as if she's been faking it this whole time. She blinks a few times to fully wake, then gazes into my eyes— brown on light brown.

"Did you just say what I think you said?"

I smirk. "Don't make a big deal out of it. There are, like, a billion emotions going through my head right now and the only one that makes any fucking sense is that I really like kissing you. I'll deal with any repercussions later."

A grin curls her lips. "I don't want to say I told you so, *buuut*, I told you—"

We're wasting too much time, so I just go for it and cut her off with a kiss.

It's deep and long and I never want it to end. Then my hands go limp because I have no fucking clue what I'm doing. This is usually the part in the proceedings where I'd unbutton the guy's pants and do some hand stuff to keep him satisfied. But what do I do for a girl?

Thankfully Aamani has some kind of sexual Spider-Sense and takes the lead. She raises my limp arms from my side and places them around her waist. I feel the curve in the small of her back. Her skin is smooth. Then she sweeps my neck with kisses. Each kiss only lasts a fraction of a second, but the pure bliss of each one makes time stand still. Then she submerges under the covers, pulling me along for the ride. We exchange smiles and then she ventures down deeper, raising my shirt and peppering my stomach with more time-manipulating kisses. Her touch is softer and more calculated than a guy's. She's not rushing like they do. She takes her time to cherish every touch, every kiss. She works her way back up to my breasts, and unlike the last person who tried to undo my bra (I'm looking at you and your Hulk hands, Calvin Mitchell), she locates the clasp and removes it in one fluid motion.

Why is all of this so much easier with a girl? Are guys really that fucking clueless when it comes to knowing what we want? If Calvin's anything to go by, then the answer is a resounding yes.

I should probably stop reminiscing on Hulk Hands and start carrying my weight in all of this. So I go to undo her bra. I quickly realize she's not wearing one. This makes me jealous because I'd love to sleep without a bra strangling my tits. After I had those bras stolen, I came up with the following equation: Bra + Crack House = Bra Stays On. Now it's a habit.

I cup her right breast and kiss her quick. I must be doing something right because she lets out a soft moan. I shush her with a smile and she giggles and whispers, "Sorry." I always thought touching another pair of tits would be nasty or mad dull, especially since I've had my own pair all my life and having tits isn't really all that great. Sports bras, crackhead pervs stealing said bras, they gave my girl Tonya back problems, having to hide your nipples when it's cold and every boy in gym class can't stop staring. Tits kinda suck. Boys put them on a pedestal. But Aamani's reaction to my hands on her body has awoken something in me and I don't want to stop making her feel this way. So I kiss them. She really likes this. Then she runs her fingers through my hair.

Just as it's getting good, Lindsay starts to stir.

Shit.

We freeze under the covers. Maybe if we don't move she can't see us.

My hand is frozen on her left breast and hers is on my right ass cheek. My heart's about to rip through my chest, it's beating so hard.

It's like Aamani said. It's my decision if and when I want to come out, and my heart's beating because I'd hate for that to be taken from me before I even know how I'm going to navigate all of this, all because Lindsay's a fucking owl and won't go to bed.

The sheets rustle.

Am I sweating? Because it feels like I'm sweating.

In the midst of me thinking about all the ways I'm going to get clowned and hated on when this gets out, Aamani cracks a smile, which makes me smile, which makes her snicker, which makes me snort, which is bad because we are not being silent.

Lindsay hasn't ripped the covers off of us yet, exposing us TMZ-style. Maybe she's still asleep or is too tired to realize that giant bulge under the covers is Aamani and me getting our freak on.

Know what? Fuck it.

I put my finger to my lips, signaling Aamani to remain silent because I'm going out to check on the situation. I pull the covers back and peek out. Lindsay has rolled over on her side with her back to us, wrapped in her blanket like a human burrito. Now she's bumpin' Rick Ross. I nod to the faint beat for a second, then pop my head back under the covers.

"Coast clear?"

I nod.

And we're kissing again.

Now that we know Lindsay is knocked out, we push our luck. She slips off my ball shorts and runs her hand up my thigh. I return the favor and pull down her Doctor Who pajama pants, which she has to wiggle out of. Then we slip away into our singularity.

CHAPTER 22

When we graduate in a month, I might never see Aamani again. She'll go off to some Ivy League school where she'll fall for someone who's comfortable in their sexuality. Or her family will move her back to India, as far away from me as possible. But no matter how far apart we end up, I will now see Aamani's face every time I close my eyes.

Basically, Aamani has forever ruined sleep for me.

The sun spills through the blinds. I squint and turn away, wishing the sun would leave me the fuck alone so I can get at least three full hours of sleep. Then I feel this weight on my chest, pushing everything that should not be pushed down, down. I blink a few times so my eyes can calibrate to the morning's smile. I look down and see Aamani, dreaming peacefully.

I never want to move from this spot. How did I fall for someone like her, captain of the STEM team, a girl? The only way I can think to explain it is by doing the math.

There are 325.7 million people in the United States, and roughly 12.7 percent of them identify as LGBTQIA+, which equals about 41,363.9 people. Not to mention there were 4.1 million people born in 2004, Aamani and I being two of them, making the chances of us finding one another, like, 1 in 0.010 percent. Now those are some shitty odds. And they get even worse when you factor in the odds that Aamani's family would choose a convenience store in Hargrove to buy, and Britt would choose the exact day of Aamani's first shift to rob it; that Aamani would beat me over the fence and I'd take a bullet that hits me in the precise nerve to severely hinder my right leg's motor skills; that Aamani would convince me to join STEM; and that she would show me the stars and it would make me crave the universe.

It doesn't add up. The math states she shouldn't be here in my arms.

Until you add the one consistent variable.

Since our first encounter, I have been the ideal variable, an element, feature, or factor that is liable to change. And whether it was my confusion of who or what I am, or how I'm perceived, I have been in purgatory, never fully committed to one side or the other, constantly battling my past and my future.

And when I account for that, the equation is clear and the math adds up:

Me + Aamani = Love

And if I'm crucified for showing that, well then: Come at me.

She's beautiful and she's . . . wait. I'm still in bed with Aamani?! I look down. My bra is on the floor as evidence.

Shit. Don't panic. No one's awake. At least the rest of my clothes are on. Maybe I can slip out before—

I don't get to finish my thought. Lindsay yawns and stretches, because of course she does.

I panic and push Aamani's head off me and roll out of bed like I'm on fire. This doesn't wake Aamani. But my good leg gets caught in the sheet and sends me face-first to the floor.

Ow.

"We have to defend Gallifrey, Doctor!" Aamani shouts as she wakes from her apparent *Doctor Who* adventure.

Lindsay looks down at me as I rub the right side of my face that just backhanded the floor. I quickly grab my bra.

"Why are you on the floor holding a bra?"

"Oh, uh . . ." I look to Aamani for help. She does nothing but rub her eyes and yawn. "Looking for my phone?"

"Under Aamani's bed? With a bra?"

Think.

"Clearly you're not familiar with Einstein's theory of location. He discovered that if you're holding something you wore when you lost an item, it will release a chemical in your brain to help you remember it. And here I thought you were up on all your scientific theories."

Nice.

"Your phone's on your cot," Aamani points out, finally joining the woken world. "And that's not a real theory."

I press my mouth into a tight line. "Thanks."

I get up and walk over to my cot, glad it's too early for Lindsay to put two and two together. I look at my phone to maintain the illusion that I've been dying to find it.

"Holy shit."

"What?" Aamani asks. "Did your phone from 2007 finally die?"

"No, I have, like, a hundred missed texts and calls."

"Well, aren't you popular," Lindsay adds.

I swipe left and read the most recent texts.

Jordan: Where R U? I'm freaking the
fuck out

Krystal: WTF CALL ME!!!

I tap on Krystal's name and wait for the ring.

She answers on the second ring.

"The fuck, yo?!" She takes a huge breath, then hesitates, as if she's unsure of what to say next. It sounds like she's been crying. I haven't heard Krystal cry since Nassir's funeral. "Where have you been?! Everyone has been calling you!"

"My bad. My phone was on silent and I just woke up. I'm in DC at this STEM thing. What's up? Everything cool?"

"Did you even look at your phone?!"

"Nah, I just saw texts from you and Jordan and called you. Why are you snapping on me?"

There's a striking silence. I don't know why, but it feels like it's a lifetime before she speaks.

"They—they got Britt."

The words don't register.

"Hold up, hold up. What are you talking about?" I almost laugh. "I just saw her. Who got Britt?"

"Some Crew niggas ran up on her last night. She's gone."

I cup my hand over my mouth and bite through my bottom lip, spilling blood, trying not to cry. It's not working. Krystal's probably still on the line, but I can't hear her. I'm rendered deaf. There's a sharp ringing in my head that feels like a grenade exploded by my ear.

What is Krystal saying? Why is she making up lies?

The ringing gradually fades and is replaced with Aamani's voice. She sounds as though she's light-years away, floating in the vacuum of space. She wants to know what's wrong. I can't tell her because then it would be real and I'll be trapped in this nightmare. I have to wake up. I need to wake up. Why can't I wake up?

I don't move as Aamani retrieves the phone and places it

over her ear. "What happened? ... It's Aamani, Lex's friend from STEM ... Krystal, we have, like, three classes together ... Yes, the Muslim one, even though I'm not and that's super offensive." She gives a few nods, listening. "Oh fuck ... that's—that's terrible."

Aamani instinctively puts down the phone and throws her arms around me, pulling me into her warm embrace. "I'm so sorry, Lex. God, I'm so sorry."

When I feel her tears on my cheek, I know it's for real. There's no escaping this nightmare. I now live in a world without Britt. Without my dear friend.

Tears roll down my cheek, I quickly wipe them away and take back the phone. People die in Hargrove all the time, I remind myself, trying anything to remain strong. It hurts to do so. Like someone put a hot iron to my heart.

"W–what happened?" I ask, trying to steady my voice.

"Kyle told me she stole a bunch of Crew shit. We're talking a whole stash and like two Gs. They found out it was her and, well ... you know how that shit go. I–I still can't believe it. Like, what the fuck, yo? I was just with her last night kicking it with Jordan and them, and now my dad's scheduling her funeral. What the fuck, Lex? What are we going to do? We have to pop back." Her voice breaks as she releases more tears.

I punch the dresser, splitting the cheap wood. "Fuck!" Lindsay and Aamani jump. I pinch the bridge of my nose, trying to collect myself. It's pointless; the whole thing keeps running through my mind on an infinite loop like breaking news on the bottom of the ESPN ticker: *I got Britt killed.* I was the one who stole the drugs and the money. Not her. I should be dead.

"I shouldn't have helped her," I mumble.

"What?"

"Nothing. I said it wasn't even their drugs. She was stealing it back for Devon."

"Who told you that? All of it was theirs. Devon even gave her the corner on 57th because she did it. She couldn't shut up about it all night, saying she blew up their car or some shit."

Our last act as friends was Britt using me. She knew I wouldn't help her steal Crew shit for Devon, so she put on that whole act of double-crossing him and needing my help so Devon wouldn't kill her. Yet the whole time she was doing it to impress his bitch-ass.

"So what are we going to do? We have to get them back. I already talked to Jordan and Kyle, and Devon said he got our backs if we want to ride out on these niggas. You down?"

I look over at Aamani and Lindsay. They're both staring at me. If I do this and it goes wrong, my future will be done. No scholarship. No better life. Just jail or a casket, the two cards it seems everyone born in Hargrove is dealt. But it was the money I stole that paid for our trip. It was my hands that took the backpack from the closet. I don't deserve a future. I deserve the hand Britt was dealt.

"Yeah, I'm in," I say.

"A'ight, hurry back. We're gonna meet at Devon's later today and figure this shit out."

I hang up the phone and start stuffing my books and the few shirts I brought in my backpack. Every time I think of Britt laid out on the corner, her still, emotionless face pressed against the cold, coarse pavement, her blood soaking the gravel, I'm drowned in a tidal wave of guilt.

"Lindsay, can you please give us a minute?" Aamani requests.

"Um, no. I want to know what's going on. Why are you both crying and acting like someone died?"

"Lindsay!" Aamani snaps. She tames her frustration. "Please. Just go outside for two minutes."

Lindsay stands and slips into her Chucks. "Fine." She whips her long brown hair and steps outside.

Aamani takes my hand, stopping me from grabbing my final book. "Finish later. Just talk to me," she says. Her voice is warm and consoling like a psychiatrist's. "What happened?"

I think about the kids at Marcus's and how they're now on their own because of me. Because I didn't consider the consequences of my actions. Because I didn't have Britt's back.

"You know that shit I helped her steal? Well, now she's dead because of it," I answer through gritted teeth.

"Lex——" She puts her hand on my shoulder. I shrug it off. "I know you're upset. I can't begin to imagine what you're going through. But this isn't on you. Promise me you won't do anything irrational."

"My best friend is dead because of *me*!" I cry, spraying spit from my mouth. "And you want me to do nothing? Nah, I'm not about to let my friend go out like that."

"I know, I know, but maybe we should just, like, tell Mrs. H and let the cops handle it. She's going to find out anyway if she hasn't already."

"So you want me to not do shit, and also snitch? You got me fucked up."

She twists her face. "What?! No. I'm not saying that. I——"

"How do you still not get it? Even after how your parents treated you. Parents, teachers, police, they don't care about us. We're out here alone. Britt was alone. I should've had her back. I shouldn't . . ." My throat clenches. "I shouldn't have helped her steal that stash."

"It's not your fault, Lex."

"Will you stop fucking saying that?! I stole the drugs and the money. It is a hundred percent my fault."

"Okay, then what's your big plan, huh?" she asks, throwing up her hands, exasperated. "Please, do pray tell how whatever stupid, 'gangsta' thing you're planning on doing is going to bring her back? How it's going to help you better yourself—your life?"

"A few people from the block and some BMs are going to bust back. We're meeting at Devon's later today."

She looks at me as if I'm a stranger, her eyes wide and taken aback.

"And you're okay with taking a life?"

I suck my teeth and petulantly look away. "Whatever. You don't know me."

"No, no, don't go getting defensive like you always do. If you can honestly look me in the eye and say you can shoot someone, then you're right. I don't know you."

"What the fuck do you want from me?" The tears have built back up and are threatening to break through.

"Listen to me, Lex." Her voice returns to that comforting melody, the one she had when we first met, the one that makes you feel loved. "This isn't you. You don't go around shooting drug dealers. Last I checked your name isn't Liam Neeson or John Wick. Britt chose this life. And you chose to help your friend when she was in need. You didn't know what was going to happen. This isn't on you."

I think back to our last conversation, Britt admitting that she's always wanted me to be the one to make it out. I miss her already. All the time we wasted this year over petty beef. Why'd you have to go and get yourself killed, Britt? Why?

"So can we please just go downstairs and tell Mrs. H and let her handle it? I promise the right people will pay for what they did."

I gather the strength to look her in her big, light-brown eyes. More tears roll down my cheeks. I don't even feel them at this point. All that remains of my feelings, of me, is sorrow, anger, and confusion. Fourteen years of friendship. The shit we've seen. We ride together. We die together. Bad girls for life. We were stupid to copy that shit. It sounds cool in the movies, but in real life they're hollow words. There's no honor in these streets. No poetic justice in the way Britt died. She's just another statistic now. A soon to be forgotten hashtag of a redundant movement.

"You do what you gotta do. And I'ma do me."

I grab my shit and head to the bus.

Britt's Instagram fills up with posts and hashtags: #GoneTooSoon #NeverForget #StopTheViolence #TrueSoldier #Grove4Life #RIP. Everyone on the bus is quiet and respectful about it. There are no sympathy apologies like "Sorry for your loss," or any of that "She's in a better place" bullshit.

I can't sit still. I'm just ready to get back to Hargrove and end this nightmare; stop this searing pain in my heart.

Mrs. H turns around in her seat behind Alan. "Hey, why the long faces, guys?"

Brian speaks on our behalf. "We just really hate Texas. Especially cowboys—the football team and their stupid *Red Dead Redemption* hats."

Lindsay seconds the lie. "Yeah, Texas can suck a dick."

"*Lindsay*, watch your mouth," Mrs. H checks her. "I know you all wanted to win, but you should be extremely proud of what you accomplished this weekend. Making the semifinals of a national tournament is no small feat. I'm very, very proud of each and every one of you." She smiles. "And I don't want to hear that kind of language again. You hear me, Lindsay?"

Lindsay nods.

I almost smile, knowing my STEM family has my back.

We're a block away from the school. I grip my backpack, ready to hobble-bolt off this bus as soon as Alan swings the doors open.

There's a tap on my shoulder and I swing around ready to throw a haymaker. I'm extra jumpy. It's Matthew. My jaw almost hits the floor. Because the bus is moving and we do not stand when the bus is moving. I know this because Matthew briefed us on the Philadelphia School District Handbook before we left for DC and informed us that fourteen percent of all school bus-related accidents occur when a passenger is out of their seat while the bus is in motion.

"This is a dark time for you. But in the end, it's only a passing thing, this shadow; even darkness must pass," he says, offering his *Lord of the Rings* necklace. He holds it out beneath his waist like we're making a drug deal.

I study the ring. "What's this for?"

"I'm aware of your recent loss. I suspect you need the power of the One Ring more than me. Imagine you're Sauron and this will give you strength."

"Matthew, I don't know . . . I can't take your ring."

"You may have lost all hope. But where there's life there's hope, and need of vittles."

I look at the ring, then back up at him. "Vittles?"

"It's a fourteenth-century word that is an alternate way of saying *victual,* which basically means food."

"Why do I feel these quotes are from *Lord of the Rings*?"

"They are indeed, specifically the first book. It is an extremely wise novel with many quotes that pertain to your current situation of grieving."

I've never encountered someone more courageous. I hold up my hair and put the necklace around my neck. And you know what, I do feel a glimmer of hope. I know this isn't the time to be getting soft, not with the task that lies ahead, but dude just gave me his most prized possession so I can feel better. So I stand, making for two bus violations, and give him a hug.

"Thank you. For real."

"You're welcome," he says, pulling out of the hug. "Now we should sit down, as there is currently a two-point-three percent chance the bus tips over and we die a horrifying death because we're standing."

He returns to his seat like it was no big deal, like he just gave me a stick of gum.

I'm going to miss my STEM family.

CHAPTER 23

I've never been strapped before, but considering what's about to go down I felt it would be a good time to start. So I swung by the apartment and took the pistol Randy keeps under Mom's nightstand. He won't miss it. Or maybe he will. Honestly, I don't care.

The cold steel rubs against my lower back and the bus seat. With each passing second, I question my decision. I'm no killer, no matter how many times I've listened to "Hit 'Em Up." But if I don't go through with this, then I'll be labeled a bitch, and I'll have let my other friends ride into battle without me, like I did Britt.

The bus passes the corner where that cop shot Nassir. It was only a year ago the corner was covered in flowers, candles, and photos of Nassir. Now it's just another corner to sell on. I don't want that for Britt. I don't want her to become a forgotten hashtag. I want her life and death to have meant something. I want the hood to know that Brittney Wallace's death will not go unpunished. That you don't mess with Hargrove.

I pull the cord and the bus stops in front of Devon's apartment building. It's funny. This place used to be a safe haven—from the cops, The Crew. Now it feels more like a tomb.

My palms are sweaty. I touch the pistol to make sure I can still unholster it quickly when the moment comes. The weight of the pistol is causing my leg to flare up. I suck it up and head inside, ready to accept my fate, to face the consequences of my actions.

I stop dead in my tracks, as Aamani, who is sitting cross-legged beside the elevator, stands.

"What are you doing here?!"

She dusts off her leggings and the bottom of her kurta. "If you're really going to go through with this, then I'm coming with you."

"The hell you are. This isn't a game, Aamani. I'm not trying to have your death on my conscience too."

"And I'm not trying to have yours on mine," she rebuts. "I'm coming."

"Aamani, fucking leave!" I bark.

"No," she answers stubbornly. "I'll leave if you leave."

I bite down on my bottom lip, pissed.

Fine. She doesn't want to listen. I'll make her listen.

I whip out the pistol from under my shirt and point it at her. She takes a step back and slowly raises her hands, tensing up. Her light-brown eyes widen, pleading.

"Okay, ha-ha. Stop playing around, Lex. This isn't funny."

I swallow the lump in my throat and steady my voice. "I'm not asking anymore. Leave. Now."

The gun is like a tambourine, it's shaking so much.

Aamani holds firm. "No. I'm not leaving you. I know everyone else in your life has, but I'm not. We're going to get through all of this together. Because that's what real friends do. So I guess you're just going to have to go ahead and shoot me."

She peers into my soul with those big brown eyes; her eyes a magical key, unlocking me. My finger grips the trigger. She tries to remain poised, unfazed. She's calling my bluff. She knows I could never hurt her. It would be like hurting myself. I drop the gun. It clangs as it collides with the dirty, cracked tile.

Aamani cautiously bends over and picks it up. "I'll just hold on to this until we can properly dispose of it. Now can we please leave?"

"No. I'm not leaving until I at least talk to Devon. I can't just bail on my friends like that. You don't understand."

"No, I get it. How about we go and talk to him *together*, and after we go get some Kit Kats and talk it out—deal?"

"Deal."

Big Lee is guarding Devon's door on the top floor. I'd call it a penthouse, but that would be disrespecting actual penthouses. It's just a shitty apartment on the top floor of a run-down apartment building. Nothing special.

Big Lee is what would happen if Shaq ate Biggie. I could do laps in his jeans and bench press his platinum chain.

"What's good, Lex?" Lee says, stepping aside to let me pass. I limp by. "Sorry about your homegirl. We gonna get them niggas though."

I drop my head at the thought of Britt. "Thanks."

Aamani takes a step forward to follow me, but Big Lee blocks her path. Forget building a wall. Trump should've hired this guy.

"And who you be?"

In my head I think, *please don't correct his grammar please don't correct his grammar.*

Aamani puts out her hand. "Aamani Chakrabarti at your service." Big Lee looks down at her outstretched hand as if he's going to swallow it whole. I facepalm. Aamani retracts her handshake. "I'm with her."

Big Lee grunts, then looks to me for confirmation. I'd leave her out here with him, but God knows what he'd do to her when she starts going on about Doctor Who, subject-verbs, and stars being black bodies. So she's probably safer with me, where I can keep an eye on her.

"She's cool," I vouch.

He grunts and steps aside.

Aamani tips an invisible hat to him. "Good day to you, sir."

I shake my head. Yeah, she's safer with me.

The house smells like we're inside a blunt. The contact high alone is enough to make you cough, which Aamani, like a noob, does. This is probably because they converted the back room into a greenhouse populated by nothing but weed plants. I'm also pretty sure it doubles as a panic room because the door has a titanium lock on it. I didn't even know that was a real thing. I thought titanium doors only existed in Marvel movies.

Devon's on the couch in the living room, hunched over a table filled with guns. There's enough firepower to arm a small nation. Kyle, Krystal, and a few other guys who worked the corner with Britt, Dre and Wallace, are in the armchairs adjacent to the couch. There's no Jordan. Kyle pops a new clip into his pistol. They're all repping BM with matching bandanas tied around their biceps; even Krystal has one. All I can think is that her parents would be losing their shit if they knew what she was about to do. I mean, it's been a while since Britt and I attended one of Krystal's dad's services, but I'd bet the Bible strongly frowns upon drive-bys.

Krystal runs over to me and gives me a long hug, like we're

CHARLES A. BUSH

family. I close my eyes and breathe her in. For a second, it feels like I'm hugging Britt.

"You a'ight? This shit's crazy."

I try not to think about Britt. "Yeah, I guess. I don't know." That's a lie. I know. I'm not okay. "Where's Jordan?"

She looks at me and shakes her head. "He bitched out. Said he couldn't jeopardize Nova. I knew he never gave a fuck about Britt."

My head drops in shame. I fear her reaction when I tell her I can't do this.

"That's not fair," I defend. "Jordan has a right to look after his future. He has a full ride."

"Whatever," she dismisses. "Fuck him."

Kyle stands and daps me up.

Devon doesn't bother getting up. He thinks he's Pablo Escobar, that just because he gives out turkeys for Thanksgiving and sponsors an AAU basketball traveling team that everyone in Hargrove is his family, but we're not. Between the drugs he populates our streets and our schools with, and how he employed Britt to transport said drugs between blocks in her backpack when she was ten, I never liked the guy. I always acted like I did because he's the kind of guy you want to have in your corner on the streets. If people know you're cool with Devon, they won't fuck with you. Or at least that's what I thought before last night, before Britt.

He picks up a semiautomatic—as if I'm not nervous enough—and turns to me.

"And where the fuck have you been?"

Devon has about four teardrop tattoos beneath his right eye, signifying people he's killed. One more teardrop and he'll look less like a gangsta and more like me at the end of *Infinity War* when my boy Groot turns to ash. For him to basically run Hargrove, he's not all that intimidating—without the arms dealer amount of guns in front of him, of course. I'll put it this way: if Big Lee is what happens when Shaq eats Biggie, Devon is what happens when Lil Wayne swears off carbs and gluten.

He notices Aamani behind me and pivots. "Yo, who the fuck let in Gandhi?"

Aamani goes to offer a handshake like she did with Big Lee. I shoot her a look like *uh-uh, that nerd stuff isn't going to fly with him.* She does the right thing and lets me do the talking.

"I was in DC. And this is my homegirl Aamani."

Devon snarls. "I don't give a fuck who she is. What's she doing up in my house?"

This is just one of the reasons why I didn't want her to come. I'm not here to play the *Explain Aamani* game.

"She's cool. She's with me."

"Yeah, she's a'ight," Kyle vouches. "She was at my party when they hit us with that drive-by."

Devon's eyes linger on Aamani as he continues to size her up. He puts down the semi and picks up a Glock instead, cocking it to make sure there's one in the chamber. He grips the handle and rests it in his lap. "They say you're cool, so I'ma let you stay. But I don't know you. You make one wrong move and I'm spilling your brains on my floor. And I just vacuumed that shit. You feel me?"

Aamani nods.

I interrupt. "Ay, I know y'all about to ride out on those Crew who got Britt, but I just wanted to tell you straight up I can't go. But whatever y'all need here I got you."

"Whatcha mean, *you can't go*?" Devon scoffs. "I thought you were a soldier. Don't tell me you're bitchin' out like that college nigga."

Krystal is devastated. She looks as if she wants to pick up one of the guns and shoot me. "What are you talking about?"

"I just..." I lose my train of thought. The look on Krystal's face, like I'm betraying her, nearly rips my heart in two all over again. "I'm just not about to roll up in Crew territory, shooting up people who had nothing to do with this. You don't have to do this either."

"Ay, don't come at Krystal with that bullshit," Devon says, speaking on her behalf. "We know exactly who pulled the trigger and where them niggas be at. And before you decide to not do shit about it, you should know they know you stole their money."

Fear sweeps across my body like a breeze. "What?"

"You think your homegirl didn't report to me like everyone else? This is my fucking hood. I let you keep it because she said you helped get the drugs. Consider it your cut."

There's too much information coming all at once. My mind is pulling in a hundred different directions.

"You ain't gonna say thank you?" Devon asks, a smirk in his voice. "Y'all young bouls is mad ungrateful."

"How do you know who shot her?"

He chuckles. The teardrops bunch up on his cheek like little jellybeans. "Come on, lil' Lex. How long you know me? Ain't nothin' go on in my hood without me knowin'."

"If you're all-knowing, then why didn't you stop them from killing Britt?"

Annoyance skewers his face. "I'ma let that slide because your homegirl died. But watch your mouth." I somehow refrain from telling him to go fuck himself. Also, that's probably not the best thing to say to someone holding a loaded gun. "The niggas that ran up on her are BMs—that nigga Troy and lil' Jerome. They runnin' with Crew now."

Troy and Jerome? The whites of my knuckles turn red. They were kickin' it at Kyle's party with us. Jerome's in my gym class. He used to flirt with Britt mad hard. They're traitors? They killed my friend? That's the biggest sin you can commit in Hargrove, turning your back on the block. How could they do that?

I guess it doesn't matter. They did it and they have to pay.

Devon puts his arm around me. His dreads smell like weed and months of unwashed hair. He holds the Glock out for me to take.

"Now tell me you ain't still tryin' to ride?"

Without hesitation, I take the gun.

"What I tell y'all?" he says to Kyle and the rest of them as if he's addressing a class. "Just like Britt. A straight ridah."

Krystal's face shows her renewed faith in me.

Aamani reaches for my shoulder.

I turn to her, trying to keep my voice down. "I'm sorry. I know you don't understand, but I have to do this. Go. This isn't your fight."

Aamani bites her bottom lip and shakes her head. "I'm not letting you do this."

"You don't have a choice. Now please go before it's too late."

"Y'all fucking or somethin'?" Devon interrupts. "What's with all the whispering?"

"I was just telling her she needs to leave."

"I'm not going anywhere," Aamani says, putting her foot down. "I'm going with you guys."

"What? No, she's not!" I quickly debunk.

Devon loses his shit laughing. "And what the fuck you gonna do, Gandhi?"

"I'm going to use this." She whips out Randy's gun. I forgot she had it.

Everyone scrambles for their piece and now there's a standoff, everyone pointing their gun at someone else.

"Who you pullin' a piece on?" Devon barks.

I try to intervene. "It's my gun. She was just holding it for me." I carefully remove the gun from Aamani's hands and tuck it in my jeans.

Everyone slowly lowers their weapon.

"Ay, Lee!" Devon shouts. "Your fat ass needs to stop thinking about Big Macs and start doing your fucking job. What the hell am I paying you for, bruh?!"

"My bad!" Lee calls from the other side of the door.

"So you think you're ready to ride with the BMs, huh?"

"NO!" I answer for her. "No, she isn't. Right, *Aamani*?" I say with emphasis, begging her not to do this.

"I'm ready," she answers confidently.

"Shit. No wonder you fuck with her, Lex. Bitch cold," Kyle says.

"We do have an extra spot in the truck because Jordan's bitch-ass bailed," Krystal points out.

"I mean, her people do stay strapped," Wallace adds. "I saw it on that Bradley Cooper sniper movie. Kids over there get rocket launchers and shit at, like, ten."

"A'ight then," Devon concedes. "Both of y'all ridin'. Let's go."

I look at Aamani with fury.

What have I done?

It's cramped in Devon's Ford. Aamani's riding bitch in the middle with Krystal and me on opposite sides of her. Our shoulders are rubbing against each other so much, if we tried we could probably start a fire. There's a heavy tint on all the windows so it feels like it's nighttime even though it's only six o'clock and the evening sun is a blood-orange hue.

Dre and Big Lee are in the car behind us for backup. They got caught at a red light, so they're several blocks behind.

I squint out the tinted window as we drive down Ogden Street, home of the open fire hydrant Britt and I used to splash in on sweltering summer nights, and the park where the boys first let me play pickup basketball with them. I grew up with these people. They're more my family than my own mother. My memories are scattered throughout Hargrove, encompassing every corner and street. And Troy and Jerome are part of those memories.

I look down at the pistol in my hand, then back out the window at the MLK mural that the Boys & Girls Club painted on the side of the vacant house on the corner of Spruce. Despite the unforgivable act Troy and Jerome committed, I can't risk a stray bullet hitting an innocent bystander or even *a* bullet hitting one of them. And if this makes me a bitch or not enough of a soldier, then so be it.

Aamani has been staring at the gun in her lap the entire ride, as though if she were to look away it would magically cock itself and shoot her. I know she's scared and regretting having ever become friends with me.

She shouldn't be here.

I shouldn't be here.

Maybe at one point I belonged here, after I was shot and before the consistent variable that is Aamani came roaring into my life like a comet. But not anymore. I'm no gangsta. I'm a supernova.

I take a deep breath to summon the courage to speak. "Stop the car," I say under my breath, looking to the front seat at Wallace driving.

"For what? Their house is right up there," Devon snarls, using the barrel of his gun to point out Troy's tiny row home.

"I don't care. Aamani and I are getting out!"

Aamani releases an exasperated sigh of relief that sounds like she's been holding it in since 2012. "Oh my God. Thank you! I was beginning to think you weren't going to change your mind. I don't even want to touch this thing." She drops the gun on the floor as if it were burning her hands.

"Nah, it don't work like that," Devon says, grilling us in the rearview mirror. "Nobody's getting out until the job's done."

"You can't keep us hostage," I protest.

"I can do whatever the fuck I want!" he barks, turning to us in his seat with his hand on the trigger. I don't know about Aamani, but I almost piss myself. "Now let's do this shit, Wallace. Pull up on these niggas slow. I told them to meet me outside to make a drop. They don't know we know they're some traitors."

"What about Lee and Dre?"

"They'll catch up. Now drive."

Right on cue, Troy and Jerome come walking out the house to the curb.

"This ain't *Fast and Furious*, nigga. I said go slow," Devon scolds.

Wallace abides and brings the car to a creep.

I tap Aamani on the thigh and nod to the door handle. She nods to let me know we're on the same page. We silently unbuckle our seat belts and then I pull the handle.

Nothing.

Fucking child lock.

Devon and Krystal ready their guns. I flash Krystal a pleading look, begging her not to do this.

She gives me a stank-eye, having lost all respect for me. "Roll the window down," she instructs, moving into position.

I do as I'm told. Aamani's hand slips into mine and I hold it tight, apologizing with each squeeze. We duck beneath the seats with our heads between our legs like we're making an emergency landing on an airplane.

Brat! Brat! Devon's automatic rings out first to commence the shots, crackling through the air like tiny claps of thunder. Krystal follows suit and lets off half her clip in quick succession.

Several bullets clang off the side of the car and Devon and Krystal drop for cover. Another bullet shatters the back window, spraying pieces of glass on the back seat. A few pieces get into my hair.

Aamani cries out in horror. I squeeze her hand tight, reminding her that I'm here and I'll protect her with my life if I have to.

"Shit!" Devon yells from behind the cover of his door. He quickly rolls up the window. "Pull off! Pull off!"

Two more shots pepper the trunk.

Wallace slams on the accelerator, peeling out of harm's way. More gunshots echo in the distance. Big Lee and Dre must have caught up.

Wallace keeps looking in his rearview as if we're being followed. "Did y'all get 'em?"

"I for sure dropped Troy's snitchin' ass. But then those two other niggas with Crew colors came running out blasting," answers Devon.

"I think I clipped Jerome," Krystal adds proudly, struggling to regain her breath. Her adrenaline is racing.

Aamani is in tears beside me, and has yet to let go of my hand.

"Yo, turn this bitch around," Devon instructs. "We're going back. They got Dre and Lee pinned down."

Aamani is going to have a nervous breakdown if we're forced to endure another shootout. And I don't foresee us being as lucky to make it out unscratched this time.

Aamani squeezes tighter like she's about to give birth, and follows it up with another cry.

I pull out my pistol and point it at Wallace with intent to shoot.

"Let us the fuck out. Now."

"The fuck, bruh?!" he says, tensing up at the wheel. "Get your girl, Krystal."

"I'm not playing with you," I double down. "Let us out."

"What are you doing, Lex?"

"Shut up, Krystal!"

Devon sucks his teeth. "Just let these little bitches out. Just know when they come for their money, I ain't got your back."

I retract the gun and toss it on the floor. "I'm cool with that."

They undo the child lock and let us out. As soon as I shut the door, Wallace peels out back toward the firefight.

I quickly wrap my arms around Aamani, holding her suffocatingly tight. I don't care if the whole world sees.

"I'm so fucking sorry, Aamani. Jesus, I–I don't know what I was thinking. Fuck, I'm sorry." I pull away to get a better look at her. "Are you okay? Are you hurt?"

She's inconsolable.

She goes to answer, but chokes on her tears, and falls back into my arms.

I hold her until they subside.

CHAPTER 24

I text Aamani, too scared I'll back out if I hear her voice.

> Me: I'm coming to the store today. We need to talk.

My phone pings.

> Aamani: Not a good idea. My parents are still super pissed. They hate you more than they hate Trump.

> Aamani: I'll come to your house

> Me: No I need to talk to your parents

> Aamani:

> Aamani: Are you insane?!?! I'm serious about the Trump thing. I'm coming over.

I pinch the bridge of my nose. She's not getting it. So I do the worst thing you can (children, don't try this at home)—I text without thinking.

> Me: You can't come over because I don't live there. I've been

> living in the crack house on
> Poplar since November. My mom
> kicked me out, I'm down to my
> last two bras, and I need to
> talk to your parents. So STFU
> I'm ducking coming over!

Me: *Fucking

Her speech bubble and ellipsis flash on the screen for a full five minutes. I'm expecting a novel.

My phone pings.

Aamani: Ok

I walk into the Super Mart. Both Mr. and Mrs. Chakrabarti are behind the register. Aamani is restocking the Kit Kats, of all things. I grin at the irony.

Mrs. Chakrabarti comes from around the counter and heads straight for me.

She starts throwing haymakers. They don't hurt or anything. She's a little, old Indian woman. The only thing hurt is my pride as I cower, soaking up her punches. "Tumhaari himmat kaise hui! Tum humaari beti ko maar daalne waale the!"

"I ... don't ... know ... what"—I try to speak in between punches—"you're ... saying ..."

I have a good idea, though. She's probably going on about how I'm a piece of shit who should stay away from her daughter or she'll be forced to strangle me with her sari.

"Mommy, stop! Ruken!"

"Mita! Mita!" her dad yells, finally pulling her off me. He looks at me and adds, "You need to leave or I'm calling the police."

Mrs. Chakrabarti stares me down while catching her breath. Tears well in her eyes, bypassing the rage. "How dare you show up here after you put my little girl in a car with strangers who had guns."

"It wasn't like that, Mom!" Aamani pleads.

Her dad wants a piece and jumps in. "I said you were forbidden to see and talk to this girl, and you disobeyed me. First you tell us you like girls and now you run around with these hoodlums, getting into gunfights. You could've been killed. This is not some video game, beta. This is your life. You need to focus on your studies and preparing for university. This girl will do nothing but ruin your chances at a good Hindu life. Bevakooph ladakee!"

"It wasn't her fault, Baba."

Her dad's about to double down on me being the Antichrist when I cut him off.

"They're right, Aamani." I turn to her parents, who cut their eyes at me. "Mr. and Mrs. Chakrabarti, I came here today to tell you I am deeply sorry for my actions toward your daughter and your store this year. The truth is, before Aamani I wasn't a particularly good person. I stole. I cheated. I disrespected anyone with an ounce of authority. I made terrible decisions like I did the other day. I was pretty much the worst. But then I met your daughter. This girl is the smartest, bravest, and has the biggest heart of anyone I know. Like, she even makes Oprah look bad." I can't tell if they're following me or not, so I switch up analogies. "Aamani's like one of those saris you make her wear."

"*Make*?" her mom resents.

I continue, focused on making my point. "Look, uh . . . what I mean is that, like a sari, Aamani is unique and beautiful, and every moment with her feels like a special occasion. She has shown me galaxies and made me strive for the stars when, before, I didn't know I was capable of leaving the ground. And for that I am forever in your debt for raising someone so magnificent."

Her parents softly smile. "But with all due respect, you're both mad wrong." Aaand they're back to frowning. "You shouldn't be ashamed of Aamani. She is a supernova who lights up all in her path. Like, so what if she's a lesbian and would rather read comics and play video games than doing all that stupid Hindu stuff? Or that she'd rather dress up like Thor than wear a churidar every day. What you guys fail to realize is that she's actually proud of her heritage, minus the whole being whored out for an arranged marriage thing—that's just not cool. If either of you would take the time to read one of her comics or actually ask her how she feels about all of this, you'd see that her favorite character wears a kurta and goes to mosque, for fuck's sake. She should be celebrated for being her, for all that she's accomplished and is going to accomplish. Because I'm telling you, this girl right here is going to change the world. Like, I may not know much, but you can take that to the bank."

Their frowns relax.

"But you are right about one thing. She won't go on to do any of it if I'm bringing her down with me."

"Lex . . ." Aamani starts.

I cut her off. "No, Aamani. They're right. I almost got you killed. You shouldn't be around me. And if being apart is what's going to allow you to be great, then I'll do it. A good friend once held me back unwillingly. I'm not about to repeat her mistake. So, Mr. and

Mrs. Chakrabarti, you don't have to worry about me and your daughter anymore. I've fucked up someone's life for the last time."

I turn and walk out.

CHAPTER 25

alf of the school and Hargrove showed up for Britt's funeral—even Marcus. If he had it his way, he'd have taken her body down to the Schuylkill River and torched it *Game of Thrones*-style. Anything to save a buck of his government stipend. He didn't even spring for another preacher to fill in for Krystal's dad, who is too busy trying to deal with his own daughter's legal problems.

The cops arrested everyone at the shootout, including Devon, who killed Troy, making for two Hargrove funerals this week. Thankfully, Krystal has the aim of a stormtrooper and only managed to clip Jerome two times in the shoulder. He'll live. He'll probably use the shooting to jumpstart his rap career à la 50 Cent. I really wish Krystal would have gotten out of the car with me and Aamani. But I know how she felt. She felt she owed Britt, that she had to be street. And let me tell you, neither of us are. I was just lucky enough to have a friend like Aamani to help me figure that out. I mean, Krystal still secretly listens to the Jonas Brothers. You can't be hard when you're bumpin' "Burnin' Up."

The one silver lining is now that Devon's locked up, there's a vacuum of power in Hargrove. Meaning The Crew are more concerned with filling that than they are hunting me down.

I'm sitting in the pew, watching the boys from the foster home bawl their eyes out as the only person who truly cared for them is lying in a casket.

"This is some bullshit," a voice in the pew behind me says. I turn. Jordan's sitting there in a sharp black suit and skinny tie, looking like an extra in a Tyler Perry movie. "Half of these people didn't even fuck with Britt. And I don't know why these fake-ass teachers are here. They never gave a fuck about her. If they did they wouldn't have let her drop out. Like, what the fuck did they think was going to happen?"

"Yeah, well, not all of us can get a full ride to Villanova," I say, part bitchy and part jelly. "Slinging was one of the only things she was good at. I think deep down she always knew how this was going to end."

His head drops as if he's praying. I feel bad because it's not his fault. I'm just in no mood to listen to people bitch.

The organ starts up another hauntingly sad tune as people begin lining up to pay their respects to the casket.

"I just . . . fuck, yo, I should've done more," Jordan confesses, picking up his head and running his hand along his waves. "I was her man. I didn't do shit. I just watched her throw her life away."

As much as I'd like to blame it all on someone else, to rid myself of the survivor's guilt that is plaguing my soul, Jordan isn't that person. Honestly, I'm not sure there is anyone but Britt to blame.

"It wasn't anyone's job to keep her on the right path. We all have choices to make and she made hers. It's that simple. You did the right thing. She wouldn't have wanted you to be in that car, to risk Villanova over some dumb shit. Just like I know she didn't want me there either."

He stands and buttons his suit jacket. It's only when I look him in the eyes I can tell he's been crying. "Thanks, Lex. That means a lot." He takes a deep, calculated breath, gathering the strength to get in line. "And don't worry, you're gonna make it out too." He flashes his dimple and exits the pew.

I wait for the line to dwindle before I go up, after everyone has fulfilled their obligation to be able to say they *attended and it was a very lovely funeral*. These people don't know the shit we've been through.

I place my hand on the casket, feeling the aged wood against my skin. I blink away a few tears and think about Britt's dead, cold body lying in the casket, a hole where her brain used to be. She's not the first young Black person to be lying with their arms crossed on this very altar and won't be the last. She has been rendered another statistic, a victim to these streets who won't even make the ten o'clock news. It's bullshit. This shouldn't be the alternative to making it out.

I don't know how, but I'm going to start my own statistic. I'll be the first Black girl to make it out of Hargrove because of her brain, and not because I can dribble or slang.

I fist-bump the casket. "I got you, Britt," I whisper.

CHAPTER 26

Each day I'm finding it harder to keep my promise to Britt, as my time to get out of here fades. It's now April, only two months of school left, and my sole acceptance letter has come from a community college in Camden whose claim to fame is they accidentally accepted a Yorkie named Mr. Fluffy. So yeah, my academic out doesn't seem imminent at this point. But what did I expect? You get what you sign up for, right? I just wish I'd have listened to Aamani and applied to some better schools. I wish I'd have known my worth pre-Nationals.

Also, not that this has anything to do with my post-high-school plans, it's just annoying the fuck out of me, but people won't STFU about prom. You'd think Christ was scheduled to resurrect again next week. I know they make a big deal about prom in every teen movie and YA novel, but really who the hell wants to dress up like they're going to the Oscars just to hang out in the gym for a few hours, drinking watered-down Kool-Aid and dancing to shitty pop songs from the early 2000s? That's going to be a hard pass for me. I can't do the Stanky Leg to "Since U Been Gone." Also, there's the little fact that I'm not trying to be that pathetic person who shows up to prom alone.

This is the shit I think about while I sit in Mr. Hilbert's class, supposedly taking notes. It's his fault no one's listening. Well, part him, part my depressing community college future, because really, why bother trying when that's the bar I have to reach? But come on, bruh. I know it's premature because we still have finals, but senioritis has pretty much kicked in for everyone. Like, senior finals are basically the definition of *going through the motions*. Besides me and a couple other late applicants, most of our class has already gotten into their school of choice.

Rachel Brown saves us and interrupts, walking in and handing Mr. Hilbert a light-blue slip, which signifies it came from the principal's office.

Mr. Hilbert skims it, then looks up at me. I turn and look behind me, because I didn't do shit. "Alexis, get your stuff and go with Rachel."

"Ooh, got 'em," Trey teases with his hyena from *Lion King* cackle. A few others join in, because apparently we're in sixth grade.

I grab my stuff and walk to the front, passing Aamani's desk. We don't exchange looks. It's too hard. Seeing her every day, knowing we can't speak, can't be us.

"Ay, deny everything," Jordan advises with a dimpled smirk.

"You already know," I say, dapping him up on my way out.

When I get to the main office my first instinct is to beeline it to Principal Garrett's office to get yelled at for some shit I didn't do. All right, and sometimes for shit I did, but honestly, who hasn't ever wanted to hijack the morning announcements to blast "Juicy"? Britt and I can't be the only ones to have ever thought of turning the morning announcements into the Electric Factory.

Mrs. Rowe, the school administrator-slash-Garrett's glorified secretary-slash-everyone's school mom, stops me. "Uh-uh, Miss Duncan, you're here to see me." She waves me over with her finger. She has long purple press-on nails that match the color of her thick reading glasses. "And pull down that hood. Actin' like you don't have any home training. I swear."

I'm confused. If I'm not here to get yelled at by Principal Garrett, then why am I here? Because school mom or not, I'm ninety-eight percent sure Mrs. Rowe doesn't have the authority to yell at me. Moments like this are when I wish I had a portable Matthew to recite the school handbook.

I approach the counter that seconds as her desk. She hands me a large envelope.

"In the future, Miss Duncan, don't use the school as your home address. We're not UPS. Understood?"

I nod, still beyond confused. So . . . no yelling?

"That'll be all, Alexis. Back to class and actually try to learn something while you're at it. It might just do you some good," she says, shooing me away with her drawn-on eyebrows.

I go back to the hall and look at the envelope. It's from the University of Connecticut, which makes no damn sense considering I know for a fact I didn't apply there.

I'd toss it if I wasn't searching for an excuse not to go back to class. I don't want to awkwardly avoid eye contact with Aamani again. Each time we do that song and dance another piece of my heart shatters. And who knows, maybe it's the first-ever water girl recruitment letter.

I pull the bold-typed stationery out and read the opening sentence: *We are pleased to inform you that you have been accepted to the UConn Future of Science Program . . .*

It's like I'm being strangled. I can't catch my breath. Is this for real? I read on. Not only have I been accepted to whatever this science program is, but I've been awarded a full scholarship.

I want to scream.

I want to do the Cabbage Patch.

I want to hop in a TARDIS and go back in time so Britt can share this with me.

I want to post it on Instagram so all the haters can see.

I can't believe this is happening.

Fuck it. "LET'S FUCKING GO!"

Mrs. Rowe pokes her head out the main office, a scorned look etched on her overly manicured face. "Have you lost your damn mind, child? I told you to go to class."

"My bad, Mrs. Rowe," I say in an exaggerated whisper, and head back to class, although there's no way I'm going back to class after this. I need a heart monitor, I'm so hyped.

I finally catch my breath and the first thought that runs through my mind is . . . Aamani. I remember her trying to talk me into applying to UConn back in our Legion of Sauron study session. Did she do this?

I have to talk to her. I don't care if we're not talking and every time she calls I send her right to voicemail.

> Me: Ask to go to the bathroom and meet me at your locker

Usually Aamani doesn't pull her phone out in class unless there's an alien invasion or she gets a news alert that the cast of the Avengers will be surprising fans at a nearby comic store. So I'm half expecting her not to text me back.

My phone buzzes.

> Aamani: Finally! OMW

I've tried everything over the past month to keep from looking at Aamani. It sounds easy, right? Like, don't look at her. It's not the Bird Box challenge. But turning away from Aamani is like trying to drown myself. I'd be lying if I said I didn't steal a look from time to time when she was sitting in front of me in class, her long black hair cascading down her back, and the small of her back showing when she bends over to fish a book out of her backpack and her graphic tee slightly hikes up.

Now she's walking toward me and the last thing I want to do is look away. She's wearing her Captain Marvel T-shirt and skinny jeans. She knows I'm staring and blushes, the hue of her freckled cheeks going from hazelnut brown to a hazelnut rose.

"Hey," she says, tucking a loose hair behind her ear.

"Hey."

Stop staring stop staring stop staring.

"I'll make this quick so you won't get in trouble for missing class," I say to the point.

"Oh, don't worry about it. I told old Hilbert I was having *female* problems. He so didn't want to touch that one. I could go to Seattle right now and he wouldn't care."

"All right, well, uh . . ." For some reason I'm overrun by nerves. "I just want to be clear that this meeting changes nothing. We still can't hang out."

"Obviously," she says incredulously.

"Okay, now that that's clear. Do you know anything about this?"

I hand her the letter. I watch her light-brown eyes dart left to right, speed-reading.

Her jaw drops, then a smile as big as the Milky Way washes

over her face. "What?! You got the scholarship! AHH! I freakin' knew it! In your face, Lindsay! In yo faaace!"

I shush her before Mrs. Rowe hunts my ass down. "What's Lindsay have to do with this?"

"Oh," she says as an afterthought, "Lindsay bet me that you wouldn't get the Future of Science scholarship based on your past grades and permanent record. She can suck on that permanent record. Sorry, I'm very hype about all this." She smiles and dives back into the letter, reading all the fine print. She's bubbling with joy.

"Yeah, but, um, why am I even up for a science scholarship from UConn? I told you I didn't want to apply."

"Lex, Lex, Lex," she says, shaking her head. "Remember when you said all whining and self-loathing that you're not going to apply to any prestigious colleges because there's no chance in hell you'd get in, and I said you're cray cray and I'll do it for you since I know all your information anyway, and you said you'd kick my ass if I did?"

I cock my eyebrow. "Yeah, vividly."

"Well, I ignored you and did it anyway and won twenty bucks off Lindsay in the process. Ah, it feels good to be rich and right about everything."

I shake my head with a slight smile, not wanting to give her the satisfaction. "I guess I should say thank you for ignoring my wishes, huh?"

"No prob. Ignoring people's wishes is what I do. Ask my parents. The whole me being gay thing was completely against their wishes."

We share a laugh. It feels good to talk to her again. It feels like the past month never happened.

"Okay, since you've actually been doing an incredible job of ghosting me, I want to take this chance while I have it to tell you something too."

"I already know you decided on MIT. Matthew told me last week when he told me he's going to Penn and Brian's going to Temple. Congrats, by the way. I'll tell you the same thing I told Matthew. I'm happy for you guys. You all deserve it. Even Lindsay. I'm mad jelly she's going to Caltech."

"Thanks! I'm pretty stoked about it. Also, my parents have never been happier about anything in their lives. But that's not what I want to tell you."

"I'm listening."

"I just wanted to let you know that in a hood miracle, what you said to my parents somehow got through their thick skulls. We sat down and had a long discussion about everything—you, my future, my comics attire, and other stupid shit that we shouldn't have even had to discuss, like trying to marry me off to anyone with a penis who practices Hinduism."

"That's what's up. I'm happy your parents are finally cool with who you are."

"Ha!" she snorts. "They are still very much *not* cool. They just changed their minds about disowning me. I guess they're, like, mildly tolerant now. You know, how the world is mildly tolerant of The Rock and Vin Diesel being gay for each other in those *Fast and Furious* movies. Clearly they're gay, but we all act like they're not. But that's not even what I've been dying to tell you. My parents and Bharti were so taken aback by your living situation this year, Bharti offered you the spare room in her house, and Dad says you can work at the store for some money until you go off to UConn. Can you believe it?!"

I nearly choke on the words.

"What? For real?"

She smiles. "Deadass. I think Bharti put something in their samosas."

"Hold up, hold up. So you're telling me I could've been sleeping at Bharti's instead of at the crack house? You do know Marvin talks in his sleep and thinks he's married to Sanaa Lathan?"

"That's what I'm saying."

"Why didn't you tell me any of this?!"

"Oh, don't even. I've been trying to talk to you for weeks and you've been avoiding me like you owe me money."

"Well, yeah, but that was before I knew your parents were moderately tolerant of me. This so confirms Bharti's legit the G.O.A.T. I can't wait to give her a big-ass hug. But even with all of this, I'm still not sure if it's a good idea for me to be in your life."

"Did you hear me? My parents are cool with it. You're going to be working at the store. And you want to know something? You said all that about me being the bravest person you know and changing your life for the better, when the opposite is true. What you've had to endure this year . . . I mean, I can't even. You're the strongest person I know. Without you I would never have gotten the courage to come out to my parents and tell them to suck a bag of gay dicks if they don't like it."

"You didn't actually say that, did you?"

"Oh my God, no. I enjoy breathing. I just said I don't care whether they accept me or not. This is me. And they'll have to deal. Mom cried and my dad nearly choked to death on his chai, but after that, it was all good."

The bell rings for the end of third period. Doors open and the hall begins to fill with students.

"So . . ." she lingers. "Can we be us again? Friends?"

I shake my head and sigh. "I mean, yeah. If your parents are cool with it."

"Yes!" she says, pumping her fist. "And I'll see you at the store tonight and take you over to Bharti's . . . no more crack house?"

I chuckle. "Yeah, no more crack house."

"Cooool . . ." she replies, awkwardly stretching out the word for some reason. "Cool, cool, cool."

I arch my right eyebrow, curiously. "Yeah, cool."

"Coolio. Coowl."

"Can we please stop saying cool?"

"Yeah, sorry. A little nervous here."

"Why?"

"Um, no reason," she dismisses. "So, uh, prom . . ."

"No. Jesus Christ, not you too. Why does everyone care so much about a stupid dance?"

"WHAAT?! It's not just a dance! It's the most magical night of our teenage lives! We'll be telling our great-grandkids about prom through the FaceTime apps that will be downloaded directly to our brains in 2089. The amazing ballroom and all the dresses and tuxedos, and dancing all night long until our legs feel like string cheese, and then there's that epic slow dance like the one in all the teen movies that's beyond romantic because everyone is forced to look each other in the eyes. It'll be like that ballroom scene in *Beauty and the Beast*. What's not to love? I can tell you this much, my parents didn't come all the way from India to not send me to prom, the most American teenager thing I can do."

I chuckle. "You clearly have never been to a Hargrove prom. Last year's was at the rec center and the senior class only raised enough money to afford a fifty-something-year-old DJ that mostly DJs polka night at the retirement home on Lancaster."

Aamani furrows her brow, considering. "I don't care if Carrot Top's the DJ. I still want to go."

"Yeah, well, good luck with that."

"It's funny you should mention luck. Because now that we're talking again, I thought I'd push my luck and see if you want to maybe, I don't know, go with me? Not as like a date or anything," she quickly clarifies. "As, like, friends. Strictly friends. No lesbian stuff."

I grin.

She looks worried.

I grin more.

"You really want to go to this stupid thing, don't you?"

"More than anything," she says, hopeful.

"A'ight then. I'll go. But only if it is in every possible way, exactly a date."

CHAPTER 27

I'm at the apartment to grab the rest of my things, mainly my sole-surviving bra, now that I know I'll be staying somewhere it won't be stolen. Good news, Mom and Randy aren't here. Bad news, I think I'm going to throw up the samosas Bharti made for me earlier. The place has never been this dirty. The counter and coffee table are littered with used needles and empty eight ball wrappers. When I lived here, she at least made an effort to hide the drugs. Clearly, she's living her best drug life without me. A horde of flies hovers over an old pizza box that has been halfway shoved under the couch, battling over the stale remains. A cockroach the size of Jabba the Hutt scurries out as I kick the box completely under the couch. I'm doing a little science experiment called *Let's see how long it takes for the druggies to find the smell.*

After tonight I'll never have to step foot in this shithole again.

I hurry to my room and toss the rest of my clothes in a trash bag. Part of me wants to wait for Mom to get home so I can see her one last time. No doubt she's a shitty mom, some would say the worst, but she's my shitty mom, and the only one I have. It's true, I hate this place, but I don't regret a second of being raised here. Hargrove is as much a part of me as anything. It was my necessity to escape that made me the woman I am today. A part of me loves her for that.

I decide to meet her halfway and leave a note. I pick up one of the free green pens they give away at the bank. I didn't even know Mom knew what a bank was. I guess she's finally looking into transferring her funds from the Bank of Under Her Mattress. But what do I write? *Thanks for being the worst, and for forgetting you pay for a family plan so I always had a phone to use. Good looking out. Fly Eagles fly!* Because that's not depressing as fuck.

A sound from the bathroom interrupts my draft. It's probably that cockroach going to take a shower. I put down the pen and go check it out, all too eager to procrastinate.

Mom is passed out on the tacky green-and-peach bathroom tile, a needle sticking out of her arm like someone claimed it as their land. Her hair is beyond matted. I pry open her eyelids to find her pupils dilated, and then I place my fingers on the small of her neck to check her pulse.

"D-d...fu...f-f...kin'...touch—"

Yeah, she's still alive.

She gives up on cussing me out and falls back into her comatose state.

A trail of dry blood runs from the needle to her elbow. I carefully pull it out. The tip is dull from having been used so much. Not some of her finest work.

The pain in my leg swells as I kneel to lift her. Thank God she's as thin as a stripper pole and barely outweighs an iPad. Even so, the pain shoots up my leg. I bite my bottom lip to push through it. I swing her arm over my shoulder as if she's a wounded soldier and guide her out the bathroom. Her deadweight doesn't help matters and neither do her pointy katana elbows, one of which is currently stabbing me in the ribs. It also doesn't help that she is in desperate need of some deodorant.

I manage to get her to bed, which of course is covered with dirty clothes that smell like vomit wrapped in a used diaper. There are chopped peach-looking chunks on two of the shirts. I gag. Using my bad leg, I kick off the clothes and make room for her to lie down. I gently place her on top of the sheetless mattress. It's the same way she used to put me to bed when I'd fall asleep on the couch watching NBA on TNT while she cranked up the R&B and did her thing in her room. Is this what *The Lion King* meant by the circle of life, tucking in your strung-out mom?

I tuck her in and roll her on her side so she doesn't choke on her vomit, which based on the peach chunks and stench is inevitable at this point. As soon as her cheek hits the pillow, she's knocked out.

I try to run my fingers through her hair, but they get caught in her naps. So I settle for a kiss on the forehead instead.

My mom, ladies and gentlemen. For better or for worse. Usually, for worse.

"I forgive you, Mom," I whisper. "And I'm sorry you're in so much pain. If there really are infinite universes and dimensions like Hawking believed, I hope you have a great life in one of them."

Then I grab my trash bag and place my key on the counter. I check the cupboard before I go, and find an unopened box of Randy's favorite, CT Crunch. I swipe it. Because fuck him.

CHAPTER 28

Lindsay closes the door behind them and shoots me one of her patent annoyed looks, flexing her eyebrows in the shape of a V. Matthew beelines it to his desk out of habit, going as far as pulling out our study packet from Nationals. I'd say I'm surprised to see him carrying around his Nationals packet almost a month after the competition, but I'm not. That's Matthew, and I love him for it. I wear his necklace every day. I keep it tucked because I'm not a fucking nerd. But I do wear it. Brian, seizing the opportunity of an empty classroom, sets up shop at Mrs. H's desk. He leans back in her chair and kicks his feet up on her desk like he owns the place.

"You guys sooo have to try this," Brian says, running his hands along the armrests. "There's so much power in this chair. I can feel it coursing through my veins. It's like sitting on the Iron Throne. Now I know why Joffrey was such a douche."

Lindsay props her hand on her hip and shifts her weight to her left side. "Why'd you call us here, Alexis? STEM is over. Or have you forgotten about team Texas and that ass kicking they gave us?"

"Effin' Texas," Brian says, having flashbacks. "If I had the power I wield now, we would have beaten the stupid *Red Dead* hats off them."

Matthew studiously raises his hand.

"You're good, Mattie. This isn't an official practice," I inform.

"Okay, then I have a question and an observation. My question is why is one of the AV club's TVs in front of Mrs. Hall's whiteboard? It does not belong there. And Brian is not allowed to have his feet on Mrs. Hall's desk, nor is he authorized to sit in her chair, as Brian is neither Mrs. Hall nor a certified teacher."

I look at Brian. "Please put your feet down before he busts out the handbook. Do it for me."

Brian sucks his teeth and drops his feet to the floor. "Fine. Keep an Asian brotha down."

"Where's Aamani?" Lindsay asks.

"These are all good questions."

"So answer them," she retorts. "I have places to be."

"Getting there. All right, so . . ." I take a deep breath, nearly passing out.

I didn't think it would be this difficult to say aloud. There's no turning back now. I close my eyes and think back on the year, all the time with Aamani and Britt wasted because I was scared of not being accepted. I think about the articles. All the Black LGBTQIA+ names in them. Even in the face of so much hate, so much adversity, they stood like giants out and proud. Some of them paid the ultimate price. For unlike the universe, our time is not infinite. Well, I'm done wasting mine.

"I'm . . . bisexual."

There's an awkward pause of silence.

Oh my God, they hate me now.

Lindsay's annoyance boils over and she shakes her head vehemently. "You made me miss my bus and watching Jordan walk to the gym in his shorts for *that*? Awesome, you're bi." She gives me a patronizing thumbs-up. "Can I go now?"

"What? Uh . . . no. There's more." I'm so confused. This is not how I pictured this going. I imagined a lot more fucks given.

"Let me guess," Lindsay continues, unimpressed. "You're secretly in love with Aamani? That's why she's not here."

"Whoa . . ." I say, nervously laughing it off. "Love's a strong word. I'd say it's more of a mutual crush."

"Mhm, we all saw you two at the reflecting pool."

My cheeks go red. "You saw that?"

"The whole world saw that," she deadpans.

"I'm with Lindsay," Brian chimes with a massive smile. "I think it's awesome!" He looks so happy for me. You'd think he was contracting mono again.

"Really? You guys don't think I'm weird for liking guys and girls? You don't hate me?"

"What? No!" Brian scoffs, disappointed in me.

"Why would you think that?" adds Lindsay. "We love Aamani. Her coming out to us didn't change that. And equally, we kinda like you, and that hasn't changed."

"Don't listen to her. We love you too," Brian says.

"Love's a strong word," Lindsay says, throwing my words back at me with a smile.

I almost laugh. They're so cool about it. I can't believe I was so scared of coming out to them. It makes me wonder if Britt would have been as cool.

Matthew raises his hand again.

I smile at him. "Yes, Matthew."

"I'm still confused. What does your sexual preference have to do with this impromptu meeting and the TV being taken from its rightful home of the AV closet? None of you would like it if I took you from your home."

"All right, here's the thing. Aamani asked me to prom—"

"I would really like to go home now," Lindsay reiterates. "This is the most useless meeting of all time. And I once had to attend an Instagram intervention."

"Hold on. Damn. I have a point. She asked me to prom and I said yes. The problem, and why I called this meeting, is she has it in her head that Hargrove's prom is like the movies and will be grand and magical and a bunch of other things it's not going to be. She even thinks there's going to be a moment like that scene in *Beauty and the Beast.*"

"That's my movie! My mom and I saw the one with Emma Watson in theaters. We legit sung the whole ride home," Brian says.

"Now as you're all aware, having attended Hargrove for four years, our proms royally suck major prom dick. Need I remind everyone when Miles nearly burned down the rec center after he lost all that money on the bum fights they were having in the bathrooms?"

"Yeah, I swore that bum with the pubic hair beard was going to win," Brian reminisces.

"Right. I'm not trying to let Aamani's magical night end up like that. She's given all of us so much this year. I want to do this one nice thing for her."

"We can't throw her a magical prom," Lindsay points out. "One, none of us are on the prom committee, and two, it's only a few days away."

"That's why I propose we at least give her something magical."

"Stop!" Brian interjects. "You had me at *Beauty and the Beast.* Whatever your plan is, count me in."

Matthew furrows his brow, considering. "Do I have to bring a date?" he asks.

"Not if you don't want to, Mattie."

"Okay, then I suppose I'm also in."

I turn to Lindsay. "That just leaves you. I need the whole team for what I have in mind."

We've backed her into a corner. She looks at us and lets out a heavy sigh, finally taking a seat. "Fuck me. I'm already regretting this. What's your idea?"

"Language," Matthew scolds.

I hug her. She breaks down into a reluctant smile.

"First we watch this movie I got from Aamani's mom, and then we pray that at least one of you has some rhythm."

CHAPTER 29

Jordan's younger brother Kevin let me borrow one of his suits, the all-black one he wore to Britt's funeral. Because, you know, nothing says *I'm about to look fly as fuck at prom!* quite like a funeral suit. The suit works though, because Kevin's shorter than me, making everything the perfect tightness to pass as a woman's suit. All the right places accentuate my curves. I make the outfit my own. I add a pair of black flats that I got from Goodwill, and a black bow tie Mr. Hilbert was kind enough to lend me. The bottoms of the flats are pretty busted. But as long as it doesn't rain, I should be good.

I take a final look at myself in the Super Mart bathroom, hardly recognizing my reflection. And I have to say, I look pretty fly. Drip drip, for sure. What can I say? I have an eye for fashion. Who knows, if this whole astronomy thing doesn't work out, then maybe I'll become a fashion designer. I may even have my own show on Bravo. Oh, who am I kidding? The whole sexy suit and bow tie thing wasn't my idea. I Googled "Janelle Monáe" and stole her look from the Grammys.

I take full credit for my hair, though. I went to Katrina's house after school to get it done. She wants to be a hairdresser and open up her own salon like her mom. She does a lot of the girls' hair on the ball team and charges half of what her mom does, which is kinda messed up when you think about how she's essentially stealing business from her mom. Anyway, she really does have a crush on Brian, and Brian pretty much ghosted her because of how we clowned him over the whole More Head Morales mono thing. I didn't realize the impact labels can have on one's life until this year—until I feared the labels that would be bestowed upon me. So I apologized for the role I played in ruining whatever they had, and promised to make amends by using my dope Cupid skills to hook them back up. She was so touched by the gesture she decided to give me a free hairdo. I wanted to go with a badass look. Something that announced the new bi and college-bound me. Something that sticks up the middle finger at the universe and says "Fuck you, I made it." So I had Katrina curl my hair and pin the curls above my temple, making a badass long faux-hawk.

"Are you ready, Lex?" Aamani calls from the other side of the door. "Are you going number two? Don't forget to spray."

"Ew, no. Give me a sec. I'm coming out."

We haven't seen each other yet. As soon as I got back from Katrina's, I rushed to the bathroom to make sure my faux-hawk hadn't collapsed in the spring heat.

I tug the ends of my shawl, making sure the jacket is tight and crisp, and I make a last second alteration to the bow tie, centering the knot. I pick up my backpack full of props needed to pull off Operation: Aamani's Magical Prom, then I take a breath and open the door.

Aamani and I are simultaneously slapped in the face by our sexy-ass doppelgängers. We're staring at each other. She looks the same but also different. It's like *Us*, except instead of horror versions of ourselves we look like celebrity versions, like somehow a Kardashian and a Hemsworth got spliced into our DNA.

Aamani looks like an Indian goddess.

She's wearing an extravagant Varanasi silk sari in hues of pink and peach, stitched with a multicolor weaving of pink-and-green floral print. The sari is long and falls like a waterfall of colors down to the floor. It makes it look as if she's walking on air. Straight goddess mode.

She smiles and I swear it's as if my eyes were only ever meant to gaze upon her.

I want to tell her how incredible she looks, but I can't find my voice. Words. Are. Very. Hard. To. Say.

"You look very beautiful and stylish, Lex," she says, looking me up and down. Oh, sure. She has no problems talking. She speak words good. "And oh my God, I love that bow tie! Very Eleventh Doctor of you. Matt Smith would be proud."

I think that's what she said. I honestly have no idea what's happening right now. I feel like I'm having an out-of-body experience and I'm hovering over myself screaming at me to get my shit together and act like I've seen Aamani in a sari before.

"Oh, man! And your mohawk is sooo cool! You look like Captain Marvel. Can I touch it? Pleeaase . . ." she asks, excitingly reaching for my curls.

I find my voice quick.

"Girl, are you crazy? You never touch a Black woman's hair unless you want to lose a finger."

She retracts her hand. "Oh, my B. I thought it fell under the same rules as petting a dog. If I let you sniff my hand first, then I could touch it."

I manage to hold in my laugh. That was pretty funny. But touching a Black woman's hair is no joke. I'm trying to save her from future finger amputation.

All of her compliments make me realize I've been rude and still have yet to say anything about her amazing sari. One of my excuses is Bharti and her parents are standing right there, camera in hand, so I'm not trying to drool over their daughter.

"I, uh . . ." I look at her mom, who looks at me like, *choose your next words carefully.* "Um, I really like your sari." Aamani is underwhelmed by the compliment. Nice going, Lex. I dust myself off. Fuck it. Let the drooling ensue. "Actually, if I'm being honest . . . you look like a billion blue stars in that sari."

The best way to secretly call the girl you like *hot as fuck* in front of her parents and mooching neighbor is to do it with science terminology.

She blushes extra hard and looks away. I notice the silver hoop earrings that open up her face. She does a little twirl, sending the floral petals dancing at her feet.

"This old thing?"

"I like your hair too," I say, looking over at her parents to make sure this level of PDA is okay. Her hair, as always, is naturally beautiful and falls effortlessly down her back.

"You like, my hair?" she asks, rhythmically pausing for a beat. Then in her best Ariana Grande voice, she breaks into the chorus of "7 rings."

I can't contain my smile. She's so damn adorable. "You're such a dork."

"And proud of it," she owns. I've always admired how comfortable she is in her own skin. Then she proceeds to rap the rest of the chorus.

I pinch my chin in thought. "Who sings that song again?"

"What?! How do you not know this? Ariana Grande. She's only the songbird of our generation."

"Yeah, let's leave the singing to her," I say with a smile in my voice.

"Okay, you two. Stand over by the milk for some pictures," Mrs. Chakrabarti instructs, waving us to the dairy.

Bharti smiles at us, equally excited. Living with Bharti this past week has been a dream. There's always food in my belly, my bras never go missing, I get to see Aamani practically every day when we drop in on the Chakrabartis, and every night before I go to bed, Bharti hugs me and says in her thick accent, "Shubh ratri" (which means "good night" in Hindi). For the first time in my life, I have someone to tuck me in. I don't give a shit that I'm seventeen. Knowing someone cares for me like she does, to make sure I'm safe and looked after before I fall asleep, is one of the best feelings in the world.

I can feel the chill of the freezers on the back of my neck.

Aamani hands her dad her phone and hurries to my side. "Take some for Instagram, Baba. We cannot deprive the world of all this beauty."

I put my arm around her and she leans into my embrace. She smells even better than she looks, like lilac and vanilla.

Mrs. Chakrabarti quickly steps forward and rips us apart like Velcro. She rearranges us so that we're standing nearly a foot apart.

"You two can be friendly on your own time when no one is around. But you are not to touch one another in public and risk being seen by someone in the community. Do I make myself clear, beta?"

Aamani drops her head in frustration and nods. "Yes."

"Good. Because Bharti will be chaperoning you to make sure you don't do anything stupid."

Bharti shrugs in apology.

Aamani's cheeks flush with rage. "What?! That's so not fair."

"I don't want to hear it, beta. I think me and your father have been quite tolerant of whatever sickness you two have. I will not let you ruin this family over some kind of phase you're going through."

Sickness? Phase? Some things will never change, no matter how "mildly tolerant" they may seem.

The right side of Aamani's lips curl as she throws her mom a snarl. Then we return to posing.

Aamani turns to me as her dad hands her back her phone. "Don't worry," she whispers. "None of these prison photos are going on the Gram. We'll take a billion selfies when we get there."

"Bet," I reply with a fist bump.

Another way to plot in front of the girl you like's parents is Ebonics—the hood's scientific terminology.

Bharti stops us before we walk into the gym.

"You two go and have fun."

Aamani and I look at each other, then at Bharti like, *wait, uh, what?!*

"What about chaperoning?" I ask.

Bharti places her hands lovingly on our cheeks, and smiles. "You both are brave and smart girls. I trust you to make good decisions. And what your mother doesn't know won't hurt her. Just don't go too crazy."

We reel her in for a group hug. "But what are you going to do for the next four hours?" Aamani asks.

She grins. "I have your parents' Netflix password, remember? I have been watching this program called *Queer Eye*. It is very entertaining and funny."

Aamani laughs and nods approvingly.

Who knew old Indian women also Netflix and chill?

I look around the crowded gym; our broke senior class couldn't afford a better venue. These are people I've spent the last four years with, some I've known my whole life, people I've tried to impress, who I've wasted precious time and effort with trying to conform to what they and society wanted me to be. I've cried with them when the streets took our friends, laughed when we roasted outsiders, and hooped with them on the block. I still have love for all these people. No matter where I go, I'll always rep Philly. But I've reserved a special place in my heart for the group of misfits in the back corner, looking comically out of place amid Hargrove's urban flair. The STEM team made me the best version of myself.

Despite it being prom, it's still a strange feeling walking into the gym after hours and have it not be for a game. I miss the smell of the hardwood, that squeaking sound the sneakers make when they rub against it, and the feel of the ball in my hands. Much like missing Britt, I don't think I'll ever stop missing basketball. But I'm not bitter about not being able to play anymore. I see now that it all led me here, to STEM, to a universe beyond basketball, and to this very moment with Aamani.

I reach over, staring down a sea of rented tuxes and dresses, and take Aamani's hand.

"We don't have to be PDA mongers," she says for my benefit.

"Why, Aamani Chakrabarti, are you ashamed to hold my hand in public?" I tease. "Don't be such a homophobe. That's not very woke."

The lines of her mouth break into a smile. And I'm not

exaggerating when I say that her smile is the supernova that ignites my galaxy.

She tightens her grip and I lead her into the mosh pit of people populating the dance floor. Everyone is so bunched together that no one is even aware that we're holding hands. When we emerge out the other side where all the tables are, people start to take notice. A few people twist their face in disgust as if we're contagious. A couple of guys from the boys' team do a double take to make sure their eyes aren't deceiving them. It's like, yes, people, the girl who once let Frank Watkins finger her in the back of the theater for the first act of *Us* is now holding a girl's hand. Deal with it.

I push up my chin and strut proudly, knowing I'm walking with the most beautiful person here.

Lindsay and Matthew are at the table. Matthew's neck deep in his punch glass and Lindsay is swiping through her phone, impervious to her surroundings.

"Hey, guys," I say, trying to get their attention. "Where'd Brian go?"

Without looking up from her screen, Lindsay points in the direction of the dance floor behind me.

Brian's popping-and-locking with Katrina. I better get invited to their wedding or I'm going to be mad pissed.

Matthew finishes his punch and looks up. "Hello, Aamani and Alexis. You both have drastically improved your attire for the evening. Kudos."

"Uh, thanks?" I say. "You have too."

Matthew is dressed like an extra from *Lord of the Rings*.

"Thank you. This is my Aragorn strider coat. My mom helped me make it to cosplay. It's made of leder and wachskordel."

"Cool," I nod. "You're definitely making a statement with that."

"As are you with your hair. You look like Captain Marvel."

"That's what I said!" Aamani joins.

Lindsay glances up in curiosity. "You both look very nice. And we already know I look very ni—"

Her face goes a shade whiter than its normal hue.

"What up, Lex? Dope suit."

I turn to see Jordan and Trey standing there, looking like half the movie poster for *The Wood*.

"Thanks," I reply.

"So, uh . . ." Trey starts, then stops. He looks down at Aamani and me hand in hand, then back up at us again. "What, you don't like dick no more? Y'all a thing now?"

I drop Aamani's hand and move to square up. "Yeah, you have a problem with that?"

He tosses up his hands. "Whoa, nah. We cool. I'm just saying, you're missing out on all of this," he says, flexing while looking himself up and down.

I snort. "I think I'll survive."

"You sure? You don't know what you're missin'."

"Positive," I deadpan. "What about you, Jordan, you cool with this?"

"Of course I am, Lex. You borrowed my brother's suit. I kinda assumed, you know," he replies with a chuckle, his dimple caving in. "As long as you're living your best life, that's all I care about. Life's too short not to."

My muscles relax. I didn't know how much his opinion mattered until now. I guess I view him as an extension of Britt, so it's really like I'm receiving her approval.

"Thing is Aamani's way cooler than you though," he adds. "Girl's got some serious style. You're lucky she likes your ass."

Aamani's head grows two sizes.

Lindsay clears her throat. "Uh-um ..."

"Oh, my bad. Jordan and Trey, this is the STEM team. This is my boy Matthew and my girl Lindsay, and that Asian over there doing the Robot with Katrina is Brian."

Trey nearly cracks a rib laughing. "What's boul doing dancing with More Head?"

"Ay, cool it with that shit," I defend.

"What? Why? Girl's given more brain than an encyclopedia."

"Because that's not her name. Just call her that one more time and watch what happens."

"A'ight, damn. Chill," he concedes. He looks back at the team and continues the introductions. "'Sup," he says, up-nodding.

"Yo," Jordan poetically adds. "That suit's everything. *Game of Thrones*?"

"*Lord of the Rings*," I correct, winking at Matthew.

"That's what's up."

"I attended one of your basketball games this year," Matthew replies. "You are very skilled."

"Thanks, bruh."

"I'm afraid your teammates are not. You lost the game by what I'm told to be an astronomical amount of points for a sporting event."

"What about my skills?" Trey asks. "You know I'm on the squad too."

"I'm unable to comment on your skill level, as you did not get in the game."

Jordan and I are dead. Man it feels good to genuinely laugh again. This past month has been torture.

"Man, whatever," Trey says with a smack of his teeth. "You

both know I always put in work when I get in. Why you think they be calling me Lou Williams out here?"

"Bruh, ain't nobody calling you that," Jordan debunks.

"H-hi, J-Jordan," Lindsay says in a voice resembling Oliver Twist asking for more porridge.

I lean over and whisper something in Jordan's ear.

He nods, listening.

"Oh, for sure. I can do that," he answers.

He looks over at Lindsay. "Lindsay, right?"

"Yes, I am Lindsay. Lindsay Ann Ross. That's me!"

He flashes that dimpled smile and she melts.

Gross.

"Would you like to dance, Lindsay Ann Ross?"

I've never seen her move so fast. She nearly pulls a hammy.

A muscle feathers in Trey's jaw. "What?! Yo, you're ditching me? What am I supposed to do?"

"What are we—dating? Go find someone to dance with, my nigga."

"I'll dance with you," Aamani volunteers. "As long as you don't use that word."

Trey looks at me for consent.

"What are you looking at me for? She can dance with whomever she wants."

"I'm just checking, because once your girl sees my sexy-ass dance moves, she might go back to being straight." He does a terrible Michael Jackson kick to demonstrate.

He clearly doesn't know how being a lesbian works.

Aamani rolls her eyes. "I think I'll be fine. You just try and keep up. Now shamone, MJ."

The four of them head to the dance floor. I can finally sit down.

My leg has been killing me, and I need to save my energy for the operation later.

"I guess it's just you and me, Mattie."

He does this confused brow-knitting thing. "You may not be aware, but there are a large number of people here."

"I meant at our table ... you know, you're right. It's just us and a room full of people, and I'm proud to be queer and disabled in front of them."

"I may be using this meme incorrectly, but cool story, bro."

I nearly fall out of my chair laughing.

Aamani and I finally make our way to the dance floor when the DJ slows it up and puts on singing Childish Gambino. I guess Trey's moonwalk wasn't as irresistible as he thought it was.

I face her and take her hand, placing my other one on the small of her back. My heart skips a beat as we lock eyes. Her brown spheres are vessels transporting us to our own universe. We sway to the mellow beat of "Summertime Magic," and Aamani rests her head on my shoulder and closes her eyes, fading into the moment. I do the same and rest my head on top of hers, smelling her passion fruit shampoo. We don't speak for the rest of the song. Our bodies do the talking.

When "Stay With Me" comes on we conform our swaying to match Sam's silky-smooth voice.

"So, is prom all you hoped it would be?"

She looks up from my shoulder. "Don't get me wrong. I'm having a great time dancing with you. Is it seeing *Endgame* on opening night levels of magical? No. Not even close. But then again, there's only so much magic to be had when you're in a run-down gymnasium that smells like locker room and weed, and whatever that is over there is going on."

We look over at Mikayla and Connor, basically having sex on the dance floor. Where's a teacher when you need one? She's assaulting his throat with her tongue while her right dress strap has fallen off and is dangling by her side, and his hands are palming her ass like the Jordan logo palms a basketball.

"Thanks for pointing that out," I deadpan. "I can't unsee that."

She half smiles.

"Hey, hang in there," I encourage. "Who knows? The rest of your prom may be magical."

She shrugs. Then she rests her head back on my shoulder, accepting her unmagical fate.

Several slow jams later the DJ returns the tempo to club level. Out of the corner of my eye I spot Matthew bundled up in his North Face, waving his hands frantically at me as if he's Flossing above his head.

I take a step back from Aamani, pulling out of our dance.

"Is your leg okay?" she asks, concerned.

"Oh, yeah, I'm fine. Just wait right here. Don't move. I feel some prom magic coming."

"Um, okay...?"

I hurry to the bathroom to change outfits. Apparently Mikayla and Connor have decided to move their public love making to the stall beside me. I hear the toilet water splash and the sound of their lips smacking together. To compound matters, changing into this thing is really fucking challenging. At one point I lose my balance and get a foot full of toilet water for my efforts. I don't know how

Aamani does it. I think this thing goes over this shawl thingy, and I put my arm through here? I don't fucking know. It's like putting together IKEA furniture, but only using the Swedish instructions. One "*how to*" YouTube video and ten excruciating minutes later, I finally get this thing on. I put on my winter coat to cover up and limp out the stall before Connor finishes and all I'm thinking about for the rest of the night is his disgusting O-face.

I meet the others at the DJ table. The DJ cuts off the music mid-song when Principal Garrett joins us. A collection of groans bounces off the gymnasium walls. Ironically it was in the middle of a Kanye song. I'd like to think that was the universe dishing out some belated justice for how he did my girl Taylor (#LetTayTayFinish).

Principal Garrett takes the mic. The four of us stand beside him in our winter coats despite it being seventy degrees outside.

"Hey, hey, settle down. We will cut the music back on momentarily," Garrett promises. Last two weeks of school or not, when Garrett speaks, people shut up. "We have a group of your fellow students from the regional winning STEM team—"

"STEM?! The fuck is that shit?!" someone shouts in the crowd. They receive a nice chunk of laughter for their efforts.

Someone follows with, "*LeBron James*!"

More laughs.

Scratch that. People *used* to shut up when Garrett talked. It's total senior anarchy up in here.

Maybe we should abort the mission.

"Will one of the teachers please locate whoever said that so I can have a little chat with them on appropriate language? Thank you. Now where was I? Oh, yes, some of your fellow seniors have prepared a special dance for you. Let's show them some respect, and then we will return to your mumble rappers and Puff Daddy—or whatever it is you kids listen to nowadays. Alexis, the floor is yours."

All of a sudden my heart is trying to tear through my chest and I can't find my breath. Is it possible to have a panic attack and a heart attack at the same time? If not, I'm making history. Why the hell did I propose this idea again? Oh, right, because I like being roasted on a colossal scale.

I somehow manage to pick Aamani out of the sea of people. We lock eyes like we did when we were slow dancing. My anxiety fades as though Aamani snapped my troubles away with an infinity gauntlet. With my body poised, it all becomes so clear. The only thing I truly care about in this moment is bringing Aamani joy.

The crowd moves back, giving us the entirety of half court to work with. We form a sad-looking V like we rehearsed, with me slightly in front of the others like I'm Beyoncé and they're the rest of Destiny's Child. I give the team the signal and we all remove our coats. People don't so much as laugh as they whisper to the person beside them, questioning what the fuck we're wearing.

Mrs. Chakrabarti let Lindsay and me borrow two of her saris, and Mr. Chakrabarti lent Brian and Matthew two of his nice kurtas. I have on a green hand-woven Varanasi sari with gold-and-pink trimmings. Lindsay's is a gray-and-black Varanasi sari with ruby trimmings. Brian is the same size as Mr. Chakrabarti, so his kurta fits him perfectly. He's sporting a block-printed Dupion silk kurta set in peach and gold. And Matthew has on a woven art silk Jacquard kurta in rust.

I give the DJ a nod to have him hit the spacebar on the track.

A woman who sounds like she's on a mountaintop starts singing a cappella in Hindi. We move our hands slowly to the sound of her methodical voice as if performing an interpretative dance.

Then the drums kick in—*bum, bum…bum-bum-bum*—and we bounce our shoulders to their beat. The drums continue to build for a few seconds before the full Bollywood beat of *Pram Ratan Dhan Payo* drops and a female chorus sings the words, "*Ni ni sa sa re re sa sa…*" in quick succession. The sitar jumps in adding almost a house music vibe to the beat, the bass jumping. We speed up our shoulder bounce so that our shoulders pop on every half note. Then the tempo slows back down, settling into an Indian club beat. The female chorus sings the words, "*Payo…Payo…Layo…Chayo…*" Then the lead singer begins to belt out the first verse.

We wind and contort our bodies like a corkscrew to the rhythm of the lyrics while at the same time pop-locking our hands in traditional Indian style as if attempting to make shadow puppets.

Over the singer's transcending voice, you can hear Matthew counting his dance steps, "One, two, three…one, two, three…"

Worst. Bollywood. Dance. Ever.

I'm thrown off and miss a few steps when Corey Hines starts nodding to the beat and yells, "This beat is flames!" Next thing I know half the crowd is nodding along as though at a Drake concert.

What is happening?

Am I having that panic attack stroke again?

Jordan and Trey are the first to come up and join us. They study our feet and take half a verse to get the moves down. A verse later the rest of the seniors on the ball team join and shortly after so do the cheerleaders. Before I know it, the whole dance has filled in behind us at center court to join in. I'm assuming everyone is either high or drunk off the spiked punch.

Aamani, who up until this point has been shell-shocked, shakes it off and comes and dances beside me. She has the entire dance memorized (she should, considering her mom suggested I do the number from her favorite Bollywood movie when she was younger).

And just like that we've turned prom into a Bollywood flash mob. If that's not some hood magic for your ass, then I don't know what is.

The song continues, the woman's hypnotic voice transcending in Hindi.

It's time for the move none of us could get down in rehearsal, which I should probably clarify we only held for an hour, but still. We seductively cover the lower halves of our faces with one hand, while fully extending our other arm and ticking our hands to the beat like a sprinkler, all while shaking our hips like Shakira. Everyone not part of STEM and named Aamani, takes a second to learn the move then starts to show why their hips don't lie. They're all waaay better at it than us. I'm not even using my leg as an excuse (though it is starting to hurt), I'm just incapable of being sexy; Lindsay's skinny ass has nothing to shake, so she comes off like your typical white girl with no rhythm; Brian is okay at it, but super cringey; and well, I'm pretty sure Matthew's doing math problems out loud at this point.

After we've busted out the Seductive Sprinkler (#Seductive Sprinkler), the dance break of the bridge kicks in with an added horn section, drums, and shredding sitar. We start weaving in and out of each other's arms, trading partners like a Bollywood hoedown, still Seductive Sprinkling with our right hands. As we prance in a webbed shape to the addictive rhythm, I can't help but feel this is the happiest I've ever been.

Shit. Do I love Bollywood music?

I'm eventually passed back to Aamani. Her smile's as bright as two supernovas. Our palms kiss as we Seductive Sprinkler and butterflies take flight in my stomach. The final verse plays us out and we revert to our beginning dance of shoulder bouncing to the beat.

The song ends with the final word "Payo!" echoing in the gym. A few cheers break out.

Trey comes racing up to me and Aamani at center court. "Yo!" he says out of breath (smoke much?). "Are all Indian songs like that?! That shit was everything!"

The DJ cuts back on Kanye to let him finish.

"Yeah," Aamani answers, proud to share her culture, "the dance and club ones are."

"Bet! I'm about to Spotify the fuck out of that! What's it called?"

I answer. "*Pram Ratan Dhan Payo.*"

I can see him try and sound out the words in his head. He eventually gives up. "I'll just type in dope Indian music. The shit will come up."

He leaves me and Aamani at center court. We stand face to face in our saris. People go back to dancing.

"Magical enough for you?"

She wipes sweat from her brow and cheeses hard.

"So magical!"

"Good," I reply, satisfied. "Now the real question is: Were we any good?"

She starts dying. "Oh . . . ha . . . oh my God . . . no!" she heaves with laughter. "You guys were missing cues left and right and were sooo off beat during the third verse. And it sounded like Mattie was playing Sudoku. But I absolutely freakin' loved every second of it! The saris and kurtas and everyone joining in—I can't believe you did all that."

I smile, content. "I'll take it."

"Would it be too cliché," she begins shyly, "if I try to kiss you after a huge Bollywood number? I mean, that's how all those things end."

My life up until this very moment has been a shit show, and I always assumed that was because it was the hand every Hargrovian was dealt. But that's the thing: life doesn't deal in absolutes, it's not some predetermined equation based on your environment, skin tone, or religion. It's an ebb and flow of messy uncertainty. And it's the variables of us that makes going on that journey so unpredictably spectacular.

I kiss her long and hard and the sparks between our lips erupt like an imploding star. I want to stay trapped in our little universe forever.

She pulls her lips away slowly. My lips long for more. Before I can say the words, she beats me to it.

"I love you."

I take my time and carefully pronounce, "Main tumse pyar karta hoon."

And who says a Black girl from the hood can't learn anything?

ACKNOWLEDGMENTS

I suppose the first person I should acknowledge is you, dear reader. Thank you for reading the book and for actually caring about the acknowledgments page. It feels good to know people actually read these things, or at least skim them.

I've dedicated my life to this book, to becoming an author. And it would not have happened without the help and support of many truly remarkable people.

First on that list is my agent and dear friend, Christopher Schelling. Google "the literary agent G.O.A.T." and his face is the first hit. Or at least it should be. I owe this man my life. To take on a young, Black, queer, debut author was pretty much a suicide mission. But through all the rejections (and there were many) and all the sleepless nights thinking this day would never come, Christopher never faltered. He truly fought for me with all of his being. He made my dream a reality, and for that, I will forever remain humbly in his debt.

Next is my editor Mari Kesselring, her Padawan Victoria Albacete, and the entire Flux team. Remember in the previous paragraph, when I bitched about those rejections and sleepless nights? Well, Mari and Flux were my fairy godparents. Which I guess would make my Kobes the glass slipper? Anyway, Flux saw me and said, "You're Black and queer, and we love it!" It was Mari and Victoria who challenged me every step of the way to do better. They were my rocks, my Dwayne Johnsons, holding me down through it all. It was through their guidance that I was able to deliver the wonderful story you have just read.

I'd also like to thank all of my sensitivity readers—Ramya Krishna, Kati Gardner, Talia C. Johnson, and friend and fellow Marvel mega fan Cara Sheridan and her sister Hannah. Thank you all for helping me champion the autistic, Hindu, and disabled communities. And to all of the WNBA players who read and endorsed the book—Betty Lennox and Danielle McCray. To Jacque Weems for helping me get the book out to female hoopers, and Tylon Harris for being my basketball idol growing up. To Kah Yangni for creating such a breathtaking cover. And a special thanks to my dear friend, Sonal K. Patel, who inspired Aamani. Thanks for telling me how hard it is to put on a sari. I hope these characters do y'all proud.

And to the city of Philadelphia. From the outdoor courts in West Philly to the Sonny Hill games at McGonigle Hall, your toughness and grit were the biggest influences on my life and basketball game. And to my childhood friends Christian Diaz and Scooter Wilkerson. We navigated it all together: traveling all around Philly for pickup and AAU games, buying knock-off clothes on 52nd Street so we could stunt at parties, and staying up until two in the morning playing *NBA 2K*. Y'all are my brothers.

To my siblings Sean, Vincent, and Alexis. Everything I do is for y'all. All I ever wanted to do is show you that someone with our skin tone can achieve anything. Never give up on your dreams. Your lives, your dreams, your ambitions matter. There is nothing you cannot do. I love y'all.

To all the people in my life who believed in me as a writer. To my lifelong friend Justin D. Harris, who reminds me every day to wear my Blackness as a badge of honor. To Scotty Bordignon (for our legendary snow days and being the best *Borderlands* partner a guy could ask for), Dylan Mello (there's still hope of fulfilling your prophecy of me appearing on Oprah), Doug Froggatt (I made sure I wrote every day), Gail Tomas (thank you for introducing me to the wonder that is storytelling), and my late friend Judy Vaughn (when I was at my lowest and thought it would never happen, you encouraged me to never give up, to shoot for the moon, because even if I miss I'll reach the stars).

And to my partner, Amanda, for bearing with me through this whole process. You gave me the courage to tell Alexis's story, which was also my own. You championed my queerness and helped me embrace it. And even after reading you section after section of the novel for critique, you always remained patient and honest with your feedback. You make me feel loved. You make me feel seen. Thank you for being you—my guiding star in the darkness.

To my grandmother, who cheered my education as much as she did when I made a basket. And to my parents. My father for putting the ball in my hands at two years old and instilling in me the work ethic to succeed at anything I put my mind to. To Geoff for raising me as one of your own. But especially my mother. You are my inspiration for all that I do. I remember those nights in the one-room apartment in West Philly, where the four of us had to share a bed. You hustled, stole, worked God knows how many jobs, entertained countless men not worth your time and beauty, did whatever you had to do to keep a roof over our heads and food in our bellies. Seeing the world through your hardships is what made me a feminist. Because I saw your never-ending strength. I saw life kick you down ten ways to Sunday, yet every time you got back up. You are the strongest person I know. The most badass. You're the supernova in my life, making me believe I can soar to the stars.

Charles A. Bush was raised in Philadelphia, and attended Cabrini University before honing his craft at the University of Oxford. In addition to writing young adult novels, he played professional basketball overseas, spends far too much time obsessing over all things Marvel, has long run out of places to store his mountains of books, and dreams of someday debating literature with Rory Gilmore. *Every Variable of Us* is his first novel. You can follow him on Instagram (@Charles_A_Bush).

3/22

LINDENHURST MEMORIAL LIBRARY
One Lee Avenue
Lindenhurst, New York 11757